Robin Blake is a novelist, art critic and acclaimed biographer of Anthony Van Dyck and George Stubbs. Though born and brought up in Preston, he has lived for many years in London.

'Cragg's first-person narrative voice is nicely judged: historically informed and reticent in the right proportions. Robin Blake's crisply written mystery offers all the pleasures of a classic detective novel and introduces the reader to an appealing new historical sleuth'
TLS

'This is rollicking stuff. Cragg and Fidelis are an engaging duo, and their first investigation is like crossing Robert Louis Stevenson with *The Archers*'
Financial Times

'Set in 1740, this book includes an involving description of life in Preston at a time when towns in such remote areas of the country ran their own affairs and kept "foreigners" at a distance . . . Cragg and Fidelis make a fine pair of detectives, and Robin Blake has written a fine first novel'
Literary Review

'When was the birth of "forensic science"? In the first of a projected series starring coroner, Cragg, and his doctor sidekick Fidelis, Blake puts it at 1740 . . . Cragg is an elegant, urbane narrator with a knack for making even minor characters come alive. Recommended'
Guardian

A Dark Anatomy

ROBIN BLAKE

PAN BOOKS

First published 2011 by Macmillan

This edition published 2012 by Pan Books
an imprint of Pan Macmillan, a division of Macmillan Publishers Limited
Pan Macmillan, 20 New Wharf Road, London N1 9RR
Basingstoke and Oxford
Associated companies throughout the world
www.panmacmillan.com

ISBN 978-0-330-51808-6

1 3 5 7 9 8 6 4 2

A CIP catalogue record for this book is available from
the British Library.

Typeset by CPI Typesetting
Printed and bound by CPI Group (UK) Ltd, Croydon CR0 4YY

Visit **www.panmacmillan.com** to read more about all our books
and to buy them. You will also find features, author interviews and
news of any author events, and you can sign up for e-newsletters
so that you're always first to hear about our new releases.

For Frank Hart

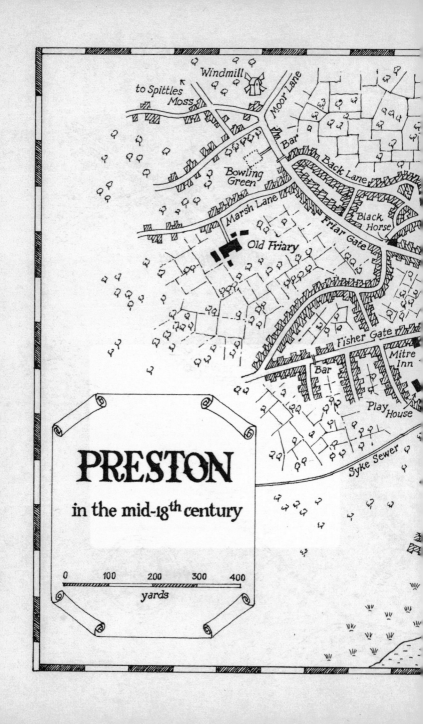

PRESTON

in the mid-18th century

0   100   200   300   400
yards

Windmill

Ribbleton Lane
to Gamull

New Hall Lane

to Wigan →

Tible Barn Street

St. John's St

Patten House

Church Gate

Bar

Molyneux Square

Market Place

Old Shambles

Red Lion

Parish Church

Water Street

Moot Hall

Bull Inn

Main Sprit Weind

Stonygate

Grammar School

Turk's Head Court

Syke Hill

Avenham Lane

Folly Field

Swill Brook

Avenham Walk

N

W E

S

River Ribble

—HEMESH·ALLES—

Chapter One

ACCORDING TO THE case notes, and checked against my private journal, it was on Tuesday the 18th of March, 1740, that a succession of disturbing events ran their course through the life of our tidy Palatinate town of Preston. That was the day on which, three hours after dawn, Dolores, wife to Squire Ramilles Brockletower of Garlick Hall, was found lying in the forest in her riding clothes, beneath an ancient oak tree.

At eight o'clock in the morning, I was sitting down to breakfast alone in the parlour when, having only just filled my tankard, I heard the brass knocker on our front door hammering. Next, a voice could be heard asking for the coroner. Finally, our girl Matty pushed a scrawny lad, whom I recognized to be the Brockletowers' kitchen boy, Jonah Marsden, through the parlour door. His eyes were popping with the import of his news.

'Well, Jonah. What's the matter?'

The boy extracted from his shirt a folded paper, which I took and opened. It was from his grandmother, the briefest of messages.

To Mr Titus Cragg, Coroner. Sir, a deplorable mortal accident has occurred. I beg you to return at once with the boy who brings this. Bethany Marsden, Housekeeper.

I studied the signature: firm, confident and businesslike. I put the paper down.

'Please elaborate, Jonah.'

The boy looked blank.

'I mean, what is this about?'

'Oh! Mistress is slaughtered, sir. In forest. This morning.'

I lifted the tankard and took a sip of beer. Twenty years in the law had taught me that a measured manner is the best project in such circumstances. I lowered the tankard again and dabbed my lips with the napkin.

'Who found the body? Was it you?'

'No, sir, I were nowhere near. It were Timothy Shipkin the woodsman found her.'

'And you say the body was away from the house and in the woods?'

'Timothy says. In Fulwood, up above Squire's own woods by the hall, under a big old oak. Seemed like she'd come down to earth, through branches.'

The night had been one of storms right enough, but Jonah's choice of words had caught my attention.

'Come down? How?'

Jonah's face twisted this way and that.

'I don't know, sir. Timothy says it seemed like Mistress dove down from the sky. Her face and hands were in the earth.'

'That's a very particular way of describing it, wouldn't you say?'

The boy did not reply, but he watched like a cat as I took another sip of beer and sawed through the slice of cold beef on my plate. And though I continued this performance of imperturbable chewing and sipping, I will admit my heart had quickened in the anticipation of interesting discoveries. I looked at this spindly messenger of death, who stood beside me with cap wrung between his hands, eyes tracking the food from the plate to my lips. I cut a crust of bread from the loaf and handed it to him. Without pausing to thank me he stuffed it into his mouth.

'So you didn't yourself see the body?'

The bread for a time gagged Jonah. He shook his head.

'How, then, did you hear of it?'

Agony filled the boy's eyes but it was not for the memory of Mistress Brockletower. In his hunger he had tried to swallow the hard crust before properly chewing it.

'It's what they're all saying at Hall. First light, Mistress went out riding, as she does,' he managed to say hoarsely, after forcing the food down at last. 'But the mare came back without her. Then us all went out looking until Timothy Shipkin come running down from woods, saying he'd found her. He told my grandma at back door and she wrote that note and sent me down here to give it you, sir.'

I rapped the note with my forefinger.

'I note that Mrs Marsden says "accident". Why did you, when you first spoke to me, say "slaughtered"?'

For a moment the boy looked terrified, as if I had asked him to prove one of Euclid's propositions. Then he screwed up his face as he addressed the question more collectedly.

'Don't know, sir,' he said at last. 'I mean, it's how Mistress were found . . .'

Jonah was shifting from one foot to the other, still watching me as I resumed eating.

'Go on.'

His face relaxed into a more neutral form of concentration, as if he were about to recite a lesson at school. Not that this boy had ever had any schooling.

'It's how she died, sir. See, Mistress's throat were cut. From ear to ear, so Timothy Shipkin says.'

And, just in case I had not appreciated the weight of this information, Jonah tilted back his head and drew his forefinger along the line that the blade would have followed: from here – to here.

Laying down the fork I closed my eyes, making a picture in my mind of Dolores Brockletower, on the last occasion that I had seen her. It was at a recent hunt – a tall, angular woman whose physical vigour was well known and whose feats on horseback had become part of local mythology.

Well known though she was, the simple demise of a squire's lady – of this particular squire certainly – would not be bound to bring much caterwauling, at least outside her own family, and perhaps not even within it. But to have the lady die violently, her throat sliced open, was quite a different matter. It might set off a small earthquake in a pocket-parish like Garlick. Well, it would be my task to quash that possibility, if I could.

I picked up the napkin and dabbed my lips. Then, clearing my throat, I leaned back in the chair, and said airily, 'I wonder . . . when Mrs Marsden handed you the note, did you happen see *Miss* Brockletower while you were at the back door?'

'Well, sir, I –'

But, before Jonah could complete his sentence, my sweet Elizabeth came running in with the folds of her apron bunched in her fists. She had heard the news from Matty.

'What a dreadful thing,' she cried. 'Dolores Brockletower dead! What happened to her, Titus?'

As she came to me I held out my hand and she dropped her apron to take it. I squeezed her slim, pretty fingers and told her the gist of Jonah's news, omitting only the explicit fact of the gashed throat.

'And so, I suppose, I will have to go over there,' I said. 'To find the truth out.'

4

Elizabeth leaned and kissed me on the forehead.

'That you must, sir,' she said, 'and go quickly about it, or else the scent will be cold.'

I had already ordered my horse to be ready at half past eight since I was due this morning to discuss with a group of cottagers in the country towards Chorley what action could be taken against a farmer illegally enclosing a piece of common land. So now I quickly scraped my plate, drained my beer and rose.

'Elizabeth, my love, as always you are right,' I said, leaning to kiss her mouth.

Telling the boy to wait for me, I strode into the hall, crossed it and swung open the door connecting the house with the office. Furzey was already at his writing desk. I asked him to represent me with the cottagers as I had been urgently summoned on coroner's business. Furzey protested that the cottagers would be disappointed not to be attended by the attorney himself.

I said, 'Just tell them the clerk always knows five times more than his principal and they'll be pacified.'

I returned to the house where the boy was waiting by the front door.

'Come along, Jonah,' I said. 'You ride behind.'

A few minutes later I was in the saddle, hoicking the boy onto the cob's rump. And so we jolted off together on the road to Garlick. It was a ride of some forty-five minutes at a gentle pace – which was as fast as I considered young Jonah could sustain. We went east down to the end of Church Gate, where the way branches to the right down a hollow way towards the Ribble bridge and the bridge-end settlement of Fishwick. But we went straight ahead, past the windmill on Town End Fields, and were soon trotting pleasantly along Ribbleton Lane. As we encroached on Ribbleton Moor the lane-side hedges and trees, which had begun to come into bud, were lively with birds twittering and building their nests.

It was apparent that news about the Lady of Garlick had already travelled to every corner of the parish, like a spider running around its web. At a squalid place called Gamull, where a row of tottering cottages lined each side of the road, people came out and called after us. At first I took no notice. But then one of them caught my attention and I reined in the horse. It was a woman whose name I knew, Miriam Patten.

'What they're saying about the wife of Mr Brockletower,' she croaked. 'Is that true, Mr Cragg?'

Miriam was a widow, ancient and raggedly dressed. She was so poor that her house was chimneyless, with just a hole in the thatch to let smoke out – and that only when she had the fuel for a fire. She was one of those who keep a cow in the house, as much to give warmth at night as milk in the morning. She was also one who, from time to time, receives a sack of coals and a bag of flour in charity from my wife, and other Preston ladies.

'I don't know,' I said. 'What *are* they saying?'

She leered up at me, allowing a sight of the blackened stumps of her teeth.

'That the Devil finally lost the taste for her society, and chucked her over the roof.'

I laughed.

'The Devil *himself*? Coming into this small parish? I think we rather flatter ourselves if we are saying that, Miriam Patten.'

I shook the reins and we rode on, leaving the draughty hovels of Gamull behind us.

This narrative, I suppose, may be read in places, or at times, in which squires are of no account – whatever levelling times as may lie ahead, or future gardens of Eden. If so, I must make it plain first that the squire was a gentleman of much importance in this particular time and place. A Justice of the Peace, a Member of Parliament in Lord Derby's interest, he owned most of the land around Garlick; the southern boundaries skirted the north-western edge of Fulwood Forest, and stretched away for half a dozen miles to the north and east. He kept a stable of expensive horses and a kennel of hounds.

And he was hated by his tenants.

Brockletower was a younger son and never thought he would inherit. In the short time since the unexpected death of his brother he'd set about remodelling whichever parts of Garlick Hall he judged improvable by mathematical architecture. He went to London and came back with a stupefying array of Italian pictures and marbles to clutter the house. The passion for these novelties is a powerful one in those whom it seizes. I remember, in Italy when I was young, how milords exactly like young Brockletower would congregate in rooms strewn with old stone fragments, picking through them like rooks behind the plough.

A wealthy, liberal, improving squire is no doubt an adornment to any manor, especially one who employs so many extra local hands in the continual knocking down and rebuilding of his house. It is how Ramilles Brockletower viewed himself and wished others to view him. And it made him angry that they did not. But his tenants and labourers, and many of the people that lived round about, continued to grumble against him, saying that a large part of the Brockletower estate was not truly the Brockletowers' by right, but had been filched from the forest – land which belonged to all the people. In their opinion the Brockletower family were nothing less than thieves of the land. It was a complaint much heard around the country in those days.

The Brockletowers, however, had always gone about their filching by scrupulously legal means. In the time of King William, old William Brockletower got an Act of Parliament that handed him the right to enclose twenty acres of the common fronting his house. This land, around the Savage Brook and the woods and wastes that stretched across the flat higher ground on either side of it, had formerly been freely grazed by the cottagers' animals, and otherwise provided their owners with inexhaustible quantities of firewood, not to mention berries, roots, mushrooms, bird's eggs, bulbs of wild garlic and nuts at various seasons. Yet by a decision of that far-distant assembly, which knew nothing of this common, or the people who depended on it, the Brockletowers had been authorized to engross the acres to themselves, and to exclude all others from the use of it. Naturally they made out it was done in the sacred name of improvement, and for the future welfare of our great nation. But the country people said to hell with the nation, and bugger improvement. It was only done for their own enrichment, the beautification of their park and better shooting for their guns.

Ramilles the son quickly let it be known he would be even more assiduous in these efforts than his father. Black Ram Brockletower, they had begun to call him, saying he was in the habit of summoning succubi to his bed, as well as that of his wife, and of holding conference with the Devil.

We turned off the bridle path and threaded our way through the trees, Jonah explaining that Mrs Marsden told him to take me here first, where the body had been found, before I went to the Hall. After a while, the largest clearing in this part of the wood came into view between the foliage and, at its centre, an oak so ancient that it was half decayed. What had been the original trunk still stood thirty feet high, but it was dead. The sockets of its fallen branches had opened up, making three or four dark portholes into the interior at various heights. But a second bifurcating trunk had grown up from the same deep-set roots and this was thriving. Its leaves were budding and preparing to spread themselves in the air.

Riding nearer, but still at a distance, I heard voices and made out a small group of men and women standing in a huddle, as if meeting together in prayer. The impression was erased when they tossed back their heads in laughter at something one of them said. I was puzzled at first by an object on the ground, a grey hump a few feet from them, lying at the foot of the tree. Then I realized this must be the lady's corpse, concealed under a sheet of burlap. As we approached, the attendant group composed their faces and began watching me sidelong. I pulled up the horse and Jonah slipped to the ground. I more methodically dismounted and walked up to the tree. The small band shuffled a little further away, except for one, Philip Barkworth (author of the witticism that had enlivened the others), who stepped forward and pulled the sacking away. I looked down at what he had uncovered.

These were manifestly the remains of Dolores Brockletower, dressed in her riding outfit of scarlet dress under a black jacket. In death she was no vision of elegance, for she had died in the undignified, rump-in-the-air posture of a pig rooting out truffles. The body had gone down on a patch of almost bare earth, with arms folded under the torso, the hands pressed palm-down by the bosom, the nose pushed into the ground that had been softened by recent rain, as if attempting to inhale the earth. I lowered myself to my haunches and squinted at the neck. A bloody gash evidently began (or perhaps it ended) just below the left earlobe and jagged downwards. Losing sight of it, I rose, took a pace back, stepped around to the other side of the dead woman, and crouched again. Here I saw, on the right-hand side, where the gash finished up (unless it had in fact started), at a spot lower down than on the other, at least two inches below the hinge of the jaw. Along the whole of its length the sloping wound was caked with a dried lip of black scab half an inch thick. In the leaf-mould below I saw the coagulated pool of gore. Suppressing a spasm of nausea I stood up and surveyed the cold, stiffening bag of flesh that had previously housed the soul of Dolores Brockletower.

There were four present, apart from the boy and myself. I looked at each of them in turn: Old Matt Thwaite, whose beard reached to his belt, the witty Barkworth, fat Jenny Milroy and pretty Susannah Shipkin.

'Where's Timothy Shipkin?' I asked. 'Wasn't he the finder? Susannah, where's your father?'

Susannah was a girl of seventeen with clear blue eyes, creamy skin, a raspberry mouth and full hips. She works as dairymaid at the Hall.

'Medad's not come home, sir,' she said. 'After he told them at Hall what he found, he didn't come back for his breakfast. Happen he's gone on to Shot's Hill. He's felling a dead beech up there.'

Shot's Hill is a tree-crested ridge the other side of the big house, a remnant of the old forest, just a hundred yards wide, with fields lying beyond it that were once part of the woodland, and are now laid to grass pasture for the squire's cows and sheep. It was strange that Timothy took himself off. For most men, the vanity of being the first finder of a woman's mysterious corpse is enough to make them stay and enjoy the glory.

'He'll be hungry, then,' I remarked. 'And what about the squire? Has he not been up here himself? The summons I had was from Mrs Marsden. But why does Mr Brockletower not come to bring his wife home?'

Thwaite shook his head.

'Squire knows nowt about it, we're thinking. He's away to York on his affairs this past seven days.'

'Is he indeed? And when expected back?'

'Our Poll says he's to come back today, sir,' said Jenny, whose sister Polly was also a maid at the house.

'Has anyone touched the body?'

'We've not gone nearer to her than we are now, sir,' said Jenny.

'None of you?'

They all shook their heads.

'We've covered her and guarded her,' growled Thwaite, assuming the role of foreman. 'But we've not looked close at her. Better to wait for you, sir, is what we thought.'

I considered for a moment, then pulled the sacking back over the hunched cadaver.

'And has anything been found? Any weapon, or object, that might have caused this injury?'

The four looked at each other.

Thwaite said, 'Not a thing, sir.'

'Have you looked?'

They evidently had not. I strode back towards my cob.

'I suggest you do. Quarter the ground of this clearing between you. If you find anything, keep it safe for me. Now I must go down to the Hall. I'll send back a cart and litter for the body. Stay until it comes, and in the meantime you may lay the corpse out before it stiffens.'

And so I left them, with a host of questions forming in my mind about how Dolores Brockletower had come upon her death. It did not look like an accident. But had it been by her own hand?

Chapter Two

I RETURNED TO THE bridleway and set the horse in a descending direction through the woods to Savage Brook, the stream that trickles past Garlick Hall. On coming into the considerable Brockletower inheritance – the Hall, its surrounding and outlying land, a fat bundle of securities, shares in toll-roads, ships and inland navigations – Ramilles had been a 26-year-old naval officer on station in the West Indies. Since this estate made him one of the wealthier gentlemen in Lancashire, he at once resigned his commission. But he returned from the navy accompanied by a surprise. He had a wife, the tall and striking-looking girl with an exotic name, a wealthy sugar-planter's daughter, so he said, whom he had encountered dancing the minuet at a ball in Jamaica.

For reasons I could not discover, the new squire took against me and my services from the start. The day after I acquainted him with his father's will, and the full extent of his sudden wealth, I received a note in his hand summarily asking me, without explanation, to send all papers relating to Brockletower family affairs to the chambers of Messrs Rudgewick & Tench, of Friar Gate, who would henceforth act for and advise him. He had given no hint of this intention on the previous day, so I replied, reminding him of how long I had served his family and asking him to think again, as I considered Rudgewick & Tench to fall short of the decent diligence required in a family attorney. I simply received a second even curter note repeating the contents of the first and indicating that I should no longer consider myself the Brockletowers' family attorney.

As I rode down towards the brook's valley, where I would turn the horse eastward to ride up towards the house, I noted the closeness of the steep slopes on either side, out of whose red earth grew the tall and ancient trees. Forty years ago the valley floor, no more than a hundred yards broad, had been cleared and turned over to park and pasture – a pretty landscape to look at from the house. Coming down to the water, I forded it, cleared the fringe of trees on the farther bank, and trotted the cob out onto the open grass of this park. The Hall was now a furlong away, a squarely proportioned, three-storey, brick-built house with numerous tall windows and a noble slate roof. Some of the frontage was masked from my sight by a cedar of Lebanon rising in front of it, and some by a screen of scaffolds, ladders and hoists, around which lengths of canvas flapped in the breeze like sails. Builders were at work modernizing the appearance of Ramilles Brockletower's home. In amongst the trees that rose up behind the house, a belt of brown and green between the slates of the house's roof and the blue sky, coils and smudges of smoke rose into the still air: the fires of the building workers' camp.

But little of this work, or outside work of any kind, was being done at Garlick Hall at this moment. In the cobbled stable yard, grouped around the drinking trough, I counted eleven men and women, indoor and outdoor servants mixing with the builder's men, who had met to exchange observations and speculations about the violent death of their employer's wife. As I approached through the arch that divided the yard from the lane, they eyed me in expectation of news.

I swung myself from the saddle.

'How do, Coroner?' greeted one of the group. 'Been up in woods?'

I knew the man as an important person in the little kingdom of Garlick Hall: William Pearson, huntsman and head groom.

'I have that,' I confirmed. 'I come directly down from there.'

Pearson nipped one of the younger men by the earlobe and propelled him in my direction, to take charge of the cob.

'Squire's not at home, so I understand,' I said, handing over the reins. No one contradicted me. 'I therefore desire an immediate interview with Miss Brockletower.'

One of the young females left the group and went in with the message for the squire's sister, while the others muttered amongst themselves, and nudged one another. I strolled across to join them by the watering trough.

'Is it true then, what Timothy says, Coroner?' asked Pearson. 'That Mistress's throat's cut and her's bled to death?'

There seemed no reason to keep it from them, and facts are preferable to gossip. So I said, 'Regrettably, that looks to be the case. We must send a cart as far as the bridge, and a litter so that she can be brought decently home. Will you see to it, Pearson?'

'Aye. I'll go up myself an'all. It's likely she's murdered, is it?'

'That is not for me to say. I must summon a jury to decide by inquest how she died.'

'Happen inquest'll be tomorrow?'

'If possible, the next day. It will be as soon as I can convene the jury.'

'And at Plough Inn?'

'You ask a lot of questions, Mr Pearson. Let me ask you one. When was the last time you – or any of you – saw your mistress alive?'

'She went out this morning,' said Pearson. 'I saddled the mare myself to be ready at six. That's her time to ride out in morning.'

'Did she leave by herself?'

A groom, Isaac Barrowford, ducked his head.

'No, she had the mare between her legs,' he murmured.

The others sniggered.

'Don't be facetious, man,' I said curtly. 'A gentlewoman is dead, and this is no time for joking.'

A few minutes later a matron of fifty, generously proportioned and with a bold handsome face, bustled out through the kitchen door. It was Bethany Marsden, grandmother of Jonah, housekeeper at Garlick Hall and a thoroughly sensible body. I beckoned her aside and we walked across the cobbles, past the barn and towards the stable block at the far end of the L-shaped yard.

'So, Mrs Marsden, this is a shocking discovery.'

'Yes, sir. I thought it best to send you the message without delay. With Squire away from home, we weren't sure, Miss Brockletower and I, if it was the county coroner that should attend, or the town. Then I remembered that you'd coronered the death of that young vagabond fellow that was found dead up in the Fulwood a year back. So Miss Brockletower asked me to write the note to you.'

'It was the right thing to do. A coroner's duty is to enquire into death within his area of competence only when it is reported to him. The Fulwood belongs to Preston town, making the jurisdiction mine. The Bailiff of Preston, Mr Grimshaw, will have to be notified also, but you may leave that in my hands.'

I was conscious of sounding pompous. Pomposity is a fault inherent in all who do legal work, and I know I am often guilty of it. I ask my reader for the same measure of forbearance that

I evidently received on that day from Bethany Marsden, who either did not notice it, or accepted it as natural in a figure like myself. I cleared my throat.

'Is, ah, Miss Brockletower very disturbed?'

'We all are, Mr Cragg. But Miss Brockletower has taken the news calmly enough. Of course – the way she is – any sudden stroke of bad news like this leaves her, you might say, in the dark . . .'

'Has anyone else been sent for?'

'Well, the first person to think of is the doctor. But, from all that Timothy Shipkin told me, he would be a mite too late. Then the magistrate, but of course that would be squire himself, and he's not here. There's old Mr Southworth at Goosnargh that's still on the Bench after thirty-odd years, but he's . . .'

She paused as if hovering on the brink of an indelicacy. I completed the thought for her.

'Not likely to be wheeling over this way in his bath chair. Precisely. Does anyone else know?'

'Oh, I should say only everyone on the estate, by now. And Mr Woodley offered to ride over to give the news to Squire Brockletower's uncle, the vicar. So he'll have heard by now.'

'Mr Woodley?'

'Mr Barnabus Woodley. The gentleman that's been superintending the works to the house. He's gone off to the Rectory this past hour.'

'When is Mr Brockletower himself expected to return?'

'This evening.'

'And have you heard from him since he went to York?'

'Oh, no, not at all. He only left seven days ago.'

'Has he not written at all, even to his wife?'

'I believe it is some time since he wrote to his wife whilst away on business, Mr Cragg.'

I ignored the tartness in her voice.

'Did you yourself see Mrs Brockletower when she went out this morning?'

'I saw her, yes. She came past the kitchen at her usual time, just after six, dressed for riding.'

'Did she speak to you?'

'No. She went out without a word. Pearson had her hack saddled. I saw him put her up and she rode out.'

'Does she always ride the same path?'

'Yes, she goes a little way down the park and sheers off across the stream and up the bridleway through the woods.'

'And you noticed nothing strange about her as she left today?'

'No. She seemed as she always was.'

'I should go in to speak with Miss Brockletower now.'

She led me back in through the yard door. I had always been a professional caller by the front door and had never entered Garlick Hall by any other way. Now, as we trotted along the wide stone-flagged passage between the 'wet' kitchen and the scullery and dairy, I breathed in an agreeable compound of baking bread, bubbling broth and the lactic rankness of spilt milk in the dairy. Mrs Marsden swung open the thick panelled door at the passage's end, and took me through to the family side of the house, which centred on a spacious hall. This was temporarily in half-light, the glazed front door and windows being shaded on the outside by the scaffolders' tarpaulins. We did not cross the hall, but turned instead up the main stairs to our left. It was an old-fashioned oak stair with massive banisters and it reared darkly up to the floors above. I stopped at the stair-foot for a moment and listened. It seemed there was still nothing being done by way of building work, and the hollow quiet in this part of the house felt expectant, like a withholding of breath.

'Miss Brockletower's sitting room is on the first floor,' said Mrs Marsden, with a trace of impatience. 'Come on up.'

We creaked up the staircase. I wondered how it would be, this interview. I had never yet been to the upper floor of the house, and had not seen Sarah Brockletower for – what? – ten years; but it was more than twenty since we had met or spoken together.

At the first floor I was led along a panelled landing, past an array of dim family portraits, whose only clearly visible details were the starched white ruffs of a long-ago fashion. At the end Mrs Marsden opened a door, and ushered me past her.

'It's Mr Titus Cragg to see you, miss,' she called out.

I took a hesitant couple of sidesteps past the housekeeper and walked into the middle of Sarah's room. The hall's shadows were clarity compared to this. The window curtains were drawn and no candle had been lit. Only a thin, morning firelight from the grate relieved the gloom.

Sarah sat beside the fire in a rocking chair, keeping it in creaking movement all the time. I have often noticed that it is a habit of blind people to rock, or sway, their heads and bodies as if keeping time with some interior tune that we – the sighted – cannot hear. Perhaps Sarah's rocking-chair habit was her way of domesticating that tell-tale impulse.

'Hello, Sarah,' I said. 'I'm sorry that we must eventually meet again only in these painful circumstances.'

'Well, Titus, it has certainly been a long time. But it is better, I suppose, to meet like this than never to meet again until eternity. I have wondered from time to time since my parents died if you would ever come and call.'

Her voice was exactly as I remembered – light on its feet, always poised on the edge of mocking, or at least being ready to mock should the need arise. But it had also been capable of a sweetness that can still make me wince, remembering it.

Sarah Brockletower. The thoughts of her that I write now do not – cannot – in any way undermine my profound, unflagging devotion to my own Elizabeth. They do not amount to anything, in fact, except the remembered tatters of a youthful love. When I was nineteen Sarah had been a difficult creature to get to know. Closeted in Garlick Hall, she never attended assemblies, fairs, fetes or the races, and was brought in and out of church on Sundays clamped to her father's, mother's or brother's arm. But then, at a country wedding in Yolland parish church, I had found myself in the pew behind hers and, afterwards, succeeded in walking her on my arm for an hour around the Green, first convincing her of my love, and after a little while persuading her to love me. I had never in my life been so eloquent. We stole a few meetings after that, when we kissed and held hands, and we exchanged letters through a servant. That was all there was in it before her mother found us out, dismissed the servant and forbade the liaison absolutely. She laid it down as law that no blind girl could ever make a wife, still less a satisfactory mother. So Sarah resumed her anathematized life, and I was sent away to the Inns of Court to think again about the constitution of happiness.

'Titus, won't you sit? Bethany, it will be best I am sure if you leave us to talk alone.'

Mrs Marsden's mouth dropped at the sides in disappointment, but she withdrew without a word. I sat on the fireside chair opposite Sarah's rocker. On the hearthrug between us her long-legged poodle lay stretched out and asleep.

'So!' she exclaimed, almost gaily.

For a moment she stopped rocking. Her face was turned, not towards me, but up at an angle, so that all I could see in the gloom were her white neck, jawline and cheekbone. Then she recommenced the back-and-forth movement.

'I believe it is the first time we have met since you grew into one of the town's most respected men, Titus. I was always sure you would. So tell me, if you please. How do you find me after all this time?'

I started. I should not have been unprepared for her directness, as she had always been the most outspoken of girls. Had I forgotten so much?

I looked at her. Sarah was thirty-seven now but, in this dim flickering light, I could hardly see her except by reconstituting the appearance she had had two decades back. I had found it a rare, flawless, serene and tormenting appearance. Even those sightless eyes had been ornaments to me.

So I could say, truthfully, 'You are just as I remember.'

She laughed.

'Not likely. Anyway you are not quite as I remember. Your voice is deeper. It seems you have acquired gravitas by attorneying, as I suppose was necessary.'

'Well, I am not here as an attorney, Sarah. As you know, your brother dismissed me from acting for this family.'

Sarah sighed.

'Yes, of course. Why *did* he do that?'

'I have never known. I believe I always gave satisfaction.'

She turned her head towards me, an ironic smile on her lips.

'So you did, Titus. Except to me, that is . . .'

Perhaps I blushed, but it did not matter. She could not see. I coughed to let her know of my embarrassment.

'Well, I am here as the coroner, enquiring into the death of your sister-in-law.'

'Ah, yes. Dolores. I had not forgotten.'

She sighed again, more deeply, raising her shoulders and letting them fall. After a few moments of silence, she said, 'So, is she murdered, Titus?'

'I cannot say that. At this juncture the law keeps an open mind.'

Her second laugh was unexpected.

'That is refreshing. The law so often keeps a closed one.'

'You seem to take this . . . event very lightly.'

'Do I? I don't mean to.'

'Do you not grieve?'

'For Dolores? Such a death should be treated as a serious matter, certainly. A grave matter, as Hamlet would say.'

'It is my duty to treat it so.'

She was immediately penitent of her levity.

'Then it shall be mine also. It was indelicate of me to refer to a pun of Shakespeare's, even though it is one of his better ones. Please tell me all you know about the matter.'

While Sarah Brockletower rocked without stopping I gave an outline of what I had seen in the Fulwood less than an hour earlier. When I finished she again brought her chair to rest, struck by a thought.

'Then my sister-in-law killed herself.'

'No woman cuts her throat.'

'No womanly woman, perhaps. But the rough-riding hoyden that married my brother might have.'

'We found no knife or razor beside her. I left some people searching around, though I do not think they will find one. Do you have any particular reason to believe Mrs Brockletower wanted to take her own life?'

'None at all. Dolores and I hardly spoke. We were not *sympathique* to each other.'

'So when did you last see . . . I beg your pardon, when were you last with her?'

'Indirectly, yesterday. She was very angry about something. I sent my maid Honor down to say I had a headache and would she be so kind as to stop banging around in the hall and screeching at the dogs.'

'Why was Mrs Brockletower angry?'

'I don't know. There seemed no reason, though my message must have exacerbated it.'

'Then why did you send it down?'

She smiled like a person tickled by a harmless jest.

'I had a headache, truthfully.'

'So her anger had no cause in the first place?'

'Honor wondered if it was a question of the time of the month, but I think not. It is more likely she was irritated by the building works. I never knew Dolores to be untowardly affected by her menses.'

There was the faintest stirring of my old feeling for her. She had always been fiercely candid about all matters not normally discussed between men and women. It was one of the things I had most liked about her.

'In any case, you did not in fact speak to her yesterday?'

'I did not.'

'Silent meals, then?'

'Dolores and I did not sit down together when my brother was from home. I took my meals up here.'

'Why is that?'

'She and I both preferred it. We are – were – of different humours, you see.'

'So Mrs Brockletower did not communicate with you at all yesterday?'

'No. She did not.'

'And it was usual, this silence between you?'

'When Ramilles is not here, yes. As I said, she and I had little to say to each other in the ordinary way.'

'Did she not even read to you in the evening?'

Sarah gave out a faint snort of derision.

'Read? I doubt she was able, unless it was a horse catalogue.'

'And on Sunday? Did she attend church?'

'She did not. I went alone with my maid Honor.'

'Was it usual for her to avoid church?'

'No. My brother preferred that she go, but when he is not here . . .' Sarah shrugged. 'My sister-in-law was not the godliest of women.'

'No,' I said, thinking of Miriam Patten's words. 'So I have heard.'

At this point I stood. It was time to get along, and it did not seem that I would gain much from further questions.

'I wish I could stay longer, Sarah, but I have much to do. If all goes well, the inquest will be tomorrow. Will you attend?'

'Is that an enquiry, or an instruction?'

'Let's say a request. I may wish to call you as a witness, you know.'

She sighed.

'Then I must be there, mustn't I?'

As I closed the door behind me I thought that, though grief has many faces, Sarah Brockletower was not wearing any of them. The fate of her sister-in-law appeared to have touched her as little as that of a fly.

I walked the length of the landing, turning each doorhandle and peering through until I came to Dolores Brockletower's own bedchamber. I went in. The room was neat and sparely furnished, and the bed rumpled, in the state she had left it after rising for her early ride. A nightgown lay across the bed. The commode had been used. On an upright chair was a dirty soup bowl and spoon on a tray. I sniffed the bowl and smelled chicken.

She had been isolated, reclusive, hardly known outside the household. It was true she had earned some fame in the neighbourhood for her fast and fearless riding, especially with the Yolland and Garlick Chase. But apart from these outings and Divine Service (which she attended heavily veiled), she was almost never seen in public, neither at assemblies, nor race meetings, nor paying calls for tea. Obviously, this shrinking from society engendered suspicion. I knew, not just from the words of Miriam Patten, that there were those who spoke of witchcraft, which in her birthplace, the West Indies, is (I believe) called Woo-Doo. Was all this talk a factor in her terrible death? I could think of an additional possibility. There had been speculation in the district as to why she had not yet provided a Brockletower heir, and some went so far as to say that all was not as it should be in this, the marital bed. Was that also a factor?

A few moments later I stood in the middle of the deserted hall with my back to the stair-foot. On my right was the room which I knew to be the squire's study and library; on my left the morning room. I made towards the latter and let myself in. Here, I guessed, I would find an escritoire equipped with pen, ink and paper with which I could write the necessary letters to Preston.

Chapter Three

THE MORNING ROOM was elegant and quiet, a lady's retreat to occupy that part of the day when the virile element is seeing to business, or in some other way having it out with the world. The male presence was, however, not entirely absent, even here. There were a couple of marble busts on their plinths, and half-a-dozen paintings on the walls, which I took a moment to examine one by one. The busts were of the Grecian sort, with eyes as blind as those of the woman I had just left. The paintings were all seascapes such as would appeal to a naval man like the squire. They showed brave men-of-war straining against the elements, their sails fat with wind and their flags streaming. Looking at these I believed I could smell the perfume of tar in the ropes and taste the salt on the breeze.

After five minutes moving from picture to picture, I wrenched myself back to the here and now. Sitting at the *escritoire*, I took paper and a pen and wrote a brief note to Bailiff Grimshaw, setting out what had happened and what steps I proposed taking towards an inquest. I then dashed off another shorter account, as a courtesy, to my Lord Mayor. Finally I addressed a few lines to my friend Dr Fidelis.

*Luke, I have been called this morning to Garlick Hall
where I find the family and estate in sad condition.
Mrs Dolores Brockletower has been found dead in the
Fulwood, the accident (if so it was) occurring during her
morning ride. Having myself seen the body in situ I have
ordered it brought home and will be grateful if you come
at your first convenience and cast a medical eye over it
– quite unofficially at this stage, you understand. I have
not yet sworn in a jury and therefore cannot request a
formal examination. I await your reply.*

*Your friend,
Titus Cragg,
Coroner*

I was just shaking the caster of sand over my wet writing when
the door was flung open and a fantastical figure stepped through.
He was dressed in country topcoat and breeches, but his wig
was far more elaborately piled and curled than would customarily be seen anywhere outside London. And he was so small
that it was not until he spoke that I appreciated this was not a
strangely attired boy, but a man of twenty-three or twenty-four.
He was extremely youthful to look at. His skin was soft, his
face had the appearance of a young rabbit, even to the bulge of
his eyes, and his voice was as light as a flute. Yet he spoke with
the emphasis of one used to laying down decided opinions to
his equals, and orders to his inferiors. It had the tone, if not the
timbre, of one who enjoyed more than anything to hear himself assert something.

'Well now!' he shrilled, his face wearing a curiously fixed
and complacent smile. 'Is company come? I did not think there
was any visitor in the house today but me.'

I stood and made the slightest of formal bows.

'Titus Cragg, sir. Attorney-at-law.'

The fellow seemed oddly delighted with these words.

'Ah-ha! A man of law, is it?'

His laugh was no more agreeable than his smile, half cock-crow and half cackle. But I remained equable.

'Until the present squire inherited, I had the honour of serving this family as their attorney,' I answered, 'though that is nothing to do with my business here today. I presume that I am addressing Mr Barnabus Woodley the . . . mason in charge of these works.'

I gestured through the window at the paraphernalia of tools, buckets and barrows beside the front of the house. Woodley pulled back his shoulders and his smile rearranged itself into a wounded pout.

'No *mason*, sir. You are addressing no rough-cast artisan. The shaping and cementing of stones is left to men bred to the job, so long as they obey instructions. No, sir, you are in the presence of Barnabus Woodley of York, architect and man of philosophy, and of taste. Have you been in Italy?'

'I have. I—'

'It was there that Barnabus Woodley discovered his true vocation, being fortunate enough to fall in with Lord Burlington at Rome, the native place of the immortal Vitruvius, and he revealed the principles—'

I roused myself to take my turn in cutting him off. 'With regret, Mr Woodley,' I stated hastily, 'I have no time to bandy reminiscences of the south.'

I am impatient with any man who speaks of himself as if he were a third person. And I had furthermore a premonition of an elaborate and tedious peroration on the Vitruvian architecture.

'I am here as coroner of the borough,' I went on, 'enquiring into the unfortunate business that has deranged this house today.'

Woodley's afflatus seemed instantly to puncture, as he subsided into a chair, semi-recumbently stretching out his legs. Even his eyes seemed to bulge a little less.

'Yes, yes. Damn me, yes. Oh dear. The coroner. Mrs Brockletower. A fearful thing and very horrible. I have just ridden to the vicarage with the news for Mr Brockletower's uncle, you know.'

He began hand-fanning himself, like a dancing-master after tripping a strenuous rigadoon.

'The vicar? How did he take the news, may I ask?'

'He is shocked but, as a man of God, not inconsolable. In his opinion she was murdered by vagabonds. The woods are alive with them. I agree with him.'

'Well, it is my duty to try all possibilities. May I put one or two questions to you?'

'Questions of what kind?'

He looked at me sidelong and, as his smile crept back, I saw the craftiness within it. Striding to the fire and turning, I clasped my hands behind my back and looked severely towards him. I wanted him to know I was in no mood for prevarication or levity.

'Of an easily gratified kind, Mr Woodley,' I said. 'Such as, when did *you* last see Mrs Brockletower?'

He sniffed drily.

'I can indeed very easily gratify you, Mr Cragg. It was yesterday forenoon. She used me rudely. I met her in the stable yard as I rode in from my lodging at the Plough Inn. She was on foot, though dressed in her riding habit, and she was far from civil.'

'In what way?'

'I greeted her and she swept past without a word. She cut me.'

'Was that exceptional sort of behaviour?'

'Certainly it was exceptional. I took the greatest exception.'

'But was it habitual?'

'Well, she was always haughty towards me.' He raised his chin and cackle-crowed again. 'Haughty-taughty! No warmth.'

'Did you give her any particular reason for this haughtiness?'

'No, I did not. She was colonial-born, you know, and she did not feel warmly towards any of the people of this land.'

'Her husband is of this land.'

Woodley held up a finger, as if in caution.

'So he is. Well, well.'

'So Mrs Brockletower made many enemies.'

'Of course she made enemies. She was of that temperament.'

'And you were yourself such an enemy – I mean, in the lady's eyes?'

Quite suddenly, as if stung, Woodley jerked himself upright.

'She was my employer's wife, sir, and I did my best to treat her courteously, which was not easy. I know nothing about her private thoughts towards me.'

'What brought you here to Garlick Hall?'

Woodley gestured to the window, outside of which someone had got to work with a hammer and chisel. The architect wore the type of expression a man adopts when speaking to a simpleton.

'Have I not told you?'

'I meant, why were you chosen and not some other?'

'You mean apart from my superior ability and taste?'

'Yes.'

'We have a connection through Archbishop Lancelot Blackburne of York. That city is my home. I have done considerable works for His Grace at Bishopsthorpe, his palace, on the recommendation of Lord Burlington, you know. The archbishop is kinsman to the squire, through his mother, I believe. So it was natural enough for me to come here on the archbishop's recommendation.'

'That is clear enough. And you're sure you did not see Mrs Brockletower after that moment – yesterday morning, when she cut you?'

'I am very sure indeed. She went into the house while I gave over my horse and got about my business with the workmen.'

'Ah! Your workmen. I must ask you about them. Was any man late for his work this morning?'

'Not that I know of. You must ask Piltdown, my ganger. He is out there now. We are hard at it shaping my pediment.'

Suddenly, Woodley jumped from his chair and took a couple of twitching sideways strides towards the centre of the room.

'Which is what I must go to now, sir. You must forgive me. As soon as idle and unpaid workmen tire of gossip, they wander off. I can't afford that. There is unaccountable trouble in finding good craftsmen. And there is a great deal of work still to be done on my pediment. And, besides, we are digging the foundation of my Grecian temple.'

'Your temple?'

He again indicated the window.

'Yes, in the grounds, out there. My Temple of Eros. It will be a destination for promenades, and a delight to those acquainted with the Grecian and Roman taste. I must show you my plans and elevations. They are exquisitely tasteful. But in the meantime, you will excuse me if I bid you good day.'

While speaking, he had begun edging crabwise in the direction of the door. A moment later he reached it, grasped the handle and relieved the room of his presence.

I returned to the escritoire to pick up my letters, and noticed a small bound journal tucked in amongst the writing paper. I lifted it and leafed through. It was a commonplace book, in which someone – Dolores, undoubtedly – had written scraps of poetry and prose that appealed to her. I turned to the most recent inscription, which read:

The Soul of a Man and that of a Woman are made very unlike.
Imagine therefore: my pain and fear.

As the lines could not be made to scan, I concluded they were not poetry. But no author or source was given. I stood for a moment before one of the two windows facing the park, trying to place the quotation. To my annoyance I could not. Perhaps she had simply made the words up: a cry from the heart.

Peering out through the clutter of scaffolding, towards the vista of forestry and grassland, I noted how my gaze was funnelled between the banks of high close-set trees to right and left. In keeping with the perspectival illusion, known best to painters and gardeners, it was a view that tapered gently but efficiently away to disappearance in a smudge of greens and browns.

But a disappearing point is also an appearing one, and now one of the smudges resolved itself as a small train of people, making their way along the road towards the house. They were following a trundling cart, with the labourer Barkworth at the horse's head and old Matt Thwaite sitting on the tailgate. The rest of the cart's load lay concealed beneath a horse blanket. This was the unofficial cortège of poor Dolores Brockletower, brought down from the woods by Pearson and his people. Tagging along behind, and occasionally leaping ahead, I could see Jonah Marsden. He continued frisking about until Pearson collared the boy and, with a few cuffs about the head, made him walk with a more respectful gait.

I left the morning room and crossed the hall, noting from the clock that it was a few minutes before ten. In the stone-flagged passage that led past the kitchen to the yard a leather-aproned drayman was rolling a great round cheese from the dairy, in the manner of a boy and a hoop. I followed him out and watched as he spun the cheese up a ramp and onto an already heavily laden cart that stood on the cobbles. Knowing his road must have been through a string of farms east of here, I stopped and asked if he had heard anything of the squire, who would be coming by the same road on his journey home from Yorkshire. But the drayman could tell me nothing.

I left him and crossed the yard to the barred gate that opened onto a path rising through the thickly wooded slope that reared behind Garlick Hall. I started up the path and in a few moments could no longer see the house or the yard for the branches and foliage, though I heard the hoof-clop of the cheeseman's horse shifting its feet, and the clack of his master's clogs as he rolled out another truckle. In the wood ahead of me smudges of smoke and the prattle of children drifted down from the builders' camp. A minute later a path levelled off and I arrived at a clearing and the camp itself.

A shawled figure was sitting, like the crone of an ancient tribe, on a three-legged milking-stool beside the fire. Over the scrawny flames was slung a pot in which some foul-smelling concoction brewed and from time to time during our conversation she would lean forward and give it a vigorous stir with a stick. Swollen-bellied children chased raggedly in and out of makeshift tents and shelters, and through the surrounding trees.

The woman seemed undisturbed by my arrival.

'Come near, come near,' she crooned in a thin reedy voice as soon as she saw me, waving a leathery hand at the sawn stump of a tree that lay close to the fire. 'I won't stand, so likely you'll want to sit.'

Looking at the woman more closely, I saw that, rather than the gammer I had thought her, she was probably of an age with myself, yet so dried, diminished and bent by poverty that she appeared twice the age. I lowered myself onto the stump.

'What is your name?' I asked.

'Peg Miller. What's yours?'

I told her I was the coroner paying an official visit.

'We are honoured, then,' she retorted, spitting into the fire.

'Are you the only grown person here, Peg?'

'Others have gone down to river to wash clothes. I mind the childer. I'm no good for the washing.'

She showed me her hands. The joints were knotted and the fingers twisted and crossed this way and that. She gave me a searching look.

'You think we don't wash, neither clothes nor bodies. Just because we wear rags and clouted shoes, don't mean we like to be dirty.'

'No such thought had occurred to me,' I assured her hurriedly. 'No doubt all human creatures will seek to be clean, if they can. Sometimes circumstances lie against them.'

She emitted a cracked wheezing laugh from her ruined mouth, and whacked the side of the cooking pot with the stick.

'Circumstances? Is that what you call them?'

She put down the stick and from under her shawl drew a clay pipe, snapped off at the stem-end and clearly many times used, but usable still. With a meaningful gesture she tipped the bowl towards me to show its emptiness and I fumbled in a pocket for my tobacco pouch, which I handed to her.

'Ta, that's kindly,' she said, digging a lump of tobacco out with her almost paralysed fingers and stuffing it artlessly into the pipe. 'So what is this official business of yours? Visitors have been almost as rare as coin since we've pitched camp here.'

I took back my pouch and told her why I had come to the Hall. She had of course heard already of the death of Dolores Brockletower. Bending and seizing a stick that protruded from the fire she pressed its smoking end into the pipe. She took a deep draw, closed her eyes and groaned with pleasure as she exhaled.

'You've likely come to smoke us out, eh, Mr Coroner?' she said with another hoarse laugh. She jabbed the smouldering stick in my direction. 'If there's fingers to be pointed, I'm thinking it'll be at us.'

Her voice was mocking rather than bitter, and there was active wit in it too. If her impoverishment had not been there before my eyes, I might have imagined she had a capacity for refined discrimination.

'Why do you say so?'

'We're poor, we are. We don't live in houses. So we must have killed that woman, would you not say?'

'No, not I,' I hurriedly assured her. 'I have to convene a court of inquest, and summon witnesses. It is not my part to accuse or find blame. Only the jury can do that.'

'But it's us they'll point at anyhow. This is what I said when my man came up and told us the news earlier on.'

'Your man?'

'Tom Piltdown. He's the ganger. I told him it bodes mischief to us, this death. We've gypsied all over the north country, we have, and we're treated like gypsies too. We are honest people, but settled folk will always call us beggars and sheep-stealers. And my poor boy always gets treated worst.'

'Who is your boy?'

'Not so much a boy now. Twenty-five is poor Sol, and a proper Goliath, but he had a knock on the head as a babby, and his mind never grew as prodigious as his body. Folk are not slow to accuse him of any crime that's on their mind, whether poaching or thieving or laughing at the King. And it'll be no different this time, I am resigned to it.'

'Please believe me, I would not jump to any such judgement. As a lawyer I am paid to be impartial. Fair.'

'Fair? Nothing is fair, only Death himself. He comes soon enough to all, as he's come to that woman this morning. As I see it, being born is only waking in the night. You bide for a bit and then . . .'

She spat into the fire again, watched it sizzle like bacon, and added, 'Then you drop off again.'

'Oh, come, come! There's so much more—'

But she cut my pious protestations short with a hoot of scorn.

'What *did* you come up here for, Mr Coroner, if not to accuse us of capital murder?'

I looked around the clearing. A dog. A cat. Some chickens. Five children playing ring-a-roses.

'No, not to accuse. Only to ask if anyone amongst you, anyone in this camp, has information about the matter. Something they have seen or heard, perhaps, even before this morning. Something that might help the inquest.'

'They haven't, not that I know of. When the men come in for their meal we shall likely talk. Then we shall hear if there's anything been seen, or not seen.'

35

'You will hold a meeting?'

'A meeting? Oh my Lord, no! We are not a Dissenters' chapel. We live close together here, so we talk.'

It was then that I heard the sound, faint at first and snatched by the wind, of female voices singing. I stood up and looked along the continuation of the path by which I had come up. From the camp it went on through the woods, and down towards the bank of the Savage Brook, and I caught sight of a small procession of women returning up it with bundles of laundry balanced on their heads. They were singing some kind of catch-song, picking up the melody one from another in the rhythm of their walking. I gave the woman before me a slight bow.

'I shall not dally to meet your friends, as I must go back down now. But perhaps I shall return, if I may. Would you be kind enough to acquaint the others of my enquiry?'

She said she would.

Returning to Garlick Hall I asked where I could find Mrs Marsden and was directed through the wet-kitchen to the dry-kitchen, and thence into the servants' hall. A desultory footman in green baize apron was polishing a bundle of silver spoons and forks at the refectory table. In response to my enquiry, he pointed the way to the housekeeper's parlour, which stood at the end of a short adjoining passage, and there I found Bethany Marsden sitting by the window at her writing table, wearing gloves, bonnet and cloak. She was composing a list. I showed her my three letters and asked how I might send them.

'To the Mayor and the bailiff as well as the doctor!' she exclaimed. 'Such important correspondence, Mr Cragg. I should be honoured to take them to town myself, if you wish. I'm riding in with the cheese-jagger.' She glanced through the window to the yard. 'He is almost ready to leave now.'

'Thank you,' I said, 'that will be most convenient. If you will carry them to my office in Cheapside, my clerk Furzey will send them on. But before you go, may I trouble you please to give orders that any servant who may have testimony for the inquest to come and see me? And I wish to speak with Mrs Brockletower's maid in any case, and to Timothy Shipkin.'

'There will be no difficulty there, Mr Cragg. I shall ask Mr Leather, our butler, to marshal the indoor servants, and Pearson to do the same outdoors. I can offer you the use of this room for your interviews, if you like. You are very welcome to it.'

'Thank you, Mrs Marsden. I shall take that up. But first I must see to the disposition of poor Mrs Brockletower. They'll be coming in with her at any minute.'

And, a few minutes after she had left me, they were. I had stationed myself at the window of the housekeeper's room, which gave a good view of the yard's entrance. The cheese-collector's cart was preparing to go out through the arch and into the lane, Mrs Marsden sitting up on the box beside the driver. Just at that moment the improvised bier on which the dead woman was returning home, with its straggle of rustic mourners behind, presented itself to come in. There was a brief *contretemps* before the housekeeper whispered into the dray-man's ear, presumably to tell him that half a ton of cheese did not hold precedence over a freshly murdered corpse. Without further complaint he pulled his vehicle back and allowed the remains of the squire's wife to be trundled in.

I immediately stepped outside and asked Pearson if there was an empty stable in which to lay the body, which, he said, there was. So I helped Gaffer Thwaite off the back of the cart and sent the rest of them on their way.

'Did you find anything when you searched?' I murmured to

the gaffer. Thwaite's toothless mouth opened a hole in his copious whiskers and he shook his head gravely.

'Not a thing, Mr Cragg sir. Not a thing, only this.'

He produced a horseshoe from beneath his smock.

'Where was it?'

'On ground, under the leaf-mould.'

'Near the body?'

'No, no. A dozen yard away.'

I inspected the find. It was worn away from use, but not rusty.

'Did you find any nails still in the holes? There's none there now.'

'No, it were just as you see it.'

'Well, it doesn't seem of any significance but perhaps it will bring us good luck in our inquest, Mr Thwaite,' I said.

Thwaite spat a thick, tobacco-stained gob onto the cobbles.

'It didn't bring the mistress owt of that, did it, though it was by when she died?'

I could think of no clinching reply to this so I just thanked him and went back inside. As I stood in the passage, about to push open the kitchen door, a servant-girl appeared at the passage end, coming from the family side of the house and wearing oversleeves and a calico apron.

'Mr Cragg, is it?' she asked. 'I'm Polly, sir. Mrs Pearson, she says I'm to come from my work and see you.'

'Yes, we must have a talk,' I said. 'Come with me, will you?'

And she followed me submissively, through the kitchen and the pantry, to the parlour.

Chapter Four

I PUT THE HORSESHOE on the mantelpiece, poked the fire and flung myself into Mrs Marsden's wing chair. Polly Milroy I invited to take the chair on the opposite side of the hearth. The whiteness of the girl's mob cap emphasized the self-conscious flush of her face. I adopted a kindly tone.

'So, Polly, you are the sister of Jenny, whom I met in the woods this morning?'

'Yes, sir.'

'And in addition you are – or were – Mrs Brockletower's personal maid.'

'Yes, sir, I was that.'

'Tell me about her.'

'What sort of thing would you want to know, sir?'

'Well, the sort of thing that might help to explain what happened. Why she's dead.'

Her eyes searched the hearthrug for an answer, but did not find one.

'For instance,' I prompted, 'had she ever told you about anything that happened to her before, while she was out riding? Was there anyone she saw in the woods, maybe?'

She made her eyes wider, suddenly excited.

'You mean meeting on purpose? Secret meetings with strangers?'

'That's not quite what I meant but, very well, were there any secret meetings?'

'If there was, she wouldn't have told me.'

'Were you not privy to your mistress's secrets? Some personal maids are, so I understand.'

She shook her head.

'Never, sir. Mistress was very private and serious. Didn't tell secrets. Didn't laugh and joke. Now I think of it I don't know why she was bothered having a lady's maid at all.'

'Well, it's usual, surely.'

'Yes, but for all the use she made of me she mightn't have been bothered. She never let me dress or undress her. I put her room in order but the closest I got to herself was when I braided her hair, or brushed it. She was always fretting about that hair. Were the ends split, was it falling out? She was always going on about it falling out.'

'Oh?'

'It didn't grow as thick as she would have liked it. She said it was fretting that did it.'

'Ah! Worrying. What did she worry about, do you think?'

'Maybe it was Squire. He . . . Oh, no. I shouldn't tell that, should I? Will I not get into trouble?'

'You must tell what you truthfully know, and I will guarantee it does you no harm.'

For a moment I despised myself saying this. If the squire should choose to punish or dimiss Polly Milroy for tittle-tattling about him behind his back, there would be little I, or the law, could do to stop him. On the other hand this conversation wasn't idle gossip. It was legally required. I cupped my hand behind my ear to encourage her.

'Go on, girl.'

'Oh, it's just that I don't think Squire and Mistress were that happy together. This last year he's not . . .'

She considered her choice of words.

'He's not gone to her at night as a husband does, or not so as us servants could tell. And people in kitchen said she didn't like it that he would spend so much time with Mr Woodley studying the plans for these works, or at the public houses in town.'

'Anything else?'

'Well, sir, about the public houses, that reminds me. She told me this herself. Squire particularly frightened her once. It seems he'd again been in Preston the night, playing cards maybe, and was riding home early through the woods, just when Mistress was out for her morning ride, going the way she always went. So he waited for her, you see, jumped out from behind a tree, so she said, like he was trying to scare her horse. Then he made a joke of it, said it was teasing. But the mistress she took it serious. To her it was not a joke.'

'When was this?'

'Last month, I think. She was sorely frighted, and I was so surprised, because she never told me suchlike before.'

'What was it about that ride, I wonder, that made your mistress take it again and again? Do you know?'

Polly shrugged.

'She enjoyed woods . . . the trees and that . . .'

'Yes, I suppose that was it. Now you said earlier that your mistress did not in general share her secrets with you, even though she did tell you she feared the squire. Which leads me to wonder whom she did confide in. I know it was not Miss Brockletower. Who then were Mrs Brockletower's friends?'

Polly's head was cocked to one side, watching the flames.

'Don't know, sir.'

I allowed a pause while she thought.

'She just liked riding. She liked horses.'

'Do you say her only friends were horses, then? Like Gulliver at the end, eh?'

'I don't know. Who's this Gulliver, sir?'

'Oh well, never mind. What was your mistress's demeanour, I mean, how did she act when you last saw her? When was that, by the way?'

'Last night, when I brought her a bowl of broth she'd asked for, in her room.'

'And how did she seem to you?'

'She was reading, I think. When I came in she snapped at me. But that's been her usual way lately, fretting and snapping at us servants. We don't like it but we must bear it, my father says, or we'll lose our places.'

'I see. Well, that will be all, Polly. Thank you.'

I was not going to get any more out of the girl and indeed the whole interview had thrown into doubt the commonplace belief that a lady is always better known to her maid than to anyone else.

The next one in was Timothy Shipkin, a gaunt fellow with spiky grey hair and a fierce light in his eyes. I knew him to be a Dissenter, a member of the Heptamerian sect who believe in all sorts of fantastic nonsense deriving from the number seven – the Awakening of the Seven Sleepers of Ephesus by the Archangels, the Seven Toes of Satan, and suchlike.

'Now, Timothy, it was you that found the body?'

'I did that.'

'Tell me how.'

He cleared his throat.

'It was like this. When Mistress's horse came back without

her, William Pearson, he sent us out to search. I went into Fulwood because I knew the forest best, and I knew the way Mistress would always ride, because I would see her at times in the woods early mornings. So I just followed, found a few fresh horse droppings, followed on and found her lying by the old hollow oak. Dead. Her throat was cut bad.'

'Indeed it was. I've seen it. Did you touch the body? Was she cold?'

'No, not quite cold she was.'

'And did you see evidence of any other person in the woods when you were searching, or after you found her? A vagabond perhaps?'

'Nobody.'

'And you found no knife or sharp blade beside the body such as might have given her the throat wound?'

'I did not.'

'Or nearby?'

'I found nothing but her.'

'And then?'

'I went back to Hall quick as I could, told what I'd found, then went to my work up Shot's Hill.'

'Why did you do that? Why not stay to help?'

'What help? She was dead. I don't mind who's dead, even the King, but there's always work to finish.'

'How well did you know your mistress?'

'Didn't know her. Didn't want to. A woman shouldn't ride astride the horse, but she did. I kept my distance lest I receive direction of the Lord and speak my mind.'

I had heard of this curious thing about Dolores Brockle-tower's manner of riding before. She seemed to have scant regard for custom, and less for the reputation of a lady.

I dismissed Shipkin, after telling him he would be called as a witness at the inquest, where I would ask him similar questions to those he had just answered.

William Pearson came in next and I asked him to detail what happened when Mrs Brockletower's mare arrived home riderless.

'She came in at the trot, wanting her provender.'

'By the way, what was she called, the mare?'

'We called her Molly.'

'Did Molly seem to have been hard-ridden at any point during the ride?'

'No, she was not in a sweat.'

'And she had on her saddle, and other tackle, in good order?'

'Aye.'

'Did you notice anything else about the horse?'

'No. Only the blood.'

'The blood?'

'Drops of blood on her neck, in her mane. Mistress's blood, you can suppose.'

'What kind of drops? Little ones . . . big ones?'

He pondered a moment, then said with deliberation, 'They were like thick gouts.'

'Are they still there – in the mane, on the neck?'

Pearson's eyes bulged incredulously. I have commonly seen the look on grooms and ostlers when they are asked (what they consider) ignorant questions about horses.

'You don't do that, man! After exercise you wash them down, you comb them.'

'Of course, yes. I just thought, in the heat of the moment . . . you know. And, er, when that was being done, was it noticed that the mare wanted a shoe?'

I rose and picked the horseshoe from the mantel.

'This shoe, for instance.'

Pearson took the shoe from me and turned it in his hands.

'The mare was soundly shod when she went out,' he said firmly. 'I made sure of it, that being my job. And when she returned she was still shod in all four. I made sure again, that *also* being my job, Mr Cragg.'

Some witnesses are like a hot cup on a cold day that should be drunk expressly. William Pearson was such a one, cooling fast towards me and, it seemed, anxious to get back to his duties. I hurried on.

'Well, what about the shoe itself? It was found not far from Mrs Brockletower's body. Does it come from a Garlick horse?'

'It looks like one of ours, but that's not to say it is. It might well be the work of our farrier Pennyfold, the blacksmith at Yolland. Then again, it might not.'

He handed me back the shoe and pushed himself impatiently out of the chair.

'Will that be all?' he asked abruptly.

Before letting Pearson go, I told him I'd want him, too, at the inquest. And then, as he went out of the room, another question hatched in my mind. This suddenly seemed of such significance that I jumped up and called him back.

'Tell me about the mare,' I said. 'What was she like? I mean in temperament. Was she difficult to ride?'

The man came back to me reluctantly, and with an audible, insolent sigh.

'Mistress, say what you like about her, she could handle a horse,' he stated. 'That mare is a very naughty one. You have to keep her to herself. Other horses, she'll bite them. She doesn't like them near. Now, I have my duties. Good day to you, Coroner.'

One by one over the next two hours the servants trooped into the parlour and then, after delivering themselves of whatever information about Mrs Brockletower they could call to mind, trooped out again. In every case they went back to their allotted tasks, the succession of small incessant functions which when added together are the life of a great house – the cheese-making, shall we say? The silver polishing, the currying of horses, the felling of beeches, the pedimentary works. Mr Spectator mounted an argument in his paper that all things pale compared to the significance of death. They had not seemed to do so in this house. If they had, the house itself would sicken and die. But its routines did not flinch in the face of mortality.

So what did I learn in those ten dozen minutes? Almost all I spoke to agreed that Mrs Brockletower had been in a fury or a fret for much of the day before she died, saying hard words to the servants and sending them scurrying around to fetch and carry. She had been calmer and quieter on the day before that, the Sunday, when she had given the day's instructions to Leather the butler, a fat red-headed fellow with the sonorous, booming voice of a dragoon sergeant.

'She asked me to find her a reel of fishing line, she did. I thought it was queer. She was no angler.'

'Did she intend to take up fishing, then?'

'She didn't want a rod, or hooks and bait. Just the line, she said.'

'What for?'

'She said it was for the hanging of pictures.'

'And you fetched some for her.'

'I did. Ten yards of it, wound on a stick. I asked her if she wanted it cutting but she says no, she's got scissors.'

And the day before that, I learned, Mrs Brockletower had been to town.

'To be measured for a dress.'

'Who is her dressmaker?'

'Talboys in Friar Gate.'

'Did he not attend her at home?'

'At first he did. But she took against his visits and preferred to go into town.'

'Why did she prefer that?'

'You'll have to ask Mr Talboys that, sir.'

I must have spoken to a dozen witnesses when, just as I had finished with Philip Barkworth – who divulged nothing I did not already know – there came a clatter of hooves from the yard. A single rider had come in, leading a pack pony slung with baggage. This, Barkworth told me, was the squire's valet, Tom Cowp, who had accompanied his master to York. Barkworth and I both hurried outside and found that Cowp had ridden in, and was alone.

Tom Cowp was a slim young fellow with a knowing look. I brought him into the parlour, still bespattered by mud from the road, to find out just what it was that he did know.

'Have you heard what happened here this morning, Tom?'

'About Mistress, sir? Yes, I heard about it on the road. People were talking about it already.'

'Saying what?'

'Oh, I shouldn't say, sir. People are that spiteful.'

I did not press him, remembering the remarks of Miriam Patten as I'd ridden through Gamull. But I noted that his demeanour was like that of the other servants, indeed like poor blind Sarah. None of them felt grief at the death of Dolores Brockletower.

'Well then, how far had the news got when you heard it?'

'I stopped in Skipton the night. By this noon I was in Clitheroe, where I heard the name Brockletower spoken. I enquired what was up. They said she was dead, and a lot else beside. People all over the marketplace were talking about it.'

'Why was the squire not with you?'

'He was with us as far as Skipton. But last night he rode away north to Settle, to speak with a gentleman about a horse he wants to buy. Told me to cut along ahead and he'd be home himself tomorrow.'

'Did you bring with you a letter or message from the squire to his wife?'

'No, sir, no letter. I was just to say that he'd be here tomorrow.'

'I see. Well, let's go back a little. What was his reason for going to York in the first instance?'

'Squire was looking at a house he might take for the races' week and Assizes, in August. And to view some horses, fast runners, maybe for racing. We visited some stud farms and other places where they had horses for sale.'

'And this horse he's eyeing up in Settle is one of them?'

'Yes.'

'So at York, you hadn't spent all the time in the city itself?'

'No. Only two or three days, looking at the house Squire might take, and paying calls. And one day we went out to Bishopsthorpe.'

'The archbishop's palace?'

'Yes. To see Archbishop Blackburne was the idea.'

Lancelot Blackburne was the most important person in York. His worldiness was the subject of much amused, or discontented, tittle-tattle. Many repeated the story that, before assuming holy orders, he had been a buccaneer in the West Indies. Some added that the Church of England had not very much changed him since, except to make him fatter.

'Did you go to Bishopsthorpe for any particular reason, or was it only a politeness to Mr Brockletower's relative?'

'You'll have to ask Squire that.'

The questions I had to ask, not only of the squire, were beginning to infest my inquiry like wasps in the roof. Dolores had been to town on Saturday. Was that significant? She had not been to church on Sunday. Did that mean anything? She had been angry – what about? And was she in truth frightened of the squire?

Then there was Squire Brockletower himself. Did he indeed go to Settle, or did he ride west ahead of his man and keep a fatal appointment with his wife early this morning in the Fulwood? After hearing Polly's account of what had allegedly happened there a month ago, I hardly dared think it. But I had no choice.

And finally the only certain witness to Mrs Brockletower's death – the horse. Why was there blood on her neck? I picked up the horseshoe and weighed it in my hands. Horses are all around us. They do the hundreds of tasks we ask of them with little complaint. How much do we in return think of them? Do we consider their natures and their needs? This horseshoe was heavy enough for a paperweight and I found myself speculating what it must feel like to be an animal with one of these nailed to each of your four feet.

Chapter Five

A NEW CLATTER FROM the yard caught my ear and, putting the horseshoe in my pocket, I went to the window. A post rider from Preston was dismounting. His hard-ridden horse's nostrils flared and contracted as it breathed deeply. He hitched the horse and drew a letter from his bag.

I went out to see if, as I suspected, it might be addressed to me. It was. As I tore through the seal I saw it had been impressed by the signet ring of Luke Fidelis. I read:

> *Titus, I am in receipt of your lines, by hand of Furzey.*
> *I cannot come today as I must operate on a fistula in*
> *ano, which I have so often postponed that my patient*
> *Mr Norris is patient no more. So Mrs Brockletower must*
> *await me until tomorrow, which she, unlike Mr Norris,*
> *will not mind. Shall we meet at the Turk's Head this*
> *evening? I will be glad to hear all of the circumstances.*
> *Meanwhile I urge you to store the corpse overnight*
> *in Squire Brockletower's Ice-house. Your friend,*
> *Luke Fidelis.*

'Is a reply paid?' I asked the post fellow, who nodded. I returned to Mrs Marsden's parlour to scribble a note assuring Luke I would be at the coffee house at nine. *I shall want to know why the Ice-house*, I added.

Having dispatched Luke's reply I asked William Leather for the key to the Ice-house, which he lifted from a hook-board in the kitchen. I then recruited Isaac Barrowford and Philip Barkworth to carry the body from the stable in which it had, until now, been laid. Hoisting the litter between them, they followed me to the Ice-house, which lay outside the confines of the yard. Here, isolated in the centre of the orchard that stood behind the stable block, on the lower slope of Shot's Hill, the fruit trees would in summer give it shade. It was a brick building half-buried in the ground and entered down steps and through a passage about five yards long. There was a door at each end of this passage, the inner one being kept closed by a spring, and thickly lagged on the inside with straw.

The interior was a double-vaulted space, built in brick and dimly lit by two lantern skylights, one at the apex of each vault, which brought not only light but ventilation. There were blocks of ice parcelled in straw and ranged on the ground along the walls. Above these, on slatted racks, were rows of wicker baskets similarly packed with smaller lumps of ice. A work table stood against the far wall. Above it, on hooks driven into the brick wall, hung a variety of hammers, picks, hatchets and saws for breaking, cutting and crushing the ice into cubes, shards, or slush for the making of the desserts that had lately become a fashionable refreshment to the palates of the gentry.

As we entered, our breath smoked in the cold air. I began manhandling the work table, a solid piece of furniture a good six feet long, into the centre of the space. Barrowford and Barkworth were taking pains behind me as they negotiated the litter down the steps and along the short corridor. There was just enough room. Barkworth in particular was breathing hard.

'Lay the litter directly on this,' I told them when I had finished manoeuvring the table.

'Why is it, Mr Cragg,' Barkworth panted as they deposited their burden, 'that the dead's heavier than the living?'

'Are they? I don't know. We must ask Dr Fidelis when he comes.'

'It's stone dead she is, and that's why,' declared Barrowford, rubbing the sweat off his hands on the front of his smock. 'And stone's pulled her soul down to bottom of all.'

Mr Spectator observes that a noble sentiment, depressed with homely language, is far preferable to a vulgar one, inflated with sound and expression. His subject is tragedy and the stage, but the sentiment applies equally, I believe, to ordinary discourse. However I did not commend Barrowford for his remark in these terms, as I found I could not be quite sure what they had meant. Instead I lifted the edge of the horse blanket that covered the corpse's face.

When I had last seen it, that face had been pressed to the ground, so that there was difficulty in viewing it properly. Now I was looking squarely down at the features. The prominent cheekbones were perhaps a little too sharply defined for the purer forms of female beauty, which authorities agree ought to tend towards softness. But this boniness was at least offset by a pair of full lips of which the alluring London actress Mrs Peg Woffington might have been proud. Presumably William Pearson had closed her eyes before loading her onto the cart. I have often noticed how as a general rule the dead body with its eyes closed looks not at all like the person who once inhabited the same flesh, not even like to that person asleep. At any rate I did not at this moment fully recognize Dolores Brockletower, whom I had seen only rarely over the past couple of years. Under this examination, closer than a man (other than a husband) might have decently given her in life, she appeared harder and bonier than she had then seemed.

What had happened to her? I made my inspection as a matter of habit, but could find no help here. In my early days as coroner, I had been convinced that to read the expression on a dead face would be to see the truth of the death itself, as if it recorded an impression of what had occurred, fossil-like. But I was soon obliged to conclude it did no such thing. Faces, which look in death as if they accused someone, turn out to have died of a seizure; others, which appear placid as a sheep, are found to have been violently murdered. In death, everything is contrary and opposite to what might be expected. But still I continued the habit, in spite of experience, of examining the faces of the dead.

I then took another look at the wound in the neck. It was, as I had already guessed, a continuous gash, and there seemed little doubt that it was what had killed her. I flipped the blanket back into place without comment. Barkworth and Barrowford were standing heraldically on either side of the door. I ushered them out along the passage and through the outside door of the Ice-house, which I locked behind me. Then I sent them back to their work.

Returning to the kitchen I replaced the Ice-house key back on the hook-board and enquired yet again if there had been any word from the squire. As there was none, and with nothing else to do at Garlick Hall, I asked William Pearson to bring out my horse. He held the head while I mounted and, before he let it go, I made one last request.

'I would like to make a trial of the circumstances of Mrs Brockletower's death, Pearson. Will you be so kind as to ride out to the hollow oak tomorrow morning *on the very same mare ridden this morning by your mistress* – what was the horse's name? Yes, Molly. Ride Molly out to the oak at seven in the morning, where you will meet me. It will only take a few minutes.'

Pearson's pitted, lumpy face looked up at me as if I was making him eat a bad almond, but he agreed to do it. Then I set off on the way home.

At Gamull, on my way back, I again saw the ragged woman Miriam Patten, who had quizzed me from the roadside that morning. She was breaking up some small branches of forest firewood outside her cottage door.

'Mr Lawyer, sir! Mr Lawyer!' she croaked as soon as I approached. 'What news? Did the Devil come for the squire's lady last night?'

'No such thing,' I told her firmly. 'It is mischievous prattle, is that.'

The woman had dropped her wood and was scrambling along beside the horse, eager for the news – as if it would feed or clothe her.

'What struck her down, then? What killed her?'

'That I cannot say.'

'Ah, you cannot say! You cannot say!'

Her tone was full of the scorn country people show in private discussions of gentry affairs. She had stopped trying to keep pace with me now and, not wishing to let her sally go by, I turned in the saddle to reply. She was standing by the roadside with her fists propped on her hips, looking after me.

'Come along to the inquest, Miriam,' I called back. 'You can hear for yourself. The jury will find out the truth, and all can attend.'

'Will it, though?' she retorted. 'Will *they* let it?'

I rode on, leaving her standing looking after me. But after

twenty-five yards I turned my horse around again and trotted back.

'Miriam – have you seen or heard tell of Squire Brockletower being in the vicinity yesterday, or today?'

'No, sir. The man's not been seen here today, nor yesterday.'

'Or at any time in the last ten days?'

'No, sir. I heard he was away to York. Any road, he's not been here-about. Why do you want to know, sir?'

'Oh, a fancy, that's all.'

I wheeled the horse, but on an impulse pulled her up again. I felt in my pocket and found a coin. Miriam still stood with her hands on her hips, looking up at me, and suddenly I had a vision of her as she must have been as a young girl forty years ago, with flowing hair and straight back. It was only a moment, I blinked, and then it was gone. She raised her withered palm and I deposited the coin there.

A few minutes further along the road I met Mrs Marsden returning to Garlick from her visit to town. She was seated beside the drayman that brought empty milk churns back to the farms. I thanked her for the safe delivery of my letters, and for the cooperation of the Garlick Hall servants in answering my questions. I explained that we had placed the body of Mrs Brockletower in the Ice-house, at Dr Fidelis's suggestion.

'It will be a good enough resting place,' I said, 'until the doctor comes for his post-mortem examination in the morning. I shall return with him. By the way, Tom Cowp's returned ahead of the squire.'

Her eyes widened in surprise.

'Why, and Squire not with him, sir?'

'He sent Cowp on ahead with his baggage while he diverted

to Settle to look at a horse. But Cowp says we shall see him tomorrow.'

We parted then and I continued on my way to the town.

It was close to seven and the light had just begun to fade when I reached Market Place. I looked in at the office to ask how Furzey had fared at the cottages, but my clerk greeted me by waving a folded paper in my face. My letter to Bailiff Grimshaw was replied to.

Ephraim Grimshaw had so far been elected bailiff four years in succession and, it seemed, the only thing that might persuade him to give up the office would be the certainty of succeeding as Mayor. He thought of himself as a consummate politician and manager of men and money; in reality he was merely rich from having a half-share in his father's leather-dressing shop, and was otherwise lazy and domineering. The business continued to flourish under the wise direction of his brother, while Ephraim banked half the profits and sought new ways to enhance the prestige of the bailiff by hosting banquets and leading ceremonial processions through the streets on every possible occasion. There was one more thing about Ephraim Grimshaw that I should mention: he hated me.

Mr Cragg, he wrote, *if you eschew the use of my officers when enquiring into this doleful event you will exceed your authority. I shall send to you tomorrow with my instructions. Ephraim Grimshaw, Bailiff to the Corporation.*

'Is it another smack from Mr Grimshaw?' asked Furzey, observing me reading the note.

I gave it to him to read and said, 'I am *ultra vires*, it seems. He wishes me to heed his instructions.'

Furzey, who knows as much of the law as I do, at least insofar as it affects the Corporation and its affairs, read through the letter then patted me companionably on the back. The action was in character. He always behaved more like my equal than my clerk.

'Well, let's see, Mr Cragg, sir. You always do exceed your authority, in the eyes of Mr Grimshaw. And he *will* exalt his own instructions. But your jurisdiction is as clear as ever, and wholly distinct from his, as *we* in this office well know.'

'Yes, Furzey. But the bailiff doesn't, and that is where our difficulty lies.'

'Shall I deal with Mr Grimshaw's communication in the usual way, then?'

I nodded and Furzey crumpled the letter in his fist and dropped it into the wastebasket.

My Elizabeth's parents lived in the village of Broughton, two or three miles up the northern road, and she had gone to visit them that afternoon with a pie in her basket. She would not be back until the next day, so I was glad a second pie had been left in the pantry for Matty to serve up for me, as I was exceedingly hungry. I washed my meal down with a glass of wine, and hurried out in good time to meet Fidelis at the Turk's Head coffee house.

But first, I strolled down Friar Gate, north-west from Market Place, to Edward Talboys's dressmaker's shop. Lamplight glowed from within, so I climbed the steps, rapped and tried the handle. Even at this late hour the door was unbolted and I pushed it open, setting a warning bell clanging on a spring above my head. I stepped in and surveyed the front room of the shop, with its counter, its bolts of cloth in their deep pigeonholes, and its hooks, buttons and ribbons displayed for sale in glass-topped cases. It was deserted but through a leather-curtained doorway at the back a tread could be heard coming down a flight of stairs.

They stopped a moment, perhaps halfway down, and I heard the dressmaker calling.

'What have you done with the scissors?'

A moment later his head appeared around the door frame, peering this way and that in the shop.

'Jerome? Is that you? Where have you been? I can't lay hands on the Sheffield cuts.'

'Ned, it's not Jerome,' I called out. 'It's Titus Cragg.'

He and I had sometimes been playmates together as children, and though our paths had since diverged I still liked him. His wife had died giving birth to the last of a quartet of daughters but he had always tried to preserve a cheerful demeanour in spite of his difficulties. He had a chubby beaming face and what hair he possessed was fair, running in a reversed fringe around the back of his head from one ear to the other. This he had fashioned in sidecurls above the ears and a short tail behind.

'Ah, Titus!' he cried as he brushed through the curtain and saw me. 'I wondered if you were my poxy-faced journeyman. He took himself off on Sunday and I've not seen the barmpot since.'

In quick, darting movements he went to the shelves and took down a bolt of grey worsted from its hole. He bumped it straight down on the counter and began unrolling it along the board's length, feeling the roll as he did so. He had unrolled half of it and palpitated the rest, when he began rolling it up again.

'No good! They're not there. I'm sure he was working from this cloth when I saw them last.'

'The scissors?'

'The scissors, yes, the cuts – a pair of my sharpest. The man's done it before, leaving tools rolled up in cloth, not to be found for weeks or months sometimes. The slovenly whelp. But now he's off somewhere, I don't know where, so I can't ask him about it. He's done *that* before an'all, going off. He's exactly like a dog after bitches. Are you paying a call, Titus, or is this business?'

'Coroner's business, Ned. The business of Mrs Ramilles Brockletower. You have heard?'

'Oh, aye, every bugger's heard. Found dead this morning in the Fulwood, throat sliced open.'

The dressmaker hoisted the bolt back into place, rammed it home and turned to me again, placing his hands flat on the counter between us.

'And she was in this shop only Saturday, ordering a gown she shall never wear.' Edward sighed. 'Nor pay for neither.'

I was grateful to him for bringing me to the point.

'Yes, so they told me at Garlick Hall. I am considering whether you ought to be called as a witness at the inquest. What can you tell me about her visit?'

'I passed the time of day, of course. But you should speak with my Abigail.'

'Abigail – your eldest?'

'It was she that served her. Mrs Brockletower always asked expressly for Abigail, you see.'

'Isn't that out of the ordinary? A rich customer like her . . .'

'Quite so. She *should* wish to be attended by the master craftsman – myself. But no, Titus, she liked his daughter better. Took a fancy to Abigail from the moment she saw her. Wouldn't let any other person attend her, not me, not Jerome.'

The dressmaker leaned forward and lowered his voice almost to a whisper.

'She *said* it was on account of her husband, that he wouldn't allow a male hand to touch her or take measurements, or a male eye to see such things being done to her. Only Abby, she said, could do it.'

'I suppose that is a natural, ladylike coyness.'

'Up to a certain point, it is. And there's no doubt my girl is a very good seamstress. Also it is her regular job to assist in fitting ladies who do not bring their personal maids with them for the purpose, and Mrs Brockletower did always come alone. But I was not even allowed into the room to see the first fitting, think of that. I mean my upstairs room, which is for private consultations, fittings and the like. Mrs Brockletower always saw Abby there, behind a shut door. She really believed it was indelicate, even a form of nakedness, to parade in front of a man in an unfinished, pinned-together dress. Well, of course, it's absurd. But she was adamant.'

'How often did Mrs Brockletower call at the shop?'

'She ordered many dresses, many. One every month or two, I should say. Perhaps eight or nine in the year. But she was fussy and the work required laborious consultation, and several visits for fitting each one. I offered that we would go out to her at Garlick Hall, but she wouldn't have it. *She* came to *us*, that was the rule.'

'So Mrs Brockletower spent the time of her visit last Saturday with Abigail?'

'Yes.'

'How old is the girl? I forget.'

'Eighteen.'

'Old enough to give evidence, then. Is she here?'

He shook his head.

'I sent her yesterday with a gown for fitting to a lady in Garstang. She will be home this evening.'

'Did they see each other alone?'

'Always, when she came here.'

'And did Abby ever say anything about Mrs Brockletower to you or her sisters? What she said . . . what humour she was in.'

'No, she was as close as one of your legal deed-boxes.'

Ned's information was going to require some further thought, and a conversation with Abigail as soon as possible. I remembered my question that morning to Polly Milroy: in whom did Mrs Brockletower confide? Perhaps now I had the answer. Perhaps she confided in her dressmaker, Abby Talboys.

I returned my hat to my head and prepared to go on my way.

'So what did you yourself make of Dolores Brockletower?' I asked as a parting shot. 'In a general way, I mean?'

'I am a dressmaker, Titus, and I have four daughters. Is there any man in this town better acquainted with what a woman wants? But I'll tell you the truth – I could never add that one up. A woman's a woman across the world, is what I say, but she was a mystery.'

Chapter Six

THE TURK'S HEAD coffee house, which was then kept by Noah Plumtree, stands off Church Gate, a couple of minutes' walk from my home. That night it was middling full. At one table two men played chess, while a huddled group around another were enjoying a theological argument. As I passed them I thought I heard the phrases 'seven sleepers' and 'my fundament!', which brought a thought of Timothy Shipkin and his Heptamerian certainties.

Fidelis had not yet come in and I wondered if he was still operating on Mr Norris, using procedures whose details I could only, and then reluctantly, surmise. I asked for a jug of negus, a couple of pipes, a pen and paper and a copy of the *Preston Journal*. Then I found an empty cubicle around whose table we would be able to talk privately.

I took the pen and made a list of possible jurors for the inquest – freeholders, copyholders and leaseholders from Garlick and Yolland and the area around the Fulwood. I would need to summon the jury tomorrow, as I had determined to have the inquest the day after, if possible. Having cobbled fifteen names together, I took up the newspaper and was uninterestedly running through a list of ships inbound to the port of Liverpool when Dr Fidelis strode in.

'Success!' he crowed. 'Old Norris is defistulated.'

Screwing up my face to discourage any further confidences on the subject, I poured him a beaker of punch.

'I would rather hear why you have expressly requested that we place the corpse in Garlick Hall's Ice-house, Luke.'

'Because it will last better there.'

'How?'

'I'll tell you.'

Settling himself opposite me he picked up his pipe and a spill. He held the latter to the candle that stood on the table between us.

'Decomposition goes more slowly when flesh is cold and even more so when it is frozen,' he continued sitting back and setting fire to the pipe. 'The philosopher and Lord Chancellor Francis Bacon tried to prove this, having heard it from trustworthy travellers to China, where the fact has been known for centuries. But Bacon caught a cold and died, you know, before the fact was demonstrated.'

'Died of a chill, didn't he?' I jested. 'The cold did not preserve him, then.'

'Your mocking only mocks you, Titus. In the far north of Tartary, the people often eat the flesh of animals they have dug out of the permanent ice-fields, centuries after the meat was buried.'

I laughed frankly at the absurdity of this.

'After centuries? Come come, it's quite impossible, Luke. I put that on a footing with Sir John Mandeville's frozen speech. You recall it?'

Fidelis evidently did not. I grant you, Sir John cannot be counted a trustworthy traveller but, then, nor can Lemuel Gulliver. I sometimes marvelled at my friend's lack of interest in English literature.

'Mandeville tells of the words being frozen as they left his and his companions' lips during an Arctic voyage. Because of this, their speech went unheard for weeks until, under a thawing wind, the words warmed up and started to sound in the air all around the ship.'

It was Fidelis's turn to laugh, this time in delight.

'Well, for spoken words to be preserved like that would be very useful, even more than the preservation of Mrs Brockletower's meat, I think. And yet, why not? The preservation of meat by freezing is a fact, after all. Why not freeze words so we can hear them later?'

I shook my head in despair. Fidelis was always confounding me with incredible claims for the future of natural philosophy, derived from his reading and correspondence. But when I tried to fill the gaps in his own education, it only ended with my being wrong-footed again. I must admit I was also disturbed by the thought of Mrs Brockletower as 'meat'.

Fidelis had laughed again, vastly amused by my discomfort.

'At all events, Titus, you must believe what I say about the preservation of meat. I occasionally see the transactions of the Royal Academy of Sciences in Stockholm, where Monsieur Laureus has been working on that very matter in purposefully designed ice-houses. These are not unlike the ones that are presently so fashionable in gentlemen's houses in England, such as Mr Ramilles Brockletower's, though he puts the installation to less serious uses.'

Having laid down his pipe he had, while speaking, been searching his pockets. Now he pulled out a folded paper.

'So you see,' he went on, wagging the paper at me, 'in depositing our late Mrs Brockletower in the Ice-house, we lend the place a nobility that it hardly receives from iced syllabubs and other trifles. If we left her there indefinitely I firmly believe she would continue uncorrupted, conceivably for centuries, like certain of the holy martyrs.'

'Or the Seven Sleepers,' I murmured.

He did not hear me. He was spreading the paper open on the table between us, smoothing its creases with his long bony hands.

'Now look here!' exclaimed Fidelis.

I looked, expecting this to be the latest bulletin from the Swedish Academy. Instead it was my letter to him, written earlier in the day.

'In this letter, Titus, you wrote "the accident, if so it was, etcetera". What do you mean by "if so it was"? Either it was, or it wasn't.'

'Yes, but at the time I wrote I wasn't sure. I am sure now that it was no accident.'

Fidelis's eyes were animated, sparkling in the candlelight. He snapped his fingers.

'Particulars, particulars, Titus! I am burning to know what I may find when I examine the body tomorrow.'

So I provided an account of everything I had seen and heard at Garlick Hall, confining myself to the facts, since I well knew how Fidelis would subsequently enjoy piling up the inferences.

'So you see, Luke, when I wrote to you mentioning a possible "accident", I did not yet have all of the facts.'

'And now?'

'I still don't know what happened. But I have established many more facts.'

'Telling you what?'

'For one thing, that she was afraid of something.'

I told him about the quotation written in her commonplace book. *The Soul of a Man and that of a Woman are made very unlike*. And, on a separate line, *Imagine therefore: my pain and fear*.

'Fear, was it?' mused Fidelis, 'fear for her life at someone else's hand, perhaps. Do you know where the quotation comes from?'

I shook my head.

'I have read it, I think, but I can't remember where.'

'Well, wherever it's from, it's about the relations or differences between men and women. The only man she had a relationship with was her husband.'

'As far as we know. But she also refers to her pain. Wanting to get out of pain is a motive for suicide.'

'Well, if she did kill herself, someone, or something, took away the blade she used.'

'Some *thing*?'

'Some animal . . .?'

'Impossible! But maybe Timothy Shipkin did.'

'I am inclined to believe him when he says he found nothing. He is a very pious Dissenter. And why would he interfere in that way?'

'But I take it your enquiries have ruled out an accident, at all events.'

'I believe so, but I am counting on you to confirm that her injuries could not have been accidental.'

'Well, from what I've heard pure chance seems an unlikely cause. No, Titus, as far as I can see, it looks like nothing less than bloody murder. Which thought calls for more pipes and another jug of negus, I think.'

He snapped his bony fingers again, this time for the potboy, then turned back to me.

'If not an accident, the cause of death would be there to see. Was anything at all found when they searched?'

I felt in my pocket and brought out the horseshoe.

'This. It was under the leaves, but not far from where she lay. As you see it is not rusty. But it did not come from Mrs Brockletower's own horse.'

Taking the shoe, he ran his eyes over it, then laid it down on the board.

'It was found just like this?'

'Yes.'

'Then it may have been cast from the horse of the man that slew her. It may be the key to finding the killer.'

'A vagabond—'

'But from the blood on the horse's neck, it appears she received her wound on horseback. How would a footpad get high enough?'

'The villain jumped up behind her and cut her from there.'

Fidelis was not impressed.

'Difficult to do, unless she helped him up.'

'Then he had climbed the tree.'

'Yes, that is possible, I agree. But it would mean the crime was done by means of a trap laid for the lady specifically. A man in the tree would have had to know she would be there and call out to her to approach him.'

'But surely you can see on whom suspicion must fall, if her killer did not chance on his victim.'

Fidelis waved his hand in a gesture of impatience.

'Oh, yes, yes. On the squire, of course. Until you speak to him – tomorrow with luck – you can be certain of nothing. But what I say is, the information you gathered about the relations between him and his wife is indicative. It points the finger directly at him.'

'But it is circumstantial,' I protested. 'It doesn't mean he must have killed her. Many couples make each other miserable without resorting to murder. And murder by Ramilles Brockle-tower is a verdict I shall very much prefer to avoid. He is still only a young man, but he is very wealthy, and of position in the county. And anyway to kill one's wife in this way, to cut her throat, would be utterly foolhardy, not to say uncouth, in such a gentleman.'

Fidelis laughed again.

'How should he do it, then, Titus? What would be the gentle-manly way?'

Covering my renewed discomfort at Fidelis's jocularity, our second pipes were brought with a fresh jug of punch. Fidelis sat back watching, as the boy laid everything on the table.

'To continue with the argument, however,' he said when he was once again puffing smoke, 'you yourself mention Brockletower's youth. He is hot-headed, maybe. And he served in the navy, where no doubt he saw and did such uncouth things as we can hardly guess at.'

'I still prefer the notion of the vagabond.'

'Because you want a quiet life. Where's your spirit? Some poor nameless vagrant dangling from a gibbet for his sins – who cares about that? But Ramilles Brockletower standing on the scaffold in his fine lawn shirt with the neck open – now that's a ship with a much fuller set of sails.'

'But where would the ship take us?' I sighed. My friend's enthusiasm for murder was making me gloomy. 'Into the unknown, Luke. The good character of the gentry is the rock on which our nation is founded.'

Fidelis was smiling. He pointed accusingly.

'You don't believe that, Titus. You say it, but do not feel it.'

'I do,' I protested. 'If Brockletower is a murderer I shall applaud his punishment. But all the same I shall wish it were not so.'

Fidelis did not pursue the point. He leaned forward, wanting to get a rational explanation of what happened in the woods to Mrs Brockletower. He was so much the empiricist that it was sometimes difficult to remember he was also a papist.

'Let us assume that the squire did kill her. We must then ask how he managed it. I say the procession of events was something like this. Brockletower gets from York to Skipton yesterday afternoon, and separates from his man. The man puts up for the night where he is, but Brockletower rides on, supposedly to Settle but in reality to the Fulwood, which he reaches some time during the night. He knows exactly when his lady rides each morning and along what route. He waits for her by the hollow oak, as your informant told us he has done at least once before. His horse, at some point, throws a shoe. When she arrives he surprises her, rides alongside her mount and, with a knife or perhaps a razor ready in his hand, slits open her throat. She falls. The horse gallops away with some of her blood on its neck. Brockletower dismounts and looks her over for a moment to check that she is dead. Remounting, he notices the shoe is missing. He occupies the rest of the day in following a long circuitous route, which takes him back home to Garlick Hall at nightfall. On the way he has the horse re-shod and, we might suppose, passes time at an inn where he is not known.'

'Well that, at least, is something we may be able to prove,' I said, still unhappy about the drift of his suspicions.

'However, we must bear in mind that facts do not necessarily come first,' continued my friend, warming to his narrative. 'We must also consider the prime cause. Death always has a cause and a reason, and the cause leads to the reason, not the other way. If you discover the cause – which as coroner is your task – you shall uncover the reason.'

'What kind of cause do you have in mind?'

'If I were you, for a case of murder, I would consider only three: lucre, love or reputation.'

'In my experience, which is quite long, hatred often comes into it.'

'Yes, of course, but hatred is secondary. It has its causation as well as murder has, and this is always, once again, one or more of the three primary matters I have mentioned. At the bottom, I assure you, Dolores Brockletower's death will have to do with the state of her marriage. The problem is that she was so close-hearted and tight-lipped. If she'd been more confiding you could proceed by questioning the confidante.'

'Well from what I have heard this evening, there may really be such a person, Luke.'

I told him of my visit to the dressmaker's shop.

'So it's possible,' I went on, 'that she found in Abigail Talboys someone she could unburden herself to, which would be why she preferred the two of them to be alone whenever she went there for fittings.'

'Good, good. This is promising. The sooner you see Miss Talboys the better.'

'She may assist with more details of the squire's joke, played on his wife at the hollow oak a few weeks ago.'

'What if it was no joke?' asked Luke darkly. 'What if it was a *rehearsal*?'

'It may have been simply high spirits. The Brockletowers were a young married couple. Such couples skylark.'

'I'll have to take your word for it.'

'They do! They flirt and joke. That's what makes it all such a pleasure.'

'Is it?'

Luke's brown, bachelor eyes were upon me, a penetrating

look. I suspected he was thinking about me and Elizabeth, and what we might do when we skylark.

'Of course it is. You must marry and you will discover.'

He picked up his rummer and drank, turning away from my remark as from something disturbing.

'Well,' he said, putting down his glass at last. 'I do not think this was skylarking on Brockletower's part. A joke is not a joke unless it is equally shared by both parties, the joker and the other. Mrs Brockletower was not amused by it. And anyway Ramilles Brockletower does not strike me as a skylarker.'

I conceded the point with a sigh.

'We have not come to any conclusion tonight,' I said. 'I had hoped your darting intellect would provide me with some new ideas.'

'Come, come, Titus, we have only just started and there are many things we need to know. Whose is the horseshoe? What is the significance of the squire's first rendezvous with his wife at the hollow oak? Why had she been in so disagreeable a humour? Why was she constantly short with the servants? Why did she cut this man Woodley dead?'

He was speaking hurriedly, like a boy turning over stones to find a worm to bait a hook. I was about to speak but he raised his finger to show he had not finished.

'In cases of unexpected disease I often find it useful to see what is new in the life of the patient; what alteration has occurred to upset the balance of their constitution. We may do the same thing here. And if we do, what is found?'

I considered for a moment.

'Building works,' I said. 'Alterations to the house. Mr Woodley and his pediment.'

'Exactly.'

'Mrs Brockletower did find the disturbance irksome,' I went

on. 'And I am not altogether surprised that she felt the same about Woodley. I do myself, and I am not required to look on his leveret's face and hear his piping voice every day. But it is not just his person that she could not abide, Luke. She resented the time her husband devoted to it – the endless discussions with Woodley over the plans, and so on.'

'And that suggests?'

'Her continued regard for her husband. She was jealous of his time.'

'All true. But does that suggest she should be murdered?'

There was nothing but dottle in my pipe. I reached for the punch jug and peered inside. It too was empty except for a sodden, purple mush of lees, lemon peel and cinnamon fibres.

'Time to go home,' I said.

Fidelis looked crestfallen.

'Oh, another jug, Titus,' he pleaded.

'No. We must ride early to meet William Pearson at the hollow oak.'

'For what purpose?'

'To try something I have in mind.'

I rose and snapped my pipe in half before laying the pieces down on the pewter tray.

'I ride at six-thirty. You will join me, of course.'

Walking home I felt pleased with my parting shot. I did not tell Fidelis of my plan in detail. But I knew he would be quite unable to refuse the lure of a visit to the hollow oak, despite his proven disinclination for early rising.

Chapter Seven

A MAN SLEEPS WELL after drinking with Colonel Negus, and I arose refreshed shortly after half past five. I made a hasty breakfast of bread and cheese while the dun cob was saddled and brought to the door. By six-thirty, I was clapping my hat on my head, ready to leave for the appointment I had made on the previous evening with William Pearson.

I stood for a moment on my topmost front step, looking around. The market-traders to my left had already set out their stalls and the place was noisy with bustle. The house itself stood right beside my office on Cheapside, facing the west flank of the Moot Hall, where the Mayor and Corporation met and the front door of which opened on the conjunction of Church Gate and Fisher Gate. Part of the market spilled over into Cheapside, and my street had become established as the poulterers' pitch, always flapping with birds brought out of their coops and hung by the legs from stall-poles. Amidst all this squawking and commotion I could not see Fidelis anywhere. But since he was a notorious slug-a-bed and my cob had been ready and waiting for a good five minutes I decided I would ride on, in the expectation that the doctor could catch me up on the road. Leaving word with Furzey to that effect, I set out.

At the parish church we threaded our way into and around

a jam of carts and coops, but I soon reached the end of Church Gate and was trotting through the suburbs under a high, dry canopy of steely grey cloud. It was not until I reached the high point of Ribbleton Moor, on which a few twists of fog or low cloud still lingered, that I heard the sound of galloping hooves coming up behind, and soon Dr Fidelis overshot us on the road, careering past on his big black gelding. He slowed to a trot up ahead, so that now it was for me to catch up with him. When I did I found my friend out of breath and less good-humoured than he had been on the previous night.

'I wish you would tell me what we are doing,' he said rather testily. 'I've missed my breakfast, which I hope wasn't for nothing.'

'No doubt you can get a plate of something when we reach the Hall,' I told him placidly. 'They press a very good cheese there. But first I want to make a particular trial at the hollow oak. You will see what it is. I have some hopes it'll benefit our inquiry.'

I was a little pleased to be able to keep him for the time being in the dark (and hungry). Fidelis was a fond friend to me, yet there will always be a certain competition between us. In this case I was sowing curiosity, in the hope of reaping praise. That may seem ridiculous in relations with a man ten years younger than myself. But Fidelis's brain was so keen that, whenever I formed what I thought a clever notion of my own, I liked to make the most of it.

Pearson was not the kind that kept his betters waiting and I was sure he would be at the hollow oak before us. And so he was, sitting astride the mare Molly. My first thought on seeing him was of Ramilles Brockletower.

'Has the squire returned yet?' I asked, without ceremony.

'I am told he has, sir. Last night.'

'You didn't see him?'

'No, I returned to my cottage at eight for my supper, and

he'd not come home by then. I left Barrowford a-waiting so there'd be someone to take his horse, and *he* told me this morning that Squire had ridden in about nine, with his horse well spurred and lathered-up. Squire'd already learned the news of the mistress. He heard it on the road, and then he rode like the Devil to get here as fast as he could.'

'Well, I hope he will be there when we reach the Hall later,' I said. 'I must see him this morning at all costs. But meanwhile we will get on with this business.'

I first showed Fidelis the place where she had lain, a patch of relatively bare earth. There had been a pool of blood under the body when I had first seen it.

'There is little blood here now,' said Luke. 'You said it was a great quantity.'

'So it was. I'm puzzled. There was a congealed pool of it on the earth, and it's gone.'

Pearson leaned forward and scanned the ground. The exposed earth was scuffed and depressed by a number of footprints. Among them he pointed to the indistinct marks of something that might have been an animal.

'Pigs most likely,' he said without emotion. 'We should've buried that blood. Too late now.'

'Quite,' I said, a little stiffly. The thought of a woodland boar gorging on the dried blood of the late wife of Squire Brockletower made my stomach turn.

'See here,' said Fidelis, pointing to the ground. 'Among these footprints, a depression that might have been made by a knee, made by someone that went down to look at the body.'

I tried to remember if I had seen this when first looking at the body. I couldn't.

'It wasn't made by me at all events,' I said, remembering how I myself had crouched to avoid soiling my breeches with mud. I asked Pearson if anyone yesterday had knelt. He thought not, at least when he went to collect the body. I asked him to show me the place where the horseshoe had been found. It was about ten yards from the tree, beside a tuft of grass. There was nothing more to show Fidelis, so I turned to Pearson to commence the experiment.

'Will you please station the mare beside the tree, over the place where your mistress lay?' I asked him.

'Shall I remount, sir?'

His voice and manner were impassive, that of a servant scrupulously carrying out the instructions of his betters, however daft.

'Yes, of course. We must all remount.'

We did so and as Fidelis and I moved to the edge of the clearing, Pearson walked the temperamental mare forward to her mark. She shied and danced a little but his horsemanship was equal to her and they were soon standing in the exact place I had indicated.

'Now, Luke,' I said, 'I want you to ride up to Mr Pearson and attempt to bring the gelding alongside the mare's flank. I want you to get in such a position as you would if you were meaning to cut her rider's throat.'

Pearson jerked up his head in a sudden show of apprehension, his hand going to the stock at his neck.

'Now, Pearson, don't be alarmed,' I reassured him. 'This is a trial, and your windpipe is quite safe.'

'Now I see what you are about, Titus,' said Fidelis. 'All right, let's try it. Head to tail, I think.'

Bumping his heels into his horse's flanks, Fidelis urged him forward. But, as soon as they approached within five yards, Molly tossed her head and snorted her displeasure, then danced backwards out of the way.

'No, no,' I instructed. 'You have to get closer, Luke, and stay longer. Try it again from the beginning. Back into position, Pearson.'

They tried again. This time Molly was even more spooked. Her eye rolled, she spun around and kicked backwards with her hind legs. Her flashing hooves found only air, but the protest was enough. I called Luke back and said I would try it myself, on my less intimidating, shorter-legged mount. But Molly could no more have us alongside her than she could tolerate Luke and his gelding. She whinnied as soon as we approached, then suddenly reared steeply, her forelegs boxing the air. Taken by surprise, Pearson lost his balance and his feet in the stirrups went up. As soon as they passed the vertical, he was lost. He seesawed for a moment but gravity had the last word and he slid backwards, and rather to one side, before toppling off the horse's rump and crashing to the ground. The delinquent mare took off as if she'd heard a thunderclap and headed down the narrow ride, veering this way and that before jinking into the trees and disappearing from sight.

Pearson sat with his legs outstretched, dazed. Fidelis immediately dismounted and went down on one knee beside him.

'Are you hurt, man?'

The huntsman shook his head. I could not tell if this was to clear it or give a negative answer.

'I've not been thrown by a horse for twenty year,' he said. '*That* hurts.'

The doctor helped him to his feet and dusted the remnants of leaves and twigs from his coat, like a mother picking up a fallen child. Pearson, not much appreciating the solicitude, shrugged him off and went to pick up his hat.

'We'd better follow Molly back to Garlick Hall,' I said, walking the cob towards Pearson and reaching down with my hand. 'Pearson, will you come up behind me?'

He shook his head.

'No, I'll walk it.'

He made off through the trees, his gait a trifle stiff. No doubt his backside had been as bruised as his dignity.

'What do you make of my trial?' I said to Fidelis as we left Pearson behind in the woods and headed down towards the brook-crossing.

'I'd say it was highly indicative,' he said.

'You mean that her throat could not have been cut by some-one on horseback?'

'No, no. I don't mean that. Molly would clearly allow nei-ther my horse, nor yours, anywhere near her. But what is the difference between our mounts and, shall we say, the squire's?'

'I don't know. I don't anything about the squire's horse.'

'You do. You know where it is stabled.'

He let me ponder this for a few moments, until I grasped the point he was making.

'Why yes, I see!' I exclaimed. 'The squire's animal is Molly's stablemate. *Ergo* they would be familiar to each other. *Ergo* Molly, with Dolores Brockletower up, would perhaps tolerate the presence by her side of an animal she knows, ridden by a man she also knows. But she would shy away if approached by strangers.'

'And the hypothesis of Squire Brockletower's guilt in this becomes circumstantially stronger as a result – wouldn't you say?'

'No . . . Or rather, yes. But, mind, not more so than that of someone else from the household.'

'That's true on the face of it, Titus. But the circumstances are less persuasive. We would have to suppose a horse was taken out of the Garlick Hall stables at night, ridden up to the woods at six where the deed was done, and returned again, with only the murderer knowing about it. The grooms would certainly have missed such a horse. William Pearson, as head groom, would undoubtedly have been concerned and made enquiries. And you would probably now have a clear suspicion as to the name of the felon. As it is, only the squire, his wife and Tom Cowp were out on mounts from the Garlick Hall stable.'

I had no answer to this, and so attempted none.

We reached the arched yard-gate of Garlick Hall five minutes later, after cantering the furlong between ford and house. A conspicuous fellow in a scarlet coat and cockaded tricorn hat, with a gilded staff on which he leaned, was waiting on foot in the lane outside. I could see from a hundred yards that it was Oswald Mallender, the Sergeant of Preston and a gigantic figure rather too burly for his clothes, whose buttons and braid strained to contain him. He stepped into our path as we approached and held up a pudgy, officious hand.

'Mr Grimshaw's compliments, Coroner. I have been sent over to assist.'

In my experience of him, Mallender's face and bearing only had two characteristic expressions, self-satisfaction and affronted dignity, which he wore according to prevailing circumstances. The first of these was now to the fore and, as usual, I found it nettled me greatly.

'Why are you lurking out here, Sergeant Mallender?' I asked sharply. 'Does not Mrs Marsden tolerate you in her kitchen?'

At once his face flipped over from smirk to pout.

'I *have* been in,' he said sullenly. 'I have asked to speak to Squire Brockletower, which was put to him, and for no reason that I can tell it vexed him. You may find this hard to believe, but he gave orders at once that I be put out of the house – *put out*, mind you.'

I glanced at Fidelis, who looked as if he were suppressing a fit of laughter.

'So it is the squire who won't tolerate you,' I said, turning back to the sergeant. 'Well, that is quite right, if you've been impertinent enough to attempt to place yourself face to face with him. It is not for you, Mallender, to confront witnesses in any inquiry, unless directed by the coroner – me!'

The bailiff took a firmer grasp on his staff and made himself as tall as he could.

'I hold the commission of the bailiff,' he stated sonorously.

I looked Mallender up and down. His official coat, though impressive from a distance, was less awe-inspiring when viewed close to, having a grubby, threadbare appearance. The nap of the velvet collar was dirty and worn and there were visible moon-shaped stains under the armpits. Grimshaw it seemed was happy to spend lavishly on his own wardrobe, but not on that of his subordinates.

'Did you not just tell me,' I asked, 'that Mr Grimshaw sent you to assist the coroner? He did not mean you to play coroner yourself. I myself shall see the squire presently and for that I shan't require a sergeant's support. However I do, as it happens, have a use for you. You can go around and begin summoning the jury for my inquest. Here is a list.'

I pulled from my pocket the paper on which I had drafted the names of possible jurors, and handed it to the bailiff. He took it reverently, as some men take Communion in church. He was picking up some of the threads of his earlier self-importance.

'I intend to hold the inquest tomorrow,' I went on. 'Be so kind as to submit the names of those you have summoned, under my authority, to Mr Furzey at my office. Let it be by close of business today.'

And so we left Mallender, passed under the arch and into the yard of Garlick Hall.

Mrs Marsden came out to greet us.

'Good-day, Coroner . . . Doctor,' she said with a coy, almost imperceptible curtsey in Fidelis's direction.

'The squire has returned at last, I am told,' I said. 'I must speak with him. But first I am afraid poor Dr Fidelis has missed his breakfast. Can you oblige with some small tit-bits to subdue his pangs?'

'I don't want to be any trouble,' Fidelis added apologetically.

'You are not, Doctor. I can offer cold roast beef and cabbage and some of our own Garlick Hall cheese with a good spoonful of old Mother Thwaite's pickle.'

I left them to negotiate the details of his breakfast and went inside by the yard door to find Leather, who, I hoped, would bring me to his master. Official dignitaries may normally expect to use a front door, but it seemed absurd to go back and round the house just to play the dumb-show of dignity.

'I call it damned impertinence.'

The squire and I were in the library, on the west side of the house. It had a handsome bay window, which looked out over a lawn in the middle of which stood a magnificent mature walnut tree. Brockletower, a curly-haired man with a snubby, apparently boneless nose and fleshy, mobile mouth, was to say the least not pleased to see me.

'A man returns from an excursion on business to find his wife is murdered. And instead of being allowed an interval – a *decent* interval – to accustom himself to the idea of being a widower, some damned lawyer or other comes along asking importunate questions. Well, ask as you like, I shall not answer.'

'That is your absolute right, Mr Brockletower,' I replied. 'I can't at present compel you, or place you under oath, or anything like. It will be different at the inquest, however. The law perforce requires—'

He swung round, his features distorted with anger.

'Damn you, sir, I *am* the law!' He jabbed himself ferociously in the chest with his forefinger. 'I am a magistrate in this county. I am a Member of Parliament.'

'You are, to be sure,' I agreed. 'But this is not a county or a parliamentary matter, Mr Brockletower. It is Corporation business, as it has to do with the death of a person in the Fulwood Forest, which falls inside the boundaries of the borough. I respect and feel sorry for your loss, but I must be firm here. I have the honour to be coroner of the town and in all questions of sudden, violent death, it is I who am the principal agent of the law. Furthermore, as of course you know, the law expects that I summon an inquest jury with all dispatch and provide witnesses sufficient to account for the unfortunate demise.'

I was careful to speak with emphasis, but without hostility. For a few moments Brockletower continued to look at me like a bulldog in blood, but he could not deny I was telling the truth. By the time I had finished he'd lowered himself into a chair and covered his face with his hands. I waited and observed, wondering if tears would presently begin seeping between his fingers. There was no sign of them. Brockletower was not one to cry before another man.

'Very well,' he said, raising his head. 'Ask your confounded questions, and be quick about it.'

'I cannot promise to be quick, but I shall try to be concise. What was the business that took you to York?'

'I intended to visit Mr Thornton of Hambleton near York to view his running horses.'

'Why?'

'I have a fancy to own some for myself.'

'And did you in fact make any purchases, of horses?'

'I did not. There was no suitable animal for sale.'

'I think you also viewed a house with a view to taking a lease on it?'

'I did. In the city of York.'

'Were you planning to take up residence there?'

A look of annoyance passed like the shadow of a cloud across the squire's face.

'Surely you know about the August week of races at York, Cragg. It is at the same time as the Assizes. Coincidentally there is a season in the city, when the Assembly Rooms attract all men and ladies of fashion. The Duchess of Marlborough herself attends. Men go to York in August to do business and sport of all kinds and I intended to do the same.'

'Did you also, on the occasion of this visit, call on the Archbishop of York?'

'I did.'

'May I ask why that was?'

'Archbishop Blackburne's late wife was a family connection of my own late mother. It was only as a courtesy that I called.'

'I understand that during your journey back you sent your servant Cowp directly home from Skipton, while you diverted to Settle to look at another horse?'

'I did.'

'And did you go to Settle?'

'Yes.'

'Passing the night in Settle and returning yesterday?'

'Yes.'

'And had you concluded any business?'

'I had not. The man I went to see was unexpectedly from

home. It was sixteen miles out of my way for nothing. I stayed the night and came back through Bowland.'

'Did you depart from the direct route in any way?'

'No.'

'I understand you learned of Mrs Brockletower's death on your way. Where and when did you receive this intelligence?'

'At one of the villages, Slaidburn. I had stopped at an inn to refresh myself. I could not believe the news, of course.'

'Yet after that you rode hard to reach here as soon as was practicable.'

'Naturally.'

'Can you think of a reason why anyone would want to kill Mrs Brockletower?'

'No, of course not. As I've just said, this . . . this murder is incredible.'

'Or could someone have wanted to injure you, perhaps, through her?'

'Injure me, by doing *that*? Talk sense, man.'

'She is from a family in the West Indies, I believe. Planters.'

'Yes.'

'Is there, to your knowledge, any member of her family, or any West Indies connection of hers whatsoever, at present visiting this country, or resident here?'

'I do not think so.'

'Do you know if she has quarrelled with anyone recently?'

'I do not know so.'

'Have *you* quarrelled with her?'

'Damn your eyes, no I have not!'

The conversation was yielding nothing beside much repetition of the word 'not'. Perhaps my questions were too bland. I decided to risk a more piquant one.

'I won't keep you much longer, sir, but there is just one last point. It has come to my attention that Mrs Brockletower maintained that you recently sought her out during one of her early morning rides, to surprise her in the forest. Is this true, sir?'

Brockletower's response to my question was clench-fisted, immediate and fierce.

'That is tantamount to an accusation that I— No, sir, this idea is utterly – *utterly* – false and a damned lie. It is close to being an actionable calumny, sir.'

'But why would Mrs Brockletower invent such a story?'

Brockletower jabbed the air with his finger.

'How would I know? But invent it she did!'

Whereupon he strode to the door, seized the handle and pulled it open.

'You may leave me now, Mr Cragg! Good day.'

I found Fidelis seated at the table in the servants' hall, with pewter plate and tankard before him, both empty. He was leaning back in his chair, gossiping pleasantly with the housekeeper.

'Ah, Titus,' he said, turning to me as I entered. 'I have breakfasted excellently, thanks to the hospitality of kindly Mrs Marsden.'

The woman beamed delightedly.

'And he is a credit to his appetite. You, Mr Cragg, have a loving wife to ensure you are well fed,' she went on, as if needing to explain herself. 'Alone in the world, the doctor has no such advantage.'

I had seen it before, this impulse of women towards my friend. Solitariness gave him some indeterminate quality that made them want to pamper him, usually by filling his stomach.

'I am glad he has given satisfaction as well as received it,' I said. 'Now it's time we paid a visit to the Ice-house. May I take the key from the hook-board?'

Carrying a candle-lantern each to help us see the corpse more clearly, we strolled down the passage, past the sound of churns clanking in the dairy, and out into the yard.

'The squire was agitated?' Fidelis asked.

'Yes. He accused me of accusing him.'

'And had you?'

'No. I only asked if it was true that he had played the trick on his wife in the forest, the one mentioned by the maid Polly Milroy. He denies doing any such thing. And what he says of his movements yesterday, and the day before, tallies with his man's prediction. He stayed at Settle, then came back by way of Bowland. He heard rumour of his wife's death along the way. His story needs testing. I intend to write to the landlord of the inn where he says he stayed.'

Fidelis stayed me with a hand on my arm.

'By all means do that, but perhaps I can make it unnecessary. I myself have business in York that I must see to soon. I might set off tomorrow, and can ask along the way about the squire's movements.'

I hesitated. My curiosity was aroused, but I wondered if I should go where it led me. It may have been an extra-legal curiosity, outside what is proper to a coroner's duty.

'That is kind of you, Luke. But tomorrow I intend to hold the inquest, which cannot be delayed. Your news will come several days too late, I fear.'

'No, no! It need not. Here is what to do. Convene the inquest, swear in the jury and bring them to view the body. Ask them to approve a post-mortem and then adjourn pending my return home.'

'I will think about it, but I don't know that they will think a post-mortem needed. And if they do, I can hardly delay for as many days as it will take you to go to York and come back.'

We walked on towards the Ice-house, passing through the gated passage between the stable block and the coach house and entering the orchard. The trees were coming into blossom and the Ice-house itself was framed by fragrant clouds of white and pink which swayed in the air above the intense green of the spring grass. When we reached the door of the building I unlocked and stood aside for Fidelis to precede me. For a moment he paused and breathed in deeply, as if preparing to savour the smell of death. I, on the other hand, felt queasy.

Then he pushed through and, as he did so, the candle in my lantern guttered. I paused to prevent it from snuffing out entirely so that by the time I was ready to enter the short passage between the first and second doors Fidelis had already gone inside. As I approached the second door, which had sprung shut behind the doctor, I was startled to have it jerked open before my face. Fidelis held the door wide and gestured inside, his face with an interrogative expression. The work bench was still there, in the centre of the cold room where I had dragged it, with Luke's burning lantern standing on it. Everything else was just as we had left it the previous afternoon, except for one extraordinary lack.

'See for yourself,' said Fidelis, waving me in. 'The body is not here, Titus. The late Dolores Brockletower has entirely disappeared.'

Chapter Eight

I STEPPED FORWARD AND LOOKED. There was no doubt about it. Except for the lamp that Fidelis had placed upon it, the improvised bier was bare.

I stooped and peered under the bench, finding the horse blanket that had previously covered the body. Pulling this out I bundled it and dropped it back on the table, then turned to poke into the corners, and the dark spaces beneath and behind the ice-filled baskets on their racks. I looked (with no rational motive) at the vaulted ceiling, as if the corpse might have floated upwards and evaporated through the skylights. All this time Fidelis watched me silently, making no move to join me in my futile search.

'I don't know what to say,' I whispered at last.

I was conscious of my head yawing from side to side, like a tortoise. My disbelief made me stupid.

'To lose a corpse, Luke! It is unthinkable.'

But for Luke Fidelis nothing was ever entirely unthinkable.

'Is it possible she was not dead at all?' he suggested, gently. 'Remember, I haven't . . . no doctor has seen her. If the throat wound was in reality rather a superficial one, she might have been in some unconscious state—'

'No, Luke,' I broke in. 'That rabbit won't run. The gash was deep and gaping. I saw the quantity of blood on the ground where she was lying. She cannot possibly have lived after such a loss of blood.'

There was another silence, and I thought of the place beneath the hollow oak where the pat of congealed blood had been, before being taken by some secretive night-feeder of the forest.

'Yes, you must be right,' said Fidelis at last, with a reluctant sigh. He shook his head at the frustration of trying to account for the unaccountable. 'And if she had woken up and found herself alive, someone would have known of it.'

'Some person must have removed the body to another place,' I said. 'But to do that without informing me is . . . well, I'd say it is against the law. Come. We must go back to the house and enquire.'

We emerged into the open air. Near a woodpile at the far corner of the orchard was Timothy Shipkin, sharpening an axe on a circular grindstone. He was furiously working the treadle that spun the stone, spouting a fountain of sparks around his feet. I motioned for Fidelis to stay where he was and hurried across to the woodsman.

'The body of Mrs Brockletower has been moved from the Ice-house, Shipkin,' I told him. 'Do you know anything about this?'

The woodsman lifted the axe head from the stone and stopped his treadling. He squinted at me as if the sun shone into his eyes, though in fact the day continued grey.

'Moved, did you say?'

'Yes. It's not there – not in the Ice-house. You work much here in the orchard. So I repeat, do you know anything about this?'

Shipkin, testing the edge of the axe with his thumb, spoke quietly.

'Know, sir? I know nothing, only I believe something.'

'And that is?'

'That she is gone. Gone out of the Ice-house. I observed you in full daylight yesterday taking her inside, but I do believe she's not in the Ice-house no more. See, it is only what I expected.'

'You expected this? How so?'

'I expected that she would walk again.'

I sensed Fidelis coming up behind me to join us and turned to him.

'Shipkin tells me he expected Mrs Brockletower to walk out of the Ice-house,' I told him. Fidelis blinked twice and addressed the woodsman directly.

'Well, Shipkin, Mr Cragg and I have considered this, you know. But she was dead, absolutely dead. She could not possibly have walked out.'

'And the door was locked, man,' I added, as a supplementary point. 'Who do you suppose unlocked the door?'

Shipkin bared his teeth.

'Unlocked? There is no need for unlocking, sir, when you walk with the Devil.'

Fidelis and I exchanged startled glances, and I turned a stern face on Shipkin, raising my finger in warning.

'That is impious and nothing but hobble-de-hoy,' I reproved him. 'Do not repeat it, Timothy Shipkin, or you will make trouble for yourself, and others.'

'I must say what I believe, sir. If belief makes trouble, that would be the concern of a higher power. I say as I said all along, from the moment I found her: it was the Devil killed her and now the Devil has taken her to live with him.'

He put his foot to the treadle and, as we retreated, the scream of steel on stone was heard again. I noticed Fidelis looking around as we walked towards the orchard gate. Everything appeared normal. The ground was covered with recently fallen blossom, over which a variety of hens and bantams stalked restlessly in search of their food. Against the rear wall of the buildings that flanked the orchard gate were stacked boarding, stones and tools used by Woodley's men, the stacks covered in sailcloth to keep them dry. A man in a labourer's clothing was at work, unfastening one of the covers in order to get at the wooden boards they protected. He was an extraordinary figure, a giant standing perhaps six foot four inches, with a huge round belly, shoulders like hams, and a prodigious bald head. In my curiosity I called out to him.

'Good day!'

The giant looked up, and it was clear at once he was an idiot. His lower lip lolled, his small, fat-enfolded eyes rolled, and the only sounds he emitted were inarticulate hee-haws.

'A freak of nature!' I whispered as we passed through a barred gate and returned to the cobbled yard. 'I believe I have met his mother.'

'I notice the bodily superabundance is compensated by a want of intellect,' replied Fidelis. 'It is pleasing to find nature balancing itself.'

In the kitchen, we found Mrs Marsden supervising the jugging of a hare. I told her of our latest encounter.

'Oh, that poor fellow!' she said, picking up the skinned hare and holding it experimentally at arm's length. 'They call him Solomon. They like a joke. That's two pounds and two or three bits, Maggie.'

She handed the hare back to the girl she was working with.

'Now, gentlemen, is there anything I can do or get for you?'

'May we go into your parlour?' I asked confidentially. 'There is a matter, which is difficult to discuss here.'

She went to the sink and rinsed her hands.

'By all means. And you shall take a glass while you do it.'

We hung up the key to the Ice-house on the hook-board on our way to the parlour. When we were sitting beside the unlit grate with welcome bumpers of Madeira wine in our hands, I asked her if anyone had taken the key off its hook – the squire, say – since I had put it back the previous day.

'Might have, sir, but not that I know of.'

'Not the squire?'

'If he went up there, which would be natural, he said nothing to me. Why do you ask?'

I told her what we had seen, or rather *not* seen, a few minutes earlier in the Ice-house.

'Well, sirs,' she said, blowing out her cheeks and plumping into the chair by her writing table. 'This is most alarming. We must ask Squire if he ordered the body to be moved, though if that is the case he did not inform me of it. Happen he did not think the Ice-house a suitable coffin-house. Shall I send him word that you would like to speak with him about this?'

Less than three minutes after she had left the room the squire himself strode into it, his face sullen with anger.

'What the Devil's the meaning of this?' he said coldly. 'They tell me my wife is not where you laid her yesterday.'

'She is not, sir,' I admitted.

'Then where is she?'

'At present, I am sorry to say, I don't know.'

He stood in the centre of the room for a few moments, scowling and tapping his foot on the floor.

'You must know one thing, at least, Mr Coroner. You are an officer of the crown and this is rank incompetence.'

I maintained my composure.

'I thought the body had been moved from the Ice-house with your authority.'

'Of course it wasn't! Why would I do that?'

'You might have thought the place unsuitable.'

The squire looked oddly uncertain, wavering between passive injury and active outrage. I have seen the same manner many times in witnesses at trial and wondered for a moment if he were acting a part.

'I didn't consider the matter.'

'But may I ask, sir: did you not go up to the Ice-house last night, after you arrived home? Or this morning, after you rose?'

'No, I did not go there. Not at all.'

'Not even to pay your respects, sir?' I ventured, looking him directly in the eyes. 'As would be so natural in a husband in receipt of such shocking news.'

Brockletower faltered under what I hoped was my searching gaze.

'I couldn't see her . . . I mean, I didn't *wish* to see my wife in that condition. I have sent to my uncle for the parish coffin to enclose her, until I can have a suitable one made. She should not be exposed to the air. She should not be looked upon.'

'Regrettably there will be no immediate use for the parish coffin,' I said. 'Unless the body is found.'

'And, I would think, no use for you either, Mr Cragg,' he said. 'I hope you can find other business to pursue in the meantime. Be so kind as to take yourself off, with your medical friend, and leave me to locate my wife's corpse. And when I have done so I shall inform you accordingly.'

A coroner who has lost a body is like a ploughman lacking his plough, a castrato cut off from his song. As we rode back to town, I confessed to Fidelis that the legal situation now was delicate.

'An inquest can only be called on a body. The real, physical corpse must be there to be viewed by the jury. In its absence, I must suspend preparations for the hearing. And yet, I *was* summoned to a doubtful death, I *have* seen the body, I *know* there has been a murder. As coroner my moral and legal obligations to investigate still press on me. Without the body I feel utterly at a loss.'

We walked our horses thoughtfully and silently for the next few minutes, and then suddenly Fidelis spoke up.

'I feel a certain loss myself.'

I was surprised.

'You, Luke? How so? You have not even seen the body yet. And I don't think you were Mrs Brockletower's medical attendant.'

'Of course I wasn't. She didn't have one, they say. I am not sure that is significant, by the way. She was young and healthy, and had no need of medicine. In any event the reason for my feeling of loss is purely philosophical. I was looking forward to performing the post-mortem. There were certain aspects of Dolores Brockletower which intrigued me.'

I was dismayed and gave voice to it.

'Intrigued? Come come, Fidelis. A post-mortem is not designed for the satisfaction of idle curiosity. It is a judicial procedure of the utmost solemnity.'

Fidelis laughed.

'Have you never looked forward to the cross-examination of a witness in court, merely because she was a pretty young woman and you might see her blush?'

'You are being frivolous. And I'm surprised to hear you consider Mrs Brockletower in the light of prettiness.'

'That is not what I meant. Only that extraneous factors often add spice to the humdrum professional round. It is rare enough that one gets the opportunity to anatomize a member of the gentry. Most subjects are of the common sort. But I would have enjoyed examining that woman in particular as she seemed from the outside such an unusual specimen, physically and in spirit.'

I did not like the trend of the conversation.

'You speak of anatomy? The word makes me shudder, especially in respect to persons of position in society.'

'Well, the Empress of Russia's gall-bladder is no different from yours, or mine, or that of this town's night-soil gatherer. And the physician or surgeon that is not intimate with the appearance and arrangement of the inner organs is of little use.'

'But, surely, the knowledge of medicines is the main thing, Luke. The immense body of treatments performed successfully in the past. The proven cures.'

Fidelis let out a brief and sardonic laugh.

'Proven cures? Most of what we doctors do are not cures at all, Titus. I'll tell you a professional secret, but you must not divulge it. Our nostrums and receipts are useless. Worse, many of them actually kill rather than cure, and even if they do *happen* to bring relief, we don't know why. As a doctor, I say civilization will not make progress until first of all contingency is distinguishable from causation, and accident from purpose.'

This was too much for me.

'My dear friend, as a lawyer I could not disagree more,' I countered firmly. 'The law is the foundation of civilized life and it is never firstly concerned with causation, but with fact, and with precedent. The first duty of the law is to establish *what happened* and only then to say *why*. Law is about truth. It seems you are saying physic is about falsehood.'

'Yes, there is the gulf between our professions, Titus. I would like to bring them closer together.'

Our talk lapsed for a few moments as we met a herd of cows being driven to dairy. For several minutes we were swamped by them, our horses raising their heads and snorting in disdain at this crowd of lowing, beshitten-arsed quadrupeds as they jostled, ungainly, past us.

'We've strayed away from the important question,' I said, once we were free of the herd and riding side by side once again. 'The missing body. Did her killer remove the corpse from the Ice-house? And if he did, why?'

'Plainly, to prevent an inquest.'

'Why?'

'Because a viewing of the body would in some way incriminate him.'

'But if he is concerned about that, he could have buried her in the forest, at or near the spot where he killed her.'

'He may have meant to, but was interrupted.'

'I think it unlikely. That part of the forest is hardly frequented and, besides, no witness, no interrupter, has come forward.'

Fidelis could not apparently think of a reply, at least for the moment. 'Well, it needs more thinking about,' is all he said. 'And I have plenty of time to do that tomorrow, while riding into Yorkshire.'

'Ah yes, Yorkshire. What takes you there?'

'A little business,' he said.

I suspected another reason.

'Is that so? Does not female society come into it at all?'

Fidelis laughed.

'I go to look at a medical instrument, Titus, a new kind of forceps to assist in childbirth that has been invented there. Perhaps I shall buy one. And there is a patient to visit on the way.'

'Those matters do not preclude the lady, but only leave less time for her, I suppose.'

I looked sidelong at my friend, but he would not meet my glance.

'It is all supposing, Titus,' he said airily.

'So will you, in all this business, have the leisure to help me discover if Brocktower's story is truth or falsehood?'

'I may, Titus. You cannot hold an inquest as matters stand, so anything I do learn in the next few days will be of help to you.'

'When do you return?'

'In three or four days. In the meantime if I have news, expect a letter. But be assured there will be no mention of any lady of *my* acquaintance.'

Shortly after this we parted, I to my office and he to a dropsical patient in the outlying village of Cadley.

But, without my knowing it, something Fidelis had said was already lodged in my brain, and would produce startling results later in the evening.

It was close to one o'clock when I reached the office. Oswald Mallender had not yet brought in the draft of jurors and I told Furzey why there was now rather less urgency in the matter, enjoying the sight of his jaw dropping and mouth falling open. I told him to tell Mallender, when he did turn up, to send word back to his jurors that there would be no inquest tomorrow after all, but that they were to stand by for further instructions. Then I passed through the baize-covered door that connected the office to the house.

Elizabeth was back from her parents'. We dined together on baked marrow and mutton and she told me how her parents fared, and of trivial matters in the village life at Broughton. I listened to this patiently for her sake, though I was burning to give a full account of events that morning at Garlick Hall. At last, I was able to do so.

'Merciful heaven,' said Elizabeth when I had finished, crossing herself. 'There is evil in that house, without doubt.'

I let her sign of the cross go without comment. She was always more the papist when she had been with her mother.

'Why do so many people think that? Why do they say Dolores Brockletower was . . .'

I couldn't find a word that was both respectful and fitted my meaning.

'A witch?' said my wife baldly. Elizabeth could always anticipate me.

'Yes, not that I like the word. There is far too much talk of witches, I think.'

'That's because you are a lawyer, my love. Law and magic, you know . . .'

I did know. I have always considered a world that admits witches and warlocks to be a disorderly one, in which truth cannot operate and law is impossible. Magic runs through the law's fingers like water. But my wife's religion obliged her to believe in such things and, wanting her guidance, I pressed on.

'Well then, why *are* the people so sure she was seized by the powers of darkness?'

Elizabeth considered the question as carefully as she considers everything, her pretty features upraised as if to confront the matter full on.

'I suppose because she was a foreigner, Titus. In the West Indies, there are frequent dealings with Satan, is that not so? Especially among the slaves.'

'What could she have to do with slaves?'

'Her father certainly must own them. But that is not all there is to this. I think she has a dark reputation because of her nature. She was dark in hair and skin, and dark in character. She did not like society, gaiety. She only liked hunting and they say that was because she loved blood. It is enough to cause gossip and condemnation. Enough to make people believe she had intercourse with devils.'

'That's true. Timothy Shipkin, for one. He was sharpening his tools near the Ice-house and I spoke to him. He claims the Devil himself came for her. I do not think so. I do not think Satan is of that kind.'

'There will be many who agree with Shipkin.'

She wiped her plate with a crust of bread, popped it into her mouth and considered as she chewed.

'I wonder that Dolores Brockletower can be so important,' she said when she had swallowed, 'that the Devil has taken the trouble to return her to life. It would be a life of servitude, I suppose. But what purpose would it serve?'

'No, this is nonsense,' I rapped out severely. 'A life is like one of those sparks from Shipkin's grindstone. It is struck, it flies briefly, but before it reaches ground it is extinguished. It does not return once it has gone. It cannot.'

'That is heresy, my love. You are denying the resurrection of the dead on the Last Day.'

'I am no theologian. But I think there is one life, and one death. The Last Day is about something else. The soul—'

'Yes, the soul – that lives on, doesn't it?'

'I think it does, but it is not a physical entity. It does not live, it exists. Has anyone ever seen it? Fidelis, who has looked into the human body, has never seen a soul.'

'Perhaps he has looked in the wrong place.'

'Well, wherever Dolores Brockletower's soul may be, it is her body I am concerned with. And whatever business the Prince of Darkness may have in this County Palatine, I don't think raising the dead is one of them.'

part of it
*

I went back to the office and picked up the traces of a difficult dispute over some burgages, which required such concentration of mind that I forgot the possibility that the Devil had visited Garlick Hall. But later in the evening, after our supper (bacon with a particularly rich cauliflower cheese) I went to my library, stoked up the fire and a fresh clay and sat for a while in thought. As the smoke rose I pondered over the diabolic beliefs of Shipkin and the others concerning possession, wraiths, succubi and all the rest of it. Such things are so easy to make plausible in speeches and sermons. But the law concerns itself with facts, and evidence. How can a rational mind view the death of the body as a transient or reversible state? It is the body that is transient like that spark I had spoken of to Elizabeth. If its end is not decisive and irreversible, it surely is not a body. A body is not like the smoke from my pipe flowing up and around, diffusing and losing definition until only the smell remains.

I realized I was now thinking about ghosts. People everywhere and in all ages have believed in these shape-shifting, half-real appearances. But when Shipkin spoke of Dolores Brockletower walking again, he was not speaking of an insubstantial wraith of that kind; he meant she had been raised from the dead like Lazarus as a physical being. But if so, for what purpose would the Devil, or any other power, do this? And did it have to be connected with the fact that she had been murdered? It might, for instance, be a chance, a coincidence, a random collision of forces, perhaps occasioned by the freezing cold of the Ice-house. Had not Fidelis assured me that coldness prevented decay? Perhaps also it prevented death itself! Perhaps—

My eyes snapped open. I had been dozing and dreaming, replete with strong cheese. But suddenly I was awake again. Luke Fidelis's dictum during our ride that afternoon had come back to me. 'We will not make progress until contingency is distinguishable from causation, accident from purpose.' It took another moment for the fog of sleep to clear, and then I grasped the corollary.

'Damn!' I said in a flash of illumination.

Dolores Brockletower's body *might have not have been taken by her murderer*. If the missing body had nothing to do with the facts behind the murder, then to find it I would have to look elsewhere. That's what Luke was suggesting I do. Look for who else required a body to be dead, besides a murderer. Look for an anatomist – and then look for grave-robbers.

'Yes, we must regard it as a possibility,' I found myself whispering, as if in dialogue with myself. 'The Ice-house is behind the stable block, remote from the inhabited parts of Garlick Hall. It is not overlooked. A visit in the dark of night, a silent removal of the body over the hill above the orchard – Shot's Hill – none of it is inconceivable.'

'But the door was not forced,' I objected.

'A lock can be picked,' I continued. 'Or the robbers had the help of someone in the house.'

'Dear God, I hope this is not true,' I devoutly wished.

These matters were troubling, as if a woman's cut throat had not already cast us profoundly enough into the wickedness of man. But an instance of resurrectionism would be a matter of serious alarm in the whole county. We had heard of such things in London, but I did not think there had ever been anything of the sort here before.

'Well, it would not surprise me if your pious hope is too late,' I told myself sententiously.

I rose, yawned, opened the bracket clock that stood on my mantelpiece and reached for the key. As I carefully wound it I considered how to set about finding the robbers, if that is what they were, and make them lead me to the body. The best procedure, I supposed, would be to identify their customer. The robbers may be will-o-the-wisps, but the one who buys the stolen goods cannot be other than a professional man, settled and in some way established.

I uncoupled the key-crank and pushed it back into its place beneath the clock. Then I rested both hands on the mantel and looked down into the embers of the fire. So I was looking for a physician, or surgeon, someone who dissects human remains here in Preston, or in the vicinity. Well, I knew of one that did. Or did once. One that had gone to Lancaster Castle to dissect the corpses of three of the rebels hanged in '15. He was long retired from professional life, but did he still cut up dead bodies at home, on the sly?

I yawned again. It was bedtime. But tomorrow I would find out.

Chapter Nine

THE HOUSE IN Molyneux Square appeared, from the outside, to be in a state of disrepair. More than one of its dusty windows was cracked, the paint and whitewash had peeled and discoloured and the exposed timbers were beginning to sag with rot. When I sounded the brass knocker, flakes of paint fell around me.

The old man came to the door himself, apologizing that his housekeeper was at market and his manservant running an errand. He wore an indoor cap on his head. I introduced myself, and he beamed at the sound of my name.

'Your father was a dear friend, sir,' he said in a fluting, breathy voice, almost a whisper. 'Come in, come in! I am Jonathan Dapperwick, by the way. Perhaps you had already surmised as much.'

I had not seen the man for years. My father had known him in their youth, but it had been some time since the good doctor had become a recluse, entirely ceasing to go into society, or even to leave his house. Some said that his nose had been eaten away by a cancer; others that he had died, and that his household had concealed the fact to preserve their places. I saw no evidence of either case in the man standing before me.

I followed Dr Dapperwick through the hallway, the darkness

thickening as we advanced further in. Without warning, a spaniel dog hurled itself out of the shadows and threatened my ankle. It did so in a playful way that I did not take seriously, but the doctor swivelled and kicked out at it, catching the poor beast full on the rump. The dog squealed and retreated.

'That animal is very fortunate,' wheezed Dapperwick. 'I dissected its mother and grandmother. Until now I have held my hand, and in fact my scalpel, in respect of it. But for how much longer, I wonder, if it continues to snap at my guests' ankles?'

The house was quiet with, except for the dog, no evidence of another living creature within. I was led into a library that contained, I would say, five or six hundred volumes. In the middle of the room stood an oak lectern, on which a folio lay open at a page of anatomical illustrations.

The doctor's indistinct voice made a contrast with his physical appearance. Apart from his sweeping gesture of welcome after opening the door, Dapperwick had kept his hands clasped tightly behind his back and now he stood before the fire in the same posture, a little bent, but otherwise an imposing figure of about six feet tall. His clothes (and the wig on its stand that we had passed in the hall) belonged to the fashion of the last reign, but I had a first (mistaken) impression of a man in robust health, with broad shoulders, a deep chest and a nicely rounded belly. Although he was more than sixty years old, he had a smooth, young visage. It was only when I took a second look that I noticed the lack of mobility in the face, a mask-like surface that merely simulated youthfulness. In addition he trembled, and displayed the results of his trembling on the front of his coat and waistcoat – dried and encrusted drops of soup, gravy, coffee and wine that betrayed a history of slopped cups, shaky spoons and badly loaded forks.

Dapperwick did not seem curious as to why the son of his

late friend Sam Cragg should be calling on him now, after years
of neglect. He was more than content simply to talk and enjoy
the company, as solitary men will. So we spoke for some minutes about my father who, the doctor revealed, had represented
him in a lawsuit in the mid-twenties. He did not offer to tell me,
and I did not ask, what it was about, but made a silent resolution to look the case up when I returned to the office. At his
request I gave a recital of my father's final illness. This had
occurred during a visit to the Buxton Spa thirteen years earlier,
and Dapperwick took a professional interest in the details.

'Your father was an able lawyer,' the old man said when I
had finished. 'Are you knocked out of the same mould?'

'I have followed my father as Coroner of the Borough,' I
said. 'And it is in that connection that am calling on you, sir.
I am sometimes directed by a jury to order a medical post-
mortem examination. But I am short of examiners. So, as well
as paying my respects to my father's friend, I had hoped to
add your illustrious name to my roster.'

'Me, sir? But I am retired from medicine.'

'From your earlier remark about the dog, it seems you still
pursue anatomy. You are, of course, remembered for your work
on the rebels of '15.'

Dapperwick shook his head disparagingly.

'I am sorry to hear that such an occasion from my young
days is still notorious. I regret the whole business. The anatomist in those cases is not only an appendage, you see. He is
worse. He is an assistant to the executioner, whose function
is not philosophical at all, but punitive. Where murderers and
thieves are cheerfully hardened to the prospect of a mere hanging, the anatomist sows terror in their hearts with his intention
of carving up their bodies and scattering their guts and numbles
to the wind. That is really no task for a man who studied at

Leyden under Boerhaave, you know. I would prefer to be remembered instead for my hands and feet.'

I was nonplussed by his last remark.

'Your hands and feet, sir?'

Dapperwick nodded towards the glass-fronted cabinet that stood against the wall behind me. Puzzled, I turned and, instead of the books that filled the other bookcases, saw a dozen glass jars displayed in a row. They contained human hands and feet cut off at the wrist and ankle and swimming in preserving liquid. I stepped nearer to look. Some were large, and some as small as a child's. Some were well shaped, others deformed. Their grey and puckered texture was disquieting, looking more like tripe than flesh.

I suppressed all expression of disgust, pretending I saw such sights every other day.

'These, er, limbs are your special study, then?'

'The extreme bodily appendages, yes. Three years ago I crowned my studies with a book entitled "The Anatomy of the Human Hand and Foot, with Supplementary Observations on Paws, Hooves, Wings, Fins etcetera". It was intended to stamp out my name for posterity in the manual and pedal fields. Unfortunately, owing to a fire at the printers' storehouse, the whole edition was reduced to smoke and ashes.'

He pointed moodily to the book open on the lectern. 'I am left with the sole remaining copy – that one there. I turn a page each day.'

'A most regrettable accident,' I said, feeling genuinely sorry for him. 'Do you not think of printing a new edition?'

'I wish it were possible. By the time of the fire the type had already been distributed and would have to be re-set, and the engraved plates were melted in the flames. To reprint the book would be ruinously expensive and I was already all but ruined. I'd be risking the debtors' prison and I could not face that.'

He looked down for a moment. I noticed that, particularly when he was not speaking, his head trembled like a man sitting inside a coach on a rough road. His lower lip was agitated, and his eyes blinked. Were these the signs of his emotion as he recollected the loss of a life's work?

'So be it,' Dapperwick continued, lifting his shoulders in a shrug. 'I am of good cheer. I have new anatomical work in progress. No point in languishing. A man must keep on. I liken my work to that of the explorers of the globe. The body is, when all's said and done, a world in miniature, much of it undiscovered. We anatomists are voyagers. Opening a knuckle, or a heel, I used to feel like Marco Polo knocking on the gates of Samarkand. We push forward. We seek after knowledge, and reveal the unrevealed. Unfortunately my own fingers are not as accurate as once they were, as you may see.'

He unclasped his hands and held them towards me, palms down. They were in continual simmering movement, the hands themselves shaking, and the fingers twitching convulsively up and down, as if playing the keys of an invisible harpsichord.

'I can no longer dissect a delicate system. The carcase of that dog I might roughly cut up still, though I doubt I would find anything interesting. But I would make a hash of the pretty hallux – that's the big toe you know – of a handsome young girl.'

I saw in his smile the barest hint of an old man's lasciviousness, as he returned his hands to their previous position.

I asked, 'How do you go on, then, with dissecting for your new investigation?'

He moved closer to me. To make sure I understood the confidentiality of his words, he cupped a shaking hand beside his mouth.

'I have a young assistant,' he confided in a hoarse whisper. 'A useful, middling anatomist, despite his youth. He comes here once a month or so, from Liverpool or thereabout. I do not publish his name.'

'And what is the subject of your investigations?'

Dapperwick hesitated, as if gauging whether to tell me.

'It is delicate,' he said at last. 'A matter of discretion. I have as yet told no one, but you are Sam Cragg's son, and therefore to be trusted. And it will out at last, when I am ready to publish. So I will tell you, but I beg you it is not for crying in the street.'

'I am all ears, Doctor.'

'You will form an idea from the title of the proposed treatise. It is to be called . . .'

He leaned even closer, breathing the four words into my ear. '*De Genitalia Virilis Muliebrisque.*'

'Good heavens!' I exclaimed, starting involuntarily back. 'That will be a remarkable work, without doubt. And a useful one. However, I understand why you do not want your competitors here in town to know about it. From my friend Dr Fidelis I know there is much rivalry in the medical field.'

By pretending to assume his secrecy was from fear of encroachment, I was hoping to lead Dapperwick into mentioning other local anatomists – his rivals. But he snorted at the idea.

'My competitors? If I have any, they are in Edinburgh, or London. There are no anatomists in this town except myself. No, I give you the title of my work *sub rosa* because of the somewhat ticklish nature of the subject, you understand.'

He tapped the side of his nose and suddenly his mouth enlarged into a most unphilosophical leer.

'Genitalia, you know. Not to be, er, raised in ladies' company. But . . .'

He leaned confidentially towards me, tapped my chest with his scrawny fist and cackled.

'. . . where would we be without 'em, eh? Eh?'

I could not immediately think of a suitable reply.

'Where, indeed?' was what I eventually managed.

I took a little turn around the library, circling the lectern until I had composed my face.

'Dr Dapperwick,' I said, 'I promise I will keep the secret of your researches from the ladies. But must I take it that, unfortunately, you will not be able to undertake any post-mortem work for me?'

He produced his quaking hands again, holding them helplessly up. Together we silently contemplated their unceasing tremors.

'I fear you must look elsewhere,' he concluded at last. 'In the absence of a good anatomist you must find a competent surgeon.'

'Ah, yes. Would, perhaps, your own young assistant be able to . . .?'

Dapperwick cut me off with a vigorous shake of his head.

'Oh, no, no, I hardly think so. It would not be proper. Did I not mention that he is very young? He knows the landscape pretty well, but not the economy. He cannot diagnose the ills. No, no. He will not suit you at all.'

After this we exchanged a few more politenesses but I doubted I could find out more. There was little point in asking the doctor a direct question about resurrectionists, as he would be certain to deny any knowledge of them. So I bid him goodbye. As I walked away from his door across the square, I looked back. He was standing at the entrance looking after me, straight-backed, his eyes blinking exaggeratedly as an extra strong spasm passed through his body, and his cap tilted sideways.

*

On my route back to Cheapside I made a diversion past Talboys's shop and called in to see if Abigail had returned yet. In the front room of the shop two high-spirited young females were making a lot of noise in choosing ribbons. Edward Talboys's attitude as he awaited their decision was that of a man with more pressing things on his mind.

'Ah, Titus!' he called out, on seeing me.

I asked if Abigail was on the premises and could I see her? He beckoned me over to the inner end of the shop.

'My Abby is here all right,' he confided. 'She has taken to her room. There was such a storm of crying when she heard of Mrs Brockletower's being dead. It was like a death within our own family.'

The giggling customers at last made their choices. I waited patiently while they gave over the money and made their way out, then said, 'So, may I see her, Ned?'

'You may try.'

Talboys called another of his daughters in to mind the shop and we climbed the stairs to the first floor, and then another steeper and narrower stairway to the small boxed-in landing of the attic rooms. Talboys knocked on one of the closed doors.

'Abby, the coroner is here, particularly to see you. You must open, you know.'

There was no reply. He put his ear close to the door, then tried the handle. It was locked.

'Abby! I am your father. There can be no doors locked against me in my own house.'

He rattled the handle and knocked again. I heard a muffled voice from within.

'Go away.'

'Abby! Is that how you speak to your father?'

His pained remonstrance had not the slightest effect. Apparently there *could* be doors locked against Talboys in his own house. And even against public officials. But I thought it unprofitable to pursue the matter just now, and suggested I call again in hopes that her docility would return. So we tramped back down to the shop where, before we parted, he spoke ruefully.

'Father of four girls, you know, Titus, and however I try I cannot get their obedience. I defy any man to rule four daughters.'

Five minutes later I was re-entering the office, where Furzey greeted me in the outer room, his face animated with alarm.

'He's here, sir. He's waiting for you. I couldn't keep him out.'

'Who, Furzey? Who's here?'

Furzey regarded me as if my lack of clairvoyance were a mental deficiency.

'*Who's here?* Need I tell you? It's Mr Grimshaw – who else? In the inner room. And even by his own lights he is huffing strong. Huffing strong as it blows off Fleetwood Sands.'

I went through to confront the bailiff.

I have never had the misfortune to see Ephraim Grimshaw stark naked, but I fancy that, in such a state, his spindly legs and distended belly would make a very ridiculous show. Fully dressed, however, he was alarmingly splendid, with silks, lace and silver buckles enough to adorn Lord Derby himself. His waistcoat alone, stretched tight around the globe of his belly, was a dazzle of gold thread. And his manner was high as the King of France.

'This is incredible news, Cragg,' he shrilled. 'In-cred-ible. You have lost – *lost!* – the body of Mrs Brockletower!'

'Well, I haven't personally—'

But Grimshaw was not to be deflected.

'Not personally? Let me correct you. You personally super-intended the deposition of the corpse in this . . . *Ice-house*. The next time you looked – *personally* again – it was not there. I call that losing, sir! I call that gross losing. In fact I call it neglect of duty.'

With a snort, he now started towards the door, shaking a raised finger.

'I shall make my report accordingly to the Mayor. And I have sent Mallender without delay to Garlick Hall, with my firm instructions to make good this distressing business by find-ing her. I trust he will not be long about it. Good day, sir.'

It took a minute or more, accompanied by a few deep breaths, to repair my humour. It was always the same when I encountered the bailiff, but this occasion was particularly pro-voking because Grimshaw had called for no other reason than to admonish me, as a school Dame pulls down the breeches of a mitching boy. After a few deep breaths I called for Furzey.

'I have never known him take such interest in an inquest. I wonder why he does.'

'I have heard something on that,' said Furzey, who was one of the best-informed men in town. To underline the nature of his information he put the back of his hand near the corner of his mouth.

'They're *saying* he has a cousin in Lancaster, with no estate and a trio of young daughters. This cousin is also Ramilles Brockletower's nearest heir after Miss Sarah and Uncle Oliver. So with three husbands to find in due course, his prospects are substantially improved if he can number Garlick Hall among his expectations. The Reverend Oliver and Miss Sarah would have only a life interest, of course, being childless. And the bailiff will be well pleased to be assured his young cousins will not become poor spinsters and a burden on him.'

This was interesting.

'In that case we must handle the bailiff warily,' I warned. 'In all matters touching on the pecuniary interests of his family, Mr Grimshaw is dangerous. Now, I have been with Dr Dapperwick this morning. Just think for me. About twenty-five years ago, did we not act for him in some matter? I don't know what it was, but the doctor suggests there was such a case, and that the results were favourable.'

Furzey frowned and jerked his head towards the ceiling, as if shake up his memory.

'The doctor and your father were friends in the twenties, all right. Not like brothers, you understand, but they drank together often enough, and borrowed books from each other. I'll go and look at the rolls. If your father ever represented the doctor, the records will be there.'

Furzey was rarely happier than when grubbing around in the firm's archive. He lit a candle and shuffled off to the basement room where he keeps all the old rolls. For the next hour, while I took up my pen and resumed the drafting of a will that I had begun before the Brockletower affair broke out, the sound of his rummaging and accompanying cries of discovery and disappointment reached my ears from below. Finally he re-emerged with a document dangling its ribbons and seals, and the light of triumph in his eye.

'I have it!' he crowed. 'The 27th of October, 1725 at the Court Leet, my Lord Mayor presiding. Dispute between Dr Jonathan Dapperwick and William Sutton, potter. I remember the case quite well now.'

I congratulated him and asked if he would outline the matter.

'It was a case of slander,' said Furzey. 'Pure slander, if there can be such a thing. A grave in the churchyard had been disturbed during the night, after the funeral of a young woman, ah . . .'

He unrolled the record and squinted at it.

'Eliza Sutton was her name, a young woman not yet twenty. There was also her child in the grave with her. She was not married, and the baby had already died in the womb when she gave up her own life giving birth to it. There, you see, it is the familiar story.'

'Who was the child's father?' I asked.

'That was Jack Hargreave, her father's apprentice. Living together in the same house, the two of them found nature more persuasive than religion. Behold the result.'

I brought him back to the subject at hand.

'So what happened to her grave, Furzey?'

'Yes, yes, I'm coming to that. On the morning after the interment it was found that a spade had been taken from the verger's shed during the night, you see. And it seemed that this had been used to attempt to excavate the freshly filled grave of poor Eliza. The spade was found stuck in the ground just beside it.'

'And the bodies . . .?'

'Had not been touched. Whoever was doing the spadework never got far enough down. He might have been disturbed, or alarmed in some way, or had an attack of conscience. But he ran off before he'd finished the job, leaving the spade behind. When it was discovered next morning, as you can imagine, it was talked about all over town. People were shocked, properly shocked.'

'Not surprisingly. A desecration like that. We might not be safe at sea, Furzey, or even in our own houses, but six feet down one does expect a certain security. So, the William Sutton that made the accusations against Dapperwick, that was the girl's father?'

'Yes. And he began putting it about loudly, in taprooms up and down Church Gate and Fisher Gate, that in his opinion the digger was a doctor of this town, engaged in the evil business of obtaining bodies and dissecting them. Then, in the White Horse Inn, he named Dr Dapperwick as the one who did it.'

'Whereupon the doctor consulted my father.'

'Who concurred that the words were actionable and drew up a complaint which was then heard by His Worship the Mayor sitting in Court Leet. Sutton could produce nothing against our client and the doctor was able to show he was attending a patient in Penwortham on the night in question. So the jury found for him. No one was ever convicted of the crime, and poor Eliza and her child lie there to this day.'

'Were damages awarded? Or costs?'

Furzey raised his index finger.

'No, that's a notable point. Particularly notable. The jury evidently remained suspicious of Dr Dapperwick. It is to be assumed they speculated (though without evidence) that he might have commissioned the attempted crime, even if he had not been present at the graveside on the night in question. He certainly never denied being deeply engaged in anatomy. So, though they found for him, they only gave him a halfpenny in damages, and didn't even make Sutton pay his costs.'

I thought of the pickled hands and feet in Dapperwick's library. He had got these from somewhere. But from freshly dug graves? I took the papers on the Sutton case from Furzey.

'The jury may have been right in their suspicions,' I said. 'It is impossible to know at this remove. And as to the disappearance of Mrs Brockletower, it cannot have been Dr Dapperwick in person. But he tells me he has a younger associate. We must find out who that is, and in the meantime I shall read through these for myself.'

I folded the paper and tucked it into my pocket. Suddenly I felt greatly in need of air.

Chapter Ten

GOING OUT OF my front door I turned to the right up Cheapside, crossed to the south side of Church Gate and entered the churchyard through the sagging, moss-covered lych-gate. It took me a few minutes of pacing up and down between the graves before I found what I was looking for, a lichen-crusted headstone on which was carved:

R.I.P.

ELIZA SUTTON

DIED 4 OCTOBER 1725
AGED 17

With her, an infant daughter.

'All that honoured her despise her
because they have seen her nakedness.
Mine eye runneth down with water.'

I stood for a time in contemplation. Seventeen. It was the same age as that of my own Eliza when we married. Children were not granted us, so we have never endured the danger and anxiety of childbirth. How could I know what it must have been like for Hargreave, her swain, or for her parents, who had carved such bitter lamentations on her stone?

But I became even more pensive over the suffering of Eliza herself. She must have realized her child was dead when the labour began. A woman feels the kicking in her womb and, I suppose, she feels it also when the kicking stops.

I moved across to a stone bench beside the path and sat down to unfold the record of *Dapperwick versus Sutton*. But before I could start reading a voice from behind startled me.

'How do, Mr Cragg?'

It was Robert Crowther, the old labouring man who dug graves and tended the churchyard, trailing a long-handled scythe. I greeted him and gestured at the grave.

'Eliza Sutton. Do you remember her?'

He leaned against the scythe, wiped his nose on his sleeve, spat, then growled.

'I do. A pretty lass, but flighty.'

'There was some talk of her grave being disturbed on the night after the funeral.'

'Aye. I mind that too. They never found the chap that did it.'

'What happened to Eliza's young man?'

'Hargreave? Flit out of the town. I've no notion where he went.'

'And who do *you* think desecrated the grave?'

He cleared his throat and spat again.

'There was talk at the time of it being doctors, you know. The kind that steal dead bodies to cut them up for the amusement of themselves and the Devil. Happen it really was one of them. Or happen it was Hargreave. I've seen that before now, a mother and child being unburied by a father crazed with his grief, or dreaming she was never dead in first place.'

After listening to two or three dry, well-worn tales of corpses Crowther had known, I left him and returned to my house. It seemed to me, suddenly, that I should be worrying about the business of the murder, and let Grimshaw and his men make whatever shift they could to retrieve the missing corpse. I had little confidence in their wit, but there was no one else to do the job. In Paris, I have read, a department of government exists – the Police – which concerns itself with all manner of crime, both discovering it and suppressing it. If we had such a police office in Preston, I dare say law and order would be more rigorously enforced than it ever can be by our magistrates and bailiff, who are more interested in making money than keeping the peace. But we would all pay a heavy price in the loss of liberty, since this Police is the very apparatus of Bourbon despotism. The English don't want French tyranny to come here. And the thought of Ephraim Grimshaw in the guise of a Frenchified director of Police was a disturbing one indeed.

I would not be able to hold an inquest unless the corpse was found. But it was my clear duty to continue to prepare for one, so that I could convene it as soon as Dolores Brockletower did turn up. During the period of waiting for Luke Fidelis's report from Yorkshire, what could I do? Then I remembered the horse-shoe. I could at least find out something about the only piece of possible evidence found at the scene of the death.

With the curve of forged iron weighing down my pocket I rode out along the Longridge road to the intervening village of Yolland. I pulled up at the village forge which served the Garlick Hall estate, lying only a mile away. The smith's name was Pennyfold.

I entered the yard where stood a coalman's dray, from which two men were unloading black sacks, and stacking them under a thatched shelter. I approached the forge itself and stood in the wide doorway, waiting for the smith to register my presence. Pennyfold was working on an iron bar that seconds earlier had been withdrawn from the hellish temperature of the fire and now glowed red as a sunset. He was holding the bar down on his anvil in a great pair of pincers, and hammering the end of it flat with a rapid succession of mighty dings. His muscles were prodigious.

'Stay back while I cool this,' the farrier shouted, though he did not turn round. He had noticed the light change as I stepped through the doorway.

Looking around I spotted on a window-ledge three octavo volumes, which I picked up out of idle curiosity. One was Bishop Taylor's *Sermons*, the second Snape's *Anatomy of an Horse* and the third Swift's *Gulliver*. A very curious trilogy.

Pennyfold had now lifted the iron from the anvil. It was still glowing, though not as fiercely as before. He took a couple of strides towards his water butt, which stood to one side, and plunged it in. The hiss was like that of a monstrous cob swan about to attack.

The smith laid the bar back down across the anvil and turned to me, wiping his hands across the front of his leather apron.

'So, Mr Cragg, isn't it, sir?'

'It is. I wonder if I may have a word.'

'Willingly. How can I help?'

Pennyfold reached down a copper mug from the window-sill, dipped it in his water butt and drank deep. Then he dipped again and offered the cup to me.

'Drink of best forge water, sir? Very good for the constitution, I guarantee. And an antidote against arsenic poisoning, you know.'

'Is it indeed? I've never heard that.'

'I am lucky never to have had cause to benefit, myself. But it's what my old gammer used to say.'

I took the mug, and sipped experimentally. The taste was metallic, or did my sense of taste merely play up to an association of ideas? I sipped again in order not to seem ungrateful and replaced the cup on the sill.

'Thank you, blacksmith. For a medicine, it's very tasty.'

'Is this on the business of the inquest, sir?' Pennyfold asked. 'I was one of those summoned by Oswald Mallender to attend today for jury service at the inn, but then we had back-word this morning. Inquest's not to be held today after all.'

'No. It has been delayed. You have heard why?'

A broad grin broke over Pennyfold's cheerful face.

'Aye, I have that. There's not much a farrier doesn't hear about any local goings on.'

'The event has amused you?' I said.

At once the man's smile disappeared, and he looked more dutifully serious.

'No, not amused, sir. Not exactly *amused*.'

'But not grieving. Is that true of people in general?'

'It may be. I don't say the parish is rejoicing, but there's not many crying. That woman, she was a stranger, colonial born. She had secrets, they say, and secrets make suspicion. She was singular, anyway. And not from here.'

I drew the horseshoe from my pocket and began unfolding the handkerchief in which I had it wrapped.

'Well, at the moment I'm not concerned with the, er, disappearance of her body,' I told him. 'The bailiff is enquiring into it, as is Mr Brockletower. She will be discovered in due course, I have no doubt. I am first of all interested in how she came by her death.'

'It was a vagabond they're saying killed her.'

'Perhaps and perhaps not. This horseshoe was found at the place in the Fulwood where she lay dead. It lay a few yards from the body. It probably has no connection with the death, but I would like to find out where it comes from. Do you recognize it as a forging of yours?'

Pennyfold took the shoe and turned it in his hand.

'Can't be certain, but it looks like one of mine all right. See the flange here?'

He put his finger on the slight rim-like projection that fit snug against the leading edge of the hoof when the shoe was nailed in place. It had three tiny v-shaped notches in its upper edge.

'These three nicks are our signature. No other local smith puts them in just so. But I'll not warrant there's none other in the country. This shoe might come from the other side of Clitheroe, or Lancaster, or away to the south if there's smiths there unknown to me signing with the same three nicks. But if it came from round here, it's one of mine.'

'And if it is yours, can you say if it's the kind of shoe you'd make for horses at Garlick Hall?'

'It's what you might call gentry quality, yes. But beyond that there was nowt special about the forgery we do for Garlick, not over what we do for other gentlemen.'

'Can you tell in any way if it fell by accident from the horse's foot?'

'Was there nails bent through holes when they found it?'

'No, I asked about that. There were none.'

'Cast shoes are usually picked up with some of their nails still in them, aren't they? But just from the look of it, I'd say this could have been taken off on purpose, because it's a well-worn shoe that's got to the end of its use.'

Pennyfold gave me back the horseshoe and reached for the rod on which he had been working before my interruption. I took this as a signal, thanked him and bade him good day, after mentioning that he and all the others remained under summons to the jury, and should stand ready to attend the inquest when the time came. Of this, he made no complaint.

The Plough Inn stood across the road from Pennyfold's forge and, feeling suddenly hungry and thirsty, I led my mount across and into the inn yard, where a couple of labourers were at work recobbling the ground. I tethered the horse to a hitching rail and went inside through the yard door. It would do no harm, I thought, to take a prospective view of the place where the inquest on Mrs Brockletower would, with luck, soon be held.

Ten minutes later I had spoken with innkeeper William Wigglesworth and looked over the barn-like room which adjoined the main building. The village folk used it for dancing, so I was informed, and for communal feasting at Yuletide, and also at midsummer if the rain fell and they could not sit at trestles on the village green. The room seemed more than adequate for my purposes and I returned to the taproom for some bread, cheese and ale, for the consumption of which I established myself in a window seat looking out at the road. I was thinking over what Pennyfold had told me. This was patently an intelligent man. His explanation of why the shoe was not cast by a horse on the spot was convincing, though it did not help me to understand how it got there. Being hardly rusty at all, how long had it lain on the ground? I could remember the weather prior to the murder. There had been heavy rain three days before, which would have made a coating of rust inevitable. But could it have been coincidental that someone had dropped the shoe at the very same unfrequented spot where a woman would die in less than three days? I didn't know the answer to that.

I reminded myself that I was no nearer to knowing *why* she had died. Pennyfold had confirmed my estimation of how little sorrow the death had caused. Mrs Dolores Brockletower was not a reputable person to the people in this part of the County Palatine. A 'stranger', Pennyfold had said. But she was also 'singular', 'not natural' and 'colonial born'. And she had 'secrets'. It all added up to one thing, the thing no one except hotheads like Timothy Shipkin, or half-witted gammers like old Ma Patten, would utter: that she was a witch; that she came from the Devil's islands; that she communicated with Satan.

The playwright Webster observes that 'detraction is the sworn friend to ignorance'. I can put that in a more Lancashire way: if you know nowt, you'll say owt.

I was satisfied that it was not the Prince of Darkness who cut Dolores Brockletower's throat. Folk only said it was because they knew nowt – about her, or about the ways of the Devil. With her Spanish name (from the Spanish Main), her riding astride, her unwillingness to go about in society, and now her violent death, she was bound to be the object of all manner of fantastic gossip. The English borough towns and countryside are not used to, and do not like, the influx of strangers, even from neighbouring places. Dark-skinned, rough-voiced ladies from far overseas will never take on, unless they go to great pains in winning people over.

For a few moments, a certain sympathy for Dolores's loneliness tugged at me, though it was apparent that she hadn't tried very much to win the confidence or love of the people around her. I remembered Sarah Brockletower's manifest dislike, and her scathing word for her sister-in-law: a 'hoyden', she called her. I trusted Sarah's judgement. If she did not value a person I was prepared to believe she had good reason for it.

My thoughts were interrupted by a thunderous sound, followed by a loud crash. A man had hurled down the stairs from the floor above and burst violently through the door at the bottom of the staircase. The next moment he was thumping the innkeeper's counter and in a loud voice calling for his horse to be brought from the stable. It was Ramilles Brockletower himself. To say he looked agitated would be quite inadequate. His face was wreathed in ferocious purpose as he stood drumming his fingers on the counter while he waited for his mount.

The squire, who seemed to be making a point of not surveying the room, had not seen me. He was so preoccupied that I debated with myself whether to speak to him at all. But at a time when Mrs Brockletower's death was talked of everywhere I felt my coroner's dignity would suffer if I appeared to avoid him in public. So I pushed back my chair and rose to my feet.

'Mr Brockletower, sir,' I called across the room in the even but sonorous tone of voice that I use in court to calm obstreperous witnesses. 'Good day to you. Might I have a private word?'

He swivelled towards me, and saw who I was. If, as Mr Spectator has it, a man hangs a picture of his mind on his countenance, the squire's mind was in a state of turmoil. The face he turned to me when I spoke his name was painted in appalled and fearful colours. But in an instant it changed, perhaps by an effort of will. His upper lip lifted fractionally on one side, his eyes narrowed. Emotion drained from him and he began thinking about his dignity and position, knowing they were not enhanced if he showed public weakness.

Squires in England believe they are little kings. They often draw a curtain between themselves and the good and honest people that sustain them. Though they know this causes them to be feared and hated, they cannot help it. In their pride I think they may even welcome popular disdain since it allows them to act freely, and with disregard for the feelings and circumstances of their inferiors, be they servants, tenants or professional men. Brockletower had behaved like this from the moment he set foot in his ancestral home after the voyage from Jamaica. He had put on the armour of cruel masculine force. To him attack and defence were one and the same, a principle which I have heard is held to be sovereign by naval tacticians.

So he attacked me.

'You can have a word with the Devil first,' he snarled. 'Lawyers!'

He pointed his finger like a pistol directly into my face.

'You are parasites, do you know that? You are the scum that forms on scum!'

The discourtesy was so gross and unexpected that I did not immediately register it. So I continued in patient terms.

'But, sir, it is my duty—'

'I piss on your duty! You have no duty to me. You are nothing to me.'

At this moment the landlord, a bow-legged fellow, came through to inform the squire that his horse awaited him, and Ramilles Brockletower strode out of the inn by the rear door that led to the stable yard, slamming it behind him.

I sat down again and took a deep draught of my beer. William Wigglesworth came up to see if there was anything I needed and I asked for a refill.

I cannot explain why, but I was moved to apologize for the squire to the innkeeper.

'Mr Brockletower is not well,' I said when he came back with my replenished tankard. 'It isn't surprising. The murder of his wife and then the sudden disappearance of her body.'

'No sir. Not surprising. And he is already a man of high passions, I can vouch for that.'

'So you see much of him, do you? In Yolland, I mean. I wonder what brought him here this morning.'

'Oh, there's no difficulty about that, Mr Cragg. He was meeting his architect. Name of Barnabus Woodley.'

'Yes, I have met the gentleman.'

'Then you know he is a very refined young gentleman, with what I call London manners. He has lodged with us since the works at the Hall were started, back in January.'

'And does the squire meet Mr Woodley here, at the inn?'

'Oh yes. Sometimes they are in the snug together, over a jug of punch. Or in the room where Mr Woodley has his drawing-table. Very close friends they are. When I've gone in with refreshments I've found them examining plans, discussing all about columns, architraves, plasterwork and what-have-you, and sometimes just arguing over art in general. The arguments are heated to a degree at times.'

'What do they argue about? Be specific.'

'All sorts. One time my Belinda went in with tea and it was pictures. Very passionate, they were, about pictures. Being a naval man, Squire favoured seaskips, while Mr Woodley, he was a landskip man through and through. While me, I'm more in favour of pictures of the chase.'

I drained my tankard, paid what I owed for the commons and returned thoughtfully to the yard. As I led my horse towards the mounting block, around which the old cobbles had been removed, I saw that a new bed of sand had been smoothly laid around it.

'I shall rough up your sand, lads,' I called out to the workmen.

'Oh, don't mind that, sir,' said the older of the two, strolling over towards me. He was glad of the chance to stop work. 'Gentleman that's just left has already done the same, but we can rake it over again quick enough.'

I looked at the sand and a thought struck me, a memory of Fidelis's keen eye surveying the damp ground on which Dolores Brockletower's body had lain. I handed my horse's reins to the labourer and crouched to look at the hoofprints of the squire's gelding. It had stood stock still beside the mounting block and the four impressions left by its hooves were plainly visible.

'By God!' I exclaimed before I could help myself.

Three of the impressions had been made by middlingly worn shoes. But the fourth, the front nearside, looked crisp and new. It looked very much as if Squire Brockletower had had cause, very recently, to get the near-fore foot of his riding hack re-shod.

Chapter Eleven

M Y FIRST IMPULSE, which I acted upon, was to run back to the smithy and bring Pennyfold across to inspect the hoofprints. I did not tell him whose horse the prints belonged to.

'That's right,' he confirmed, lowering himself to his haunches and closely eyeing the marks in the sand. 'The near-fore's a new shoe. The others are worn, and should be replaced soon.'

'Is the new one produced from your forge?'

He considered the question, drumming with his fingers on the breast-piece of his leather apron.

'No, it's not one of mine I should say. It's not easy to tell from a print like this, but it's got a mite less of width than we would allow for. But why do you want to know if it's one of ours, sir?'

I again produced from my pocket the shoe picked up in the Fulwood, crouched down beside him and pressed it into the sand beside the impressions of the worn off-fore shoe left by Brockletower's horse.

'For a comparison. I want to know if the impression of this old shoe, that I showed you earlier, has the same degree of wear as this horse's three worn shoes. Could this old shoe, in fact, be the one that the new shoe replaced?'

'For a true match you will have to press down much harder, sir. Think of the weight of the horse.'

He reached forward, resting his fingers on the shoe where it lay, then with a grunt pressed firmly downwards before carefully lifting the crescent of iron up again. He examined the impression.

'Well, it's near enough the same, as you see.'

'But not conclusively?'

'Not conclusively. Approximately. It may indeed be the old shoe that the new one replaced. Then again it may not.'

'Thank you, Mr Pennyfold,' I said, taking back the horseshoe from his hand. 'I must be satisfied with that.'

Five minutes ride from the inn, along the Preston road, is St Michael's Church. This is not one of those piles from the Middle Ages, the stones of which, having got a good strong scrubbing from time, show forth a blurred surface, lacking edges and definition. St Michael's Church, with its vicarage across the road, was built in brick at the beginning of the reign of King George the First, and it was wonderfully crisp and new. The prime mover had been the former vicar of Preston, Mr Peploe. When he heard that the Christians of Yolland faced a three-mile trudge to Longridge to attend divine service, he'd established a curacy and raised enough money to build this plain little church for the village. Not long afterwards Yolland was made a parish, and old squire Brockletower got the right to name his brother as its first parson.

As I reached this spot on the road I could clearly see the church porch, with its four small-scale Grecian columns. The Very Reverend Oliver Brockletower himself was standing under it. The afternoon sun, which had been playing chase with the clouds, sent down a beam from the south-west that lit him just as you might see in an Italian picture, to indicate divine benevolence towards a praying friar or saint. Not that Mr Brockletower was a saint, or anything like. Very Reverend he may have been, but his chief reverence was for wine and worldliness. Nor was the priest, at this moment, devoutly praying. Having blinked a few times in the sunlight, he turned and locked the church door with the large iron key in his hand.

Being a genial man of the world was the way the world preferred Oliver Brockletower to be. Aside from the circles that Timothy Shipkin moved in, people liked their vicar to ride to hounds, to dance, to play at cards and the fiddle and enjoy the robust consolations of roast beef and port wine. The English don't want a vicar to be an impoverished hermit, living half out of this world before he is ready to leave it for good. How can a man run to the aid of others if he is weighed down by self-reproach, self-pity or self-loathing? Who can hope to be absolved of the reluctance to leave this life, if the absolver himself knows nothing of life's pleasures? In Spain it may be different. In England we want our men of God to have tasted life.

The sunbeam still gilded the Reverend Brockletower's wig, which hung down the sides of his face like the ears of a sheep. But then, as if abandoning the effort to sanctify him, it dipped behind cloud. I called out a greeting and slid from my horse as the vicar launched himself unsteadily down the path to greet me. He showed none of the distaste that his nephew had earlier displayed, but welcomed me ebulliently and with outstretched hand.

'Coroner Cragg! What brings you into my humble parish?'

I told him only that I had been looking over the room I wanted to use for the forthcoming inquest. He pursed his mouth and shook his head, which set the loose skin under his jawline flapping.

'But that is an inquest you will not be holding now, I fancy.'

'Not today, no. Without a body—'

'Precisely! No body. And who is to say if this *nobody* will ever be found, eh?'

He looked pleased with his conceit. He almost laughed and I realized that he was the worse for drink. Very much the worse. The syllables of his words were eliding, the consonants here and there exchanging places.

'If her body is not actually consumed, I am confident it will be found,' I insisted.

Mr Brockletower turned to me with a kind of leer.

'Not actually consumed, you say? Ah, yes, very possibly. But I suspect her soul, her *soul* is already consumed, you know. By fire!'

He set his dewlaps wagging again.

'We are all sinners, you know, all sinners. But that one . . .'

He tailed off and as he breathed out I could smell the wine on his breath. Just what was he telling me? It was not very usual for the Reverend Brockletower to speak in the voice of a vicar – of sin and the like – when not actually mounted in the pulpit. In society he preferred to discourse on music, poetry and horse-racing.

'Shall we take a turn around the churchyard?' I suggested. 'In the interests of the inquest – should it ever be held – I would like to know a little more about Mrs Brockletower's character.'

'Willingly, Mr Cragg. The clergy must always assist the civil power, if to do so does not conflict with our spiritual duties.'

His tongue had a lot of trouble with the word 'spiritual'. It came out as 'spurtchal'.

So we set off along the paved path that circled the church. Catching his foot, he almost tripped on an uneven flag, but I seized his arm before he fell.

'When you spoke about sin just now,' I asked as I steadied

him, 'did you mean to imply that Mrs Brockletower had been an unusually sinful person herself?'

Having recovered his balance and his composure the vicar straightened his wig.

'Oh, yes. From what my nephew has told me she was quite wicked in herself, you know. Ramilles came to me very stricken in his conscience. His marriage was troubled, very troubled indeed.'

A conscience-stricken Ramilles Brockletower sounded unlikely, but I did not remark on it.

'It has been suggested,' I said, 'that Mr and Mrs Brockletower were out of countenance with each other because she had not conceived a child – an heir for Garlick Hall.'

'I am struck that you should say that. I was of the same opinion and mentioned it to him. And do you know what he did? Scoffed. Said his wife was not going to conceive by *any such* means.'

'I don't understand.'

The vicar came to a halt and turned to me, grabbing my forearm in a histrionic gesture, his breath breaking against my face in stale, crapulent gusts.

'Dark matters, sir. Very dark.'

I thought of the things Dolores Brockletower had stood accused of in the popular mind.

'Not witchcraft, surely? I myself do not credit it, but there has been talk that she dabbled in such things.'

The vicar frowned. My question seemed to perplex him for a moment.

'No, no,' he interrupted. 'Not the dark arts. Not the machinations of the Evil One. Though I should not be surprised to learn she was familiar with those, since we know her origins, do we not?'

He spoke with a sigh, and without malice. For a moment silence fell between us until with a jerk he resumed his shuffling stride. He had lost the thread of his narrative.

'No,' he went on. 'I refer to those mysterious matters the, er, offices of the bedroom, and so forth.'

This at last was a solid hint to get hold of.

'And such offices are . . . distasteful to Mr Brockletower in some way?'

'Without any question. And that was the very word he used: what had once been a delight had become distasteful. It is why he desired to alienate her. That was my point, you see. That he wanted to divorce her.'

'Good heavens! *Divorce?*'

In my astonishment I had raised my voice. In our part of England the word divorce, in reference to marriage, is so rarely heard that it invariably causes sensation. The vicar in his cups had just confided a piece of almost incredible news.

I went on, 'Did he come to you for advice on this matter?'

'Indeed. He asked me if I knew about the procedure whereby he could obtain one. Well, I told him I am merely a clergyman who warns men not to sunder marriages. How would I know about the means to become di-div-divorced – you see? I can hardly pronounce the word, it so revolts my tongue. But I did caution my nephew. I reminded him he would damage his own material circumstances by such a course, she being, as I believed, the only daughter of a Jamaican sugar plantation with enormous pecoon . . . pecuniary expectations. My nephew inherited my brother, the late squire's, estates and I know for certain they were encumbered with very considerable debts. And as you see for yourself at the Hall, the spending still goes on.'

'Do you know if the present squire pursued the question of a divorce? Perhaps by consulting elsewhere?'

At that time a divorce required an Act of Parliament.

The fleshy underchin wobbled again.

'I do not. We had the one conversation and he never returned to the matter. I felt it would be an indelic . . . an in-deli-ca-cy to refer back to it myself.'

'And can you remember when exactly this conversation took place?'

He stopped walking to consider for a moment, stroking his chin.

'Not exactly. A matter of seven or eight weeks ago. Before the beginning of Lent. Shall we say that?'

The Reverend Brockletower and I set off again. Soon we had completed a circuit of the church and I already had much to think about. I offered to help with him back to the vicarage but he declined the offer, as if mildly affronted. After bidding me farewell he tottered across the road to his vicarage gate. I mounted my horse and set off again on my way to town.

Ten minutes later, well on along the rutted road, I was musing on the marked difference between the bibulous, amiable uncle and the taut, enraged nephew. For a moment I found myself seized with a resentment of my own against the young squire, and the way he had spoken to me.

'Scum' indeed! If anyone was scum . . .

For a moment I wanted to ride directly to Garlick Hall and throw the insult back in the squire's face and his entire class.

Sometimes I can glimpse what had so excited the Levellers of the last century. The landowning class that lords it over us is an idle and pampered regiment. Most of mankind struggles to eat and have shelter, which consumes their time and strength. The landowner has no such preoccupation. His life is like an Italian opera in which time is a measure of pleasantness and gratification, with occasional entr'actes for the conduct of business.

And yet – and yet – though the habits of the landowner may be as indulgent as a household pig's, he is also a provider, and a spender. If all of us lived in cottages, without great houses to bring great works into being, life would be very mean. Costly navigations, new roads, agricultural improvements and philosophical advance would come to an end. There would be no great churches, no ironworks, no ships of the line, no Baltic or East India trade, no lace, or wine, or sugar, or tobacco. How then would we all live?

The classes of society are links in a chain. Willy-nilly they have their positions; they do not choose them, nor are they chosen for them, unless by Providence. Considered in this aspect the rich are less operatic and more like the kings and queens of Sophocles, who cannot exchange roles with the chorus, as the actors that play them can. In this light the rich are more pitiable than contemptible.

After I had suppressed the temptations of levelling, and in contradiction of my views during the discussion with Fidelis in the Turk's Head coffee house, I began to consider Brockletower in the character of a Sophoclean king, driven to wife-murder. The tragic drama that I wrote in my head was persuasive. He meets her on foreign station and brings her, an heiress, home as his wife. It becomes evident soon enough she will not conceive. The local people evidently do not take to her and she makes few if any friends. The companionable amusements and pleasure of, what the marriage service calls, mutual society – 'with my body I thee worship' – begin to pall. Worse, even, she reveals character traits and amatory tastes previously hidden from him, which he cannot support. The excitement of a woman, exotically encountered, is lost in the humdrum surroundings of home. Intoxication is succeeded by a headache and a sour taste in the mouth. Sexual activity ceases.

What does a man do in these circumstances? She is pouring scorn on him at every opportunity. She nags, rages and calls his virility into question. And he begins to hate her.

So he turns his mind to putting her aside. But divorce is a ruinous as well as a tedious procedure, and besides would mean that he forfeit his wife's sweet sugar wealth. With these reflections his thoughts stray down a darker path. He knows her habits, knows precisely where to find her alone and vulnerable. And so events follow the path that Fidelis had plotted for me two nights before. He departs on his journey to York, dismisses his servant on the way back and rides through the night to the Fulwood, where he encounters Dolores at the hollow oak, kills her and returns home hours later, having had his horse re-shod.

I admit I had performed a volte-face about Brockletower's guilt. It was all plausible to me now, but there was a caveat: no one had seen it happen. Nothing had been heard, only gossip and idle talk. Would a jury be convinced enough to bring in the finding that I had previously been so averse to: 'murder by Ramilles Brockletower'?

A verdict of murder by person (or persons) unknown would be all that was required of my court. But now I found myself nurturing a desire to have the killer of Dolores Brockletower found and punished. She might not have been an amiable lady. But she had not deserved to die in that way. I wanted her killer brought to justice.

Chapter Twelve

AFTER CLEARING THE parish church and vicarage, the road to Preston soon passed through a peninsula or outcrop of the old Fulwood. It was no longer a part of the common forest, having been annexed two generations ago by the Brockletower estate, though they had not yet cleared it for pasture or planting. Much anger and some grief had been provoked by the appropriation. The woods were a useful source of fuel and rabbits for the poor, and more than one of the squire's ricks were burnt that summer. But the Brockletowers had made good their claim with legal parliamentary measures, and (as my father gravely used to tell me) where Parliament shoots, the mark is always hit. In the meantime, it must be admitted, the people's fuel-gathering and rabbit-snaring went on as before.

No sooner had my road penetrated this contentious belt of woodland than I came up to a long timber cart, hitched to a pair of heavy horses, standing on the wide grass verge that separated the road from the trees. Two great trunks, roughly sawn to length, had already been loaded, and men were at work trimming a third. Supervising the work was the squire's woodsman Timothy Shipkin. As soon as I saw him, I recalled a small but (as I thought) important thing that I wanted to ask him.

I called out and Shipkin walked across. He had the face of a man who could think of better things to do than bandy words with an official from the town. Yet he couldn't be faulted on the ground of superficial courtesy.

'How do, Mr Cragg?' he asked, automatically swiping his hat from his head to reveal the stiff, abundant bristles of his grey hair.

'Hello, Shipkin,' I replied and, thinking I would approach my question by a round-about way, gestured at the work going on behind him. 'What are you doing here?'

Without shifting his feet Shipkin rotated the upper half of his body until he could nod in the direction of the timber carriage.

'Nothing but what you can see. Fetching some timber to make spars.'

He held the position for a moment then swung round to face me again. 'They're for that architect, as he calls himself. For the supposed temple of his.'

'Ah, yes. I have heard about it. I imagine you take a disapproving view of such works – pagan temples and the like.'

He shrugged his thin shoulders.

'It's not a building concerns me, but what folk do in it. I'm told this one is for doing nowt in, but sheltering from rain. If that's right, I am content. Rain comes from our creator, but so do the means to shelter from it.'

Surprised that Shipkin had taken a tolerant view of Barnabus Woodley's folly, I steered the subject away from architectural morality.

'Well, I'm sorry to call you from your work. Have you come directly from the Hall today?'

'I have that.'

'Is there any news about this matter, the disappearance of your mistress's body?'

'None, sir, not when I was there. That were three hours since.'

'And I wonder if the man Mallender was there, the bailiff's sergeant?'

'The one in the dirty red coat? Aye, I saw him poking about.'

'Did he make any discoveries?'

'Him, sir? He's not the capacity. If one of them heavy horses were stood behind the door of his parlour I reckon he couldn't discover it.'

I think I smiled but, feeling I should administer a mild rebuke, said, 'He is the bailiff's man, you know, so we must extend him courtesy if possible. Well now, there was one more thing I wanted to ask you. It's about your own first finding of the body of poor Mrs Brockletower. A small detail.'

'What's that, sir?'

'When I examined the spot where she lay, which I did very closely, there was a depression in the earth beside her. It seemed to be the imprint of a knee.'

Shipkin adopted a look of mild scepticism.

'A knee, you say?'

'Yes, an imprint – where I imagine someone went down on one knee beside the body. To look more closely at it, I would imagine. Was it you that made it? Did you kneel beside Mrs Brockletower in that way when you first came upon her lying by the hollow tree?'

Shipkin is the only man I have ever met who frowned with his whole face. His countenance was so deeply and expressively lined that when he concentrated his thoughts, it was not just the forehead that contracted. The declivities that criss-crossed the cheeks and chin, the fissures that descended from each side of the nose, the mouth and around the bulb of the chin, and the cracks that rayed out from the corners of his eyes, would all deepen and contort. They did so now, as he attempted to locate and root out the answer to my question from his memory.

'Don't rightly remember,' he said warily at last. 'And what would it signify if I did?'

I ignored his question. A religious enthusiast is an obstinate clown, in Mr Spectator's estimation. But that sage had never met Timothy Shipkin, who was no fool and (as I could tell from his tone of voice) already knew the precise answer to his own question. The dint in the damp earth might signify much. It might be the only indication of another person present when Dolores Brockletower fell bleeding to the earth. And, if that were the case, it was surely the mark of her murderer.

'Do you at least recall noticing this knee-print yourself?'

Again his face tightened, but after a moment he shook his head.

'I do not. Happen it was one of the others that went up after me.'

I shook my head.

'They told me none of them went as near her as that. So, if you do at any time recall doing such a thing, please send word. It may be important evidence. Now, I will take up no more of your time and be on my way. Good day, Shipkin.'

I kicked my horse's flanks and was off again, dissatisfied that Shipkin's defensive wall had not been breached. I had covered only about two hundred yards when my mind received a kick as sharp as the one I had given the horse. I had seen in a rush the import of my metaphor of the wall. It had been produced out of my intuition that Shipkin was on the defensive, that he had something to hide. Suppose, I thought, that what he had to hide was full knowledge of the murder. And, to go one step further, that he knew the killing had not after all been done by the squire. And, finally, suppose he knew this because Timothy Shipkin had done the deed himself.

It was a completely new and contrary hypothesis to the Greek tragedy I had previously constructed.

When acting as coroner or legal adviser, I always try outwardly to show a firmness of decision. No judge, jury, or client can have confidence in a man whose views will forever jump about like fleas on a mattress. But, when I secretly interrogate myself, this solidity deserts me. Though I tell no one except Elizabeth (from whom I hide nothing) I will often doubt my own powers of decision, dithering inwardly about which coat to wear, the black or the brown; which meat to eat, the flesh or the fowl; which wine to serve, the port or the claret. And so it was now. Having, as it seemed, fixed firmly in my mind the idea that the squire was the murderer, I was now hopping off after another suspicion.

But I could not stop myself. The theory formed itself with alarming rapidity in my brain. It enumerated the points suggesting Shipkin's guilt. First, wasn't he hostile towards Mrs Brockletower, particularly her masculine way of sitting a horse? Second, hadn't he indisputably been there at the scene of her death (though oddly going off immediately to Shot's Hill to fell a dead beech: from one death to another, you might say)? Thirdly, wasn't he a member of a millenarian group, in whose distorted opinion an act of violence against a sinner might not necessarily contradict the teachings of Our Saviour? And finally, being a forester, did he not have frequent recourse to sharp instruments, such as might be used to cut a person's throat?

Yes, I thought, there might be a case against Shipkin. But I would have to dispose of one awkward fact. The man was a pedestrian, whereas Fidelis and I had already mutually concluded, almost *pro certo*, that the cut-throat had been mounted. How could an earthbound Shipkin have managed the business? This and other questions jingled against each together like coins in my pocket as the horse and I jogged along the road to Preston. They had not resolved themselves by the time we arrived back in Cheapside.

'Timothy Shipkin is no murderer,' said my wife with decision, lying against the bed pillows as pretty as ever in her lace-fringed night-cap. She looked up from her sampler to watch me as I pulled off my breeches. I had been telling her after supper what the vicar had said. The squire's desire to sever himself from his wife had astonished her, but reinforced her suspicion that Ramilles Brockletower had murdered her.

I cannot say why I had chosen this particular moment to extenuate the case against the squire by admitting, with a tiny itch of shame, of my suspicion towards Shipkin. Perhaps the act of undressing had made me more confiding, though, of course, I would have told her in the end anyway.

I struggled out of the rest of my clothes and pulled the sleeping gown over my head.

'I think he might be,' I said, diving into bed and reaching out for her. But she wriggled away from my touch.

'Ow! Your hands are cold. Warm them up, Titus.'

I rolled onto my back with a sigh, and folded my hands together across my belly. Elizabeth resumed her stitching.

'Tell me why you suddenly suspect poor Shipkin.'

'I met him on the way back from Yolland this afternoon. He was loading tree-trunks he'd felled in the spur of forest that the road passes through.'

'And?'

'He told me Mallender has been poking around at Garlick Hall, looking for the body. Found nothing, not that I would expect him to. Shipkin didn't think much of his powers either.'

'Nor do I. Nor does anyone. But go on.'

'I asked Shipkin to think back to when he'd found the body of Dolores Brockletower. I asked if he had gone down on one knee beside the body.'

'Why would he do that? To pray?'

'No, no, to look more closely. To inspect the neck wound. There was an impression in the ground in about the right place, and it seemed to be that of a knee. I wanted to know if it was Shipkin's knee.'

'I see. And was it?'

'He couldn't remember, which I find unaccountable. When such a momentous thing happens as the discovery of a dead body, I would say that a person remembers every detail. Wouldn't you?'

'Not always. The shock might wipe the memory away.'

'I'm wondering if it was deliberate loss of memory, and he knows more than he says, but is trying to keep his distance.'

She frowned, pressed her lips together and made a pout. I could not tell if she was concentrating on what I was saying or on her embroidery.

'Only yesterday,' I went on, 'he told me the woman was a consort of the Devil. If he really believes that he might think it his religious duty to hasten her on the way to hell.'

Under the bedclothes I sent my hand as an experiment across the gap between us. When I found some flesh she whacked her own hand down sharply onto the eiderdown above.

'Your hand is still cold.'

Reluctantly I took back my hand.

'What's your opinion of Shipkin, then?'

Letting her work rest, she lowered her head to the pillow and studied the ceiling.

'I don't think he can have done it, Titus. I've met the fellow. He's a religious man and would show the guilt, shock and remorse of any foul act he had committed. And besides, Shipkin has never been known to do any violence to anyone, not even to raise his hand.'

'There are consummate hypocrites, my dear.'

'Yes, and I never saw one that I could not see through.'

I sighed. She was right. My wife has formidable powers in reading character.

'Well I wish you *could* see it in him,' I said despairingly, 'I've no particular feeling against Shipkin, in spite of his obnoxious seven sleepers. But if there must be a guilty party—'

'I know.' Elizabeth's interjection was sharp and discomfiting. 'You would much prefer it to be him. But is a woman's style of riding really sufficient provocation to murder? I know what is behind this. It is not that you *believe* Shipkin is guilty, you only *want* him to be. And, of course, he is very convenient to your suspicion. The poor man's a born outsider. His trial and execution would leave the social order undisturbed. Not so if the squire turned out to be a wife-killer, Titus. Then our whole little society is implicated. But this is no reason to convict an innocent man in the place of a guilty one. Shame on you!'

'It would be shame on me, of course, if he were innocent. But, you know, Shipkin may still be guilty. Though I must admit . . .'

'What?'

'Well, there is one circumstantial reason to support Shipkin being what he says he is. The man does not ride, whereas there's every reason to believe the assassin was on horseback. Fidelis is of the same opinion.'

Elizabeth picked up her sampler, laid it on the bedside cabinet, then subsided into her pillow again.

'That settles it, Titus,' she said brightly. 'If Dr Fidelis says Shipkin is telling the truth, and if I say the same, it must be the case. So pursue the squire, and leave the woodman alone.'

She turned on her side towards me and laid the back of her fingers against my cheek.

'Now,' she murmured, 'is there any likelihood of your hands being warm at last?'

Chapter Thirteen

ON THE FOURTH morning after the death of Dolores Brockletower, I was awoken by a gunshot. No – I can only have been partially awoken, since I immediately heard another shot, and then a third. I understood that they came from the gun of Ramilles Brockletower, and then I saw him standing up to his waist in the rising morning mist, firing again and again into the woods. His target was the shrouded figure of his wife as she flitted between the trees, like a hunted nymph desperate of her life. Then I opened my eyes and saw the casement window swinging in and out, being hammered against its frame by a squall of wind and rain.

I yawned and rubbed my face. Mrs Brockletower as a nymph! That's the dream-world for you. A wrinkled mirror distorting what it reflects.

Elizabeth, an even earlier riser than myself, had already quit the bed. I groped for my watch on the bedside cabinet and found the time was half past six. Then I too sprang up, crossed to the window and pulled the delinquent casement shut. The weather was grey, gusty and rain-sodden. I turned and hurriedly pulled on my clothes. It was an indoors day in prospect.

As I breakfasted I considered what I had to do this day. I was still concerned, above all, about the missing body of

Mrs Brockletower, since I had no faith in Oswald Mallender's ability to find it. The man might have been adequate for hauling naughty boys home by the ear to be thrashed by their fathers, or chasing washerwomen off the riverbank when they strayed too close to the salmon traps. But this was a challenge far beyond the scope of his feeble intellect. I doubted that he had even glimpsed the possibility of Dolores Brockletower's remains having been purloined for sale to the anatomy trade.

I myself was beginning to warm to this particular idea. True, it changed the philosophical status of the body's disappearance. Instead of being a necessary consequence of the particular facts of the murder (whatever they may be) it became, under this hypothesis, a random contingency. But it was nevertheless appealingly simple, requiring just two elements to make it run: someone on the lookout for a body, and a simultaneous widely advertised death. The questor would then have had the simple task of going to Garlick Hall at night and helping himself, with only one complicating obstacle: how a stranger could turn the lock of the Ice-house. But I was hopeful that this would not prove insurmountable.

The balancing possibility was that, in hopes of avoiding an inquest, the body had been removed by the murderer himself. It was equally plausible and a lot more desirable philosophically, since the solution to the one crime automatically became the key to the other. Mallender's wits were perhaps just quick enough to grasp this. Had he got as far as suspecting the squire? I doubted it and, if I was right, his 'poking around' at Garlick Hall under Ramilles Brockletower's own supervision was more likely to lead him astray than to put a discovery in his path.

I therefore decided that, after allowing Grimshaw and Mallender a free hand for twenty-four hours, and nothing coming out of it, it would be as well to pay Mayor Blackburne a call. I needed to enlist the support of a higher authority before renewing my own assault on the problem.

Nathaniel Blackburne was from a family widespread in the county and beyond – one of his distant relatives was Lancelot, the present Archbishop of York – and had been born one of the fourteen children of Jack Blackburne of Dutton, a country manor standing twelve miles to the east of town. Tall and handsome, though now approaching sixty, Nat had lived in our town as long as I could remember and risen to the mayoralty after amassing a fortune in the cheese trade. It had been one of his drays that I had met at Garlick Hall on the morning of Dolores Brockletower's death.

On the whole, Mayor Blackburne's tenure had been a beneficial one. The town certainly appeared to have increased in wealth, and he had shown a deep mastery of civic politics, not least in his handling of Grimshaw. The Mayor could not have prevented the bailiff's election – the Grimshaws controlled too many votes for that – but if the bailiff's ambition was a strong and fiery tincture, the Mayor kept its bottle-stop firmly in his own hands. Grimshaw was allowed his showy parades and personal adornment, but the Mayor made sure to confine him to a subsidiary role. It was the sort of control a father has over a son that he cannot disown, yet does not trust.

Blackburne's other care was the politics of a wider sphere: he had the county to deal with. This represented a greater power than any he faced inside Preston, and it continually sought to obtain advantage over the town, imposing on us and squeezing us of revenue.

Having crossed Cheapside and entered the venerable timbered structure of the Moot Hall, I found it was this external view of the Brockletower killing that most preoccupied the Mayor at that moment. And, by this, he meant primarily how it was regarded by the Lord Lieutenant, Edward Stanley, eleventh Earl of Derby.

'You had better know,' he told me in his chambers when I informed him of the reason for my visit, 'that Lord Derby is following all this with the closest attention. The very closest. Imagine what he must think. The wife of our MP, sitting in his interest, murdered in this horrible way! His lordship is no fool. He realizes that young Brockletower's whole future is in the balance. And if he is forced out of Parliament, his lordship would have an expensive by-election to fight.'

'Has Lord Derby already found Mr Brockletower guilty of killing his wife, then?'

'No, no, don't be absurd, Cragg. He is the fairest of men, but he is thinking ahead. He is thinking: *what if*? That is how we should all think. Tell me, in your opinion, is it conceivable that Ram Brockletower could have done this thing? I cannot think it so. Surely it was a stranger, some wandering footpad or other.'

'Do you mean, could Mr Brockletower have done it in himself? Or are you concerned with circumstantial probability?'

'Oh, I don't doubt he *might* have done such a thing. He suffers grievously from anger, and I never thought that his West Indian marriage was anything but precipitate and unfortunate. But under the circumstances, how could he be the murderer? Wasn't he away from home in Yorkshire at the time?'

'I'm afraid I cannot speak of the circumstances, even to you. It is better if nothing comes out until we have found the victim's body and can hold an inquest.'

'As you wish. Finding the body is of the first importance.'

'Mr Grimshaw insists its loss was a matter of carelessness. Let me assure you, Mr Mayor, it was not. It was an act of wickedness hard to anticipate or prevent. So we must find the body, and the person who removed it.'

'The bailiff is inclined to jump to rash conclusions from time to time. But you have my confidence in this, Titus. What can I do to help?'

'We need a proper search by a disciplined body of men at Garlick Hall. Mr Grimshaw has thought fit only to send a one-man search party: his fellow Mallender. Mallender is large, but not large enough. In my opinion we need a troop of soldiers.'

The Mayor looked dubious.

'Well, much as I desire to help you, it's not for me to say. Only the Lord Lieutenant can call out troops and whether he would agree to do so for something like this I can't say. You'll have to go and ask him yourself which, fortunately, you won't find too difficult. You will find him at home at Patten House.'

I went back to the office, meaning to write a note to be sent round to Patten House asking for an interview with the earl. But I was forestalled by Furzey, who stumped into my room brandishing a letter for my immediate attention. It had been delivered half an hour before, and bore the Lord Lieutenant's seal. His lordship had anticipated me.

> To Titus Cragg Esq., Coroner of Preston, Good Sir, I
> would be obliged if you would attend me at my house
> here in Preston at your earliest convenience. Derby.

Within the boundaries of the County Palatine, a summons from Lord Derby has the force of a Command Royal. He enjoys prestige, magnificence and wealth. He is not contradicted and his summonses are acted upon precipitately.

Of all the Earls of Derby, this one was Preston's own. Patten House, a fine tall structure, wooden-framed but topped by a battlemented tower, stands right in the centre of town. It came to his lordship through his mother, who was a Patten, and he lived there when he was only Edward Stanley, before he inherited the title from his cousin, the tenth earl. With the title came big houses at Knowsley towards Liverpool, and Lathom Castle at Ormskirk and a London house too. But Patten House remained his favourite town house in Lancashire and he returned here to conduct his estate business, and that of the vaster estate of Lancashire, which he held in his charge. He came to be sociable, too.

Patten House is known to anyone who has seen Preston, since it is by a margin the largest and best private residence we have. It stands on the north side of Church Gate, on the other side from the church, but a little to the east, and back from the road. So one approaches it through a noble gate and porterhouse on the street and is then funnelled along a path walled on each side to form a 'chimney', which leads to the main door.

Just within that door, on the left, was a small writing office, in which his lordship's man of business and a clerk held sway. I greeted them and passed the time of day until a young footman appeared to lead me wordlessly across the flagged hall and up the wide blackened-oak staircase to the first floor. We strode across an anteroom and the servant swung open the door before announcing me with sonorous self-importance.

I found Lord Derby sitting stiffly in an armchair near a large old-fashioned leaded bow window. His legs were crossed, his face half turned towards the light and his chin lifted. He wore his everyday buff coat but at the same time a formal wig, an odd look. Opposite him stood an easel supporting a small stretched canvas on which a portrait painter was at work. Standing at his elbow, and holding his palette, was a bored-looking youth whom I estimated to be seventeen.

'Come in, Titus,' called the earl without altering the

position of his head. 'Take a seat. This is Mr Winstanley. You do not object to our talking in his presence? He endeavours to complete me phizzog before I go to London at the end of the week.'

I said what we had to discuss was in its nature confidential, and would it not be better if we were alone? The earl cheerfully agreed and sent the painter and his boy to wait in the anteroom. Winstanley made no verbal objection though he was clearly put out at being put out.

Lord Derby then rose, stretched, removed his wig and strolled around the easel to examine Winstanley's work. I joined him. The sitter was fifty, and looked it, but Winstanley, without sacrificing verisimilitude, had cunningly contrived to make him ten years younger. I did not mention this, but I did ask why only the visible flesh of the head, neck and face appeared, of which the latter was cut off along the forehead at the wig line. The effect was disconcertingly fragmentary.

'I cannot say,' Lord Derby replied, as if the matter was of little importance to him. 'We must presume Mr Winstanley knows his business. He works the face from life because, he says, it is the only important aspect of a portrait. For the rest, he scuttles back into his studio and in due course one sees the finished canvas. Do you think the face is like?'

I had to think quickly to answer this possibly forked question.

'In this incomplete state the final effect is difficult to judge, my lord. But it appears very lifelike.'

His lordship gave me a shrewd look and returned to his chair. I sat a little uncomfortably on the narrow window seat.

'Well,' he said with a sigh, 'one does not have one's portrait done to gratify oneself. It is a dynastic duty. All my ancestors are lined up along the walls of Knowsley, so I must take my place amongst them, what? Now! To business. I am very concerned about this affair concerning the wife of my old friend Brockletower's son – now, of course, his *late* wife. What do you know about how she died?'

I had known the earl for several years when he was no more than a comfortably situated baronet. We had even provided him with some legal services from time to time. So I felt no restraint in giving him an account of the last three days, though I made sure to concentrate on the facts rather than my private interpretations of them. But his lordship immediately arrived at similar conclusions without any prompting from me.

'Of course young Brockletower must fall under suspicion in this,' he said when I had finished. 'It seems quite possible for him to have ridden to the Fulwood and killed his lady when he was supposed to be out in Yorkshire. As to why he should have done so I would not venture an opinion. Knew his father pretty well, of course, but this boy's a stranger to me. Met him a few times at Parliament, and we've conversed once or twice at assemblies here. He's said to be a shade hot-headed. What do you think of the case, Titus? I value your acumen highly, you know.'

His manner was condescending, of course. But we lawyers are accustomed to that from our noble clients.

'It may have nothing to do with the case, your lordship, but if I can put it like this, the natural affection of the marriage had somewhat cooled lately, as far as I have heard from members of the household.'

Lord Derby snorted.

'The natural affection always does, sir. It's no reason to resort to assassination.'

'No, not usually,' I agreed.

I felt it better to treat what the Reverend Brockletower had told me about his nephew's wish for a divorce as a confidence.

'There is also the question of her body disappearing,' I went on.

'Ah, yes, that. Most interesting. In addition to killing her, did the young fellow also purloin her body from the Ice-house? That's the first question. And the second is, if he did, why did he?'

I gave a submissive cough and said, 'The only reason that comes readily to mind is that the murderer wanted to make it impossible for me to hold an inquest. However, I think it quite as likely that a third party stole the body, as an act unconnected with the reasons for murder itself.'

Again Derby smartly caught my underlying meaning.

'Body-snatchers, you mean?'

I shrugged. 'There's no record of such a crime ever having been committed in this town. On the other hand, it is on the increase in our nation, we are told. So I cannot discount the possibility that body-snatching has indeed come to Preston.'

'Hmm. We must hope not. And we shall have to find her, anyway. Nat Blackburne tells me you are unable to proceed to an inquest else.'

'For an inquest we must have a body. That is why I wonder if you would sanction the dispatch of a party of soldiers to form a search party in the grounds and park of Garlick Hall.'

'Soldiers, you say? I don't see why not. We need this matter cleared up one way or another. If I am to endure the strain and expense of a borough election, I would like to know as soon as possible.'

'From where will you detach the soldiers, if I may ask?'

'From my own regiment, naturally. Some of them are at camp not far away. I will send to their captain and instruct him. I would think the search might be instigated tomorrow or at latest on Sunday. The captain's name is Fairhurst, Frederick

Fairhurst. I shall send him a warrant and tell him to cooperate with you in person.'

'I am obliged to you, your lordship.'

'And I to *you*, Titus. We must speak again when I return from London in ten days, but keep me informed of any discoveries in the meantime. And make good use of Fairhurst's men. WINSTANLEY!'

The painter and his sullen boy returned to the room as I was going out. Closing the door behind me, I looked back. Lord Derby had replaced his wig, turned his head towards the window and was adjusting his chin to the required position.

A note from Ned Talboys awaited me when I returned to the office. It told me that his daughter Abigail still refused to come out of her room, and was being kept alive on little other than warm milk and biscuits. But she had expressed a wish to talk to me specifically. Would I pay a call at my earliest convenience? As it happened my earliest convenience was now.

I quickly picked up my hat again and hurried away to Friar Gate.

Chapter Fourteen

THE DRESSMAKER LED ME, as before, up the narrow flight of stairs to the attic. He knocked on his daughter's door.

'Abby! This is your father. I have Mr Cragg the coroner with me.'

After a moment we heard her voice, a little shrill and evidently from just behind the door itself.

'Father, you are not to come in. Please go down. When you have gone I shall let Mr Cragg in.'

Grumbling about the whimsy of all young girls, Ned stumped back downstairs. As soon as his footsteps were no longer audible, the catch on the door was released, the door swung open and Abigail stood before me, wearing a white nightshift and heavy woollen shawl.

'Please come in, Mr Cragg.'

I did so, feeling oversized and ungainly under the low and sloping ceiling. It was a plain bedroom with a bed, a washstand and a tiny iron fireplace in which a thin spiral of smoke drifted up cheerlessly from a single blackened log. Beside it was an armchair. Abigail motioned me towards it.

'Sit there, if you please, sir.'

I did as she asked while she perched herself on the edge of the bed, pinching her hands between her knees and fixing me with an intense gaze. She was an undeniably pretty young woman, though at this moment her hair was tangled and the whites of her eyes showed pink traces of weeping.

'Mr Cragg, are you enquiring into the terrible thing that happened to Mrs Dolores Brockletower?'

She spoke hoarsely, almost in a whisper, but I noted that she spoke well, and with intelligence.

'Yes, that is so,' I replied. 'I understand you knew her particularly, Abby. I wonder, is there anything she said to you that would help at the inquest?'

Abigail appeared taken aback at this word, as if she had not foreseen it.

'Oh! I wanted to speak only to you, sir, in private. I should not like to . . . give evidence in the court.'

I spoke as gently as I could, as a parent tries to coax a child out of its hiding place.

'You might have to, Abigail. But it isn't difficult, truly. You would be among friends.'

'Oh, but it would be difficult! It would be right hard to speak these things publicly and in front of people.'

'You have some evidence to tell, then?'

'Yes, to tell you. But not the whole world.'

'Let's start with that, then; with you telling me. Shall we?'

She closed her eyes and hesitated for a few moments, then made up her mind to plunge in.

'See, I was always Mrs Brockletower's choice for a dress-fitter. She said she didn't like my father fussing around and mumbling at her with a mouthful of pins. She said dressing a woman was a woman's business, and that was that. She liked coming here, though. In the end she was visiting us such a lot that she was not just a customer. She seemed more like a sister – to me, anyway. And don't say: as if I didn't have enough sisters already. I am the eldest and have not the consolation of an older one. So I welcomed it when Mrs Brockletower called me her dearest little Abby, and petted and kissed me when we were alone, and said I was her only friend.'

'Are those the words she used – her only friend?' I asked.

'Yes, and she would tell me things, too, private things about her and the squire.'

She saw that I wanted to interrupt her again, and held up her hand to stop me.

'No, sir, let me go on. I will answer your questions after, if I can.'

I nodded and composed myself to listen to the remainder of her tale.

'It was like this. I have a beau, sir, and Mrs Brockletower used to want to know all about him and what happened between us when we walked out alone together. Intimate things, you know, the sort of things that no respectable girl could repeat without blushing. But she coaxed such things out of me and she did make me blush a great deal, but in return (as she said) she would tell me similar intimate matters about the squire and how it was between them. Not that I asked, you understand. Only that she seemed to want to requite my tales about G—, about my young man, with tales of her own. To make things equal between us, that's how she put it.

'So that's how I learned that Mr and Mrs Brockletower had become unhappy in their marriage since arriving in England. In the West Indies, when he was a naval officer, they had been happy and now here in Lancashire she could not forget what she had lost. She said it was like her happiness and pleasure in her husband had slipped from her hands. Now he was cold towards her, and she to him, without wanting or meaning to be. I was sorry for her. She had a rough side to her, as everyone knows, but I could also see the sweet side.

'About four months ago something happened. It was partly because of Mrs Brockletower's questions about me and my young man, and me wanting to have something new to tell her. Anyway I was walking with him in the fields down near the river one Sunday afternoon, and we came to a barn, and he took me inside, and we . . . we lay down in the straw. I didn't mean it to happen, sir, not for a moment. But it did and now I think in a way Mrs Brockletower had inflamed me, with her questions and that. She had kept pressing to know if I was still . . .'

'Still what, child?'

She answered in a whisper I could only just catch.

'A maid, sir.'

After another moment's pause she cleared her throat, squared her shoulders and continued more audibly.

'She would taunt me shockingly, sir. "Don't tell me you are still intact," she would say, not believing me when I said I was. And so, after that particular Sunday, I was able to tell her I was no longer, she seemed delighted, laughing and praising me for doing this thing that, in my heart, I knew I ought to be ashamed of. But I got over my shame, and the young man and I still took our Sunday afternoon walks, and that haybarn still saw quite a lot of us, until . . . well, it happened.'

'What happened?'

'You must be able to guess, sir.'

'I think I can, but you must tell me.'

Again her voice diminished to almost nothing.

'I was with child.'

Having been sufficiently prepared for this news I showed no surprise, though I tut-tutted and dear-deared a little, before I asked her when this had happened.

'At the start of March, sir. That was when I began to feel the changes, like.'

'I see. Go on with your tale, Abby.'

'Well, first I told my young man, and his response was spiteful. That's the only way I can describe it. He said he would not marry me and would deny everything, and leave the town for London, or the colonies, if need be. I was so terribly afraid of what would happen to me. So I turned to Mrs Brockletower and asked her for advice when she next came to the shop. And she was right good to me, and promised that she *would* help me. And she did, and all, or would have done. She had thought of a way. But now she is gone and I've got no hope.'

She began sniffling.

'How was she intending to help you, Abigail?' I put in gently.

'She said she would arrange everything.'

'In what way?'

'She said she would give me money and a place to go where I could . . . have the baby. And then after a while she said she would take the baby to Garlick Hall, and bring it up as her own.'

I had maintained an unshockable front up to this point but suddenly surprise burst through.

'Good God, child! Is that what she proposed to do? Adopt? Truthfully?'

'Yes. Yes. She told me that she was certain she herself could never have children, but that Mr Brockletower wanted an heir, which was part of the reason for the difficulties between them, you see. So this appeared to her as the perfect answer, for everybody.'

I found myself speaking rather severely.

'I don't think she was speaking for everybody. The perfect

solution for you, young lady, would be marriage, as I am sure you are aware. Everything else is more or less an imperfect solution. Have you not spoken to your father about all this?'

She shook her head.

'And what about the young man? Can he not be induced to do his duty?'

'It doesn't matter, sir. I do not love him and I no longer want him. I would refuse him even if he trailed behind me all day on his knees.'

I sat and pondered for a moment.

'Let me get something clear,' I went on. 'Before Mrs Brockletower spoke to you about whether or not you were a maid, you had done nothing untoward in that regard. Is that right?'

'No sir, I had not.'

'So Mrs Brockletower can be said to have encouraged you, even *incited* you to, er, misbehave with your young man. Would you agree?'

'Well, yes, sir, I suppose she did that.'

'And she had already gone to considerable lengths to gain your friendship, your confidence.'

'She was very friendly, sir. I believe we *were* friends.'

'Now tell me one more thing. You are explaining all this to me. Not your father, or the vicar of the parish, or anyone else who might reasonably be expected to direct you rightly in the matter. Why? Is it because you want my help, or because you want to help me?'

'Because you came to call on me the other day, sir. I asked why and my sister told me it was because you were enquiring about Mrs Brockletower's death. I wanted to help find out why she is gone. I want to know who did it, and why. To get justice for her, that would be something. Me, I cannot be helped, not now. I am past help.'

She started crying properly now, pressing her hands to her face so that the tears leaked through between the fingers. I thought it time to speak sternly to her.

'Nonsense, Abigail. No one is ever beyond help, unless one is to believe the theology of John Calvin, which I personally do not, and nor should you. Now, I want you to promise me you will tell your father about your condition. If you like, I will speak to him also. But I want you to tell him first. The poor man needs to believe his eldest daughter trusts and loves him enough to confide in him. Will you do that?'

Abigail raised her head and wiped the back of one hand across her mouth and nostrils, and then did the same with the other, sniffing loudly as she did so. It seemed her courage was returning.

'All right, sir, I will do as you say. I will tell him today. If he should strike me dead, do not be surprised.'

I allowed myself to smile.

'Your father is not a man of violence. He will be distressed, of course, but he knows these mistakes have been made before, and have been resolved before.'

And so I left her, and went back down to the shop, where I found Ned carefully cutting a length of cloth.

'You will be glad to hear,' I said, 'that Abigail is of a mind to speak to you now. It is an unhappy tale, but you had better hear it from her own mouth. Don't be hard on her, will you?'

'Hard on her? I shall only be happy that she can trust me with what's getting at her.'

I nodded at what he was doing.

'So you found your cuts at last?'

He held his scissors up with the blades separated to form an X. 'No, we didn't find them. I had to buy new.'

I left him and returned to the office. Furzey greeted me with a sardonic smirk.

'Don't put your feet up just yet, Mr Cragg. Now Captain Fairhurst's sent a note round to say he will be at your disposal in the Magpie and Stump tavern at one in the afternoon. That would be about now.'

I found the captain in civilian clothes and drinking wine. He was accompanied by another man who wore the uniform of a sergeant and was sipping from a tankard of beer. The pair sat at their table with what looked like a sketch-map open in front of them, conferring together.

To drink familiarly with one's sergeant may seem an unsoldierly thing to be doing, and to my eye Fairhurst seemed an unsoldierly figure. He had bow-shoulders, gap-teeth, and a squint that gave his round and dimpled face the superficial appearance of a gargoyle, partly comic, partly malign. He introduced his companion as Sergeant Sutch.

'My sergeant is fittingly named, Mr Cragg,' Fairhurst told me with a momentary giggle. 'Can you guess in what way?'

I paused and looked the sergeant over. He was a grey-haired and weatherbeaten figure who seemed by comparision with the officer, every inch what he was supposed to be: upright, commandingly tall and very squarely built. But I had to confess I could not see in what sense his name was so suitable.

'Because he will lead his men in "sutch" of the missing corpse – you see?'

Fairhurst leant forward slightly and let out another guffaw, accompanied this time by a stuttering fart, which I clearly heard and would shortly smell. I simulated a smile, noticing at the same time that not a muscle of the sergeant's face had moved.

'Well, never mind that, to business,' Fairhurst went on as if nothing had happened. 'We must discuss the details, but first: what will you drink?'

I took a seat and said I would join him in some wine. I then asked if he had received the Earl of Derby's warrant.

'Yes, I have it here, I warrant you.'

This occasioned more detonations, of laughter and of wind, as he drew from his pocket a folded paper carrying Lord Derby's seal. He gave it me and I looked it over while he spoke to the potboy, ordering wine and more beer for the sergeant. In the warrant his lordship requested and required Ramilles Brockletower Esq of Garlick Hall to render every assistance to the military detachment under the command of Captain Frederick Fairhurst in their efforts to find the missing body of Mrs Brockletower. The warrant encompassed searches of the house, outhouses and grounds of Garlick Hall, and of any other of his lands and property whatsoever, as might be required by Captain Fairhurst in furtherance of his task. It was properly and correctly drawn up and undoubtedly had the force of law. I passed it back to the captain.

'This seems satisfactory, Captain. Tell me how you propose to proceed.'

'Sergeant Sutch should tell you.'

The sergeant took a judicious draught of beer, laid down the tankard, wiped his mouth with his hand and looked at me with a steady, confident, almost mocking gaze.

'First may I say, sir, how gratified I am – ah-hem, *we* are – that you have chosen to employ trained men in this matter. You can never do better than a soldier for a search. A band of estate workers, to take an instance of those who might otherwise be deployed, understand nothing of thoroughness. To begin with, half of them is going to be women. They go about it in a way I can best describe as being like a flock of farmyard chickens, pecking around without system or sense. They think of a likely place and go to look there, and when they find it empty they do nothing until they think of some other likely place, and then they scurry off to look into that. And so on, sir, aimlessly.'

He was speaking with such gravity, purpose and rhythm that I had nothing to say, but could only nod my head inanely in time with his sentences.

'Now, the trained man,' he went on lifting a finger, 'that is to say the soldier, gets down to the job under principles.'

He solemnly lowered his finger to the paper on the table in front of him.

'So tomorrow, under *principles*, as I say, I shall take twenty men, sir, and they shall fairly put a comb through the grounds of that estate. We shall form a line, with each man representing one of the teeth of that comb, and draw the line across the ground that we wish to search. In that way nothing whatever is missed.'

His finger rapped the paper on the table.

'This is a rough plan of the area, which I myself drew up after making a reconnaissance this afternoon. I have divided the ground into sections, an inner ring here, consisting of four areas nearest to the house, and another ring consisting of these nine outer areas. We shall clear them one by one in number order, to make sure we miss nothing.'

'Admirable,' I commented, with absolute sincerity. 'As you say, it is good to go by a system.'

'It is essential.'

'Yes, of course, essential. But what about the house?'

'A search of a residence requires a different method and is

inclined to create greater disturbance. I therefore propose, with your agreement, to omit the house until after we have finished in the gardens and park. That way, if we find what we're look-ing for outside, the disturbance will not be necessary inside.'

'Very good. Very good indeed, Sergeant,' said Fairhurst ardently.

I agreed. Sergeant Sutch seemed an altogether exemplary figure and I turned to his captain and told him as much.

'Yes, yes,' cried Fairhurst, clutching Sutch's shoulder. 'I call him *Sergeant Argent*, that is to say, worth his weight in silver. Of course, I *would* say gold, but that would spoil the conceit, you know.'

I raised the glass to my lips and drank the wine down quickly. Then, before the captain could conjure any more con-ceits, I stood up.

'Well,' I said, 'you are at liberty to execute the warrant when you like – tomorrow, perhaps, Sergeant Sutch?'

'Ay, tomorrow,' said the man. 'We'll march down there at first light. Don't worry, sir. If she's there, we'll find her.'

After thanking him, I put down my glass, made my excuses and left.

Chapter Fifteen

'I SAW THAT Mr Woodley in Market Street this morning,' said Elizabeth. 'What a strange type of man he looks. More a boy than a man.'

We were talking in bed that same night, curled together in a comfortable embrace. I had already told her the story of my day, of the revelation by Abigail Talboys, and my encounter with the clumsy persiflage of Captain Fairhurst.

'Woodley has bulging eyes, like a baby,' I observed. 'But, though he may look boyish, he walks like a dancing master.'

She laughed merrily.

'I can hardly believe he has the job of putting up big houses for rich people to live in. I would never employ a babyface like that to give me a roof over my head, Titus. I wouldn't feel safe after.'

'He's no younger than you are – twenty-five, twenty-six? And you, I perceive, are no child.'

Since my hand was caressing her right breast at the time, I was very much engaged in verifying my last statement.

'But he is unnaturally young-looking – just like a china doll.'

'He's got more brains than a doll. He's clever. Though in my opinion he's also a bluffer.'

'A bluffer? Is he not what he seems, then? Is he not really an architect?'

'Oh yes, he is an architect. Anyone can call himself an architect, it seems. One day there may be an inn for architecture as there is now for lawyers. But it is probably far off.'

'He's a liar, then? There's bluffers that are powerful liars, I think, and others that are not liars, but such fools to themselves that they persuade everyone else of the same foolishness.'

'Woodley's the second kind. He may be a fool—'

'A fool with brains!' she broke in.

'Yes, which is the most unfathomable kind of fool. But he believes absolutely in himself. On the other hand there is something fantastical about him. He reminds me of a genie who should be in a bottle but got out. What was he doing when you saw him?'

'Coming out through the arched entrance of Molyneux Square.'

'Was he indeed? I wonder why he would go there.'

'He had an abstracted, thoughtful look about him, that is all I can say.'

She raised herself up on an elbow and kissed me.

'And now, I must sleep. Tomorrow I am taking some food around the Moor cottages. We have Mr Broome's cart ordered for seven o'clock. We'll be loading a hundred loaves and a whole barrel of pickled herring to give away.'

I returned her kiss fondly.

'Good night, then, my sweet miracle worker,' I said, turning to snuff out the bedside candle.

In the morning I rode back, in spring sunshine, to Garlick Hall, wishing to see how far Sergeant Sutch's men had progressed. I found them, a dozen fusiliers, tramping up and down a part of the garden which sloped away on the south-east side of the house, between it and the Savage Brook which flowed past at a distance of less than a hundred yards. Standing at a right angle to the house was a long hothouse built of glass, with a chimney emitting a continuous thin stream of smoke from the boiler.

The soldiers carried ash poles and were poking the ground in the flower borders and beneath the shrubs and hedges. Above them by the house itself I found the sergeant with the squire's gardener, an aggrieved, animated, wiry little fellow by the name of Benjamin Lowry.

'Who's going to mend all the damage these men are doing?' I heard Lowry wanting to know, bouncing up and down in agitation. 'Some of the plants your men are trampling are rare and valuable, never mind sensitive. They'll die from getting scarified like this.'

The soldier replied in his calm and measured basso. If that voice were an instrument I swear it would be the lower register of the bassoon.

'I have my warrant, Mr Lowry, from the Lord Lieutenant himself. It directs me with the force of the law to conduct this search. Not you, nor even the squire, can countermand it.'

At this point Sutch noticed my approach and swung round, touching fingers to his scarlet and white hat, bound with golden braid.

'Good morning, Mr Cragg, sir. We have a fine day for the combing. You've come to enquire of any finds, no doubt.'

'And?'

'Nothing yet, sir – or nothing of importance.'

But at this point there was a shout from one of the men, who had paused at the crossing point of two grass walkways. The rest of them broke the line to gather around him, and two spades were brought up.

Lowry gave a cry when he saw the spades glinting in the sunlight.

'My new turf!' he cried. 'I have just laid it. They can't . . . I won't allow them to put their spades to my new turf.'

The soldier had evidently seen for himself the chequered pattern of freshly laid turf and, quite reasonably, decided there might be something lying beneath. As Lowry launched himself with a stumbling gait towards the knot of soldiers, it was clear to the sergeant and myself, as we followed, that he would not be in time to stop any digging. He had covered only half the distance when the first spade was driven cruelly into the grass, while Lowry screamed at them that the turf was still young and tender and they must treat it gently. But the soldiers' style of digging did not even approximate to the gentle spadework of a lawn-keeper. There was no careful peeling up of the new sods, no making a low wall of them in bricklayer's style ready for re-use, before getting into the exposed earth below. When we reached the searchers, the hole in the grass was already a ragged cannonball-crater, and Mr Lowry was clutching his head and moaning as if in actual pain.

To make matters worse, there was nothing to discover beneath but one or two writhing earthworms that the spades had cut in half. With a shrug the soldiers fanned out again, to resume their positions as the teeth of a comb. They left the hole and the mound of earth they had dug with as little compunction as a mole leaves behind his molehill.

After watching the combing for a few more minutes I left the sergeant, saying I must go and find Mr Ramilles Brockle-tower. I intended to speak with him about my own progress in preparing the inquest into his wife's death, and was anticipating a difficult, unpredictable conversation.

In the end there was no need for me to seek out the squire. I was rounding the corner of the house, from where I intended to approach the front door, when I saw him striding purposefully towards me, the heels of his boots banging the paving stones of the house's forecourt. As he bore down on me, impatiently negotiating the various piles of stone, slate, wood and other building materials that Woodley's men had left there, I could see he was yet again distempered. As he stamped up to me I wondered when in his life he had last laughed or capered or skimmed a stone across a pond for the pleasure of breaking the water into animated patterns and sunlit sparkles.

'This invasion of soldiers is disturbing my household, sir, and leaving a trail of destruction behind it in my grounds. And it is distracting these men who are working on my house, taking their minds off the job so that they work too slowly. It's intolerable. I shall bring an action against it, sir. An action!'

An action? That would have to be against the Lord Lieutenant, which seemed a far-fetched threat. I adopted a light, cheerful tone, as if I had not perceived his words as a threat at all.

'Well, they are not a bad band of men. They are trying their best to keep within the bounds of their commission.'

'Then they should keep off my gardener's lawns and borders. They're trampling valuable plants and flowers. What next? Will they smash the glass of my hothouses and pluck my peaches and pineapples?'

'Good lord, is there really such fruit so early in the year?' I asked innocently, well knowing there couldn't be. 'It's a wonderful contrivance, a hothouse.'

'Be damned to you, Cragg, don't try and take a rise out of me. Abandon this futile poking around and pack your soldiers off to wherever they came from.'

'They are not mine, sir, and it is not for me to call them off. These are Lord Derby's militia and his lordship does not think the exercise futile. And, I'm afraid, the search must include the lawns and beds. But I shall ask the sergeant on your behalf that his men refrain from breaking any glass, or plucking any fruit.'

At the mention of Lord Derby, Brockletower fell silent. He knew there were some powers against which his bluster was of little avail.

'Mr Brockletower, I have one small question to ask.'

'Yes?'

'Did you on your travels have one of your horse's hooves re-shod?'

'Curious things you want to know. But, if you must know, yes. At Settle, he cast a shoe. I stopped at a wayside farrier's.'

'Thank you, sir.'

I cleared my throat and adopted a slightly harder tone. This was to show that I was now about to raise a matter less easily dealt with.

'I fear I must, in addition, broach a more delicate subject.'

The squire sighed deeply, and closed his eyes.

'Must you, sir?'

'I must. It concerns your own relations with your late wife.'

Brockletower's only reply was a bitter, croaking laugh.

'You laugh,' I observed.

'Yes, I laugh. And that is all I do.'

'Very well, allow me to go on.'

I had changed my tone again, and was speaking with the utmost softness, as to a skittish horse.

'You and Mrs Brockletower were not blessed with family – I mean, with progeny. It must have been a cause of some distress to you both.'

He turned to me with an unexpected look of anguish, eyes wide open and mouth crushed. Had I made a crack in his shell?

'Is that correct, Mr Brockletower?' I persisted.

He seemed to teeter on the brink of speech for a few moments, then fell right in, head first.

'See here, Cragg. A man that wants an heir is desperate. He thinks about it all the time, he dreams about it.'

The words were tumbling off his tongue. He was near to gabbling.

'Without an heir a man's like a ship without ballast. Even without a compass. Barrenness is exactly what the Book says it is: a curse, because it knocks the compass needle off its pin. It knocks the purpose out of life.'

'But there's a ready remedy, surely,' I put in. 'The law allows a man to adopt an heir.'

'Adopt? I am a naval man, sir. I would no more bring another man's child into my family than crew one of His Majesty's ships with a gang of mulattos and lascars. Such things are for buccaneers, and houses of ill-pedigree. I must have my dignity, don't you see? Dignity is honour. Nothing is more important.'

'Did Mrs Brockletower agree with you about adoption?'

But now he was silent again, moodily pushing a stone around on the ground with the toe of his boot.

'You do not answer me,' I persisted. 'I fear I must repeat the question. Much hangs on it. Did Mrs Brockletower, on her part, wish to adopt a child?'

He mumbled a reluctant reply.

'She asked me to consider it, yes. I don't see why much should hang on that.'

'Was this recently?'

'Oh, two or three weeks ago. A month at most.'

'And did you consider it?'

'Of course not,' he replied, regaining some of his briskness. 'I dismissed the notion out of hand. I have told you why, and now will you tell me what these questions are about?'

174

Not wanting to lose momentum, I ignored the last demand.

'Squire, I wonder if you asked her if she had a *particular* child in mind, for the adoption?'

'Of course I did not! Such a thing never occurred to me. It was enough that I had quashed all further conversation on the subject.'

'And how did she respond to your quashing?'

'She sulked.'

'So you quarrelled?'

'No! Why don't you listen? I said that *she* sulked. Sulking was one of my wife's prime accomplishments.'

'But communication did break down between you on this matter.'

'Yes, of course it did. On that subject, it broke down completely, to my entire satisfaction.'

'Did you consider breaking off communication with your wife . . . in any more drastic way?'

'What do you mean?'

I drew a deep breath and without further thought launched the question towards him.

'Is it true, Mr Brockletower, that you considered separation . . . divorce, even?'

He turned to me with suddenly renewed ferocity.

'*Divorce?* Has someone suggested this to you? Who have you been speaking with?'

He raised his eyes upwards and his hands too, in a gesture of hapless understanding.

'My uncle! You've been gossiping with my reverend uncle. You know he is a sot? Nothing he says is reliable. Nothing he says will stand up as evidence in any court, not even your own miserable gutter-court of inquest.'

'You are jumping to conclusions, Mr Brockletower. No one

is speaking of evidence in court. I am merely trying to determine Mrs Brockletower's state of mind at the time of her death.'

'Why? Why would *you* want to do such a thing? In what precise way is it any business of yours?'

'You yourself are a magistrate,' I went on, my voice straining to convey patience and peacemaking. 'You know that I must hold an inquiry into the death, because of its suddenness and violence. The ultimate responsibility, I agree, is that of the empanelled jury. But I must preside over the proceedings, and my duty entails calling proper witnesses and marshalling the facts so that a coherent narrative of events prior to the death is put before that jury.'

At this Brockletower raised his index finger and shook it at me.

'Ah! But you have no body, sir. You cannot hold your inquest without a body. I know the law to that extent, at least.'

We had come almost full circle in our exchange, and I permitted myself the small pleasure of closing it.

'Which is why we are searching your estate,' I told him. 'And why we must go on until we find what we are looking for.'

As I left the squire I felt a peppercorn's weight more sympathy for him, after the glimpse I'd had of the more relenting side to his character. Virile ferocity may be necessary for the advancement of civilization across the world, but it gives way to more domesticated emotions from time to time. On the other hand, Brockletower had neither confirmed nor denied his reverend uncle's story about his desire for a divorce.

In hope of getting nearer to the truth of this, I strolled around the side of the house and into the yard, entering by way of the kitchen. I found it in its usual condition of heat, steam and brothy smells. Bethany Marsden was in supervision of a sturdy girl with bare forearms who was mixing a duff in a large bowl.

The housekeeper did not ask about the search and I did not mention it, but I did request the opportunity to speak to Miss Brockletower. A few minutes later my request had been granted and I was seated in the same chair I had occupied before in Sarah's darkened room, opposite her rocker.

'Well, Titus! Events have taken a theatrical turn indeed since we spoke last. I hear the sounds of men outside, quite different in tone from those of Mr Woodley's builders. Are they by any chance a search party for my late sister's body?'

I told her about the soldiers, and the methods they were applying.

'"Combing", is it? I like the notion.'

I asked if I might speak with her so confidentially as to exclude her relating the matter even to her brother.

'As he is my brother and protector, that is too much to ask,' she said. 'But let's say I shall not reveal anything without warning you first, and in any case not without very good reasons. Will that satisfy you?'

I said it would.

'Then what is it you want to discuss?'

'First, your own feelings about Ramilles. Are you affectionate, the two of you?'

'That question comes close to prurience, Titus.'

'It must seem so. But I trust your judgement of human nature, Sarah, and I am trying to form an estimate of your brother's nature – his character and temperament.'

'You want to know if he killed her, in other words?'

I flinched. Her directness had once again abashed me.

'Hypothetically, yes.'

'So be it. Hypothetically. Let me think. I don't think I know the answer. He is my baby brother and as a baby I loved him. I would cuddle and kiss him endlessly, wishing I could see him. But later he became a very selfish boy, wrapped in his own concerns. He did not bother himself about me and I hardly knew him. And then he went to sea. When he returned a dozen years later with his wife there was a great deal of reserve between us. So, although I respect him as my brother because it is my duty, and as one whom I had once truly loved years ago, I do not now love him well enough to say no, he cannot be a killer. There! You must be satisfied with that. I've told far more than I should.'

'You have expressed yourself finely, Sarah.'

'Never mind finely, I've told the truth. I hope that is all you need to know.'

I looked into the fire, and then at her poodle lying on the hearthrug. The words she had just spoken, 'one whom I had once truly loved years ago', might be meant for me, too. 'Wishing I could see him': had this also been what she had felt about me? Sadness at the way human feelings can be changed by time and distance overwhelmed me. During our juvenile walks arm in arm, in the clumsily phrased messages we exchanged, and the words we spoke between kisses, it had been Sarah's blindness that bound us most tightly together. I told her she would never need sight, because I would always be her eyes. And she told me – I remember her words exactly – 'How can I hope to see more happily than through my Titus's eyes?'

But now this same function that I'd wished to perform was done by a poodle, and her sightlessness, which had made our babyish love so potent, had fallen like a curtain between us. So was I, in relation to her, no different from all the rest of the seeing world? I saw, at least, how utterly changed I was since we had first known each other. The boy who had wanted to be nothing but a blind girl's trusted Cicero was now a man of the world, who thought nothing of driving frightened people to tears with his questions. And the girl – she was still blind, and still alone, though no longer a girl.

'Why are you silent, Titus?' she demanded sharply. 'I do not like it, you know. Silence to the blind is like darkness to everyone else.'

'All right, I shall come straight out with it. There is a story going about that your brother and his wife had become so unhappy that he wished to part from her.'

Sarah gave a gasp and clapped her hands to her cheeks. At last I had surprised her. I went on.

'You will understand how important it is that I find out the truth of this. Do you know anything about it, Sarah? Did he confide this to you?'

She shook her head.

'No, he did not. But . . . part from her, you say? Well, I am shocked. There is no surety in the affection between men and women, is there?'

'It is only a tale I heard. But it does perhaps fit the case. After our last talk, it was apparent to me that the couple were not happy.'

'They were not particularly happy, no, but most people are not. Such a step! Separation? Divorce? I was privy to nothing of the kind. You must ask elsewhere.'

It seemed she was signalling the end of the interview. I began to take my leave when she stopped me.

'Before you go, I do have one piece of advice, Titus. Look to Mr Woodley for the source of the wickedness in this house. I consider him an evil influence, ever since he kicked Jonathan.'

'Jonathan?'

'My dog.'

At the sound of his name the dog raised his chin from his

forepaws and gave Sarah an enquiring look. She tilted her chair forward, stretched out her hand until it found his head and stroked it as she explained.

'Jonathan and I were walking together alone in the park, as we often do. He is on his leash and I allow him to take me where he likes. I fool myself that it gives him a sense of freedom and dignity but the poor creature's driven by his routines and mostly does the same round every day. First we visit the cedar tree, which he circles several times before cocking his leg. Then it's down to the gardener's toolshed under which live rabbits. And on to various other places that his nose leads him to. It's so curious. Jonathan is happy to be my eyes but for his own purposes he employs his eyes less than his nose.

'Anyway on this occasion he led me into the wood, well, not exactly into it, but along a tongue of the lawn that makes a grass walk curving into the trees. Quite suddenly Jonathan got excited and he pulled the leash out of my hand, then ran off ahead barking. A few seconds later I heard Mr Woodley shouting at Jonathan in the coarsest language that he shouldn't go in there, that he'd have him shot if he did, and then I heard a penetrating yelp and Jonathan came running back to me. I can only suppose that Mr Woodley gave him a violent bunt with the toe of his boot, as he was still whimpering when he reached me. So we turned around and came home.'

'Did Woodley speak to you?'

'I don't think he even saw me. As I said, the walk curves sharply to the right. I was standing around that bend and out of view, or so I think.'

'And what business did Woodley have in that place?'

'Why, don't you know, Titus? The end of the walk, that's where they're building this temple of his. But I don't think a man so cruel to a dumb animal should be building temples.'

She fondled Jonathan's ears.

'Which is why we call him Jago, isn't it, Jonathan?'

'Jago?' I said, a little puzzled. 'Forgive me, I don't . . .'

She sighed.

'You are dull-witted today, Titus. I refer to Jago, in *Othello*. Take my word for it, Mr Woodley is not to be trusted.'

Chapter Sixteen

Outside, I found the troopers a hundred yards from the house and sitting in a circle under the shade of the great cedar of Lebanon that rose from the middle of the lawn. They were dividing loaves of bread and taking turns to drink from a breaker of beer. A smartly turned-out horse stood picking at the lawn nearby. This belonged to Captain Fairhurst, who had ridden over to review Sergeant Sutch's progress.

'Well, Mr Cragg,' the captain called out as I walked towards them. 'The men are enjoying success!'

Nonplussed, I turned to the sergeant.

'You don't mean you've found what we're looking for?'

'No, no, sir,' replied Sutch hastily between chews of his bread. 'And, though we don't know where it is yet, we do know much more about where it is *not*.'

Producing from his tunic pocket the sketch map that I had seen at the tavern in town the previous day, he unfolded it and traced with his finger a circle around the square, which represented the Hall.

'We can safely rule out these four areas in the immediate vicinity of the Hall, which I have cross-hatched as you see. I have also sent three men to go through the workmen's camp, which I set aside as a separate area of search. We shall now proceed, under system, to the outer ring, which has seven defined areas. We shall work our way through these one by one.'

'Will you finish before dark?'

'That will depend on how much digging we must do. I hope we can.'

'And they may not need to finish at all,' broke in Fairhurst, with one of his crowing laughs. 'About the whereabouts of poor Mrs Brockletower: before dark we are in the dark, but in daylight the lamp may yet be lit!'

Unwilling to engage with these elaborations of wit, I wished them luck, returned to my horse and rode back into town.

When I reached the office, Elizabeth had not returned from her mission to the Moor. I put the Brockletower case out of my mind, and applied myself instead to drafting a complicated trust deed. Saturday is Furzey's *dies non* and I was so absorbed in my solitary work that midday came, and went, without my noticing. It was half past two when Elizabeth returned, her cheeks glowing from her exertions.

'We got rid of nearly all the food, Titus. But Mr Broome's horse went lame and we had to return home. Have you eaten?'

I told her no.

'Then quickly! Come through to the house. I'll feed you and tell you about my adventures.'

As I sat down in front of a plate of pickled herring and a half loaf of bread ('I told you we couldn't quite give it all away,' she explained, a little ruefully) Elizabeth told of the hovels she had been into, and of the mixed response of the poor people in receiving her charity.

'Some of them spat when they saw me, as if I were the cause of their destitution. They took the food anyway, of course. But I have marked down two or three cottages where the ingratitude is truly discouraging, and I shall not be visiting them again. But now, I *must* tell you something else. The whole countryside is talking about the death of Mrs Brockletower. And do you know what they are saying?'

I said that I didn't.

'They are on fire with the notion that she was a werewolf, Titus. A werewolf, who roamed the woods at night. She transformed herself by a belt that she put on, made from the hide of a real wolf. She brought it with her from the West Indies, they say. The night she died in the Fulwood, she had met the Devil himself, and it was he who tore out her throat. And as she lay dying she transformed back into a woman, which was how she was found as she was – on all fours.'

It was a variation, though more elaborate, of what Miriam Patten told me when we met at Gamull, during my ride with young Jonah to the Fulwood on Tuesday.

'So what do they say about William Pearson's testimony, that he saddled her horse and watched her ride out in the morning? And all the others that saw her in the morning before she went riding?'

Elizabeth shrugged.

'Only that they were lying, or under some spell.'

'This is nonsense! I doubt there *are* any wolves in the West Indies. Surely you don't give credence to this kind of talk.'

'No, of course not. But it is interesting, don't you think?'

'I think it's twaddle.'

'I don't say she *was* a werewolf, Titus. But the idea must have come from somewhere.'

She shuddered briefly, betraying something in herself more deep-seated than academical curiosity about this phenomenon.

'It came from the ravings of half-starved brains.'

Elizabeth reached forward and picked an uneaten shred of

herring from my plate, tilted back her head and delicately dropped it into her mouth.

'Yes, well, that's a possibility,' she went on, after she'd swallowed the fish. 'But in a bushel of lies there is a grain of truth. And there was definitely something odd about that woman. If there *were* werewolves—'

'There are not!'

'But if there *were*,' she insisted, 'and it was proved Dolores Brockletower really had been one, the discovery would not surprise me at all.'

I returned to the office and my work on the trust deed, but now I could not concentrate as I was still hoping for news from the search party at Garlick Hall. But I was even more distracted by the imaginary spectre of Dolores Brockletower as a she-wolf, running and running by moonlight through the woods with bared and bloody fangs.

For supper we had Elizabeth's economical invention, being rissoles of yesterday's salmon, minced with spinach, capers and breadcrumb. Afterwards I left her embroidering by the parlour fire and went into my library. Feeling a tiny pricking of guilt, I began taking down books that might yield further information on lycanthropy. As I knew quite well, stories of transformation, or metamorphosis, run deep in literature and pagan religion. The myths of the Greeks and Romans teem with them and Ovid had merely collected all of the ones he could find. I looked up what Mr Spectator has to say about Ovid's stories: 'Here we walk upon enchanted ground,' he says, a phrase to stiffen the hairs on the back of one's neck, if any phrase can. But stories of people becoming animals, more particularly metamorphosing into wolves, are not only cases of Ovidian enchantment, but of satanic business. And they appear to have much to do with cannibalism.

Lycaon was the first lycanthrope, I read. He was older than Zeus and lived before the flood, which, in part, was his fault. He had dished up the flesh of his own sons in a stew for a banquet, to which he had invited the gods. But his murderous impiety was discovered and he was condemned to roam the trackless wilderness as a wolf, tormented by an insatiable hunger for human flesh. He was not destroyed until the great flood was summoned to obliterate all living wickedness.

In old tales from Asia Minor I found the same creature, but now in female form – a woman guilty of frightful sins. For seven years she was condemned to transform each night into a she-wolf, first devouring her own children, then those of her neighbours, before ranging ever wider to spread fear and havoc throughout the land.

Finally, after more than an hour of turning pages, I happened on a remarkable passage in Verstegan's *Restitution of Decayed Intelligence*. I read:

> The werwoolfs are certayne sorcerors who having anoynted their bodies with an ointment which they make by the instinct of the devil, and putting on a certayne inchaunted girdle, doe not onely unto the view of others seeme as wolves, but to their owne thinking have both the shape and nature of wolves so long as they weare the said girdle. And they doe dispose themselves as very wolves in wourrying and killing most humane creatures.

My first thought was to take this immediately into the parlour and read it to Elizabeth. I quickly suppressed the impulse. I did not want to frighten her, but there was something else. I was more than a little ashamed at my own curiosity, and at the faint pulse of pleasure, repulsive but undeniable, that I felt when reading about this absurd hocus-pocus. So I quietly posted Verstegan back to his shelf, and hurriedly returned to the parlour.

Although my wife's religious beliefs did not lean towards the established church, she never failed to come with me to Divine Service on a Sunday morning. Her habit was to slip out before eight and go, by herself, to the discreet house where her co-papists gathered to worship – with, on most Sundays, Luke Fidelis among them. She then came back to breakfast with me at nine and, forty-five minutes later, we stepped out into Cheapside and walked arm-in-arm the short distance from our home to St John the Divine, the parish church, arriving in time for the ten o'clock service. She did this purely out of duty and the wish not to embarrass me in front of the townspeople. She was not permitted to take Communion, of course, but her mere presence was proof that she honoured me, and it made me proud. It is for such everyday tokens of affection that I love her, as much as for her sweet character and her beauty.

This morning I carried in my pocket a sealed letter delivered by the postboy a few minutes before we quit the house. It had come from Yorkshire and was addressed in the hand of Luke Fidelis. I had not yet had time to open it, though I could hardly contain my impatience to know what news it contained.

Mr Brighouse, our vicar, was a contrast to the rotund and ruddy Mr Oliver Brockletower. Stick-like and shrivelled, though he is no more than my own age, his ministry was benign enough, but blighted by his complete inability ever to say or do anything interesting. His sermons were particularly painful to hear, though he regarded it as his duty to preach at considerable length, and in a thin, scrannel monotone.

As usual, he creaked to the pulpit with the face of a

condemned man climbing the scaffold ladder. He announced his text, and the congregation settled in for up to an hour of prosaic moralizing, unsalted by a modicum of wit or enlightened learning, yet hedged about by thickets of qualification, gloss and biblical quotation. They did not mind much. As the sermon washed over them they lapsed into the embrace of their own thoughts and daydreams. Some quietly dozed, others went into a reverie, or drew up mental lists of things to do in the week ahead. People animated by real religious passion were meanwhile having their spirits lifted at the Dissenters' Meeting House along Fisher Gate, or (like Elizabeth) had received the Sacrament in their own peculiar style beforehand, at the papists' chapel.

I eased Fidelis's letter out of my pocket and gently broke the seal, keeping my thumb on it to muffle any cracking sound. Then I unfolded it, careful to keep it below the rim of the box pew, and began to read.

Dear Cragg,

I am now at York but yesterday attended my consumptive patient Mr Templeton at Harrogate. He is a co-religionist to me and though a young man of my own age he is not only gravely ill but reduced further by the bite of the recusancy laws. I expect him to require Last Rites before we reach the solstice.

But I know you will prefer to hear news of the matter that has been puzzling us at home. Some of my enquiries have yielded interesting results, though I fear you may find others disappointing.

I shall spill the disappointing news first. I have been following Mr Brockletower's supposed returning route in reverse, and I found that people along the upper Ribble valley remembered how he passed through, riding hard

*and yelling other traffic out of the way. They knew
the reason for his haste of course: the finding of Mrs
Brockletower's body had already reached that part of
the county. It was about three in the afternoon when he
rode through the village. Further along my eastward road
I came to the village of Slaidburn where the squire had
stopped at the inn for food at midday on Tuesday, and
where they told him of what had happened at Garlick
Hall. It is a remote, fell-top place but a post rider had
come through from Clitheroe on his way north to Kendal
and brought the information, which he himself had heard
in the marketplace that morning. You will observe that
this does not yet preclude that Mr Brockletower was in
Fulwood early in the morning. He could just have ridden
from there to Slaidburn in four hours. But when I reached
Settle eight miles to the north-east, I again found the story
he told us tallying. He had certainly spent the night there,
as he said, at the largest inn. The landlord told me he had
arrived at seven the previous evening (Monday the 17th)
and taken a room. Supper had been eaten in the chamber
(mutton chops, cheese and claret) and he had not been
seen again downstairs until he paid his account and rode
away at eleven the next morning. I do not think this is
consistent with his having been in Fulwood during the
early part of the morning. To do so he must have used a
different horse, and the time was not sufficient for him
not only to make the journey, but to dispose of the
exhausted horse afterwards without anyone's knowledge.
And to get back into his bedroom without being seen
would have been no easy matter. That is all I can write
now. I will write again from York.*

L.F.

I folded the paper and discreetly slid it back into my pocket, while Mr Brighouse's voice wheedled on. My mind went back to the indiscreet revelations of his clerical colleague, the squire's uncle. According to these, Ramilles Brockletower had become angry with his wife – a theme that was, by chance, under consideration at this very moment in Mr Brighouse's sermon. He was quoting (as he told us) Proverbs, chapter 6, and its warnings against unbridled passion.

' "Can a man take fire in his bosom, and his clothes not be burned?" ' the vicar squeaked, raising a twig-like admonitory finger. ' "Can one go upon hot coals, and his feet not be burned?" '

I did not think Mr Brighouse knew a great deal about fiery bosoms, for a more passionless man could hardly be imagined. But I rather liked the words. And I was taken even more by what followed.

'If I may be permitted a profane aside,' Brighouse continued, 'one of our secular writers (of the reign before last) closely echoes the sentiments of Scripture in commenting on "how pernicious, how sudden, and how fatal surprises of passion are to the mind of man". Although these are not sacred words, they are sensible ones, and all men would do well to take heed of them.'

I was startled by the quoted words, for I thought I knew them. But from where? I silently repeated to myself twice and three times: *pernicious . . . sudden . . . fatal*. And then, with delight and surprise, I placed them. Surely they were from the *Tatler*, the words of Mr Isaac Bickerstaff (as was the paper's conceit) writing upon . . . Upon what? I could not remember.

I determined to look it up in my four-volume edition of that excellent forerunner and companion of my darling book, the collected *Spectator*.

*

In my library, with a few minutes' leisure before dinner, I looked up 'passion' in the index of my bound edition of the *Tatler*. I found that the vicar's reference had been to one of the numbers in volume III, where Bickerstaff reflects on the differences between men and women, and recounts the murder of a Mrs Eustace by her husband. This was interesting enough, but there was more, very much more and of such momentousness that a few minutes later I was excitedly telling Elizabeth about it over our Sunday meat.

'It's the most surprising discovery. I don't know if it is chance, or part of a design. But it seems to bear on the Brockletower case.'

'Go on.'

'As you know,' I said, 'the *Tatler* was written every other day by Sir Richard Steele, pretending to be Mr Isaac Bickerstaff, a retired gentleman who commented freely on coffee-house news, political gossip and anything that took his fancy. The vicar's quotation on passion is from Bickerstaff's story of Mr Eustace, a landowner who lived together with both his wife and his sister. The two women were always arguing and in these disagreements Eustace invariably took his sister's side. And then he killed his wife, in her bed at night, as Othello kills Desdemona, but with a dagger rather than by strangling. He stabbed her, my dear, and was himself shot dead by a constable while making his escape.'

Elizabeth clapped her hand to her mouth.

'What a shocking thing, Titus! Why did he do it?'

'That's one of the points of interest. No reason is given. But the story is preceded by a discussion of the different tempers of men and women. Sir Richard suggests, I think, that Eustace's motive for murder was not explicit, but implicit. His mind was poisoned with the notion that male and female are in essence irreconcilable. *Ergo*, he could never agree with Mrs Eustace, or she with him, and that his only recourse was to murder her.'

'Then his mind was deranged. Why are you so pleased with this horrible tale?'

'Because when you think about it, there are extraordinary affinities with the Brockletower case. And, when I was in Garlick Hall's morning room on the day of the death, I found a commonplace book in her writing table. The last entry was a quotation "The Soul of a Man and that of a Woman are made very unlike". I now know where it came from. Can you guess?'

'The same *Tatler* essay?'

'Precisely. I have just seen the same words in my own edition. But there was one thing more. Dolores had added six extraneous words: "Imagine therefore: my pain and fear".'

'Not words from the *Tatler*?'

'No. These are not the fictional Bickerstaff's words. I think they are the real Mrs Brockletower's. So what should we make of that?'

Elizabeth laid down her knife and fork and thought for a moment.

'That she was reading the *Tatler* and was struck by similarities in the situations of Mrs Eustace and herself.'

'The husband's passionate rages, sharing the house with his sister.'

'Yes, and discovering those parallels naturally made her fear for her own safety.'

'So it appears,' I agreed. 'And how right she was!'

Chapter Seventeen

T HE SILENCE OF night lay across the town. All I could hear was the coming and going of the night-soil man. But it was not his cart's squeaking axle that kept me awake. I could not sleep because of the Brockletower inquest, of thinking exclusively about it, even when I wanted to think of other things, even when I was exhausted. I dreaded, most of all, an open verdict, or 'murder by person or persons unknown'. Her killer must be known, I said to myself, over and over. And it was my task to know him.

My hope (and simultaneous fear) of quickly assigning guilt to Ramilles Brockletower was probably dashed, for Luke's enquiries showed he had a formidable alibi. The distance between Settle and Preston was surely too great for him to have done the deed with his own hand, and on his own horse. So much for my speculation about the fresh shoe I detected on Brockletower's horse at the Plough Inn. He might have got to Fulwood by riding furiously on another, very fast and fresh horse. But it seemed unlikely that he could have exchanged horses in secret. And how did he dispose of his first horse in the meantime? Were we all, in some way, bamboozled?

I lay with these thoughts revolving in my brain like windspinners until I heard St John's clock striking three. I sat up in bed, rubbing my temples to ease the torrent of thought, then got up and walked around the house in my nightgown, ending by lighting a candle in the library and taking down once more volume III of the *Tatler*. I re-read Isaac Bickerstaff's reflections on the struggle between reason and passion and how the man Eustace had allowed his passion to master him and make him kill his wife. I looked with particular care at the passage from which Dolores had taken her commonplace inscription: *There is a sort of sex in souls . . . and the soul of a man and that of a woman are made very unlike, according to the employments for which they are designed. The virtues have respectively a masculine and a feminine cast. What we call in men Wisdom, is in women Prudence . . .*

It seemed doubtful theology to me. Can there really be a gender to sins and virtues? I prefer Mr Spectator's argument, that it is the temptations that differ in men and women, while the sins they call forth are of an intermediate sex. I replaced the *Tatler* and brought down the *Spectator*, to enjoy again that essay and its measured cadences. But at once I found a jar in the first sentence. 'Women in their judgements are much more gay and joyous than men.' That was not true of Squire ~~Bannister~~ and his lady, at any rate: they had been as dour and misanthropic as each other. Perhaps this very mismatch of husband and wife was the reason she wrote of her pain and fear.

What, if anything, was Woodley's role in all this? Sarah had implied he was the Jago of it, the false witness, the seed of evil planted in the family. In Shakespeare, Jago murders by proxy of his master: in this case, had he done it with his own hand?

By now I had grown thoroughly cold but I did not mind, as I find to return to bed chilled is a sovereign cure for insomnia. I found the bed beautifully heated indeed by the body of my sleeping wife and so dozed off as her warmth seeped into me.

*

By ten in the morning I had a note from Captain Fairhurst, received not half an hour before. He wrote that the search had resumed today, as only five of the seven outer areas of Garlick Hall could be combed on Saturday, before it became dark. Nothing had been found, but the captain declared himself an optimist. 'Operations were suspended for the Sabbath,' he wrote, 'but I feel it in my gut that we will find something today.' My own feeling was that, if we relied for guidance on Captain Fairhurst's gut, little of fragrance would emerge.

I turned over once again my thoughts of last night. I'd believed them at the time, with the hypnotic certainty one forms in the middle of insomnia. If Woodley was a Jago, he had poisoned the squire's mind. Or had I merely constructed from these strange events a kind of story of the sort seen in plays, romances and novels?

At breakfast Elizabeth immediately noticed my distraction, and my yawns, and said my eyes were sunken into my face, so tonight I must drink an infusion of fennel and borage in milk and brandy to soothe my sleep. She promised herself to prepare the posset for me.

At half past ten Furzey called out to say the post had come with another letter from Luke Fidelis in Yorkshire. I opened it with eagerness, hoping it would contain something, or anything, that might make solid the airy speculations of the night.

And I was very happy to find that it did.

> Sir, I have the honour of continuing the account
> of my enquiries here in Yorkshire into the activities
> of Ramilles Brockletower during his recent visit.
>   At my inn on Micklegate I fell in with a man of
> trustworthy, respectable appearance named Abraham
> Cooper, who told me his brother-in-law works as a

*confidential clerk at Bishopsthorpe, the palace of the
Archbishops of York, writing letters and memoranda
for His Grace. You will remember that we have been
wondering just what business Squire Brockletower had
with the archbishop. I am happy to say that I am now
in a position to tell you what it was.*

*You will be aware that, because of his Lancashire
connections, the archbishop owns estates in our county.
So, I made out that I was a tenant of the archbishop
myself, here to do business about my tenancy. I indicated
that a private conversation with this relation of his might
be of considerable value to me. Mr Cooper was agreeable
and invited me to his house, where we found the
brother-in-law playing a game of backgammon beside
the fire with his sister, Cooper's wife. The brother-in-law
was introduced to me as Peter Sumption. After a few
minutes' idle chatter, Cooper told Sumption that I was
interested in Bishopsthorpe. I took up the story, saying
that I was Ramilles Brockletower's neighbour, and knew
that he had paid a visit to the archbishop last week. And
I admitted further, pretending to be shamefaced, that I
was consumed by curiosity to know what business it was
that Mr Brockletower had with the archbishop, in case it
was on the matter of a boundary dispute between myself
and Brockletower.*

*Sumption looked suddenly like a conspirator, winking
and nudging me cunningly. 'I am a trusted servant, sir,' he
said. 'And I must be faithful to that trust. Unless, that is,
by a stroke of ill-fortune, I am left with no choice but to
be unfaithful to it.'*

*He spoke in an insinuating way that unmistakably
invited me to follow him up. I said, 'And how might
that come about?'*

He held up a finger. 'There is a way, to be sure, in which we might try the case, whether it is to be fortune or ill-fortune, faithful or unfaithful.'

'What way is that?'

He gestured at the gaming table. 'Why, with a game of backgammon, sir. My stake shall be my trust as the archbishop's servant, and yours a small matter of three guineas.'

Puzzled by this turn in the conversation I asked him what he meant.

'Well, sir, if I win the game, I am three guineas the richer and you none the wiser. On the other hand, if you win, I shall tell you all you wish to know in return for nothing. How's that for a wager?'

I turned quizzically to my host, thinking, what den of thieves have I fallen into? Cooper just shrugged. 'Peter do love to play gammon with a stranger,' he said with a laugh, then adding more seriously, 'Give him his game and, if you lose, you must pay up. But beat him square, and he'll keep his word. He always do, in spite of everything. And,' (added in a whisper behind his hand) 'he ain't such a player as he thinks he is.'

So I put my three guineas down and we played. My host was right. Sumption was not at all the hand at backgammon that he considered himself. Ten minutes later I was in an unassailable lead, having packed my fourth house with my men while he had a couple of his own sitting on the bar, unable to get back on the board. I won by a gammon and, with an oath, he leaned back and began stuffing a pipe in readiness to keep his side of the bargain. But he swore that he would never repeat any of what he had to say outside of that room, or to any official person, and he would deny it if put to him. I told *him to go on, for I would never reveal him as the source of the information, on my word as a gentleman.*

'Very well,' he said, sitting back in his chair and applying fire to his pipe. He seemed to trust me completely, though I believe whether he did or not hardly mattered. Sumption was, as I was about to discover, a man who never felt so alive as when holding forth to an audience. He cleared his throat. 'The meeting between Ramilles Brockletower and Archbishop Blackburne . . .' He cleared his throat again, more forcefully. 'It happened within my actual hearing, my writing office being in a small room with a door giving into the archbishop's audience chamber, you understand. I could not help overhearing, and what I overheard I think you will find of unusual interest. Indeed, it shocked me. Mr Brockletower had come to the archbishop to enquire about a divorce from his wife, sir, no less! He felt this to be an absolute necessity as their differences were irreconcilable. Well, when he heard this my lord laughed uproariously and said show him a couple in the country not in the same condition, but Mr Brockletower persisted, saying he was desperate, that his wife was barren, and the Brockletower estates wanted an heir of his own blood, and much of the same.

'My lord the archbishop then grew serious, speaking very gravely to Mr Brockletower, who by the way is, I believe, a kinsman of some sort. He warned him that divorce was not to be undertaken lightly and was anyway quite impossible without an Act of Parliament. It was not within his power to do anything but recommend the members and Lords to pass such an act if it were laid before them. But recommendation alone would not be enough to secure the divorce, oh no! Three further

conditions must be fulfilled before such a procedure could be successful. The first was money, a golden stream of it, with lawyers and writers and messengers and stationery all to be paid for at parliamentary rates, not to mention the money expended on, ahem!, getting the votes themselves, if you see what I mean. Some of the richest men in the land have had their fortunes drained, utterly drained, by these procedures, leaving them with nothing but copper coin to count.

'The second attribute was time, for it might take a year or more before such a measure found room in the parliamentary calendar. And finally there had to be due cause. Criminal conversation on the part of the one you are suing was the most promising of these. In other words, adultery, he said, booming out the word, adultery by his wife, with another party. Her shame must be proved, with witnesses, beyond doubt. So, he asked Mr Brockletower, had there been any such criminal conversation, and Mr Brockletower blurted it right out that yes, he suspected so.

'I heard very little more because at this moment the servant came in and announced dinner, so my lord took Mr Brockletower into his dining room for a meal which was likely to be a long and rich affair, judging by the archbishop's girth. The last thing I heard him say was that he wanted to know all the details of Mr Brockletower's family life, and Mr Brockletower assured him he would tell all. The archbishop laughed loudly and said he was all agog.'

Now these exchanges look black for the squire of Garlick Hall, except for the fact that Sumption will never admit to a court that he heard them. That Brockletower was considering divorce comes as a complete surprise. But

I am also struck by the behaviour of the archbishop. He seemed vastly amused by the whole conversation. Nothing offends or shocks him, though he is primate of York!

Now that I have passed an hour or two in the coffee houses of the city, I realize that Archbishop Blackburne is far from being conscientious in his enforcement of the law of God. But there is more. I have heard something of Barnabus Woodley, who as you may know has been resident in this city. I have heard particulars about him that I will not write in this letter, but communicate to you when we next meet in person. With God willing, this should be on Tuesday, towards evening, or perhaps Wednesday morning. Meanwhile, I am, sir, your affectionate servant, Luke Fidelis.

I had no time to think about the letter because now another note came by hand of a soldier, this time from Garlick Hall and written by Sergeant Sutch. He asked that I ride out there at once, the 'once' underlined.

I rode off under warm sunshine, going by way of the North Moor, where the annual races are held. The open country gave my old cob the chance to run in his ponderous way, so that only twenty-five minutes had passed by the time we plunged down the lane leading directly to the gates of Brockletower's wood-enclosed park. Five minutes later I was dismounting in front of the house itself.

I was feeling happy because, though Sutch's message contained no hint of what I might expect at the Hall, I was sure that he must have recovered Mrs Brockletower's body. If so, my inquest could at last resume and I would sleep better tonight.

But I was premature: there had been no such find. Instead the soldiers were gathered in a group confronting a similar number of workmen, not estate workers, but the men engaged in Woodley's building works. The workmen were standing at the edge of the trees, at the start of an ornamental walk. They were plainly intent on blocking the soldiers' way along the walk. At that moment I realized what this walk was: the one up which Sarah's dog had run, the one that led to Woodley's garden temple.

I walked across the lawn and stepped between the two groups of men.

'What is this?' I said to the man standing in front of the builders, who I supposed was their foreman. He merely swore and spat, so I swivelled back to face the troops. I could not see Captain Fairhurst anywhere.

'What is the reason for this stand-off, Mr Sutch?' I asked.

'We are trying to inspect the temple, sir,' Sutch replied, coming towards me. 'It is the only place we haven't searched. The builders have been keeping us away from it, they have even threatened us with breaking our heads if we come near. So I thought it wise to put off searching it until we have exhausted other possibilities. But now we have searched every other part of these grounds and can be put off looking into this temple no longer. Yet these men are still preventing us. Captain Fairhurst is not here; nor is the squire. That is why I sent for you.'

I swivelled back to face the murmuring knot of builders.

'Are you?' I challenged. 'Are you obstructing the king's men?'

Piltdown, the ganger, a wiry, deeply weather-beaten fellow in a protective leather apron and carrying a wooden mallet, spoke angrily from the front.

'One of us has been beaten by the soldiers. He's bruised and got a black eye. And that was after they stormed through our living quarters, pulled down all the tents, and frighted the women and childer.'

'Nevertheless, a little restraint would—'

'Restraint be damned. My men are very vexed that these soldiers should come and rough up freeborn Englishmen, and destroy their shelters. Now we are waiting for Mr Woodley. I have sent word to him. His orders were no one is to disturb the work in progress at the temple – no one, whoever they be. And if we allow them to go there, and there is damage, we shan't be paid a farthing while it's repaired. That's usual.'

'Why should the works be damaged? The soldiers only want to look.'

Piltdown spat again.

'Mortar is wet. Stonework's not secure. And I've seen the ruin them soldiers do. They went through our camp like a twisting-storm. So until Mr Woodley comes and says otherwise, we cannot allow them in to knock pieces off the temple.'

'These troops have the Lord Lieutenant's warrant,' I said mildly. 'You cannot prevent their search, you know, not law-fully.'

'We are just awaiting our own orders,' he repeated stub-bornly. 'Mr Woodley has told us if anyone damages the temple we must all answer for it. It is Mr Woodley, not us, mind, doing the preventing.'

The man was clearly a born troublemaker. I decided on a firmer tone.

'And my cat reads Horace, Mr Piltdown! Come come, man. Mr Woodley is not here. As far as I can see, it is *you* who are in the way. Clear off out of it, and let the soldiers do their duty in the Lord Lieutenant's name.'

My words had no beneficial effect. Instead, quite suddenly, a clod of earth came flying from the midst of the gang and over my head. It landed in front of the soldiers with a wet thump, accompanied by derisive hoots from the builders.

Now I heard a bustle among the soldiers behind me and turned again. Aggravated by this sally, Sutch had lost patience. He now ordered his men to pick up their weapons and, with a rapid run of *trick-track* sounds, they began fixing bayonets. I had a summary vision of the horror that might be about to unfold.

'Sergeant!' I called out. I was aware that my voice was cracking with anxiety. 'Sergeant Sutch! Have great care. We do not want violence here.'

'It will not be violence, sir, but merely the exercise of power.'

'That is sophistry!'

'As you prefer, Mr Cragg. But whatever the case, we must force home the Lord Lieutenant's will in this.'

'I am told a man of yours beat one of them. Is that true?'

'A slight quarrel. We searched the workmen's camp. A few tents were unavoidably pulled down. Some dirty names were called and the one that called them received a rap on the nose. He deserved it.'

'Well, Sergeant, be that as it may, I still think—'

But Sutch was in no mood to hear what I still thought. He brushed past me and took a step or two towards the builders and let fly a parade-ground bellow.

'Listen here! I call on you for the last time in the King's name to move aside, so we may do His Majesty's business of making a search of the building site behind you, known as the Garden Temple.'

I flicked a glance towards the scaffolded front of the house. A group of estate servants had gathered at its near corner to watch the goings-on. Seeing William Pearson among them, I ran over at the double to join him.

'Where's the squire?' I gasped. 'If ever he was needed, it's now. Someone must calm this confrontation. They will not listen to me.'

'Squire's away from home to Lancaster, Mr Cragg. The bailiff's sergeant is somewhere about. He's supposed to be on Corporation business but spends most of his time in the kitchen drinking Mrs Marsden's port wine. I've sent young Jonah to get him.'

'What can *he* do?'

Pearson smiled and showed me the palms of his hands.

'Not a bloody thing! Nor me, nor you. These are soldiers, trained to fight, while those builders are rough-necked incomers, and very half-witted. Also one of them's been assaulted. They likely won't back off till one lies dead, with a bayonet in his chest.'

Timothy Shipkin standing beside him gave out, not exactly a laugh, but a kind of triumphant yip.

'The churning of milk bringeth forth butter, as Scripture sayeth.'

Pearson ignored him.

'Not you, nor I, nor that dolt Mallender can change these men's minds, Mr Cragg,' he said. 'Happen the bayonet will.'

I looked around in desperation at what was looking increasingly like two armies in miniature squaring up to do very unequal battle. The soldiers were forming a line, making ready to march forward and sweep the nuisance aside by force. I could not comprehend the immediate necessity of this. I called out impotently for them to stop and consider, to wait for reason to reassert itself over anger and discontent. No one was listening. The soldiers continued to ready themselves, while the group of builders, each of them armed with some sharp or heavy tool, murmured amongst themselves, seeming to be bracing against the shock of an attack. I saw in their midst the towering figure of Solomon, the idiot I had spoken to when Fidelis and I were leaving the orchard on the day Mrs Brockletower's corpse went missing, and whose mother I'd met at the camp. He was hoisting above his head a great iron-headed sledgehammer. It seemed cracked heads and worse injuries were in prospect; or something even worse than injuries.

And then quite suddenly everything changed. Two figures appeared silently, serenely, between the contending groups, walking slowly and without fear. One was the dog, Jonathan, I had last seen dozing in front of Sarah Brockletower's fire. The other was Sarah herself.

Chapter Eighteen

SARAH AND JONATHAN advanced to a point about halfway between soldiers and builders. No sooner had the two groups of men registered her presence than they fell silent, then began shifting their feet and exchanging uneasy comments, murmuring to each other out of the corners of their mouths. The dog sat on its haunches and lolled its tongue.

I was still near the house with Pearson and the others. Now, in sudden panic, I set off, half-running down towards Sarah, wanting to haul her, physically if necessary, out of harm's way. But I pulled up before I had covered half the distance between us. I realized she had not strayed by chance into the middle of this *rencontre*, but had placed herself there with a purpose. What was more, I thought, she was of strong enough character to succeed in that purpose, which was of course to make the peace.

Turning her head this way and that, Sarah tried to assemble the various sounds she was hearing, to make a picture in her mind of what she could not see. One of these sounds was the approaching tread of Sergeant Sutch. He came towards her in a bustling manner, then inclined his head and spoke quietly into her ear, causing her to turn towards him.

Now I could see her face. It looked paper-white, and pinched.

Seeing her in daylight I realized that Sarah's extreme pallor was not face-powder, or even the effect of spending most of her time out of the daylight. She was looking sickly-pale and exhausted. Her voice in the other hand was clear and sharp and audible to all.

'No, I shall not move away. Is it you in charge of the soldiers?'

Again the sergeant spoke inaudibly. Sarah's reply was loud, scornful and audible to us all.

'You mention the King, sir? And the Lord Lieutenant? I may be stone blind, but I think neither gentleman is with us now. In my brother's temporary absence I am the proper authority in this place. And I demand that you stand your men down. I will have no violence. These workmen of Mr Woodley, though they do not live permanently on the estate, are employed on my brother's business and they shall not be threatened.'

Sutch hesitated, looking short of ammunition with which to reply to Sarah's withering fusillade. At the same moment we heard a scattering of stones and Jonah Marsden came at speed around the far corner of the house, and careered across the gravelled forecourt like a skidding ninepin. Behind him was the sweating figure of Oswald Mallender in hot but not very close pursuit. Having caught sight of the soldiers and workmen confronting one another, he began shouting, and waving his arms.

There was no sense in coupling Mallender's arrival with the reassertion of reason. At the sight of him the soldiers gave a cheer more of satire than encouragement. I strolled forward quickly enough to reach Sarah and Sutch before Mallender did. I put my hand on Sarah's shoulder – the first time I had touched her for almost twenty years.

'Sarah, it is Titus,' I said. 'You are safe, now. The danger is past, I do believe.'

Though her face was as strained and pallid as ever, Sarah laughed.

'Danger, Titus? But I saw no danger! That is the advantage I have over you. I am glad you are here nevertheless. Tell me, who is this arriving at such full cry?'

In speaking these words she raised her voice in order that the approaching Mallender would hear them. He faltered in his advance and then, not quite knowing what to make of Sarah's presence, adopted the strategy of ignoring her and of striding across to harangue the workmen instead.

'You men! You are in breach of the peace. The bailiff's peace. The Lord Lieutenant's peace. You must give over, you know. Give over and . . . and disperse.'

A jeer followed by general laughter came from the men. Mallender turned and came back to where Sarah and I were standing. Immediately a figure broke from the crowd behind and stalked after him. It was the ganger, Piltdown.

'Let's put an end to this, now,' I said as he approached. 'It's time to parley the dispute. Mr Piltdown, what is your objection to the soldiers entering your Temple of Eros?'

'It is not in safe condition. Columns might fall. Foundations sink. The whole lot collapse.'

'You are intending to stabilize it before completion of the work?'

'What would be the use of the place otherwise?'

'Then complete that work of stabilization,' I said simply. 'Then it can be searched.'

Not liking the sound of this, Mallender butted in.

'The bailiff's orders are—'

But Sutch overrode him.

'They might bury anything hidden underneath with rubble and mortar. We couldn't allow that, Mr Cragg.'

'Precisely so,' huffed Mallender. 'It might be just what the bailiff has asked me to seek.'

'Under supervision, then,' I went on. 'Suppose Sergeant Sutch posts one reliable man to watch the proceedings, and make sure nothing is buried in cement.'

Mallender looked as if he would object further, and Sutch looked doubtful, but instead of hearing them I turned back to Piltdown.

'You would not object to the presence of just a single soldier on the site to see that all is above suspicion?'

Piltdown mumbled the concession that he supposed this would be better than to have the whole platoon crawling over the site, but he'd have to ask Woodley. Sutch knew his freedom of action was limited, and he now found it further curtailed with the appearance of Captain Fairhurst riding at a rotund trot towards us. Ignorant of the battle that had so nearly been fought, he sprang from his horse and joined us, smiling globularly and rubbing his hands together in a businesslike way. I told him immediately of the imbroglio over the searching of the Temple of Eros, and the joke that must have been ready on his lips immediately died there. Pop-eyed and deprived for the moment of words, he swung his face in turn towards me, Sarah, Sutch and Piltdown, and back to me. I then put to him my idea for a resolution of the dispute, to which he listened attentively. After a moment's thought, and a vigorous rub of the hand to his jaw and jowl, he subscribed to the plan.

'I see no reason against it,' the captain decided. 'As long as a lookout is posted who has a sharp pair of eyes in . . . in his . . .'

His head yawed tortoise-like once more.

'In his head,' he completed.

'Good! Excellent! Let it be so!' cried Sarah, who had been

listening carefully to these exchanges. 'Mr Piltdown and Sergeant Sutch – you must shake hands on it at once.'

'Just one moment, Miss Brockletower,' said Mallender, stepping forward with his arm and fat hand extended, as if to carve a way back into the dispute. 'I hold the bailiff's commission, and I would advert you that we are not—'

'Oh, I doubt the bailiff can hold sway here, Constable. Are we not on a gentleman's property? Are they shaking hands, Titus?'

'Yes, Sarah,' I told her a moment later, 'they are shaking.'

And so, though with no great warmth on either side, they were.

'Good work, Titus,' whispered Sarah as she took my arm to walk away. 'That was a parley you can be proud of.'

'Not me, Sarah,' I said, with feeling. 'I only drew up the treaty. It was you who prevented the war.'

'Is it possible that it is really there?' asked my wife, straightening her bonnet and picking up her basket. We were preparing to go together to our garden to stock up the vegetable larder.

Immediately after Sarah Brockletower's successful démarche at Garlick Hall I had returned to town for discussions with my client, Mr Septimus Patch, about certain complicated entailments to his will. For a while, therefore, my mind was entirely unoccupied with the affairs of Garlick Hall – a considerable relief – and I did not go through to the domestic side of the house until near four o'clock. It was then that Elizabeth proposed we walk out together to gather leeks and carrots.

Opening the front door, I sought clarification.

'That what is where?'

'That the missing body is hid in this temple?'

'For all I know, my love.'

We left the house and struck out across Market Place. This funnels at its north-western corner into Friar Gate, and we were soon walking along that street, which curves in a shallow S-shape as far as the town Bar, where it continues as the Fylde road. Our garden lay to the left of this road, one of three thoroughfares that fork away from the Bar across undulating terrain towards the north and west of the town.

'Well, in my opinion, to hide the body like that is a barbarous thing! And why, in heaven's name?'

We were passing Talboys's shop and I caught a glimpse of the dressmaker at the counter speaking earnestly with a customer, scissors in his hand and a tape-measure draped around his neck. I reminded myself I had not yet told Furzey to place Abigail on our witness list for the inquest.

'I didn't say it *was* there. I said—'

'But, if it is, everything is explained, Titus. The workmen blocked the soldiers from entering the temple because they knew it contained exactly what the soldiers were seeking.'

'Yes, but I was given a perfectly plausible—'

'Titus, they were ready to *fight* the soldiers.'

We had left Talboys's behind us and were making good progress down the gentle slope of Friar Gate.

'Even if they were,' I replied, 'which I doubt, the likelihood is they only wanted to prevent their work on the temple being undone.'

'Building works undone! Is that a cause to give your life for? Is it something to make you face muskets with those spikes stuck on their nozzles?'

'Bayonets,' I said mildly. 'Fixed to their muzzles.'

'It would have been carnage. Blood running on Squire

Brockletower's lawn. Wounds beyond the skill of any surgeon, even of Dr Fidelis. And more work for the coroner directly after.'

'As a matter of fact that is just what Timothy Shipkin foresaw while it was happening in front of our eyes. "The churning of milk bringeth forth butter" is what he said.'

'*Butter?* That's an odd remark. What has butter to do with it?'

'Well, it's from the Book of Proverbs.'

Elizabeth gave me a slightly wounded look.

'Oh, Titus! You know very well that I have not been brought up to know the Old Testament as well as you, or Timothy Shipkin.'

So I completed the quotation for her.

' "And the wringing of the nose bringeth forth blood. So the forcing of wrath bringeth forth strife." So Timothy was right, in his way. Someone was indeed forcing wrath, but I think it was Sergeant Sutch and his men with their method of searching. The building men had seen the damage soldiers do when they go over a place; they'd been over their camp, after all. And any damage to the temple would have to be put right before Woodley paid out any wages. Then, one of them was struck by a soldier, and not as a joke. Their ire was up against the militia, but they knew the limits of their power. No, if you ask me, this was no more than a case of chained dogs barking.'

'Well, you were on the spot, Titus. But I do wonder if they were about to let slip their chains.'

'That would mean they were all party to the conspiracy. And for what reason? Do you think they murdered her too? What have they to do with this affair? Why would they steal and then conceal a body?'

'Why, to sell it later to an anatomist.'

We were getting close to the limit of the town now, the Friar

Gate Bar, near which stood the remains of the Friary itself, which had been adapted as our House of Correction.

'Perhaps we should talk of other things now,' I protested, marvelling at my Elizabeth's readiness to discuss any matter without blushing.

'No, Titus, if you please, let us talk of this. Did you yourself not believe that selling to an anatomist is the likely motive for the body's first removal from the Ice-house at the Hall?'

'I am led to believe, if that were the case, it would not have been buried or concealed, but handed on immediately. Freshness, you know. I really cannot go into detail. But, anyway, besides this fact, I am not aware of any ready purchasers for that sort of merchandise in this town, or anywhere around here.'

'Yes, you are!' she retorted fiercely. 'Dr Dapperwick is a notorious anatomist.'

I had already given Elizabeth an account of Thursday's visit to Jonathan Dapperwick.

'Dapperwick is too reclusive,' I stated. 'And too crippled in the hands. He could not profit by this.'

'Then this young assistant of his, the one that he mentioned to you. We do not know who he is, or where he comes from, or anything about him.'

I considered the matter. There was something in what Elizabeth was saying. This young anatomist just might be hot-headed enough to take such a risk. It was impossible to make a judgement until we knew his identity. But it deserved further investigation, I was thinking. Tomorrow, possibly.

We were now through the Bar and had walked up a slight rise past the bowling green, and the windmill, which commands the approach to the town from that direction, and made another fifty yards along the road before arriving at our garden's gate. I opened the padlock with one of the keys attached to my watch chain and pushed it open. Like all the gardens hereabouts, the half-acre plot was enclosed by high wattle fencing and supported not only vegetable beds and fruit trees but a couple of beehives, a small flock of hens and a dovecote. As always when I came here I looked upon it with satisfaction – a place in which the flow of time became pleasantly sluggish, and the cares of business dissolved like mist in sun.

We got about our business, I to lifting the leeks and Elizabeth the carrots. But after a few minutes, with her basket full enough, she wandered up to inspect the beehives and see how busy their inhabitants were in the spring sunshine. A moment later I heard her scream.

'Titus! Over here! Titus!'

I got up from my knees and ran towards her. She was looking down at the ground behind the hives. A man lay spread out there on his back, with his arms by his sides but his head at a grotesque angle. His eyes stared, and his purple tongue stuck out.

It was the architect Barnabus Woodley.

Chapter Nineteen

BEFORE I COULD stop her, Elizabeth was on her knees beside him, loosening the stock and the shirt at the throat. There was much dirt on the front of the shirt.

'Please God, let him be alive,' she prayed. 'Let him live.'

I moved to her side and knelt in the same way, touching the back of my hand to Woodley's brow. It was cold as marble.

'We are much too late. He's been dead for hours.'

She clapped her hands to her cheeks.

'It's Mr Woodley, isn't it? Oh dear! Oh dear God! Is there really nothing to be done?'

She was in distress, almost crying. I touched her elbow.

'No, nothing. Come away.'

I drew her to her feet and began walking with her as quickly as she would allow me towards the gate.

'But why? Why here?' she protested. 'Why in our garden? What was he doing here?'

These were the same questions I was asking myself.

'I don't know, yet. But I shall find out.'

We reached the gate and went out into the road. I turned her towards me and held her by the upper arms. Her eyes were wide and filling with tears.

'Don't cry,' I said. 'There's nothing we can do for Woodley

now, except be just to him in death. Go back at once and tell Furzey what's happened. I'm staying here. We cannot leave the body alone. Furzey will notify the bailiff's clerk and then help will come. Woodley has to be removed to some suitable place. The House of Correction would do. Tell Furzey to suggest it. Now go!'

When she had gone I went back and stood beside the body, trying to make up my mind about it. One's response to a death depends on one's relation to the deceased. Woodley and I had been the next thing to strangers. We had met, but in an entirely superficial encounter, as if making the opening moves in a chess game. They had not revealed Woodley to me as a person, but only as a rather strange type, and one I had not liked very much. But now the sight of his corpse, inside its blue coat, prodded my conscience. The remarkable wig was missing, revealing a head of brown hair pulled into a pigtail at the nape. Poor histrionic Woodley. If the world's a stage, he had fallen through the trap-door in mid-performance.

Yet to pity the architect was useless, as I had already reminded Elizabeth. It didn't in any way advance my under-standing of how he came to be lying dead in this garden, and of who killed him. How, for instance, did he come in? I returned to the gate and examined it. The lock had been intact on our arrival. Dead or alive, Woodley could not have come in that way. So I walked the perimeter of the garden outside the fence – a few steps along the road and then I plunged into the narrow pathway that separated my garden plot from my neighbours'. Similar pathways snaked around and between all the plots here-about, making a kind of maze, walled on each side by tall lattice fencing that was overgrown with climbing plants to form high hedges, all but impenetrable. But in one place, well in from the road, I found what I was looking for. A ragged hole had been hacked right into the fence, large enough for a man to pass through to my garden. I looked down at the surface of the path beside the hole. There were hoofprints faintly discernible in the dry mud. A horse had been here, and recently, though the path was not intended for horses. Whoever rode this horse in must have done so with the sole purpose of breaking the fence and entering my garden unobserved.

I forced my way with a little difficulty through the hole and stood once again inside the garden. I was certain Woodley had come in by this means. But in what condition was hard to know. Had he walked through himself, or been dragged? And who had made the aperture? On the ground just inside it lay a hatchet, which was not from the stock of tools I kept in the garden. I picked it up and weighed it in my hands. It was well-balanced and sharp. No doubt it had been the means by which the fence had been breached.

I went back to the body. The exposed face was scratched and grazed, but there was very little blood on it. Still holding the hatchet I knelt and used it to lever the rigid body up and over, until it was lying face down. I now saw that a single savage wound had been inflicted on the back of the head. The blood had gushed down the man's nape and neck and soaked his shirt and coat to the small of his back. I looked closely at the split in the skull. It was like a notch, about four inches long. Carefully I placed the hatchet's blade against the lip of the wound. It fitted exactly.

'Stay! Don't move, there!'

A booming voice echoed around the garden and I looked up. Sergeant Mallender was coming towards me, holding up his hand. With him were two constables, followed by Bailiff Grimshaw, who was bustling in through the gate with a look of officious determination. I rose to my feet. Mallender and his two acolytes – they were the brothers Esau and Jacob Parkin – arrived breathlessly and surrounded me while Grimshaw hurried to catch up.

'Well? What are you waiting for, Sergeant?' the bailiff called as he stumbled through the leek bed, kicking a hen out of his way. 'Take this man up! Can't you see? He has a weapon in his hand and a body at his feet. Do your duty, man! Arrest him, at once!'

They had taken my coat and I was sitting in my shirtsleeves, on the filthy mattress of a narrow pallet, looking into the beady eyes of the only visitor so far allowed me. The brown rat, up on his haunches amidst the stinking straw and cleaning his whiskers fastidiously, was staring back with the fixed attention of someone who has just asked a question, and wants a reply.

Grimshaw, his face set in an expression of grim delight, had brought me with Mallender and the Parkin brothers in an ostentatious parade up Friar Gate, across Market Place and into the town lock-up. This occupied part of the cellars of the Moot Hall, a clammy, subterranean accommodation reserved for those taken up and awaiting a charge, or their trial, or the judge's sentence. These cellars extended beyond the above-ground perimeter of the building, and it was plain my own cell lay directly below an area of the market itself. The space was faintly lit by holes in the ceiling that had been drilled through the market's pavement, so there were spots of light high above my head shining like constellations. I could hear market traders' faint cries, the clop of hooves, and the rumble of barrows. The whole point of a prisoner is his exclusion from normal life. I had been incarcerated for only an hour, but these ordinary sounds were already making me feel painfully alone.

The walls were thick, but I could make out the sounds of

other prisoners, hammering the doors for water, food, or some human contact. Not all of them were suspected felons: there would be strangers among them, condemned by Grimshaw and his cronies as interlopers and awaiting expulsion from the town. These were, by definition, friendless in town, and therefore hungry. I could hear their beseeching cries – 'Bring bread! Bring meat!' – which made me conscious of my own hunger.

With squeaks and groans the door had swung open and I heard the voice of Ephraim Grimshaw.

'Well, Cragg, this is a pretty pickle of a mess you're in.'

The bailiff stepped inside, attended by the gaol's keeper. The brown rat scuttled out of the way.

'Am I? I should say that was you, Grimshaw. You have unjustly imprisoned His Majesty's coroner on a specious excuse.'

Grimshaw sneered.

'Did I? You were found with a dead body at your feet, in your own garden, holding the weapon that, as seems likely, inflicted the fatal injury. Even a coroner is not immune from suspicion in such a circumstance.'

'I went there with Mrs Cragg. The body was already lying there, and it was cold. The weapon was also on the ground. I picked it up to examine it. That was after I had sent my wife to find Mr Furzey, and tell him to inform you, which I presume is what happened. You know quite well I didn't kill the fellow.'

'That will be for the Mayor alone to decide.'

'In the meantime I demand that you let me out of here.'

'That too is for the Mayor.'

'Can I have pen and paper?'

'No.'

'A candle then, and a visitor? I am sure Furzey's out there, asking for me.'

'Possibly.'

'Then let me see him.'

As Grimshaw considered the request he sighed, which made his gleaming waistcoat shimmer in the gloom. Suddenly he swivelled and made for the door.

'All right,' he said over his shoulder. 'If your man is up there, we'll send him down. But you won't be out of here until the Mayor bails you.'

'Bails me?' I protested. 'There's nothing to bail me for.'

But the bailiff and gaoler had already left. The heavy iron-bound door thudded shut behind them.

Furzey appeared ten minutes later. Tucked under his arm was a linen-wrapped parcel and, in his hands, a flagon and a lighted tallow candle. The dancing light of the candle animated his face and I wondered if it was only the effect of this that made him appear likely to laugh aloud at any moment. In the event, he didn't laugh, though I suspected vast amusement at my situation on his part.

'So, here you are!' he exclaimed. 'How you got yourself into gaol would bamboozle philosophy. Mrs Cragg sends food and beer.'

He stooped to place the candle on the floor, and the package on the bed beside me. Then he unstopped the flagon and handed it across, watching critically as I tipped beer into my thirsty mouth.

'Let's just apply ourselves to getting me out of here, shall we?' I asked a little testily, as I laid the flagon down and turned my attention to Elizabeth's food. It was half a loaf of bread and some pieces of ham. I was truly ravenous.

As I tore at the bread and ate it, turn by turn with the ham, Furzey gathered himself to leave.

'You don't need to eat so desperately. I'll see to it. Mayor upstairs'll have you out of here within the hour.'

Furzey's parting words cheered me, but presently it grew dark outside and the candle, which my clerk had 'forgotten' when he left me, burned itself to nothing. My spirits dwindled with it as no word came from upstairs. I could see nothing in the pitchy dark and was by now shivering uncontrollably from cold. I hammered on the door, shouting for a blanket and, eventually, the leather-hooded turnkey appeared. I tried to talk to him about my release but he only grunted. He proffered a horse-blanket, then pulled it back as I made a grab, wagging his finger. I found a coin in my pocket, which he took. Then he threw the blanket at me with a menacing growl and pulled the door shut. Disconsolately, I wrapped his coarse offering around my shoulders, took a last pull from the beer flagon and, with only my inquisitive (and now invisible) rodent for a cell-mate, I lay down in the dark to think about the afternoon's events.

Who was the late Barnabus Woodley? A peculiar sort of man, Elizabeth had said. And Fidelis had learned 'particulars' of him that he could only pass on by mouth. Would these provide reasons why someone wanted to kill the man?

One or more of his workmen might have. If Peg Miller's words meant anything, none of the gang or their women thought highly of their employer. On the other hand, if they had killed him, would they have engaged in the *rencontre* with the soldiers? That only happened because Piltdown – so he claimed – had been threatened by Woodley with a stoppage of wages if damage occurred to the building works. The gang would hardly have run the risk of death by musket fire on the threat of a man they knew to be already dead.

I returned to the more dramatic idea that Woodley had in some way come between Squire Brockletower and his wife: that he was their Jago and betrayer, their poisoned mouth, 'more fell than anguish, hunger or the sea'. But if this were true, what did

Woodley know? What did he tell Ramilles Brockletower? And could he have carried through his role as the squire's Spartan dog or bloodhound as far as cutting her throat? I doubted it.

I ran through one supposition after another, but in my particular situation there was one central fact that I could not remove from my thoughts: that it was me, and not the murderer, that lay here in prison. From being the agent of inquiry, I was suddenly the subject of it. But why had the body been brought to my garden and left there? *Cui bono?* Who gained by this crude attempt to incriminate me? Falsehood was outrunning the truth in every direction, I thought, as I fell asleep at last to the sound of the rat, darting this way and that through the straw to scavenge the breadcrumbs I had dropped from my supper.

The rusty hinges of the cell door screeched and I awoke. Light penetrated in scattered spots through the holes in the ceiling. It was morning.

'Wake up, sir! Wake up! It's Furzey back again.'

I rolled into a seated position and rubbed my neck, stiff from lying without a pillow.

Furzey held a paper in front of my face.

'Your manumission. You can come out.'

'You said it would take an hour,' I groaned. 'It's been all night.'

Instead of replying, Furzey turned and walked out, past the turnkey who was standing immediately behind him holding a lantern, and a thick bunch of keys threaded onto an iron hoop. I followed, stepping out across the cell threshold with that slight hesitation which all prisoners feel upon release.

'Last night Mayor had the toothache, displacing all other business,' my clerk explained over his shoulder as we made our way along the dripping passageway that led to the stairs. 'There was nothing I could do.'

We passed door after door, all closed and iron-bound, from which issued whining, sing-song appeals for relief in response to the sound of our tread.

'Did you not think of Lord Derby?' I replied. 'He would not have let me stay incarcerated in this hellish place.'

'His lordship is on his way to London.'

'And it was no good applying to Bailiff Grimshaw, I suppose.'

Furzey snorted.

'Hardly. He's hardened his heart against you. '

Soon we had climbed back to the daylight. As we left the Moot Hall the sun was bright, and my spirits lifted, though I felt much in need of clean linen and a shave.

Elizabeth greeted me at home with a shriek, some brief tears, and a set of fresh underwear. Less than an hour later, having breakfasted, I was sitting in Gilliflower the barber's chair in the Shambles, with lather covering my lower face. The street door opened and shut behind me.

'So, did the prisoner reflect with profit on his crimes?'

The laughing voice was not that of the barber. Luke Fidelis had come in.

'The lock-up is a bad place for reflection, Luke,' I retorted. 'Cold and damp. Rats. The incessant cries of the damned in one's ears. But what about you? Did you meet the lady, and buy the forceps?'

'The less said about any lady the better, Titus, but the forceps are a ridiculous contraption, and positively dangerous to the unborn, as anyone can see except the conceited fool who invented them.'

'When did you get back?'

'Not until late, and half dead, so I dived straight into bed. Didn't learn of your incarceration until Furzey told me at your office, a few minutes ago. What in heaven's name happened?'

I related my wife's discovery behind our beehives.

'The body was cold, you say?'

'Quite cold.'

'Had it stiffened yet?'

'It was stiff as a log.'

'And had you yourself been in the garden during the previous twenty-four hours?'

'No, not for days.'

Luke laughed again.

'And yet you were arrested! The stupidity of our bailiff is boundless.'

'It isn't stupidity. It is vindictiveness.'

'That's the same thing, in his case.'

'I don't think so. Grimshaw wanted to demonstrate his power. That was his whole intention. He knows I didn't kill the architect.'

Gilliflower finished with my face. After patting the remnants of soap from my jowls he allowed me to rise. As I paid him, Fidelis took my place in the chair.

'Come with me to look at Woodley,' I said. 'They have him in the Old Friary.'

Fidelis took out his pocket watch.

'I am expecting a caller at my lodging in thirty minutes,' he said. 'But he will not keep me long. Come then and I will go with you. We have much to discuss.'

Chapter Twenty

FISHER GATE LEADS west from the Moot Hall, just as Church Gate heads east. Both these thoroughfares are lined by a mix of houses, ancient and new, but generally well found and creditable to the town. They lie along the length of the high bluff, or ridge, which runs parallel to the north side of the Ribble valley, placing us between the river to the south and the moor and forest to the north. It is our height that gives the town its healthy and advantageous position. Houses on the north side of Church Gate and Fisher Gate look out across to the moor, but those on the south command a prospect of river and the old road that snakes across it and away to the villages of Leyland and Chorley and the undulating country beyond. Far fells lie to the east while in the west the flat marshes stretch to the coast.

Fidelis lodged on this more favourable southern side of Fisher Gate, at the house of Lorris, the bookbinder, of whom I was a good customer and friend. I had myself secured the rooms for the young doctor after convening an inquest on their previous tenant, Lorris's aged father-in-law, who had created a vacancy by fatally setting fire to himself. Repaired and repainted, the rooms were pleasant and spacious, on the top floor of the premises, looking onto the street on one side, and over the roof of the playhouse to the distant country on the other.

Admitting me to the hall, Lorris's lady gave me a quizzical look. She clearly already knew where I had lodged overnight – as, I guessed, did most of the town.

'It was a cruel thing, Titus,' she said. 'The bailiff is no friend of ours after this.'

'Thank you, Joan. He has his reasons for what he did, I must suppose.'

'Not reason enough, anyway.'

A big-boned lad came clumping down the stairs, carrying a leather valise, the contents of which clanked metallically. Glancing at him, I realized it was the young artist's assistant who had waited in the anteroom at Patten House during his master Winstanley's audience with Lord Derby. Having collected his greatcoat, he departed with only a mumbled farewell and I asked Joan Lorris if she knew his name. She did not, only that he had arrived ten minutes before to see Dr Fidelis.

The doctor himself came down a minute later, in coat and hat. I said goodbye to his landlady and we set out.

'The young fellow I have just seen leaving the house,' I said as we crossed Fisher Gate and started down Chapel Lane, which cuts through to Friar Gate. 'What's his name?'

'That's George.'

'I've seen him at Patten House, with the portrait painter Winstanley.'

'He's Winstanley's assistant, or apprentice. And according to himself with more talent below the joint of his thumb than Winstanley in his entire body. They've been staying at the Bull whilst painting his lordship.'

'Was George here to paint you, too?'

Luke laughed.

'No. I am not yet ready to be made immortal. George takes a strong interest in the anatomy of the body. He came to borrow some instruments, because he wants to dissect a fox, so he says. Dr Dapperwick with whom he has taken instruction is so long retired and so poor that he has none of the latest engines and contrivances.'

'Dapperwick!'

In my excitement I jumped ahead of Luke and turned to stop him in his tracks.

'I saw the doctor last week at his house, just after your departure for York. It was part of the inquiry into the missing body. He obviously couldn't help. But he mentioned he had a young assistant, whom mysteriously he would not name.'

Fidelis nodded.

'That's George. Dapperwick employs him chiefly as a draughtsman, but he has helped him in dissection too. Dapperwick has palsy and his fingers are all but paralysed.'

'I have seen them. But why would a boy artist, of all people, want to learn anatomy?'

We resumed out walk.

'George holds,' said Luke, 'that in order to draw the outside of the body perfectly one must first become intimate with its inside.'

'And he says he has a fox to dissect, does he? Suppose his fox is really a lady. Suppose it was your friend George that stole that corpse from Garlick Hall – which is still not found, by the way.'

'George would not do such a thing by himself. He has no connection with the Hall and is not yet sixteen.'

'Young as that, is he? I would say seventeen or eighteen, by his looks.'

'He appears old for his years, but still wouldn't commit such a crime, I am certain. He's called to be a painter, not a transported criminal.'

'If you say so, Luke. You know the boy.'

'Can we think of who else might have purloined the body?'

'There are the building workers at Garlick Hall,' I said, 'Let me tell you what happened there yesterday.'

By the time we turned out of Chapel Lane and reached the end of Friar Gate I had told him about the previous day's stand-off between workmen and soldiers.

'It's suspicious,' Fidelis agreed as we rested a moment at Friar Gate Bar.

'Yes, but I'm damned if I know where it gets us to.'

'It helps, Titus. Consider this: the men professed to be concerned about damage to the temple, in case Woodley would not pay them. But this would not concern them if they knew he was dead. It's a beautifully balanced proposition. If the men killed Woodley, the corpse is not hidden in the temple; and if it is in the temple, they must not have killed Woodley.'

'But I say again, where does that lead us?'

Fidelis gestured to the ancient stone remains of the Friary on the other side of the Bar.

'Let's have a look at Woodley. Maybe he can tell us something.'

The friars' church had long ago been pulled down, but the surviving buildings were put to use by the town as a House of Correction. Unlike the Moot Hall lock-up, where I had spent my uncomfortable night, this was a place for the proven malefactor, once the Mayor had passed sentence of imprisonment. The friars' cells were the sleeping quarters and the refectory was the workshop, while the old kitchens, scullery and wash-house still functioned in their original capacity. We found Woodley lying still fully clothed on a table in a room close to the latter. It was pervaded by the smell of slimy water. I thought how little this delicate man would have enjoyed his situation, had he been aware of it.

His white shirt-front was browned with dirt, so that it almost matched his breeches. The arms lay straight and close to the body. Testing the stiffness of the arms, Fidelis looked as best he could at the inside of the coat sleeves, then at the throat, before turning his attention at last to the head-wound. He tilted the body, inspected the dried blood down the back and then began carefully feeling the slim body all over, pinching and palp ating the muscle and flesh from shoulders to ankles. He looked closely at the scratches to the boyish face, eyed and smelled the inside of the mouth, did likewise with the blank eyes, and the hands. Finally he opened the breeches and examined what lay within.

'I think the rigor is past its extreme,' he said at last when he had returned Woodley to modesty. 'If so, he was killed yesterday, early in the morning.'

'And he died from the head wound?'

'Undoubtedly.'

'Struck from behind, then.'

'Only if you assume he was attacked. I have seen injuries like this in men who fell drunk from their horses, though I admit in this case the skull is more deeply split.'

'Consistent,' I suggested, 'with assault by a hand-axe?'

Fidelis leaned again over the broken cranium, running his finger into the jagged, bloody crack.

'That would do it,' he murmured. 'But why are you so specific?'

'I found such an axe near the body. Grimshaw has it now. I was holding it in my hand when he came to the garden. He pretended to believe I'd just used it.'

'The villain!'

'Quite. If you have seen enough, let's go up to my garden. It's only five minutes from here. I'll show you where I found the weapon.'

Within twenty minutes we had looked over the whole garden and toured its perimeter. We noted the complete absence of blood on the ground where the body had lain, proving this had not been where Woodley died. I showed Fidelis where I found the hatchet, inside the breach in the fence, and we agreed that, from the fence's appearance, it looked as if it was penetrated from the outside by someone who'd arrived on a horse (the hoofmarks were still faintly visible), using the hand-axe for the purpose.

'Here's what I think happened,' said Fidelis. 'Woodley was killed somewhere else, possibly with the axe, and brought here across the rump of a horse. The bringer dropped the axe after breaking through the fence. Then he dragged the corpse from the horse and into the garden. The soil on Woodley's shirt-front and inside his sleeves, and the scratches on his face, are there because the killer had hold of the feet, or legs, with the face and body turned down and the arms going up as they trailed in the dirt.'

'Couldn't the face have been scratched before Woodley died? A fight of some kind?'

'No. The flesh was damaged, but not bleeding. It happened when his corpse was dragged along the ground.'

'So once his killer had dragged the corpse to the selected place, he arranged it tidily, with the arms along the sides.'

'Yes.'

'So at that point the body was still limp?'

'Exactly. The whole thing was done within five hours of the murder, or he would not have been able to rearrange the arms without forcing the shoulder-joints, which he did not do.'

'This has been most useful, I think.'

I realized that the last thirty minutes had been stimulating. The vile chamber I'd been forced to spend the night in had gone from my mind and I forgot the bailiff's deliberate injury to me and my pride. I was enjoying myself and so, I could see, was Luke Fidelis.

'Come away,' I said. 'and let's get a drink. There's more to talk about.'

We sat in the parlour of the Friary Bar Inn with a bottle of claret between us. I thanked Fidelis for his two letters from York, and told him they confirmed what I had found out independently: that Ramilles Brockletower had wanted to divorce his wife. I asked that he complete the story of his enquiries there.

'I shall,' he said, 'but let me deal first with the squire's movements on the night before Mrs Brockletower died, when he was on his way home. I have now ridden the whole road from where Brockletower stayed on the Monday night, and am convinced he could not possibly have made the journey to Fulwood, killed his wife, and returned to his lodging in Yorkshire in time. In short, I am certain that, contrary to our reasonable suspicion, he was not his wife's killer.'

'Well, I never wanted that to be true.'

Fidelis raised a finger and smiled his clever and faintly vulpine smile.

'But he may have procured someone to do it.'

'I know. But who?'

'Well, it is something else that my friend the backgammon player confided. It concerns Mr Barnabus Woodley. He was known in York.'

'He certainly styled himself Woodley of York, as if he owned the city.'

'But if this fellow Sumption is right, the city disowned Woodley. He came there, it appears, from Lichfield. And after a stay of less than a year word followed that he had been investigated by the Dean of Lichfield about a fraud he perpetrated on the cathedral, after he was employed in some repairs.'

'What fraud?'

'They say he absconded with fifty pounds that he did no work for.'

'Had he done anything like it before?'

'When he fell under suspicion at York, the Recorder wrote to fellow recorders in the cities Woodley is known to have lived in: as well as Lichfield there was Bristol, Exeter and Plymouth. The man had fallen under suspicion in each place before moving on.'

It took me a few moments to absorb this startling information.

'Did they not take him up in York, then, to answer the charges?'

Fidelis shook his head.

'Archbishop Blackburne would not allow it. He was charmed by Woodley and, besides, has a deadly dislike for the Bishop of Lichfield. So he protected Woodley and gave him work at Bishopsthorpe and elsewhere. It was he that recommended him to his cousin Ramilles Brockletower. The archbishop is notoriously dissolute. People in York say he looks kindly on all sins except matricide.'

'So Woodley lay under suspicion. But was he a murderer?'

'If he was, and Brockletower paid him to kill the fair Dolores, the squire might well have felt that Woodley himself shouldn't continue to breathe.'

I took a deep draught of wine and refilled my glass.

'Yes,' I said, refilling my glass. 'He might very well have felt that. And it might have been the very reason he decided to absent himself on a trip to Lancaster.'

At that moment there was a voice, loud and urgent, outside the door. I heard my name. Then abruptly William Pearson burst into the room.

'Mr Cragg,' he panted. 'I've brought a horse from your home. Mrs Cragg said it was best, to save time, as you must come, and quick. Mrs Brockletower's found, sir!'

As I rose, Fidelis hesitated.

'I wish I could come with you, Titus. But first I must attend the Mayor. His toothache requires prescription.'

'We shall meet later,' I told him. 'No doctor can afford to leave a mayor in pain.'

Hurriedly Pearson and I left Fidelis and took Moor Lane, the road that skirts the town to the north. Pearson gave me a detailed account of what had happened at Garlick Hall since I was last there, scenes from a drama in which Timothy Shipkin had again played a climactic role. On the previous day, strengthening work had continued at the Temple of Eros, overwatched by the militia man posted by Sutch. But by evening word had come of the death of Barnabus Woodley, upon which the workmen's camp fell into despondency and then truculent anxiety. Neither the Temple of Eros nor the Hall's pediment were fully finished. They wanted to know who would complete the work, and what about their pay if they were to be laid off?

Led by Ganger Piltdown, a group went to the squire, who had returned from his business engagements in Lancaster. Closeted in his library, he would not see them. Back in the camp there were loud words and cuffing fists, not least among the women. At dawn next morning Piltdown and simple Solomon were missing.

At just the same time, Shipkin, as he made his way to work

towards Shot's Hill, came upon the same Solomon stumbling through the woods. He was carrying in his arms a large, long bundle wrapped in sailcloth. When he saw Shipkin coming towards him, Solomon was immediately alarmed. He let his burden roll to the ground and made off at a run into the trees. Shipkin came forward to examine what had been dropped, and found the canvas to be a large bag, and that this had been used to make the improvised shroud of a human body – Dolores Brockletower's.

'It is remarkable that this is the second time Timothy Shipkin has found Mrs Brockletower's body,' I observed. 'Was Solomon alone?'

'Timothy saw no one else with him. But day was not fully broken, and light was not the best.'

In the midst of my own excitement, I wondered if the woodsman himself had been disappointed in the discovery. He had declared the dead woman raised by diabolic force, a delusion further strengthened by the local talk of werewolves. His certainty would have to be revised now.

As soon as Shipkin raised the alarm, the sergeant was sent for, and he instigated a thorough, military manhunt in the woods, though this was called off by noon, without result. The squire might have had little stomach for my presence but, in view of the return of his wife's body, he was forced to send Pearson to fetch me. Meanwhile orders were given to bring her to the Ice-house, pending my arrival. There were to be double sentries at the door.

I went first to the Ice-house, just to be certain of the identification. I entered, doffed my hat and then clapped it back on to ward off the cold. Mrs Brockletower lay once again on the central table, but now enclosed in the sailcloth bag, of a type I had seen before at building sites under use for the storage and transport of the longer type of tool – two-handled saws, surveying poles, and the like. Whatever its original use, such a bag was well suited to the business of smuggling a corpse.

I pulled the bag open and looked upon the dead one's face. It had become bloated and discoloured since my last sight of it, taking on a surface appearance something like a universal bruise, the skin all yellows and browns, mottled and marbled by blacks and blues. But it was without any doubt at all the face of the late mistress of Garlick Hall.

I felt deeply oppressed by this sight, and by the cold and gloom of the place. So, having made my verification, I quickly slipped back outside. Nothing now could be done about these remains until Dr Fidelis came, but I hoped on the morrow he would conduct his post-mortem examination. So after a brief word of encouragement to the two sentries (warning them to keep each other awake at all costs) I hurried back to the house, where I found Mrs Marsden and secured the use once more of her sitting room as my headquarters.

I asked the housekeeper when Mr Barnabus Woodley had last been seen at the Hall. It was in the morning of the previous day, early, before the squire's departure to Lancaster. Woodley had attended the squire in the library, and 'the squire was in a terrible rage with him, for the servants heard through the library door violent shouts and curses, such that none dared knock or enter, even though the fire needed attending to'. I asked if there was a servant in the establishment brave enough to go in and ask the squire if it would be convenient for me to speak with him, of practical matters connected with the inquest. Picking up the gauntlet herself, Mrs Marsden said she would do it and, a few minutes later, she returned to say that the squire would see me at once, in his library.

Chapter Twenty-one

THOUGH IT WAS bright day outside, the library was darkened by the shrouded scaffolding that still clung to the front of the house. Brockletower, sitting in the gloom, appeared to have given himself up to despondency. I found him wigless and wearing slippers and biting his nails in an almost crouching attitude on the edge of an armchair. He was looking down at a slim polished box in cherrywood with brass fittings, its lid closed, which lay at his feet on the Turkey carpet. As I came in he looked up briefly and then set his gaze downwards again.

'So! No longer the gaolbird!' he remarked acidly.

'No,' I answered neutrally. 'That matter could not be laid so easily at my door.'

'It was laid in your garden.'

'Not by me. But I have not come to talk about my innocence.'

Brockletower was stroking the highly polished surface of the box with a flattened hand.

'What, then?'

'Principally about your late wife: the inquest.'

Brockletower fetched a heavy sigh, like a child's.

'Why go through all this?' he said. 'Should death be a matter of public titillation? All you do is rake over cold coals. The dead should be buried with dignity. My wife should be allowed to go into the night without fuss.'

'We cannot do that. We must establish how her end came. The agency of it.'

'The agency was some vagabond, surely.'

'I cannot make that assumption. A suspicious death has been reported to the coroner, Mr Brockletower. As magistrate you know that my duty in such cases is not ambiguous. It is the law.'

His head dropped and I remembered how he had issued me with a ringing challenge when I previously made the same assertion. *I am the law!* he had said. All such fight was gone out of him now. What had done for it? Grief, perhaps. Or guilt. Or despair.

'But this post-mortem examination you intend,' he continued, with a suggestion of trembling in his voice, 'surely *that* is unnecessary.'

'I cannot agree,' I said. 'I value my friend Fidelis's skills. No witnesses have come forward to tell us what happened to Mrs Brockletower, so we must rely on physical evidence. The doctor may uncover some cause, some painful disease let us say, which would assist our understanding. I shall therefore ask the jury to authorize a formal examination, which I am sure they will do.'

Brockletower shook his head slowly.

'She was not ill. I would have known.'

'I shall of course note that. The jury will be glad to place it in the scales of evidence.'

Brockletower heaved a deep breath, shuddering as if even the act of respiration cost him dear. 'You do not like me very much, Cragg, do you?'

The question caught me unawares. At a loss for an answer, I began to stammer something when he cut me short.

'Of course you don't. Nobody does. My father was cold-hearted, and my witch of a mother wasted no chance to contrast my vices with the virtues of my sainted brother. Sister Sarah conceals her true feelings under a smokescreen of loyalty, for which she has her own excellent reasons. Likewise, my servants and tenants keep their counsel, but I would wager that they too find it hard to love their squire. But let us come, finally, to the one who has most recently left me – my *wifely companion*. That *person* had come not to like me at all, in any guise or at any price, and told me so to my face.'

I could have found a few words contradicting all this, though it was probably for the most part true, and I felt no obligation to bandage Brockletower's self-pity with lies. So I merely glanced at the mantel clock and said, 'It is not proper for me to speak of such matters, sir. Instead I must now ask about Mr Woodley, and when it was you last saw him.'

He turned his face to me briefly, then looked away again, as if it were painful to meet another human gaze.

'I interviewed him early yesterday morning in this room, before I rode to Lancaster. I was told upon my return, late at night, that he was dead. That is all I can tell you.'

'You quarrelled, I have heard.'

'I gave him a piece of my mind, yes.'

'What about?'

'The works. Costs, delays, matters of that kind.'

'How do you think he died?'

Brockletower gave an exaggerated shrug, as if trying to disburden himself of something.

'One of his workmen, I suppose. They are ruffians. They came down in a mob, baying to see me, you know. I had the idlers turned away.'

Beyond the window I could hear the sound of a whistling

man and the creak of an axle passing the window: a barrow loaded perhaps with stone or brick or sacks of sand.

'They are not idle now,' I observed. 'They're working again. They still hope to be paid, I suppose.'

'Ha!'

It was a laugh of pure contempt. I cleared my throat and rose to leave.

'The inquest will convene early tomorrow morning at the Plough Inn and, if the jury authorizes it, the post-mortem will no doubt follow in the forenoon. I trust I shall see you at the inn, sir, and that you will give your evidence.'

As I spoke I noted that the squire had begun gently to shake, seized by some new inner quaking. His face, already grim, was now set in a mask of desperation. When I rose to leave him, he sprang to his feet and reached out to detain me by gripping my forearm. He was behaving like an actor at Drury Lane.

'Cragg! Look, I am humbling myself, and I don't do that lightly. I am begging you, beseeching you. Don't proceed with this plan. Don't ask the jury to have this doctor cut open her . . . her body. I cannot bear the thought of it.'

As gently as I could I prized his fingers from my arm.

'I am sorry. But I must.'

His face instantly hardened again, then he turned away.

'Then there is nothing for it. Do not refer again to anything, *anything*, I have said in this room, Cragg. I shall deny it if you do. You understand?'

I said that I did, but gave him no assurance.

The afternoon wind was gusting and the trees that stood in massed ranks around the house and garden were as restless as the sea. I left the yard by way of the arch and skirted the side of the house until I reached the front, where I found operations had recommenced on the facade and pediment, under the direction of a fellow who, I gathered, had for years been Piltdown's second-in-command. Of the ganger himself, there was no trace.

The work had evidently reached a critical juncture. Three men were getting ready to raise a large piece of masonry in the shape of a beam up the side of the house, securing it to a stout rope that hung down the facade. It was part of the parapet that would run around the edge of the roof, or so I guessed, for the stone rested on a neat stack of similarly proportioned dressed stones.

I stood and watched the proceedings. The three men who had tied the rope in place now took the strain and began hauling on the rope's free end. The rope ran up to a pulley mounted on a sturdy wooden bracket that protruded above the roof, passed over the wheel and returned to the ground, where its other end had been securely tied to the stone block. A fourth and a fifth man stood waiting on high to receive the delivery.

It was a heavy pull and I could hear the men grunting, the rope groaning and the pulley squeaking as they hauled it upwards in jerky fashion. When the stone had reached a height of some thirty feet they paused for breath, while the man at the rope's end laboriously wound it around his body for extra security.

At this precise moment we heard an inarticulate, almost bestial cry behind us. It had come across the lawn, from the direction of the trees that surrounded and obscured the tongue of grass that led to the hidden Temple of Eros. I turned and to my astonishment I saw Solomon, the man-child, trundling towards us across the lawn. He had his arms extended and he was uttering a sound that seemed compounded of the lowing of an unmilked cow, and a pig's slaughterhouse squeal.

The reason for Solomon's obvious distress became clear

when we heard a second voice issuing from the trees beyond. It was a sonorous parade-ground shout – the voice, as none of us doubted even before we saw him, of Sergeant Sutch.

'Lay hands on that man! In the name of the King, arrest him I say! Stop him!'

The voice was followed immediately by the man it belonged to, emerging from the trees in zealous pursuit of his quarry like a hunter that has flushed a hare from the covert. He proceeded towards us at a regular, military trot, the various accessories of his uniform, pouches, powderhorns and the like, flapping up and down in time with their owner's step.

Before I had time to take adequate stock of these events, the enormous form of Solomon was abreast of me. I reached out, and my fingers briefly closed on a fold of his shirt, but he battered my hand away with his clenched fist and blundered on.

He seemed to be making with purpose towards Piltdown's deputy, a dark and sallow man who spoke with a Welsh accent. Solomon was extending his arms imploringly as he continued to groan and squeal and stumble towards the only man who, as he may have thought, could save him from the sergeant's wrath. The Welshman seemingly in no mood to assist, or possibly misunderstanding the appeal as a threat, dodged round to the other side of the heap of stone blocks, where he adopted what looked a pathetically inadequate, half-crouching defensive pose.

The three men on the rope, with backs turned and bent to their task, were not in a position to apprehend their colleague, nor even to apprehend the danger he brought. Anchored to the rope like boats at their moorings, they were unable to act in any way at all. But, in the event, none of us could perceive the disaster that was about to befall. Solomon careered on towards the stack of masonry, his bewilderment made more fearful by the barks of the sergeant behind him. As he reached it he hesitated for a fraction of a moment, then lurched to the side in an attempt to run around the stones and reach his object. Unfortunately at that moment an empty bucket was caught by a swirl of wind and blew over to roll in front of his feet. In tripping over it he collided with the three rope-haulers who, taken utterly by surprise, wobbled, staggered and let go of the rope. The forward two successfully got out of the way at once, while the other, with the rope-end wound about him, was spun around by the falling weight like a top before he flailed to the ground and rolled himself as quickly as he could to safety. The rope whipped from his fingers as the heavy stone's descent continued unchecked.

Stopped by the collision, Solomon was standing between the rope and the descending beam. In a moment his head and neck came into contact with the rope, which was still spinning like a vortex. It seemed to flick around him for a moment, and then became tightly wrapped around his neck. In the next moment, giving out a sort of strangled cough, his enormous bulk was whisked upward into the air as easy as a dandelion seed. A split second later the massive stone beam crashed with awful finality to the ground. For a moment Solomon continued to ascend, but then jerked down again and settled.

We had all jumped away from the crashing beam. Now we collected ourselves and looked up. The massive bulk of Solomon Miller was hanging by the neck and gently revolving in the breeze. A fraction of a second after the stone struck the ground we had all heard the sickening crack of his neck breaking.

Chapter Twenty-two

THE CRIES OF dismay seemed to have no effect on the squire, who resolutely stayed in his library, but it caused the servants to run out, the women clapping their cheeks and the men blaspheming in shock. Taking command, Sutch supervised the lowering of the body.

'I thought I saw someone in the corner of my eye, in the woods,' he explained, 'spying on the work. Dodged behind a tree, he did, when I looked at him directly. So I went in and flushed him out of cover.'

'An unfortunate ending, Sergeant, but you could not have foreseen it,' I told him.

With his great bulk stretched out in front of us, there was no doubt Solomon was dead and, feeling that the matter was in good hands, I asked one of the grooms to bring round my horse. There was nothing further I could do here, and I still had Mrs Brockletower's inquest to arrange for the next day.

As I waited, one of the labouring men approached me and plucked at my sleeve. He wanted to know if Solomon could be laid in the ground as soon as they had had his wake, this being customary among them. I considered for a moment. Solomon had lost his life violently and suddenly, and under normal circumstances that would require an inquest. But in this case I was certain one was not needed. The hanging had happened before the eyes of half-a-dozen witnesses, and no one would disagree about its nature: quite evidently accidental. Most importantly one of those witnesses was myself. As coroner, I would be able to assert the cause of death to the Mayor and borough officers and, since those gentlemen would not find it very palatable to lay out cash for an inquiry into an explicable death, they would be satisfied. I told the man to go ahead and bury Solomon as soon as he wished.

'I wonder about Peg Miller, the woman whose acquaintance I made at the builders' camp,' I said to Elizabeth as we sat down to our meal that evening of leek soup thickened with potatoes, followed by boiled mutton. 'She is Solomon's mother. He is being waked at this moment, but I wonder how the death has affected her.'

'As it would any mother, Titus. She must be distracted and inconsolable.'

'Oh, I'm not so sure. There is something peculiarly philosophical about Peg. I believe she possesses what Mr Spectator calls equality of mind. Do you know the passage?'

She laughed.

'You and your Mr Spectator! I sometimes think I am married to both of you, and am a bigamist.'

She meant the gibe friendly, so I went on.

'But it's a famous essay. He states that Equality of Mind is the capacity not to over-value our earthly existence. You see it enables us to understand instead that life on earth is only 'the circulation of little mean actions'. I am sure such opinions are by no means more rare amongst the common people than in refined society. Solomon cannot be said to have been much favoured by nature. Perhaps his mother could conceive that, in the life to come, Solomon might be happier and more useful than he had ever been in this, and that his passing could therefore be borne with fortitude.'

'Oh, Titus! You sound as if you were in court. Think. He was a human being, this poor Solomon. He had the feelings of a man, and a soul of his own too. The woman bore and breeched him, and loved him no doubt as passionately as any mother. She would not consider her son in that light. No woman thinks her son mean or useless.'

'Old Mrs Brockletower did, of Ramilles. He told me so himself this very day. He said she never did love him as well as she loved his older brother. He also says his wife was equally cold towards him.'

'Did he say that? It is a remarkable admission from a proud man. And to someone he does not know well.'

'He wanted something of me. He was trying to elicit my pity. He did everything short of going down on his knees begging me not to have his wife's body opened and medically examined.'

'What? Is that what you intend? Examined by Dr Fidelis?'

'Yes.'

'Well, I would say Mr Brockletower's feeling is natural. I also would object. He does not want her cut open. It is a violation, and horrible, and against religion. The buried body should be all of a piece, so that it may rise again entire at the end of the world.'

I sighed and shook my head.

'I do not think Ramilles Brockletower is a very religious man,' I said. 'I do not think he believes quite the same things as you, my dear.'

'Shall you examine him at tomorrow's inquest? If so, you will be able to find out.'

The next morning it rained. Now, it may strike the reader as superfluous to say that this has a dampening effect. But the encroachment of damp is not only a question of sodden hats and wigs, bespattered stockings and flooded shoes. It is also the human spirit and its finer natural capacities that become cold and soused on a wet day. So, when I set out for the Plough Inn, under a continuous and perfectly uniform downpour from a muddy sky, I immediately found myself worrying about my jury and how well they would apply themselves to the task.

But I need not have. At some inquests, where little of interest or importance is for consideration, there may be difficulties in assembling a quorum of jurors, let alone in keeping them awake. A vagabond had died in the Fulwood a year previously, and few of the freeholders I summoned cared strongly enough about the case to heed the call. I was obliged to make do with a panel of only seven somnolent freemen. But just find a box of silver in a ploughed field and folk will fight for the right to decide if it be treasure trove. A murdered squire's wife is as fascinating as a silver hoard, so there was little danger of apathy. I was not surprised to find that, out of the sixteen I had originally slated, fourteen men reported eagerly for duty, each one burning, in spite of the damp day, with the fire of curiosity in their bellies. I assigned two of these as reserves, and promptly empanelled the remaining dozen.

The landlord had prepared his public room for the occasion. My place was a chair with a high ladder-back at one end of the room, behind a good-sized oak refectory table. This was provided with a pen, penknife, ink, sand-shaker, quantity of paper, jug of water, drinking-glass and the brass hand-bell with which

I mark the various stages of a hearing. I did not have the table to myself. On my right sat Furzey, who had his own writing materials and would act as clerk. On my left, ranged in two rows of seats along the side-wall of the room, were the jury seats, which were directly faced, on the opposite wall, by a single carver chair for the use of the witnesses. Finally in the main body of the room the public seats were arranged facing me in rows, as for an audience at the theatre. The first two rows would be reserved for witnesses and behind these, separated by the space of two vacant rows, the public's own seating was arranged.

I took my place without ceremony and surveyed the already packed hall. Under the drumming of rain on the roof, it was buzzing like a beehive. I saw Bailiff Grimshaw, his waistcoat flashing red silk and silver braid. Near him was the great bulk of Sergeant Mallender, the man's enormous buttocks distributed across two seats, and with small rivers of water flowing off him to the floor beneath. I saw Bethany Marsden sitting companionably with her grandson, Jonah, who'd originally run to me with the news of Dolores Brockletower's death. I saw many of the other servants from Garlick Hall, numbers of respectable town and village people and, at the very back, behind the last row of chairs, the standing room, reserved for the lower orders. In the midst of the smocked and straw-hatted flock stood Widow Patten, the crone from Gamull who had informed me on that first day that Dolores Brockletower's death was the Devil's work. I felt glad to see she had taken up my invitation to attend, and (so I hoped) witness the confounding of her superstition with rational explanation.

Giving a vigorous shake to my hand-bell, I called silence and turned towards the jury. I gave my usual homily about the weightiness of their task, and then proceeded straight to the swearing. One by one they stood and read the oath from

Furzey's printed card, which they passed reverently from hand to hand. Then I told them to elect a foreman and, as they whispered about this amongst themselves, I sat back in my chair.

After a brief interval of attentive quiet, the audience had resumed its low-pitched drone. I immediately noticed Sarah Brockletower arriving on her brother's arm. He was talking to her urgently. They made their way by degrees up the hall, ignoring all attempts to speak with them, and settled in the front row of the witness seats. Sarah looked calm, though pale. The squire was agitated.

The jury finished its deliberation quickly enough, and George Pennyfold came over to tell me he had been elected their spokesman. I was glad of the choice. I thought him dependable.

Once that was settled, our next duty was to view the body. I announced to the room that the fifteen of us – myself, the jurors and the reserves – would have to walk over to Garlick Hall, making the best of the rain. I would then reconvene and begin to take witness evidence. I asked those giving testimony not, in the meantime, to go far away as I expected we would return for the resumption within the hour.

And as the jurors filed out of the hall, bundling themselves into coats and cloaks, I noticed our landlord standing importantly just outside the door. I took him by the elbow and drew him away from the crowd.

'Mr Wigglesworth, you have heard the news of your former guest, Mr Woodley?'

Wigglesworth nodded.

'I have that, Coroner. He was up at dawn the day before yesterday and took a crust for his breakfast away with him in his riding coat pocket. I never saw him again. Owed me almost six pound, he did.'

'I suppose you may ask the squire for the money,' I said. 'If you dare.'

I now saw Luke Fidelis striding towards the inquest room, having clearly just arrived from town.

'Luke!' I called.

He came over to me.

'When we leave, follow ten minutes behind,' I said quietly. 'You shall operate straight after the viewing.'

At some point during our walk, along the long straight lane known – oddly, since it is quite level – as Cow Hill, the jurors threw off the chilling effect of the rain and began nervously to make light of the business, and to laugh jauntily amongst themselves. It was in this spirit of quite inappropriate jolliness, bred no doubt from nervousness as to what they would soon be faced with, that the jury arrived outside the Ice-house, where two rain-bedraggled militiamen were still on guard. We huddled together to light the lanterns we had brought with us. It was George Pennyfold that led the jury in, with lantern held high, while I acted as sheepdog, herding and chivvying them past the soldiers and through the narrow passageway that led within.

I doubt that any of the jurors had stepped into such a place before, and as they did so their previous levity was instantly punctured. The lamplight slewed and sliced through the gloom as the lanterns swung in their hands. They huffed and blew and pulled their wet coats more tightly around them. The space was narrow and, by the time we were all inside, completely congested.

In an inquest, the viewing is a serious, almost a sacramental business, and I like to imbue it with appropriate solemnity. The narrowness of the space obliged me to shove my way past the jurors but, having done so, I was able to take my place at the corpse's head, and to rearrange the other twelve in a suitable pattern. Foreman Pennyfold stood on my right, with four others lined up beside him, while five more were ranged on my left, and the remaining two jurors proper occupied the far end. The reserves stood just behind, at their shoulders.

'You are here soberly to inspect the body,' I said in a low, even, warning tone. 'This is in order to fulfil the law and to inform your later deliberations as to the cause of death. You must take note of anything that might lead us safely to a conclusion on that.'

So saying, I gently drew apart the lips of the canvas enclosure to reveal the dead woman's greasy, discoloured face, and the jury gave a collective shudder and caught their breath. That we are forever in the presence of death is a familiar idea, but unless you are a Dr Fidelis, or a fighting man like Sutch, the matter may be largely an abstraction. To confront a murdered corpse in a dark, freezing cellar is quite another thing. The jury was unsettled, though they had different ways of showing it.

'I feel sick.'

'Woe to her that is filthy and polluted.'

'She stinks, anyway.'

'Let's see her throat, where it were cut.'

'And then let's get out of here.'

A murmur of assent to this suggestion rippled through the room, and some of the jurors pressed handkerchiefs to their noses.

'No,' I insisted, 'we cannot and must not leave until you have all seen the body entire.'

I indicated that jurors further down the table should help me to open the covering and reveal the corpse's whole length. They did this gingerly, as if it might at any moment explode.

But when it was done, Dolores Brockletower lay in her riding habit of black tunic and voluminous red skirt, spread before our eyes.

'Are we not to see down to her buff?'

The question came tremulously from Adam Pimlott. In his twisting face, I could see lewdness struggling with fear, or nausea. I shook my head firmly.

'It will be sufficient for you now to see the neck wound.'

But Pimlott persisted.

'But Mr Coroner, sir, I heard it's the custom to behold the body naked.'

'So it is, usually. But in this it would not be right, as you must agree. She is a gentlewoman.'

I looked to Pennyfold to lead them away from this unseemliness and he did not disappoint.

'Aye,' he said, with a firm nod of his head. 'It would be an indignity.'

'Then let us examine her neck, which you can see plain.'

Her flesh felt ghastly cold and a little pulpy as I placed my index finger on the chin and prodded it to one side. This exposed the slash in her neck, which was clogged with congealed blood exactly as if it had been roughly caulked with pitch. None of the assembly was inclined to inspect this very closely, though it brought a new round of gasps when I turned the chin the other way and showed how the wound had completed a near half-circuit of the neck.

'The gash is a handspan in length, as you see,' I observed. 'Are we agreed?'

And, dumbly, they nodded their heads.

Once that part of the viewing was over the jury became more at ease, as I could tell by the way their conversation over poor Dolores's remains began to dissipate into irrelevance.

'She got a beautiful pair of boots, she has,' observed Abel Plint at the opposite end of her from myself. As a cobbler, he was professionally interested.

'Course she has,' murmured Horatio Gumble, a smallholder who also leased land, discontentedly, from the Brockletower estate. 'Never owt but the best for her, and all likely paid for out of my rents.'

'Got a beautiful two of something else an'all,' said young Anthony Maybridge, with a suppressed snigger.

'Wonder when Squire last laid his hand on them things,' remarked Thomas Thorne. 'Not recently, I'm thinking.'

'Not in the last week, leastways, or so I hope,' added Maybridge.

There were the noises of simulated vomiting and cries of 'Leave off!' from one or two of the younger jurors.

'Not for a bit longer than that, though,' said Thorne, his voice swollen with insinuation. 'Squire's far too fond of that girlish builder chap, so I've heard.'

'Shall we change the . . .?' I began.

'Over at Plough all hours,' Thorne went on unstoppably. 'So William Wigglesworth told us the other day.'

'Yes, I were there. He said he were in and out of that Woodley's room the last few weeks like the man was his lady-friend.'

'His *catamite*, you mean?' added George Pennyfold.

One of the jurors, Peter Gardner, did not know the term.

'His what, George?'

'His bardash is that, you clown.'

'Well whatever you might call it,' said Maybridge sagely, 'Squire's headed for hell-fire on *that* road.'

'They do say there's many like it in the navy,' said Gardner.

'The question,' said the blacksmith, 'is not exactly what

passed between Squire and Woodley, is it? Did she suspect? That's the point. That poor woman – did she think she knew something?'

Although I had begun to feel scandalized at the turn the discussion was taking, this last rumination by Pennyfold made me realize that something important was being said, and that I must take notice. There was talk already of Ramilles Brockletower's hidden life. And if secrets are whispered about, even if they are only common scandal, they must be looked at with care and judgement, or the inquest will lose public credit. Behind all nefarious deeds, all crimes and acts of desperation, there are secrets, which both sustain and explain them. It is an essential part of every inquest's business to examine rumours and secrets.

Also, it brought back to my mind the drunken confidence imparted to me by Ramilles's uncle, the vicar, in the Yolland churchyard, and the reputation Woodley had gained in Lichfield and York. I silently warned myself that if additional suspicions of deviant behaviour were now to surround this case, they would have to be considered by us. On the other hand, they would require the extremest care in handling. Ramilles Brockletower himself, I reminded myself, would be present to hear them.

Then I looked at Pennyfold and thought what a just question he had asked! *Did* she know? Or even suspect? And if she did, where did that leave us? With a violently jealous wife – a wronged woman – a broken heart – a vengeful, outraged spirit?

'Diabolic!'

The word had been growled by Tom Avery, one of the reserve jurors. He went on in the style of a chapel preacher.

'That is a dark deed done by Satan and his minions constantly amongst themselves, and they—'

'Tom!'

I held up my hand in warning, but he was not to be easily quelled.

'No, Mr Cragg, I must speak out because you must understand. Hell commissions the filthy practice on earth—'

'It isn't your place, Tom Avery.'

'—to *weaken* our manhood and destroy God's law. I insist upon it!'

I slapped hard on the part of the bench that was nearest my right hand.

'Tom, no! It is I that insist. You must not speak. You are a reserve juror. You are here to follow our deliberations with care, but not to take any part in them. You will only do so if called upon to join the empanelled jury.'

'But when I hear of abominations I must—'

I shook my finger at him.

'You must not. You must be silent. That is the law. Now hush.'

Tom Avery subsided but his outburst had its effect on the others and they began a discussion of their own about the rumours that had been circulating. These centred frankly on Dolores and lycanthropy and I found the common lore on this matter, of men into wolves and vice versa, remarkably well informed. At least, they agreed broadly with the account I had read on the previous Saturday evening in Verstegan's book.

'Devil gave her an ointment, so they say, when she were a girl. She brought it with her from the Indies.'

This thought came from Gregory Matchet, and soon he and Horatio Gumble were exciting each other by it.

'Yes, and she kept it secret in a brass pot, under her bed no doubt,' Gumble babbled, 'and then when she fell out of happiness with Squire she took to smearing it on herself—'

'Smearing it all over her body,' said Matchet with a certain lascivious relish.

'And then out and roam the woods at night, she did.'

'To cheer herself up.'

'Aye and as a wolf she must have killed that fellow they found dead in the Fulwood last year.'

Although I usually try not to interfere with a jury's conversation, however absurd, I could not let this pass.

'Gentlemen! Horatio, Gregory, I'm telling you, don't be daft. I held the inquest on that fellow in the woods, and he was killed by a bolt of lightning hitting the tree he had sheltered under during a storm.'

'Happen such a werewolf has fiery breath,' argued Gumble. 'Scorched him she did. Same outcome as a lightning strike, that.'

The idea appealed to the jury as a whole and there were burbles of agreement from around the table. But these were interrupted by a sudden savage shout from George Pennyfold.

'My arse! This woman here may have been anguished, but she wasn't possessed by Satan, nor any other devil. And as for this diabolical ointment, where is it? Has anyone seen it? Or this brass pot she kept under her bed? Where's that? It isn't there. Now, come out. We can do no more here and this cold is crippling your common sense.'

The last remark may have been true. The rainwater that had earlier soaked our clothes had become infused with the chill rising from the blocks of ice around us, and we were all trembling. Our lively discussion had warded off the knowledge of it but, no sooner were we reminded, than we began to feel it. There were a few mutterings against the foreman's words, and against werewolves and diabolic possession, but the jury seemed suddenly to wish for nothing more than to leave the Ice-house and never if possible come back.

I seized the opportunity this presented to me.

'Before we go out,' I said, 'there is one more piece of business. I respectfully request the jury to commission a post-mortem examination by Dr Fidelis, who waits outside for the purpose.'

'An examination? Why? What's he going to find?' put in Gumble, with a degree of wounded truculence.

'Happen, traces of that ointment you and Gregory are so determined she had on her, eh?'

This was Pennyfold. I ignored him.

'The doctor will look for any suspicious pathology,' I explained. 'By that I mean traces and signs in the body that may help us in our inquest's task this afternoon. If he can set about it without delay, he will have his testimony ready for us before the end of the day. Is it agreed? Raise your hands.'

Dispirited by the cold, they all did so, and after refolding the canvas around Mrs Brockletower's body, we trooped out of the Ice-house.

Chapter Twenty-three

W HILE WE HAD been occupied in the Ice-house, the prevailing leaden clouds had begun to break up, revealing patches of blue sky. Rain still scudded over us in bursts, but the blue patches were fast increasing and we knew we would be dried by sunshine on our walk back to the Plough Inn. Meanwhile, Luke Fidelis had arrived with his medical bag and was standing in conversation with the two militiamen. I took him aside and told him the medical examination had been approved.

'Then I'll begin immediately.'

'How long shall you be?'

'That depends on what I find. There may be nothing, which sometimes takes longer. But a couple of hours will see it done, in any case.'

Standing in front of the Ice-house in the middle of the rising slope of Squire Brockletower's orchard, one could look down at the yard of Garlick Hall and see the face of the clock that surmounted the gateway's turret. It was only just gone half past ten.

'I shall expect you before one o'clock, then.'

But Fidelis detained me with a touch on my arm.

'I was followed here from the village by Oswald Mallender.

At this moment he's down in the house, warming his arse at the kitchen range.'

'He was admitted?'

Fidelis shrugged.

'There's only the senior parlourmaid in charge. He will have bullied his way in.'

'Did you speak to him?'

'No. He kept his distance from me.'

Mallender could only have one thing in mind: obstruction. He was bent on it, he enjoyed it, and he was made for it.

'Keep it that way,' I said. 'Have nothing to do with him. Fix your mind on what you have to do.'

'I ought to have your written warrant for the examination. With Mallender about . . .'

His request was just and I should have anticipated it.

'Yes, of course. But I have no writing materials here, and besides it will be better if Furzey drafts the note, I think. I will send it by runner as soon as we get back to the inquest.'

I turned and set off after the jurors, who were already half-way down the orchard. I had covered only ten yards when it struck me that Fidelis ought to send word if he were in any way delayed beyond the specified time. So I turned and, as I did so, an unexpected figure popped out from behind the Ice-house and joined the physician.

'Who . . .?'

But no sooner had the question formed than I recognized him. I hastened back to my friend, who smiled apologetically.

'A little ruse, Titus,' he said. 'I was not sure you would permit me an assistant in the operation, so I intended that he remain out of sight until you left. However, now you have seen him, may I introduce young George, an artist of considerable promise?'

I looked the boy up and down as he blushed a deep crimson.

'An assistant, you say?'

'Just for the day. For this procedure. He doesn't expect any payment.'

I blew out my cheeks, thinking.

'It is not quite regular and I am wondering if he is a little young. Fifteen, isn't he?'

'He is uncommonly tough. His strength and sense will be of much help to me, and he can learn much for himself at the same time. You will become a patron of the arts by agreeing to this.'

I turned to the tyro himself.

'What do *you* say, boy? Are you not afraid to deal with a dead body like this?'

George shuffled his feet. 'No, sir. The dead can do me no harm.'

So I agreed to his being taken on, and went on my way, hastening to catch up with my jurors. Traversing the yard, and passing the Hall's kitchen window, I looked in to see Oswald Mallender there. He was sitting on a bench by the fireside gulping down a bowl of steaming pottage, while his own damp clothing steamed likewise in the warmth.

On arriving back at the public room of the Plough Inn, we found that several of those present, including the bailiff, Squire Brockletower and Sarah, had crossed the yard and entered the inn in search, like Mallender at Garlick, of the warmth of a fire. For the majority who remained, William Wigglesworth had served hot punch at a farthing a glass, with buttered spice-bread. The offer had been taken up with enthusiasm and we found the hall filled with loud conversation and laughter. An improvised concert had begun with a trio of musicians, using my table as a stage, playing lively jigs on a fiddle, bagpipe and tabor. Below them the front rows of chairs had been pushed out of the way and a gaggle of girls were dancing. Encircled by hooting hand-clapping youths, they whirled and stamped in shocking abandon. Among them I noticed several Garlick Hall servants.

Tom Avery was even more dismayed by the sight than I. Unable to decide between covering his eyes or his ears, he found a middle way by clapping one hand to his right eye and the other to his left ear. At the same time he jigged up and down on the balls of his feet out of sheer indignation, an action that could hardly be distinguished from the dance itself.

I looked for Furzey. Never one to lie fallow, he had brought some writing from the office and I saw him sitting in his place at the table, apparently absorbed in work. His foot, however, was moving up and down, keeping time with the tune. I strode forward and roared for the musicians and dancers to stop.

'This is a court of inquest, and by heaven you shall respect it, or be answerable.'

I had bellowed these words as loudly as I could and no doubt, as Elizabeth said to me with much laughter when I told her about it later, my face turned the colour of a boiled beet-root. But the words had immediate effect. The music faltered into silence while the revellers stood still, some of them hanging their heads. Then I swept through their midst, pushing them this way and that with my arms to reach the table.

'Furzey,' I said sharply, 'why did you not stop this disgrace-ful exhibition?'

As the musicians, their instruments tucked in umbrage under their arms, began to clamber reluctantly off the table, Furzey laid down his pen and stretched his back and arms.

'Because I was enjoying it,' he said with a frank and simple smile.

I closed my eyes and took a deep breath. Elizabeth once told me that Furzey was my jester. Or, put another way, that he performed the function of the slave whispering into the ear of the triumphant Roman general, reminding him to come down to earth.

Sometimes, it was hard to be grateful for this service.

'Let's just get on with the business,' I said, seizing a clean sheet of paper and handing it to him. 'Please draft a warrant for Dr Fidelis authorizing a post-mortem examination on Mrs Brockletower's body.'

I waited while he did it, then sealed and signed the warrant and crooked my finger at young Jonah Marsden, in the public seats, to come out to me.

'Run with this to the Ice-house at Garlick Hall,' I told the boy. 'Give it straight into Dr Fidelis's hands, and nobody else's, mind!'

When he had gone I held out my hand to Furzey.

'We must proceed. Have you the list of witnesses?'

From the bundle of papers before him my clerk extracted a sheet on which he had noted those whom I intended to call, listed in order. With this in my hand I shooed away the musical trio, supervised the restitution of the witnesses' chairs in neat rows, sent word into the inn that the inquest was about to resume, and rang my bell for order.

It took a little longer, and several more shakes of the bell, before everyone was seated, the doors were banged shut and we were ready to get started again.

My father, as learned an antiquary as he was in the law, taught me that the English inquest and the coroner who presides over it, are very ancient institutions, with origins fogged by time. The proceedings therefore rest not on codices and legal precedents but on real remembered events. So, as far as possible, I liked to design my inquests as a teller shapes a tale. To put that another way, an inquest is a kind of play whose theme should catch and hold the attention of the jury and the public from the very start. The proper way is not to plunge straight in with the ultimate question – who killed Cock Robin? The inquest starts with the circumstance prompting the question: that Cock Robin has been found as a corpse, in such-and-such a place and manner. It starts, in other words, with the testimony of Cock Robin's first-finder.

Accordingly, Timothy Shipkin now stepped onto the stand, and was sworn. For a man with no particular position in society, he cut a confident, even an imposing figure as he took the oath. The audience was so rapt that the scrape of Furzey's pen could be clearly heard as I led Shipkin through his movements after dawn on the Tuesday of the previous week. Although it was not my business to try to prove the man a liar, the court needed above all to be sure that he was telling the truth. But probe as I might into how the body was disposed, whether he moved or interfered with it, whether there was any knife or razor to be seen beside the body, or signs of anyone else at the scene, his account in the courtroom tallied precisely with what he had already told me of these questions. He was a model of steadiness in all he spoke.

The jury and public nodded their heads as one when Shipkin described himself doing something they approved of, but broke out into murmurs of dismay when something untoward came up, as when he described the victim's wounded neck.

In retrospect I wish I had not asked my last question. I put it to him with a wish to clear the air, but it had the opposite effect.

'Before letting you go, there is just one more matter,

Mr Shipkin. You are aware, are you not, of the talk in this neighbourhood of some *supernatural* element in these events?'

The witness's sharp-set eyes glowed, as if by fire shining through ice.

'Aye, that's right.'

'And that the subsequent disappearance of the body of Mrs Brockletower gave a certain credibility to the idea?'

'Some said so.'

'Were you one of those yourself?'

'You know I were, Coroner. I told you it.'

'So you did. But now that the corpse is found being carried away by a man, not a devil, do you not modify your ideas?'

For a few moments he looked at me, and then turned his flashing eyes towards the jury.

'I stand by them,' he said. 'I say the woman was killed by the demon Asmodeus, seven times destroyer of wedlock, as the Book of Tobit tells us. She was brought away from her resting place by a man right enough, but a strange one, touched in his body and his head by the diabolic influence of Asmodeus. So I think.'

He turned back to me and repeated defiantly, 'So I think.'

Shipkin's invocation of Asmodeus had sent a ripple of excitement through the jury, and the entire room. I saw the reserve juror, Tom Avery, cast a glance sideways at his neighbour, meaning he'd known this from the start. But the murmuring was not all of the same kind. Perhaps half of those present, no doubt the less educated and less rational portion, were with Tom Avery, both thrilled and terrified by Shipkin's claim. The others I guessed were as sceptical as I. The squire, seething rather than sceptical, was pursing his lips as if ready to empty his lungs through them.

'That is not a fact, Mr Shipkin,' I said as resoundingly as I could. 'It is an opinion, and one based on an apocryphal tale.'

I turned to the jury and raked them with a warning look.

'Therefore it is not evidence. You jurors must discount it. Mr Furzey, you will note that in the record, if you please.'

The scratch of Furzey's writing was lost under one or two cries of dissent from the back of the room. Taking no heed, I excused Shipkin and he left the stand. Next up was William Pearson.

The head groom of Garlick Hall began by describing what had happened early on that Tuesday morning: how he had prepared Mrs Brockletower's riding horse, Molly, how she had ridden off alone, and how (roughly an hour later) the horse had returned without her, with blood on her mane and neck. He had ordered searches by all men that could be found in the yard and house, including Timothy Shipkin, who had been in the kitchen. He said he knew the direction in which the lady might have headed and asked should he walk up there? Pearson told him to do so. Forty-five minutes later Shipkin returned with the news that he had found the mistress's body under the old oak, whereupon Mrs Marsden wrote a letter to me, which was sent by hand of her grandson, while Pearson sent a small group of estate and house servants to the woods to watch over the body until my arrival.

Bethany Marsden sat down next in the chair and confirmed Pearson's evidence in every respect. When I asked about Mrs Brockletower's demeanour in the days before her death, she repeated what I myself had heard when questioning the servants on the day of the event itself. Her mistress had been fractious, vexed, peremptory and preoccupied. When I asked why, she could only pull a perplexed face. She did not know.

I released her, dipped my pen in ink and ran a line through her name on the paper. Some noise in the hall distracted me and I looked up to see Mallender's unwieldy form making its way towards two unoccupied chairs. Meanwhile, I consulted my witness list. The next name was that of Woodley, but of course he would now be the subject of his own investigation.

Then came the squire. I looked up at him, sitting rigidly and silent beside his sister in the front rank of chairs. By contrast, he had been anything but immobile during the evidence of the two *three* witnesses heard so far, fiddling and shifting restlessly about, his face set in a scowl. Knowing this would not be an easy passage of evidence, I braced myself and said, 'Mr Brockletower. Come forward, if you please, sir.'

At this there was a collective sigh of satisfaction from the audience. This was the evidence, above all, that they had come to hear. This was the prurient peep into the life of the wealthy and powerful that they craved. For the next few minutes not a sound would come from them as they followed every nuance, every jot and tittle of the proceedings.

Brockletower took the oath in the acid manner of a school-master reading a list of his pupils' misdemeanours.

'Thank you, Mr Brockletower,' I said. 'Now, please would you tell us when you last saw Mrs Brockletower?'

'Morning of the 10th of March, Monday. I was leaving for York. She was preparing for her usual early morning ride.'

'How long did you plan to be away?'

'I intended to be back by the 17th, Monday.'

'But you did not in fact return until the 18th?'

'No. I made an unplanned visit to Settle on the way back, after sending my man home ahead of me.'

'What was your business in York?'

'None of *your* business.'

'But it is this court's business. Was it to look at horses?'

'You already appear to know, so why do you ask? Yes, it was.'

'Only that?'

'Only that.'

'Not to meet the Archbishop of York?'

He looked startled.

'How did you—?'

'You did meet Archbishop Blackburne, did you not?'

'Yes. Paid a call. Nothing unusual there. He's my relative. A matter of courtesy.'

'Very well. Coming back to your wife for a moment, you have heard Mrs Marsden say that she was ill-tempered on that day, the day you were to return. Can you think why that may have been?'

'No. I wasn't there.'

'One would think she would be happy rather than angry on that day of all days . . . the day on which her husband was due to return home, after a week's absence.'

'*Would* one? You speak for yourself.'

I took a deep breath. There was nothing for it but to plunge.

'I must put it to you plainly, sir. Was your wife unhappy in her marriage, Mr Brockletower? Were *you* unhappy?'

The effect of my question was everything an expectant audience could hope for. The Squire of Garlick's face suddenly flushed with blood. He rose to his feet in a paroxysm of anger and brandished his fist.

'That's an insolent question, by God! It is beyond all propriety. It is the question of a damned blaggard.'

He held the stance, with his fist upraised. The room had fallen utterly silent, as if even to breathe would be enough to staunch the flow of the drama.

'Regretfully, I can only repeat it, Mr Brockletower,' I said. 'Isn't that the real reason you went to York?'

'Of course it was not!' Brockletower thundered.

'Was not your journey in reality to seek the archbishop's advice?'

'Advice? Advice? About what, sir?'

'About—'

I never finished my sentence. At that moment the door of the room burst open and Fidelis's temporary assistant, the young painter George, burst in at a run. The door bounced off the wall and the bang brought the entire room out of its trance. Everyone craned round to see the cause of the disturbance, whispering and exclaiming in frustration.

'Message!' George gasped. 'Message for the coroner!'

He looked up and down the room, his cheeks strawberry red from exertion. He must have run all the way from Garlick. As soon as he spotted me he began striding down the room between the audience and the wall, his boots booming on the bare floorboards. Reaching the table he held out a folded paper on which I recognized the handwriting of Luke Fidelis.

'You must come, Coroner,' he panted. 'You must come at once, Doctor says.'

I took the note from his fingers. In the side of my vision I saw that Ramilles Brockletower had slumped back into the witness chair. He pressed his face into his hands and gave a groan as, slowly and deliberately, I began unfolding the paper.

Chapter Twenty-four

I READ:

Dear Titus,

Something utterly unforeseen has appeared, and everything is changed. I urge you to adjourn and come to the Ice-house. Adjourn until tomorrow at the earliest because this extraordinary turn will require some consideration. And come alone, except for George. But come quickly! Luke.

I made no attempt to complete the suggestion I'd been putting to the squire in the witness-chair, but immediately stood up with Fidelis's paper in my hand and addressed the court. A contingency, I announced, had occurred that regrettably forced an adjournment until the next day. There was a brief flutter of comment. I ordered the jury to return at nine and (with faint hope of their compliance) to discuss the matter with no one in the meantime; the squire and other unheard witnesses I asked also to return; the public I cordially invited back; and Furzey I directed to lock the room as soon as it was vacated. Then I gave a final ring of my bell, abandoned my place, and strode out rapidly with young George scurrying along behind.

Everyone present had been awed at this sudden histrionic suspension of the inquest. As I rode out of the inn's stable yard five minutes later, with the apprentice painter sitting up behind, hardly anyone noticed our departure, so vigorously were they debating events as they spilled out of Wigglesworth's room and into the sunshine. So we headed off, neither questioned nor pursued.

'So what is this, George? What has happened?' I asked as we cleared the village and took the road to Garlick Hall.

'Doctor Fidelis says I'm not to tell, sir, but to let him.'

'I must be patient, then.'

But the way in which I dug my heels into the horse's flanks was anything but patient.

Luke Fidelis was slight and, with his thin face and wispy fair hair, not a commanding figure in a physical way. But at this moment, standing in his bulky leather apron before the steps that led down to the door of the half-submerged Ice-house, he looked as grim and substantial as a slaughterman. Beneath his cool greeting I discerned enigmatic, inner puzzlement.

'What in heaven's name is this, Luke?' I called as I sprang to earth. 'Where are the guards? I hope you are not going to tell me we have lost Mrs Brockletower for a second time.'

I meant this to be jocular. His reply brought me up short.

'I wanted the guards out of the way. They are down at the house drinking beer. And as for Mrs Brockletower, we have, in a way, lost her.'

'Lost her? Luke, what has happened? Is the body *gone*?'

He shook his head.

'No. It lies where you last saw it.'

'Thank heaven. Don't joke with me.'

'I do not.'

'Then tell me what you mean.'

Fidelis shook his head.

'I won't tell you. I'll show you. Come inside.'

We filed down the strait sunken passage between the two doors. It was no longer a novelty for me to enter the Ice-house, but I still felt the chill invading my soul as well as my clothing and skin.

I saw in the lamplight that the table was covered with the same horse blanket we had used when first bringing the litter and its burden here a week ago. The litter had been taken away. So had the long canvas holdall that Solomon had used to transport the corpse. But in a pile, roughly folded on top of an ice basket, I saw the red skirt, black bodice and assorted white underclothes that Dolores Brockletower wore, in a pile topped by the boots that Abel Plint had so admired. I found the sight of Dolores's clothing affecting in a way that was hardly rational. I glanced back at the table and realized that now the contours and outline of the thing beneath it were even more sharply and evidently those of a human being.

Luke took up his position on one flank of the table and motioned me to stand opposite, with the boy artist at the foot.

'Be prepared, Titus,' he warned, taking hold of the edge of the blanket that lay above the head. 'This is something I cannot explain.'

Slowly he drew down the blanket, first showing the mottled and glacial face. He gestured at it, as if in question.

'This is her face,' I whispered. 'Dolores Brockletower.'

'Naturally,' Luke replied. 'But wait.'

He continued to draw the blanket down, past the neck, wounded and black-gashed, the shoulders, and the breasts. These had perhaps lost some of their tone post-mortem, for they sagged to this side and that, and were mottled and marbled by decomposition. Making no comment, Luke continued to draw the covering away from the ribs, navel-knot and belly, where, for just a moment, Fidelis rested. I contemplated the torso. There was no jagged, roughly sewn wound from breastbone to abdomen, such as had always previously appeared when such examinations were ordered.

'You are playing with me, Luke,' I whispered again. 'How can you have found anything? She is not cut open yet.'

Fidelis smiled thinly.

'You say "she". Who is "she"?'

'This dead woman, of course!'

'A dead woman? Judge for yourself!'

With something of an actor's flourish he swept the blanket entirely away, whirling it up and casting it aside in one movement to reveal the remains of Dolores Brockletower lying before us on the table, stark naked from head to foot.

'Good God in heaven!' I cried.

I looked down in disbelief, and then up at the torso, and again down below. How shall I put this? At the fork of the legs was not what belongs to any woman. What we saw there was small and perhaps ill-formed. But it was, beyond dispute, that of a man.

It was indeed an extraordinary, unforeseen turn, and unforeseen is the raw head and bloody bones of legal epithets. Every lawyer knows this: random events are the sworn enemy of diligent casework. The higher your stack of precedents, the more vulnerable it is to toppling by the salvoes of chance.

'You are the doctor, and the natural philosopher,' I said a few minutes later in the open air. 'So what is it we have just seen in there – a male, or a female?'

After the astonishing revelation of the Ice-house we did not linger, but came out immediately, being careful to lock the door behind us. I posed my question while sitting with my friend on a fallen branch that lay in a pool of sunlight between fruit trees. The spot was a little higher up the sloping orchard looking down over the Ice-house towards the yards, outbuildings and rear facade of Garlick Hall. I was grateful to be warmed by the sun after the severe jarring I had just received.

I would have been gladder still of the comfort of an answer to my question, but for once my friend was at a loss.

'I simply cannot say,' admitted Fidelis. 'I am helpless. I have seen many deformities in my time, but never one like this. A woman who is at the same time a man, a man that is also a woman. That is natural madness.'

'When it's known that . . . this *person* was not as she seemed it will alarm the people, that's certain. They already suspect an irruption of evil here. Now it will only be confirmed. Is there no explanation in natural philosophy we can give them? Is this a freak of nature, or truly something outside nature, Luke?'

Fidelis took off his hat and rotated it thoughtfully in his hands.

After some moments he said, 'It turns everything over, you see. If there were any two absolutes in this life, I would have said it was the separation of the sexes. Until now.'

I was struck by his manner. Luke Fidelis, who is usually so sanguine, and so precise, was no less confounded and confused by this than I.

'Well, it resolves one puzzle, at any rate,' I said. 'The entry in Dolores's commonplace book. It was not just the story of Mr Eustace that disturbed her, though it must have done so. It was also the question of sex and souls. She didn't know how to fit her own case into the system.'

'What did she write? "Imagine then: my fear and pain". She was afraid for her own soul, for its integrity.'

'For its very existence.'

Of the three of us, it was the young artist who seemed the least perturbed. Having deposited himself at a few yards distance he had produced a sketching book and a piece of black chalk and was now absorbed in making a careful drawing of the Ice-house. I suppose his calm was natural, because as a stranger to the town he had no preconceptions of Dolores Brockletower in life. Having known her, seen her, accepted her as a high-ranking woman and a wife, it was hard for Luke and myself to discover at the flick of a blanket that she had all the time been a monster, a double-sexed mongrel, an affront to nature and decency.

'We must appeal to someone who can pronounce on this definitively,' I said.

'Definitive is a word in law, my friend, not in nature.'

'Yet we must know what this means. We want an authority on the question.'

'An authority? In this town? London or Edinburgh might offer us one, but there's no such person here!'

And then it burst on me, like a brainwave breaking.

'No, Luke,' I said quietly. 'You are wrong.'

I got to my feet and walked across to where the boy artist was at work. Crouching behind his shoulder, and squinting to sharpen my eyesight, I looked over his work. It was rough but extraordinarily like, the small sunken building appearing on his page in just proportion, and from just this viewpoint.

'Now, I am told,' I said, 'that you know someone in this town who should take a very particular interest in what is inside that Ice-house.'

'Yes, sir. I was thinking just the same.'

'Then we are agreed. But will he come out here, and view it himself?'

George shook his head decisively.

'He never leaves his house. He might want to come, but he would not be able to, I think.'

Fidelis joined us now, and peered over my head in order to study George's work for himself. I turned to him.

'We refer to old Dapperwick, Luke. He interests himself particularly in genitalia. Did you know? His library is lined with casts and bottled samples, I've seen them myself. If anyone can speak with authority on this sort of question, he can.'

Luke straightened his back and stretched his limbs. He seemed a little put out, as if I had questioned his judgement, or his knowledge of the world. Then, taking my arm, he drew me a little distance out of George's hearing and spoke through compressed lips.

'I don't know Dapperwick, but have heard he's senile. Would he have anything useful to say on this?'

'Yes, he is old, sick and reclusive,' I said, 'but not entirely mad. He forgets the day of the week, but he remembers his grammar and rhetoric. I wish we could fetch him here to make an examination. But at the least we can go and talk to him about this.'

Fidelis rubbed his chin.

'We can do better, Titus. I shall finish my examination – it's essential to look inside the body – and as I do so our young artist shall make drawings.'

'Which we will take directly to the venerable doctor for an opinion. Excellent! What do you say to that, George?'

The boy, who had looked so withdrawn and passive in his work, now looked re-animated. He closed the book with a snap and rose to his feet.

'All right,' he said. 'I don't mind. I can start now.'

*

Leaving the surgeon and draughtsman to their work, I decided to stroll down to the yard and then up the path to the workmen's camp. I hoped to learn more about poor Solomon and his escapade with this out-of-the-ordinary corpse. I wanted to know how and why it was in his possession because I believed this would tell me who knew its secret, and what consequences that knowledge had had.

As I made my way up the path through the dense wood that rose behind the Hall, the trees were still dripping from the morning's rain as my nostrils filled with the spicy smell of wet humus and leaf-mould. I listened for the sound of laughing children echoing down from the camp. But I heard none and, on arriving at the clearing where I'd first talked with Solomon's mother, I found it was a camp no longer. The tents were gone, the shelters dismantled. The ring of stones that had enclosed the fire had been disarranged, some of them kicked away, while within it was only a mess of sodden embers. The stool the woman had sat on lay overturned, its three legs pointing to the sky. In just a few hours they had all packed and gone.

I picked up the stool by one of its legs, meaning to take it back down with me to the dairy, from where it had probably originated. But first I wandered about a little and soon, in a corner of the former camp, some distance from the fireplace, I found a long mound of freshly turned earth and lying on it, having already keeled over in the rain-softened soil, a roughly fashioned cross.

I set the stool down and sat upon it to contemplate, for a few minutes, the unconsecrated burial place of poor simple Solomon. I guessed he had been put hurriedly in the ground without much ceremony. These people were not godly. His mother was not godly, certainly. She would not care that there had been no priest to recite words over her son, or that this was not consecrated ground. No one else cared, or would care, what happened to these itinerant labourers as they migrated from place to place, and job to job. What had been the woman's simple idea of human life? A night waking. I wondered if that was all any of them believed.

Then I thought about Solomon himself. That this fool, fogged in his thought and confused in his speech, had been the solution to the disappearance of Dolores Brockletower's dead body, was in reality no solution at all. Soon we would be digging for knowledge in the half-buried mind of Dapperwick. But to do so here, to dig for knowledge of Solomon's motive, in a being born without reason into a life without purpose, would have been perverse and unprofitable.

All that could be said was that he was not only a fool, but a tool. But whose? Knowing what I now knew about Dolores Brockletower's peculiar nature, I would have said this must be the squire. The body's disappearance would have been very much convenient to him, if there was any likelihood of its being viewed naked by a jury, or medically examined for an inquest. In a man of his standing, to have it publicly revealed that his wife was not fully a woman would bring down a shame and notoriety that he could never outlive. But I found it hard to conceive that he dealt with Solomon directly. I supposed instead that he did so through the medium of Solomon's employer, Barnabus Woodley, and that Woodley had operated through his foreman, the ganger Piltdown.

Oh well. The ganger had gone and Woodley was dead. Perhaps we would never know the truth in detail. I rose and picked up the stool, which I carried back down the path to the yard of Garlick Hall. Once there I saw Fidelis and the boy coming towards me. They were now ready to bring George's drawings to Molyneux Square, to show to Jonathan

Dapperwick. How fast they had worked! Hurriedly I deposited the stool by the kitchen doorstep for the milkmaid to find it and bustled away to collect our horses.

'I must tell you,' said Fidelis, as we jogged along the road, with George mounted behind Fidelis. 'Obstacles were laid in my way before I could even begin my task this morning.'

'By Mallender?'

'He was behind it. Oswald Mallender came up to the Ice-house after you left us. He gave me a letter signed by Grimshaw over the bailiff's seal, forbidding the post-mortem. There was another communication for the soldiers, in which the bailiff instructed them to bar me from entering the Ice-house. He waved it at the soldiers and told them to let no one into the Ice-house. These papers must have been prepared before the inquest even began. The obstruction was premeditated.'

'The Devil it was!'

It was the effrontery of this that surprised me, not the fact of it. Grimshaw stood for the interests of men like Brockletower. It was their plumage he borrowed to feather his own nest, while justice and truth could go to hell.

'The squire must have put him up to it. With his feelings about me, you know, Grimshaw would be willing enough to conspire with him.'

'Ephraim Grimshaw is a poltroon.'

'But a powerful one. However, on this occasion, his letter has no more legal force than a page out of *Mother Goose*. You had my authority to proceed with the examination. That weighs heavier than all his seals.'

'But that was the rub, Titus. I didn't have it, not at first. The soldiers barred the Ice-house door and refused to let us pass. Even when your note arrived, I couldn't persuade them to let us begin work. The soldiers were illiterate. Only when Sergeant Sutch appeared and read my warrant did I gain access.'

'The squire must have asked Grimshaw to intervene. Didn't I tell you he was all against your cutting his wife open?'

'Yes. And now we know why.'

'But now that you *have* cut her, what result?'

Fidelis shook his head.

'None, Titus. It was necessarily a rapid survey. The anatomy was so strange and confused that I could make nothing of it. But I saw no disease in the principle organs. And there were no wounds, new or old, except the one we know about. The stomach was empty.'

'The empty stomach doesn't signify. The servants told me she never broke her fast until after the morning ride. Now, let us pick up the pace. I am impatient to hear Dapperwick's opinion.'

Chapter Twenty-five

'A CAPITAL EXAMPLE of hermaphroditism, is that!' exclaimed the author of *De Genitalia Virilis Muliebrisque*.

Dapperwick's fingers were fluttering moth-like over the page of George's drawing-book, which lay open before him on his library's writing table, around which we all stood: the old anatomist, the young artist, Luke Fidelis and myself.

'Am I to understand,' Dapperwick continued, 'that the original of this subject is lying dead less than five miles from here?'

'Yes, at Garlick Hall,' I told him.

Dapperwick's trembling fingers traced the outline of the naked corpse. Taking a downward viewpoint, George had drawn it with astonishing accuracy and truth, not only the outline, but the actual flesh of it, and with the complete illusion of three dimensions.

'I only wish I could look at this in the flesh,' Dapperwick went on. 'I have never seen one, you know. They are exceedingly, *exceedingly* rare. But no. It is impossible for me to go to Garlick Hall, or anywhere outside this house. Quite impossible.'

His lips were pursed and faintly dribbling, but the eyes set in his masked, immobile face were on fire. They were like the eyes of a chained dog pulling at his tether for a piece of meat just out of reach.

'That is a great pity,' I agreed.

A thought struck him and he raised his head, darting a bloodshot glance towards me.

'Can you not trundle it here to me, Mr Cragg? By cart, or litter, or . . . somehow?'

I shook my head.

'I fear that is even more impossible, sir. It is against the law to move or remove a corpse that is under inquest.'

'Oh, well. Fiddle-de-dee. Nothing to be done.'

Dapperwick returned his hungry gaze to the full-length drawing, then turned the page, where a detail of the genitals appeared, equally accurate and in considerably closer detail. He stabbed the image with his forefinger.

'Oh, wonderful! It is exactly as described in the medical treatises. Exactly!'

'I only know of such things from Ovid's *Metamorphoses*,' I remarked.

Dapperwick nestled the knuckles of one hand into the palm of the other and rubbed or screwed them into it. It seemed like a gesture of enthusiasm at my mention of the Latin poet.

'Ah yes! Ovid, you know!' he squawked. 'A far better natural philosopher than is generally recognized.'

I looked at Fidelis interrogatively. Was the old man being satirical? It appeared not. Without drawing breath and with his whole head vibrating from increasing excitement, Dapperwick enlarged on his admiration for Ovid.

'Ovid celebrates change, transformation, you know. I regard that as a vital principle in nature. As you may therefore surmise I say "Foo!" to those who maintain all species were fixed unchangeably at the creation. Modern poets such as Mr Pope who spout about the ladder of creation being immutable. Pure stultiloquence, sir. Living things are not eternally separated into impermeable envelopes marked "apple" and "pear", "camel" and "leopard", "male" and "female". Under the right conditions, an apple may be grafted to a pear, a camel to a leopard, is it not so? Something of the same happens in cases like this.'

'Please elucidate, Doctor,' I asked.

Dapperwick tapped George's drawing.

'Well, as Dr Fidelis will of course be aware, Dr Leeuwenhoek's microscope taught us a few years ago that the male *seminum* contains animalcules, like shoals of tiny tadpoles, swimming around it. The question then arose, are these in fact embryos? Their matter is disputed. Dr Burton of Wakefield, with whom I correspond, contends the woman's egg is the embryo-in-waiting and the animalcules are nothing but carriers of an electrical energy that, as he puts it, delivers a kick to the egg that propels it into life. Much as I respect Dr Burton as a man-midwife, I contradict him on this. In my opinion, the little tadpoles *are* veritable embryos. In the *seminum* they form a community of males and females – the males no doubt issuing from the right testicle and the females from the left, as Aristotle teaches – but once precipitated into the womb, they begin to contend with each other to get to the safety of the woman's egg, which is their nursery, in effect. The first one to establish itself there proceeds selfishly by locking the door, as one might say, to keep all its competitors off.'

'In that case how do twins come about?' I asked.

The doctor smiled at me indulgently, as at a female pupil who asks a question cleverer than she knows.

'Ah! Twins! In such cases, you know, *two* have burst through the egg's door simultaneously and are forced somehow to cooperate. And this is very germane to the subject under discussion.'

With his finger he rapped George's drawing again.

'I believe it is a variation of the process of twin-making that results in the hermaphrodite. Sometimes, very occasionally, these twins become engrafted one in the other and are born as conjoined monsters. But in a handful of such cases (which, you know, are already very rare) a male and a female become completely merged and a single hybrid individual, both masculine and feminine, results. A monster, but not necessarily a hideous one. Which is what we have in George's fine drawing here. There is no witchcraft about it. It may be very uncommon but it is natural, perfectly natural. And rather, um, beautiful, too, in its way.'

'Do these, er, hermaphrodites always appear the same? Anatomically, I mean.'

'Oh no, they come in various arrangements. With or without *testes*, with or without the vagina.'

'And may such creatures become pregnant, and bear a child?'

'Curious you should ask. But, in answer, I think an analogy with the mule may be drawn. A mule is the intergrafting of a horse with a donkey, and it is utterly sterile, as everyone knows. So is the hermaphrodite. Tales of hermaphrodites marrying and impregnating each other are delightful, but I fear poetical.'

He turned to Luke.

'I hope you agree, young Fidelis.'

My friend answered diplomatically.

'I do not have a view, Doctor, as I have never until now had occasion to consider the matter. But I expect the Royal Society will give a ruling in due course.'

Dapperwick's preternaturally unlined face registered a trace of disappointment that Luke had not endorsed him.

'True . . . the Royal Society . . . true enough.'

We fell silent for a few moments, while Dr Dapperwick tapped his chin thoughtfully with his fingertips.

'It is very strange,' he said at last, his voice audibly thinner, and rasping slightly as if a reed needed changing. 'I seem to remember having such a conversation as this in a dream, a few days ago. I fancied I received a visitor whose conversation turned after a while to individuals of mixed sex. And I dreamed that he asked me the same question as you have: is it the general view that they cannot reproduce? And I admitted it is not.'

He shook his head sorrowfully.

'The whole field of generation is greatly argued over, you know. But, yes, it was strange, my dream. You might say predictive, yes. You might say auspicious.'

'May I ask who your visitor was, in your dream?'

'Oh, just some young fellow. He was unknown to me. He wore a most remarkable wig, though. An unheard-of, monstrous thing, such as one often meets with in dreams and nightmares.'

We three walked across Molyneux Square a few minutes later. Fidelis broke the silence with a slight laugh, though a mournful one. I thought I could tell the reason.

'Sense and senility,' I said. 'How is it possible for the two to be so thoroughly mixed in one man?'

'I find it no more incredible,' he replied, 'than the mixture of male and female in Dolores Brockletower. Rather less, I think.'

'But there is one important question, Luke. Can the unfortunate Dapperwick reliably tell the difference between a dream and his memory? That dream-visitor of his, the one he mentioned, was perhaps no dream at all. He really had a caller, and I know his name. My wife saw Barnabus Woodley coming away from Molyneux Square on Friday last. You see the significance, Luke?'

'Woodley the architect was the visitor? Yes, that is striking.

Woodley asking about the fertility of hermaphrodites? Now that's surpassingly interesting. Shall we sit a few moments?'

We had reached the green in the centre of the square and Fidelis was indicating one of the curved marble benches that stood on scrolled feet at each of its corners. George plumped himself down at one end of the seat and opened his sketchbook. Taking chalk from his pocket, he began to draw. Fidelis and I sat down on the opposite extreme of the semicircle.

'It cannot be a coincidence,' I said. 'Woodley must have known Dolores Brockletower's secret.'

'Yes, either from the squire or directly from her.'

'From the squire, I would think. The two men were close, while there was a strong dislike between Dolores and Woodley.'

'But why would he, of all people, concern himself with her possible fertility?'

'That's hard to guess. Not only did the squire and his – what shall we call it? – consort? – his consort then – not only was there in *fact* no prospect of a direct heir of the Brockletower blood coming from their union, but both of them *knew* it, beyond any doubt. And must have from the beginning.'

'So they must,' said Luke, with another rather heartless laugh. 'The anatomy that George has drawn so prettily for us was well hidden under fine dresses and hunting clothes. But it could never have been concealed in the bedroom. I'm thinking Brockletower was not a dupe when he married his Dolores – or, at any rate, he could not have remained so for long after.'

But something else was on my mind.

'Yes, Luke, but it also makes them unlike other couples that do not become parents, do you see? The latter continue almost into old age to hope, and pray, and perform superstitious rites, because they cannot explain their barrenness. The Brockletowers could never have had any such hopes. Whatever form their intercourse took—'

'Did not the vicar of Yolland tell you something about that?' interrupted Fidelis.

'Not specifically, but he did strongly suggest certain,' I dropped my voice, 'irregularities. And, as I say, whatever they did was not going to result in a child under any circumstances.'

'What did they do, sir?' asked George, still sketching industriously but all the while listening with long ears to every word.

I ignored him. He was too young.

'But my point is that all this accounts for Dolores's interest in the Talboys girl, and her being with child.'

'Which she actually promoted,' Fidelis said, 'from what you told me.'

'Excellent! You think exactly as I do, Luke. Dolores Brockletower does appear to have encouraged the girl to put herself in the way of pregnancy.'

Luke rose and dusted his breeches.

'And my guess is,' he said, 'that Mrs Brockletower was premeditating the adoption of the child by herself and her husband. But I am afraid I must leave you now. I have a patient waiting.'

I held him back for a moment.

'The truth about Mrs Brockletower must be kept a close secret, Luke. For the time being, anyway. Is that agreed?'

'Agreed,' he said.

I turned to George.

'Agreed, George? No telling of this, not even to your own shadow.'

George nodded his head and I turned back to Luke.

'Let's you and me meet later,' I said. 'At the Turk's Head coffee house in three hours' time.'

We three did not part finally until we had passed under the covered alley, or tunnel, that connects the square with Market Street. From there Fidelis hurried off to his consultation, while the boy and I turned the other way. The mention of Abigail Talboys had reminded me that I wanted to pay a visit to Talboys's shop. At the top of Friar Gate, George told me he too must leave me, to rejoin his master at Patten House.

'He is finishing the portrait of Lord Derby. Well, the face.'

'I suppose he will return to Warrington to complete the figure,' I remarked.

George made a sound that might have been interpreted as a scoff.

'Not him.'

'You mean he will finish it here?'

George made the sound again.

'No, he will cut out the face and send it to Mr Van Aken in London.'

I stood still, in amazement.

'Why? Who's Van Aken?'

'He sticks the faces that others paint on a canvas, and paints the body around it – clothes, hands, wig. He's famous for his drapery.'

'Good lord! Is that how it's done now?'

'By Mr Winstanley it is.'

'You do not approve?'

'I think an artist should be a complete man. Not one that farms things out.'

'Your master is trying to get the best possible result, I suppose.'

'No. He does it because it makes him feel more important. Only the face matters to him. It is all he can be bothered with. The rest is for others.'

'Lesser beings, he thinks?'

'Yes. He's God Almighty, him.'

'So when we view the portrait at last, it will only be my lord's face we see. The body will be that of another person?'

'Not another *person*. A lay-figure. That's a puppet made of wood. A toy in toy clothes.'

'Couldn't *you* do the drapery for him, George?'

'I'd refuse and he knows it. I'm not to be treated as less than he.'

Such confidence, in a mere boy and apprentice, took me by surprise. I decided to caution him about it.

'To think like that could cut short your indentures, George. Only a particularly patient master will endure insubordination. I hope Mr Winstanley is patient.'

I said this in as kindly a way as I could.

'Only a patient apprentice will endure a bad master,' he said, looking me boldly in the eyes. 'And I am not patient, Mr Cragg. Time with Dr Dapperwick or Dr Fidelis is better spent than it is with him.'

Though I was itching with curiosity to know if Abby Talboys had had an inkling of Mrs Brockletower's unusual *physiologia*, the real purpose of my visit to the Talboys was to tell her I would, after all, be needing her as a witness at the inquest. I found her father in his shop, unpacking some newly delivered rolls of Nottingham lace.

'Eh, Titus!' he exclaimed when he saw me, and came round the counter to clap me on the shoulder. 'Bailiff locked you up, but could not keep you. You bested the man!'

I had not bested Grimshaw – not yet – but I thanked my old friend for his sentiment. Then I asked after his eldest daughter.

'Abby is to go to Yorkshire,' he told me. 'To her late

mother's sister at Gargrave, a good Christian woman. She will give birth there and stay on after.'

'You will miss her.'

He laughed, for with Talboys good humour cannot help breaking through.

'Eh, I'll miss her work. Not her wilfulness.'

'And you'll be a grandfather, before I am even a father. Think of that.'

'Must I think of it? I have enough trouble with fatherhood. Four daughters and three still cluttering my home!'

'I wonder, Ned . . . has Abby told you anything more in detail about her conversations with Mrs Brockletower?'

'Not me. She tells me nothing. But here she is and you can ask her your questions in person.'

Abigail had come in from the street, carrying some packages.

'Abby,' said Talboys, 'Mr Cragg would like a word. Would you like to take him up to the fitting room?'

Abby seemed neither welcoming nor hostile. She led me briskly up to the first floor, and into the room that looked out over Friar Gate. It was furnished with a couple of dressmaking dummies, but otherwise resembled a comfortable parlour, with upholstered chairs, polished furniture and a fire burning in the grate.

I sat in one of the fireside chairs while Abby put her purchases on a sideboard.

'I am to make a journey into Yorkshire, Mr Cragg,' she said. 'As I shan't be returning soon, I have been shopping for necessaries.'

'Yes,' I said. 'Your father told me. It is a good solution.'

'Judging from letters to my father, my aunt does not think so. And nor do I. I will be spoken to roughly on arrival, no doubt, and put to work with the pigs and chickens. I am out of favour, in disgrace, but the fault is all my own.'

She was standing at the window, looking not at me but out into the street.

'Not entirely,' I said. 'There is someone else who takes half the blame.'

'Oh, you may forget him,' she said huffily, spinning around and briskly removing her bonnet, which she laid beside the parcels. 'So, what is it you want to speak to me about?'

I told her that I would still need her as an inquest witness tomorrow, but that there would be no need for her to reveal her pregnancy.

'It will be enough for you to tell the court that Mrs Brockletower told you during your private sessions together that she very much wished for a child, and that she hoped to be able to adopt one. That is the only testimony the court will need.'

Abigail pressed her hand to her forehead, like one soothing a headache. Then she turned to me, her face breaking into a charming smile. She had excellent white teeth.

'I am relieved, Mr Cragg,' she said. 'It had been preying on my mind that I would be terribly frighted, speaking in public about being with . . . you know.'

'Well, no one need know about that who doesn't need to know.'

I looked around me.

'Well now, this is the room in which ladies have their fittings, is it?'

'Yes, sir.'

'Mrs Brockletower included?'

'Yes.'

'So it is here that you often talked so intimately, as you described to me the other day?'

'Yes. This is where we talked.'

I coughed and shifted in my chair. How on earth was I going to put this?

'Did she ever speak to you, I wonder, about exactly why she was childless?'

'She only said it was impossible for her to conceive.'

'Without saying why?'

'Yes.'

'And you formed no idea yourself on the subject? That there might be some physical deformity, say.'

'Physical deformity? What can you mean, sir?'

'In the way her body was made. I imagine a dressmaker knows her customer in that way better than most – taking measurements and so on.'

She looked at me intently for a moment.

'Why do you want to know this?'

Her voice was sharp, and edged with emotion as she went on.

'Mrs Brockletower was a good friend to me. I will not have her talked of as being deformed.'

'I am sorry, Abby. Sometimes a coroner must ask displeasing questions.'

She turned back to the view from the window.

'Well, I cannot answer yours. If there *was* anything, I knew nothing about it.'

'Then we shall speak no more of the matter.'

I rose and moved to stand beside her. The afternoon traffic in Friar Gate was mostly of carts and packhorses trundling empty churns and barrels of unsold produce back to the country from Market Place. Abby sighed.

'A farm girl, that's me from now on, sir. A slave of the muckheap, pigsty and cowshed. I had hoped for a life of more refinement. Not to be, now. I'll never get a husband that isn't coarse, and a bumpkin.'

She was probably right. She was bonny all right, but with no dowry, and a little bastard in tow, her stall in the Gargrave marriage market was not likely to be under siege. I tried to boost her hopes.

'Abby, you are pretty and you have wit. Some fellow of dependable means and good sense will come your way. Hold out for that, will you?'

This time she smiled tightly, with closed lips. I could see she did not believe me but perhaps, with time for reflection, she might one day. So I found myself hoping as I gently took my leave.

Chapter Twenty-six

AFTER LEAVING ABBY TALBOYS I returned home. Legal correspondence does not stop merely because one is in the middle of an inquest so, having had a bite to eat, I intended to go from the parlour into the office. But first I allowed myself a quarter of an hour in the library, getting down the fourth volume of Tonson's *Miscellany* of poetry, stoking the fire and settling into my chair beside it.

Turning the pages I soon found what I was looking for: Mr Addison's rendering in English of the fourth book of Ovid's *Metamorphoses*, in which was embedded the lovely, liquid story of Salmacis and Hermaphroditus. It is a brief tale, told in a single scene. Hermaphroditus, handsome son of Hermes and the goddess of love, strips for a bath in a woodland pool, fed by a stream that gurgles under the protection of the nymph Salmacis. Seeing him naked and powerfully swimming, she so strongly desires him that she hurls herself into the water and locks her arms around him. Their passion is such that (I read)

> *Piercing each the other's flesh they run*
> *Together, and incorporate in one:*
> *Last in one face are both their faces join'd*
> *As when the stock and grafted twig combin'd*

Shoot up the same and wear a common rind:
Both bodies in a single body mix,
A single body with a double sex.

I shut my eyes, imagining the picture – a beautiful image of the very act of love, in which my beloved and I strive so strenuously to unite, to merge each into the other. My own person may be a little distant from Hermaphroditus, son of beautiful and illustrious parents. But Elizabeth . . . Elizabeth is the perfect vision of a nymph, or so I thought, and think.

I jerked awake. An hour and more had passed, and I had slept. I hurried into the office, where Furzey greeted me with a superior look.

Later, letting Elizabeth know I would be dining out with Luke Fidelis, I put on my hat and strolled across Church Gate to the Turk's Head, where I found him in one of the confidential booths, smoking and drinking Burgundy wine. I joined him in the wine and called for a pipe, telling him of the poetry I had been reading. Fidelis is not one for poetry, not even when I mentioned Ovid's use of the word intergrafting.

'It is exactly the conceit used by Dr Dapperwick,' I explained. 'I believe it is what he meant by saying the poet is a better philosopher than most realize, and that he had thought the thing out.'

'No,' Luke muttered. 'Dapperwick is merely happy to find poetic support for his daft theory. But as evidence it is not worth spitting at.'

I told him he'd be a better man if he loved poetry more, and he countered by maintaining I'd do better to prefer reason to rhyme. So, differing amicably, we poured more wine and I asked Fidelis what he had been doing. He pulled a book from his pocket.

'After leaving the Mayor, I also did some reading, though rather different matter from yourself. It is Dr Thomas Allen's account of the Hampshire hermaphrodite, Anne Wild, born in the last century. It is among the Transactions of the Royal Society.'

He tapped the book with his index finger.

'Wild had the sexual equipage of both the male and the female,' he told me. 'But since at first she appeared to have no penis, she was raised as a girl until something remarkable occurred.'

I was agog.

'What?'

'*Presto!* A male organ appeared and for three years she was more like a boy. Then, just as suddenly, her menses began to flow, which continued for another two years until, suddenly again, she began to have a beard. After that her body increasingly resembled a man's.'

'So she became a man, after all?'

'Never entirely. She could be aroused by either sex. Listen to this.'

He opened the book and read aloud.

'"One night as she was making merry with her companions she cast her eye upon a handsome man and became so much in love with him that the excess of her passion made her hysteric."'

He closed the book once more.

'So Anne Wild was capable of feeling both as a man and as a woman, depending on the circumstances.'

'What happened to her?'

'The article does not say. She lived and died in obscurity. Without Dr Allen's intervention we would not have heard of her. The country people had been superstitiously afraid of her at first, no doubt, but probably came to tolerate or even grow fond of her in the end.'

'It is better than being exhibited in a circus show, which might have been the case. But it isn't easy to see how she can have been happy.'

'She must have been tormented. I do wonder about the veracity of this author when he states she was making merry. Her life must have been a continual puzzle, a torrent of questions. The same goes for Dolores Brockletower. Waiting for your arrival, I have been trying to calculate the number of those questions.'

'And have you succeeded?' I asked. 'How looks the balance sheet?'

'It is divided into three columns: moral, medico-philosophical and legal.'

'I am interested in the legal column, of course.'

Fidelis held up his finger.

'In which the prime question asked is, what was Mrs Brockletower's legal status? Was she male, or female?'

'I think I know the answer. But tell me first the philosophical position – the medical one.'

'All right. Medically speaking, she was as Dapperwick described her: a hermaphrodite. Compared to the Hampshire case, she seems more female on the surface. She had the voice, skin, bosom and shape of a woman. Of course under her shift, in layman's terms, were a cock and balls, if somewhat reduced in size.'

'And the latter, I think, are the items that solve the legal puzzle. Medically she may have been of intermediate gender, dressed she may have seemed a woman, but the genitalia I fancy made her legally a man. *Ergo*, if she was legally male, her marriage could not have been valid. What flows from that?'

'We encroach on the moral column here. What flows is the disgrace of the husband.'

'Yes, and his financial ruin, too. Think of the debt-encumbered estates that his uncle told me of. She – let's call her that since we don't have another pronoun – she had inherited property and securities that kept him from sinking. She was wealthy.'

'Jamaican sugar.'

'Yes. And sugar is sweet. But if the marriage is sour, the husband cannot have the sweetness of the money. Her family will recoup the lot. I'm thinking this might be considered a motive for favouring murder over divorce.'

Luke shook his head.

'No, Titus. I see it as a motive for keeping her alive. Or, if for killing her, only in such a way that it could not be detected. A violent slaying of a kind we have seen would be bound to trigger an inquest and an examination of the body – as it did. That was the last thing Brockletower could permit.'

Fidelis was right, of course.

'Oh dear,' I reflected, 'we already knew it was impossible for him to have killed her in person. But I was beginning to hope that, since it appears the squire wanted an end to his marriage, we could show he killed through an accomplice, whilst he skulked in Yorkshire. But, if what happened in the Fulwood was the wrong kind of killing to be explained by *that*, I am no further on.'

'You *are* further on, a little. He certainly didn't kill her, or have her killed. We can say that. But you can be fairly sure he stole her body from the Ice-house – using an accomplice also, I would think.'

'Piltdown?'

'Why not? His woman's son was found in possession of the

body. But it was all done at the squire's behest, I am sure. He was forced to it by the inevitability of an inquest following the murder.'

'Which still goes down as committed by person or persons unknown,' I said, with an exasperated groan.

For half an hour we continued to turn over these questions until, quite suddenly, the coffee-house hubbub of card players and politicians stopped, as is conversation in a theatre when the curtain rises. Fidelis and I looked out of our booth to see the cause.

'I'll be damned,' whispered my friend.

Ramilles Brockletower, in his riding clothes, had made an entrance from the street. With every eye on him, and awed whispers flurrying in his wake, he stalked wordlessly into the room, checking each table until he reached ours. I saw his eyes bulge fractionally when they met mine, after which, still saying nothing, he spun around and crossed to the internal door that led through to the kitchen and the stairs. The keeper of the coffee house, Noah Plumtree, was standing there in his apron. The two men conferred and Plumtree stepped aside to allow Brockletower's passage through. I noted that under his arm the squire was carrying something. It looked like the polished cherrywood case I had seen the day before on the floor of his library.

As soon as he had left, the chatter rose again sharply, as the room filled with speculation.

We ordered chops and another bottle of wine and, while we awaited our food, I told Luke about my meeting with Abby Talboys, and her blighted prospects in the Gargrave farmyard.

'The silly baggage,' he said. 'She should have been more careful.'

The chops arrived and I was hungrily preparing to cut myself a slice when I felt a tap on my shoulder. It was Noah Plumtree leaning towards my ear.

'Compliments of Mr Brockletower, Coroner,' he said. 'He asks would you be so kind as to attend him in our upstairs private room?'

The cherrywood case that I had seen in the Garlick Hall library rested unopened on an oak table in the centre of the private room. It was about the size of a closed gammon board, with brass catches and corners.

Ramilles Brockletower stood awaiting me, with his arms folded, and head lowered. As soon as I entered he roused himself and strode behind me to the door. With a rapid movement he turned the key, snatched it from the lock and slipped it into his pocket.

'There. We are alone.'

He coughed, a formal clearance of the throat, and went on.

'We've had our differences, Cragg. But can we agree on one thing, at least? Ours is a race of endless airs. Don't you loathe the prattling, the cozenage and the cupidity of it? Worst of all is its preoccupation with damned trifles and trivialities. Every thought of the human race makes me heave with nausea.'

This frontal assault on humanity was, to say the least, unexpected.

'Have you taken me from my supper just to preach misanthropy?' I asked.

He had begun moving slowly and aimlessly around the room, tapping his chin with his fist. It was a good-sized room floored in a polished wood, which enabled Plumtree to let it to a dancing master for his weekly classes.

'Preach. That's good. But I am no divine, Cragg. I have sailed across the oceans. I have seen men disembowelled. I never felt a feather's weight of pity at the sight. I was weighed down only by a ton of disgust. I have witnessed diseased human flesh bubbling like soup over a flame, sir. Then I have witnessed it swelling up and exploding! When will your painted people, your dancing masters and fops, face *that*? I would devoutly like the Deluge to come again. Indeed I would, wouldn't you? And this time let's agree that Noah and his brood shall perish with the rest. Let everyone be swept away. We are all vermin, are we not?'

'Your views are too extreme for me.'

He started, as if it were his turn now to be surprised.

'But I am given to believe you are a clever man, and the possessor of a good library.'

'I have a library, yes,' I admitted.

'Does your reading not lead you, then, to the same conclusion – distaste for every living man, woman and child in creation?'

'Well, people are less tidy in person than they are in books, I grant you, but I—'

'That's not what I mean. I am speaking of the people who write the damnable books! Authors, sir, authors!'

He was becoming increasingly excited, raising his voice and gesticulating.

'No better than those they scribble about. All are the same.'

Brockletower pulled a book from his pocket and threw it on the table, where, beside the cherrywood case, there stood a pair of candlesticks. Between these lay a silver pen tray containing a bunch of quills, and the book struck the tray, pushing it across the polished surface and over the table's edge. The tray and quills scattered across the floor's polished boards.

Ignoring the spilled pens, he pointed at the book.

'She gave me that to read. Marked one passage specially for me, and I know why. She did it to goad me, torment me.'

I reached and picked up the book. It was volume III of the collected *Tatler*, a duodecimo edition, smaller than my own octavo, and in a binding not at all as well kept, but rubbed, scratched and broken at the hinges. There was a ribbon in its pages, and I opened it at the place, already feeling sure which passage I would find. And there it was: the story of Mr Eustace.

'A paltry little tale,' commented Brockletower, 'of paltry people, with paltry concerns. I am ashamed she should think us comparable.'

'Are you not, then? The circumstances seemed similar to your wife, I think.'

'No, no, they were not a bit similar. Did you know I am hereabouts called "Black Ram". You remember *The Moor of Venice*?'

'*Othello*? Strange you should refer to that. Only the other day I—'

'Now *that's* similar. You know what the Black Ram did to the White Ewe?'

He laughed derisively.

'That would be funny if it wasn't so damned sad. My wife would have me her own Othello, in every way but the colour of my skin.' He pulled up his sleeve, and briefly showed me his wrist and forearm. 'But I doubt Venice valued his wife more than mine was valued in the Jamaican circles in which I found her.'

There was a moment's silence.

Wanting him to continue, I prompted, 'How was that?'

'Think, man, think! It was impossible to calculate her worth out there! A barocco pearl! Nothing like it had ever been seen before. Looked as a woman, and fucked as a man. You don't hear of that very often.'

I remained attentive. The man was out of his mind, but not incoherent.

'I stole it from them, their pearl. I had known her but a few days, a few days, when suddenly I found that I would risk everything for her. Of course it was criminal to be married, but only if people knew about her. I thought no one would ever find us out. Her father gave me his blessing, naturally: he was more than glad to be rid of her. But look what she's done now – made it all public, planned my ruin. Woodley saw that. He told me. But his idea of saving me . . . that disgusted me as much as *she'd* come to disgust me. A gallows or a mollyhouse. Bad, bad choice.'

'How did she plan to ruin you?'

He jabbed his finger at the book, which still lay open in my hand.

'As his wife ruined the feeble Eustace. My wife wanted the same thing as happened to her, you see: to die at my hand. By that time her barren, monstrous life, her *self*, was as horrible to her as it was to me. I told her I did not like her enough to kill her and hang for it. I offered instead to send her back to Jamaica but she told me she would rather die than go back. And now she *is* dead, and I am condemned, though I did not kill her. I have read the story she found in that book, you see, and I know how it must finish. But unlike the other man, the husband in the book, I did not kill my wife, though she wanted the world to believe that I did.'

He was standing now with the table between us. His hands slid down and over the polished case that lay in front of him, his fingers fiddling with the catches. Suddenly he snapped them, flipped the lid up and showed me what the box contained. Nestling together muzzle-to-handle in a bed of red silk lay a pair of duelling pistols.

'One of these,' he went on, 'is the means by which you, sir, are going to do away with me. You have initiated this business with your meddling and snooping. I know this because I have been with my uncle today. The old fool's tongue has been running away, and told you of things that must be concealed. So now it is for you to complete the task. And, as you do it, this other piece will be the simultaneous instrument of your own death, at my hands. Just like the story. Come on, man, both are loaded. Let us duel, let us die point-blank. Take your weapon and begin.'

I backed away, thinking what little use it would be to argue with him. He was crazy.

'Why did you kill Woodley?' I asked, in desperation to keep him talking. 'And why bring him to my garden?'

Brockletower's restless movement stopped, and he frowned, as if struggling to remember the details.

'He knew, you see, about that creature. Foolishly I had made him my confidant. I had reached a point when I had to confide, and I thought he was my friend. He stole the body when I asked him to, and arranged to hide it. But then he wanted money, the villain. So I met him on the road from Lancaster in the night, pretending I had been there for the money, and would pay him. I paid him, all right. I had the means with me: crude, and not gentlemanly, but efficient, silent and swift. The night was dark and no one saw.'

'And my garden?'

'Why not your garden? I feared the gallows. I wanted you to bear the burden instead of me. So I took him there at night.'

'Why would I want to kill Woodley?'

'How would I know? Because he was loathsome and a cheating extortioner. Because of some quarrel between you.'

In one movement, he seized both guns from the box, one by

the conventional grip and the other – evidently the one meant for my use – by its barrel. He sidled around the table and advanced towards me, his own pistol pointing to the floor while he thrust the other's handle in my direction.

'Take it, damn you! Don't back away! It's time to finish this.'

I cast a wild look towards the door. I remembered it was locked and the key in Brockletower's pocket – so no way out there. A sideways glance towards the nearest of the two casements informed me that it was a few inches open. I considered it as a means of escape for a moment, before dismissing it. I would not be halfway across the sill before Brockletower fired, killing me almost certainly with a bullet in the back even before I had bounced off the cobbles.

I had never fought a duel either with pistol or sword and was altogether ignorant of the martial arts. I agree with Mr Spectator in scoffing at the duel because it is a system designed exclusively to kill men of courage and honour, whilst preserving the lives of cowards.

I did, however, know that duels are staged only when each contestant is accompanied by a friend to hold his coat. I grasped this fact as a means of playing for time.

'If we are to duel,' I said, 'we shall need seconds. Mine shall be Doctor Fidelis, who was with me below in the saloon. Permit me to go down and fetch him. At the same time you must nominate a friend of your own.'

He glowered.

'Friend? Is it not yet clear to you, Mr Coroner? I have none.'

'But think,' I said hurriedly. 'Without seconds, we cannot honourably fight. As a naval man you must appreciate how such things are arranged in civilized society.'

He was brought up short by this argument and the hand

that had thrust forward the reversed pistol dropped to his side. I considered immediately hurling myself at him but when his left hand went down, his right (as if counterbalanced) came up, this one holding the second pistol in the firing position. I was looking down its barrel.

'If you will not duel with me,' he said, his voice choking with emotion, 'then you give me no choice. I must kill you in cold blood, and then afterwards myself.'

'But think of your sister,' I protested. 'You know the legal penalties of suicide. She would be left destitute.'

He waved the firearm in a circle threateningly, and then showed me the one in his other hand.

'I shall do it with your weapon, sir, so that when we are discovered, they will assume death was by mutual shots, and that you killed me. That scheming creature, supposed by many to have been my wife, tried to do the same to me, you know: to have the world believe I killed her. Frightened to be put into unconsecrated ground. Feared being buried at the crossroads, with a peg malleted through her shrivelled heart.'

I had no time to reflect on these interesting words, for now Brockletower's resolve suddenly hardened. He straightened his arm and aimed the pistol directly at my face. The muzzle was three feet from me so that I found myself looking along the top of the barrel, past the cocking-hammer and his cuff, then straight along the arm to his eye, which was narrowed and concentrated on its target. I saw his thumb come up and hook itself over the hammer as, with a dry and, it seemed, unnaturally loud click, he cocked the piece. Breathing heavily, I took a reflexive step back, and then another, until I could go no further. My back was to the wall. I was now expecting to die in a matter of seconds as, like a lunging fencer, Brockletower came in pursuit by stamping smartly towards me once, and then again, to re-establish the yard of distance between his gun and my face.

But he was concentrating all his attention on me, and not on where he was placing his feet. He had also forgotten the bunch of pens he'd spilled a few minutes earlier so that, when his feet landed on them, he was unprepared for their roller-like effect. His feet slipped uncontrollably away from each other so that, with no time to adjust his balance, he teetered, his arms jerking and his head snapping up. A moment later he went flailing to the floor and, as he did so, the back of his head struck the corner of the table. At the same instant his finger pulled the trigger and the gun exploded with a deafening crack, the ball smacking into the ceiling. As the squire landed, the undischarged piece broke from his other hand and spun across the boards.

He lay still, stunned and bleeding from the head, with a look of staring incredulity on his face. I collected my wits, then scooped up the dropped pistol, and cocked it. I was still trembling and my heart thumped, though my fear was relieved. For a moment I was on the edge of killing him, until reason prevailed. I released the hammer and stooped to pick the key from Brockletower's breeches' pocket. With this I opened the door, stepped out and relocked. From the top of the stair I saw the landlord and a group of his customers looking O-mouthed up at me, brought from their pleasures by the sound of the shot. They spied the pistol in my hand and shrank back with a collective gasp.

'Are you well, sir?' called Noah Plumtree in an awed and trembling voice. 'We heard the shot. What has happened? Have you killed him?'

'I am well,' I replied, 'but Mr Brockletower is not. He is injured, though not by gunfire. He took leave of his senses and tried to shoot me, but accidentally fell. He struck his head and fired into the air. Go fetch a watchman to guard him until he is taken up. He's insane and will have to be arrested.'

Fidelis shouldered his way through the bodies jamming the doorway until he was standing at the stair-foot.

'Injured, is he?' he called out. 'I'm coming up, Titus.'

He took the stairs two at a time. Half a dozen others made to follow him, but I stopped them.

'Mr Plumtree!' I called, 'see to it that no one else comes up to the room.'

I unlocked the door and pushed it a few inches open.

'Mr Brockletower,' I called through the crack. 'I have brought the doctor to see to your wound.'

I pushed the door wide and we went in, looking around. The curtain billowed away from the casement, which was wide open, and the candlelight flashed and flickered in the draught. Of the squire, the only signs in the room were the open pistol-case still lying on the table and, on the floor beside it, a small pool of blood.

Chapter Twenty-seven

I LEANED OUT OF the window, with Luke beside me. A horse, hard-ridden, was clattering away towards Church Gate. I withdrew my head.

'He has gone. Back to Garlick, probably.'

'If, as you say, he's lost his reason, perhaps he should be pursued. He might endanger the people there.'

'He is out of his wits, all right. He admitted just now that he is Woodley's murderer. We shall send word to his sister through Mrs Marsden, explaining what's happened, and warning them to be on their guard. There are still Lord Derby's soldiers on hand, if need be.'

I stooped to the floor to pick up one of the pens that, a few minutes earlier, had saved my life. Gently Luke took it from my fingers.

'Your hands are shaking, Titus. You are still shocked. Let me write for you.'

Luke drew up a chair and sat down at the table. An inkpot, a stick of sealing wax and a sheaf of paper lay ready for use, and on the top sheet he immediately noticed a faint line of indentation.

'Someone wrote on the previous top sheet.'

He looked under the table and saw a waste-paper basket.

He reached inside and fetched out one crumpled sheet, which he flattened on the tabletop.

There was just one half-line of writing, in a scrawled hand. I leaned forward to read it. *Ephraim, I cannot sustain this. My way of life—* That was all.

'The squire wrote this before he sent for me. I wonder what it was he could not sustain?'

'Finishing the letter, anyway.'

'Maybe he abandoned this and drafted another,' I proposed.

'No. The indentation means this was the last sheet used. Now, at the time of writing, he expected to die shortly. This would have been his last statement.'

'But why was he addressing himself to the bailiff?'

'We must ask the bailiff, though I do not think he will help us.'

Luke flipped open the inkpot, squared up the paper and briskly wrote a note to Sarah Brockletower, which he sealed and handed to me. Then he rose and walked slowly around the room, noting everything he saw. He carefully examined one corner of the oak table.

'This is where he struck his head, isn't it?'

'Yes.'

'I can see the blood.'

Going downstairs, we found the Parkin brothers, Grimshaw's constables. Ignoring their knowing smirks, I stood them down, saying the danger was over. Then I gave the note Luke had written, with a shilling, to Noah Plumtree, who had a postboy on hand to ride with it express to Garlick Hall.

I felt a mixture of emotions. Though tingling with shock after my confrontation with death, I was at the same time profoundly tired. More surprisingly I felt hungry. I crossed the saloon to the table that Luke and I had occupied, picked up my cold, uneaten chop from where it lay in a congealed pool of fat, and walked with it to the door.

'I'm going home,' I told Fidelis, tearing off a chunk of meat with my mouth and chewing rapidly. 'This has been a long day.'

He walked with me up Turk's Head Court and towards the Guild Hall and Cheapside. It was a gentle evening, the air still as the light slipped into gloaming. Approaching my door I looked back in to Market Place, now empty but for the stall-holders' detritus, a few pedestrians criss-crossing its open space, and a figure I recognized sitting beside the water-fountain. I took Fidelis by the arm and guided him to follow me.

'Before I go in, there's someone over there I want you to meet.'

Peg Miller was crouching on the fountain steps, with a tin cup in front of her to collect alms. The cup was empty.

'Mistress Miller,' I said. 'I hope you remember me.'

She tilted her shrewd face towards me.

'You are the crowner.'

'I am. May I present my friend, Dr Fidelis?'

She responded to him with a lady-like inclination of the head. I noticed some of her clothing was also that of a lady, in particular a riding jacket, which rather hung about her, as it was several sizes too big. As were the good boots on her feet. I went on.

'I thought you and yours had left the vicinity. You struck camp at the Hall.'

'Mr Brockletower ordered us off Tuesday. He sent up his bulldog, Pearson. Mr Woodley'd already gone, and now I hear he's killed. I'm not sorry, except for there's never a penny of money for us, though they owed a month's wages. This is why I am waiting here, to see my Lord Mayor. I want justice.'

'Justice?'

'For my boy Sol that we buried back at Garlick Hall.'

'He has *escaped* justice, Peg. He was caught absconding with a body under inquest, which is a serious offence, you know. But now, after this accident, no one can touch him.'

'True, he has escaped. But I want justice against them that used him. And then I want payment of what is due for my man's work the past month.'

'Your man – Tom Piltdown?'

'Yes, him that *was* my man I should say. I've broke with him now, because I know what he did.'

'What did he do?'

'Mr Woodley knew. Now you shall have to ask Squire.'

Fidelis dropped to his haunches, so that his face was level with Peg's.

'Was Tom the father of Solomon?' he asked.

She turned her head to the side and spat.

'Never. I might have wished it. I been with him five year, and with Sol's father it were more like five minutes. I never even knew his name. And, if Tom were that lad's father, happen he'd have been kinder to him.'

'Was he unkind to Solomon, then?'

'I'll say no more till I see the Mayor.'

I took out my purse.

'Don't count on him seeing you,' I said, peering inside. 'And look out for a fat man in uniform called Mallender and his two ferrets, the Parkin brothers, whom he will surely set on you if he finds you here begging openly. But meanwhile I hope you will eat something.'

I dropped a crown into the cup.

'You're most welcome,' she said with simple grandeur.

'I see at any rate you have good clothes on your back, and

boots on your feet,' observed Fidelis, as he felt in his pocket and contributed a further shilling.

Peg Miller looked down and smoothed a crease in her jacket.

'These are the dead woman's clobber,' she said.

'Mrs Brockletower's?'

'Squire cleared out her wardrobe. Wanted rid of it. Sent a big roll of clothes and shoes up to the camp for us women to share around. The sizes are all too big for me, but clean and strong at least. The younger girls wanted her fine stuff – the ball gowns that look like they've never been worn, fancy undergarments, stockings. Silly. I like to keep warm, me.'

The conversation with Peg Miller had the effect of calming me. Going home I sat down in my fireside chair and told Elizabeth how I had met the Squire of Garlick Hall in the Turk's Head, and that he had tried to kill me. I was perfectly even-headed and able to make light of it: I had had a momentary brush with danger. That was all. A bad dream, and now over.

Nevertheless my wife rushed to the kitchen and brought me a cup of wine with a few hartshorn drops in it.

'It'll help the shock, Titus,' she said, sinking to the floor by my chair and resting her arms on my knees. 'Drink a bit and then I want to hear every detail of what happened.'

So I told her, ending with an account of my encounter in Market Place.

'I was wrong about Peg,' I admitted.

'How wrong, Titus?'

'I was wrong when I said she would be philosophical about her Solomon's death. She is not. She is angry and she has come to haunt the town, wanting justice.'

'That's what I thought she would be like. A mother. But what kind of justice can she get?'

'None. No one will listen. There is no justice for people like her; not for those that haven't a threshold to cross at night-fall.'

'Nor for many of those that have.'

'Maybe not. But there's another reason also. When he died, Solomon Miller had himself been wanted for the crime of stealing a corpse. It hung over him as heavy and deadly as the block of stone that actually hanged him.'

'He was not really guilty, though. He was a simpleton and put up to it.'

'That's true. The immediate instigator was Tom Piltdown, the ganger who lived with Peg. She's broken with him now, because she says he took advantage of her idiot boy. But don't think the likes of Ephraim Grimshaw are going to pursue a charge like that. Piltdown is gone. The trail of accusation reaches above his head to Woodley – who's gone too – and then as far as the squire. Grimshaw regards himself as hand-in-glove with the gentry. He won't agree to cudgel Brockletower on Peg Miller's say-so, you can be sure of that.'

'Well, from what you say, the squire has done a good job of self-cudgelling. He killed Woodley and admitted it. Now he's running.'

I lifted my glass and drained it, then yawned deeply.

'Running? I wonder if he can. He is desperate but he is also injured. I say he will be found, but the question is, what will he do when they have him at bay?'

The hartshorn drops did their work. I slept well, and dreamlessly, and awoke early, feeling refreshed and ready for the resumed inquest at Yolland. Over breakfast I determined in my mind how to proceed. Brockletower's madness the previous night was more than a brainstorm or temporary aberration.

There was no chance he would be able to continue his evidence. So I would call Sarah, his sister, and Fidelis as witnesses. Fidelis would tell just what he had found in his examination post-mortem. Whatever happened I reckoned it was going to be a day of revelations.

For once Fidelis was at my door before I was ready to leave, carrying his medical bag. He took me aside and felt my pulse, then examined my eyes. I told him I was quite well and felt no after-effects from the evening before. After laughing at my belief in the hartshorn, he seemed satisfied, and we rode away together. I explained how I would conduct the business, and then we reverted to the subject of my frightening interview with Brockletower in the Turk's Head.

'At one point, he was raving about Shakespeare's *Moor of Venice*. Thought he was Othello himself, and Dolores was Desdemona.'

'And was there a Jago in the plot?'

'He implied it was Woodley, which I too have suspected.'

'Have you? Maybe the real Jago was inside himself: at some point that part of him turned against the very thing about Dolores that before had fascinated him. Her monstrousness. It was all very well in alien Jamaica, but just try to domesticate it here, in Lancashire, and the case is hopeless.'

Fidelis gave a single, heartless laugh.

'I think, in the first instance, his intentions towards her were not criminal,' I said. 'He raged against humanity more hotly than Dean Swift, but he didn't want to kill his wife. He wanted her back in the West Indies, and out of his way.'

'So we already know he didn't kill her personally, and now you're saying he didn't order her killing either.'

'I am certain he did not. She had come to fear him as much as he hated her but her fear was more bitter than his hatred.'

'That is part of the reason she left the words from the *Tatler* story in her commonplace book about the souls of men and women being different. "Imagine therefore: my pain and fear". It must have been bad for her, Titus. A war in her nature – half man, half woman. That is why she wanted us to imagine her pain and fear.'

'Yet there is more to it than that,' I said. 'She gave her husband the Eustace story to read. Brockletower believes she wanted him to kill her just as Eustace did in the story. She wanted not only to die, but him to kill her and pay for it with his own life. This is the darkest of the secrets we've uncovered. But since Brockletower did not kill her, even that doesn't tell us how she died.'

'And you are heading in a straight line for the finding of murder by person or persons unknown.'

'So it looks. That's better than self-murder, but an empty assertion all the same. I wish we could avoid it.'

We arrived at Gamull where, like a wraith fated to haunt me whenever I passed through, I saw the wizened, hag-like form of Miriam Patten standing in the road.

'Stop!' she croaked.

'Are you not coming over to the inquest today, Miriam?' I asked. 'I saw you there yesterday.'

She stood before us with her legs parted and her bony arms flung out sideways as if trying to turn a running pig.

'Eh, Mr Cragg, there's cause for another now,' she called out.

'Another? Another what?'

We pulled up our horses to hear her better.

'They sent word,' she said. 'I been told to wait and divert you.' Fidelis laughed.

'Divert us, Miriam? What are you going to do, sing "Tom Bowling"?'

'You what?'

She cupped her hand behind her ear, looking puzzled and twitching her head slightly to the right, then the left, and then back again.

'You say there's cause for another,' I said. 'Another what?'

'Of your inquests, they're saying, and you must go again to the hollow oak. They've found Squire lying there.'

I looked at Fidelis, then turned back to Miriam.

'*At the hollow tree in Fulwood?*'

'You heard. So they sent word that I must wait for you, and tell you.'

To my old cob's great surprise I gave her a double kick and urged her into a slow and stately, but palpable, gallop towards the Fulwood.

It was still not nine o'clock when we came to the hollow oak, our mounts blowing hard. William Pearson, with two others, stood below it, but it was what lay at their feet that compelled the attention. Here, on more or less exactly the spot where Dolores Brockletower had fallen less than a week earlier, was the body of her husband, not lying flat but twisted around, with his face turned upward and his eyes staring open in a look of frozen surprise.

An old man and woman, dressed in filthy rags, stood nervously by, he protectively gripping her by the arm. These were the finders. I dismounted and approached to question them. The pair were a married couple who had been gathering wood with their granddaughter, so they said. More likely it was setting illegal rabbit-snares that had brought them so deep into the forest. In either event, they had found the squire lying on the ground and sent their granddaughter running for help while they stayed to mind the body.

'Did you recognize the man?'

'We did that. It's Squire.'

'Where is your granddaughter now?'

'After she brought Mr Pearson here from Hall, he sent her away to find you, sir. First she went to leave word at Gamull for you to come here, instead of going to Yolland. Then she will have run on to Yolland in case you had already passed through.'

'And what time did you find him?'

The old man gave his wife an apprehensive look.

'What d'you mean, time?' he asked cautiously.

'Of the clock.'

He looked at me as if I were mad.

'There's no clock here, sir. We're in woods.'

'I know that, man! But was it before or after sunrise?'

'Half hour after, no more,' he said.

That meant about three hours ago.

'Did you touch the body at all? Was it warm, or cold?'

'Oh no, no! We didn't touch it. We wouldn't dare touch it.'

'Well, was his horse nearby?'

'Yes, I caught it. It were picking grass, on top of that bank. I tethered it and it's still there.'

He indicated a place fifty yards away, where the forest floor rose to a clearing that was covered with grazing. I saw and recognized the horse as Squire Brockletower's.

I circled the body and crouched to go through his pockets. I rolled the body over to get at the right-side pocket of his coat, which was lying under him. It contained a pistol, apparently the one he had picked up from the floor at the coffee house. It was not loaded. Nor had it been cleaned since its last firing – which I presumed to have been the accidental discharge at the Turk's Head. I pushed the pistol into my belt and investigated the breast pocket. It contained a letter, the seal broken and the handwriting not the squire's. I stood up.

'Luke, can you tell the manner of death?'

Fidelis took my place beside the body and began his examination by opening the squire's clothing. I unfolded the paper I had found, and began reading silently to myself.

My dear sir, consider it! You were born to enjoy more worthy attachments than you ever had with that thing. I can well comprehend the hold a person like her – or him – no, let's say 'it' – gained over one such as yourself, but . . .

Luke Fidelis remained busy over the body but Pearson and the old pair had been drawn towards me like cows to a gate, and were looking curiously down on the paper in my hands. To the two old ones the letter could mean nothing, however closely they inspected it, but Pearson might have read it. So I walked away from them among the trees.

. . . but soon, in place of the attractive idea you encountered in Jamaica, you had perforce to accommodate the unattractive person here in Lancashire. And, having done so, you received less and less, and eventually nothing at all, of pleasure, so that at last you had only an impediment to pleasure. Well now, the impediment is removed! All that remains wanting is assurance that no person shall ever know the truth of it. I can give you that assurance. I have the truth stowed and safe from all eyes. All that remains is for your recompense to seal it up for ever. Five hundred guineas shall satisfy us both and the rascally coroner shall never find the truth.

His conclusions, should he do so, would expose the great secret to the world and surely end all your interest in Jamaican sugar. You will be hounded from society, from the county. You know you have my undivided loyalty always. Five hundred will do it! Your most affct friend, Barnabus Woodley.

Quickly I folded the extortionate letter and stuffed it into my coat. 'Rascally coroner', indeed! I returned to the others, who stood craning towards me, expecting to hear something of the contents of the paper. Instead I asked Fidelis what he concluded.

'There's a head injury, which has been bleeding. It must be the one he got when he slipped last night and his head struck the corner of the table. Also an arm appears to be broken and he has an injury to his cheek and chin – probably done by falling from the horse. But most important there is a bullet wound.'

'He was shot?'

'Yes. In the belly. The ball came out through his back. It is almost certainly what killed him.'

He pulled back the coat and I could see a blackened and blood-stained hole in the lining. I pulled the pistol out.

'Don't tell me he discharged this in his pocket?'

Luke shook his head.

'Yes, but he may not have done so deliberately. I think he fell from his horse and the gun went off when he hit the ground.'

'Or he was thrown.'

'Fell, I think. He had taken a severe blow to the head. He probably fainted; perhaps the injury caused a bleed within the brain. Such a thing is more likely under the pressure of strong emotions.'

I sighed.

'So he may have got what he wanted, after all. Accidental death.'

'But what brought him here, Titus? To this place, of all places?'

'Maybe he intended to shoot himself here, on the spot where Dolores had died. As a kind of . . . what shall we call it? A poetic resolution of all his entanglements. He certainly deliberately re-loaded the piece. It had been discharged when he picked it off the floor at the Turk's Head.'

I instructed Pearson to ride fast to Garlick Hall. He must let them know what had happened and if possible prevent Sarah from leaving for the inquest, then return to meet me at the hollow oak. Meanwhile I direly warned the two ancients of their duty to keep a watch over the corpse until I or Pearson returned, however long that might be.

With these orders I set a course for events to repeat with some precision those of a week earlier. What had been done then for the wife, had to be done now for the husband: a watch put on the body; an urgent message sent up to Garlick Hall; instructions given to prepare the Ice-house for a second tenant. There was no need this time, however, for a tumbril to be trundled up the road. The squire's horse might not have been bred to pack duties, but to carry the remains home was a last service he could do for his master.

There was another difference between now and then. Hurrying away with Fidelis to Yolland, I set my duties out in a clear arrangement one by one, like ninepins in the alley. The squire had died, as had his wife, within my jurisdiction. I had been summoned to the corpse according to the correct form, and it was plain that an inquest would be needed. Well, as luck would have it, one was already sitting. I only had to splice the two hearings together by swearing the existing jury anew on this second matter, and I could proceed without delay to show them the second corpse at the ideal location for its viewing – the site where it was found. There would be, as far as I knew, nothing irregular in that, though Furzey with his long forensic memory would be quick enough to tell me if there were.

Chapter Twenty-eight

WE ARRIVED AT the Plough Inn, several minutes after nine, to find that Furzey had not only caused the doors of Wigglesworth's public room to be unlocked, but had let in the public. Their number was vastly greater than on the previous morning, and so was the hubbub: it was clear that the peasant granddaughter, arriving ahead of me, had spread the momentous news of a fourth death connected to Garlick Hall. My first concern, then, was whether Sarah was here, and knew her brother's fate.

There were still people crowded around the door, trying to force the entrance to the inquest, although the room inside was already at capacity. As I approached I saw Bailiff Grimshaw in the ruck. As the latecomers barged and brayed around him, his gold-braided hat was pitching and bobbing like a cockboat.

'Cragg!' he bellowed, catching sight of me and jabbing the air with a stubby finger. 'I hold you responsible for this disorderly mob.'

I waved at him cheerfully, as if I had not caught his meaning, and skirted round the pack until I found Wigglesworth.

'I hope Miss Brockletower hasn't come yet,' I said, raising my voice to be heard.

The landlord leaned close to my ear.

'In my parlour, sir.'

'Oh! Then I had better go in to her. Later I would like to wagon my jury a distance of some two and a half miles. Is your passenger-vehicle available for use today?'

'It is that, sir. I can have horses between the shafts in ten or fifteen minutes.'

'Will you do that, please?'

Wigglesworth seemed reluctant.

'At whose expense would that be, sir?' he asked. 'At your own?'

'No, no! The town will pay out of coroner's expenses. Add it to the account you submit with the hire of the room.'

Sarah was sitting beside the fire with the dog Jonathan and her maid Honor. She had not removed her cape and bonnet, nor lifted the black veil that hid her face. I had come in without announcement, but she knew at once it was I.

'Titus,' she said in a clear, high, strained voice. 'When you come to visit me it is always to give news of another fatality. I am beginning to think of you as an angel of death.'

A number of stools were stacked in a corner behind the parlour door. I lifted one of them down and placed it beside her chair.

'Angel of death!' I said, lowering myself onto the stool. 'That is a new way of describing a coroner. So you already know what has happened?'

'I've heard that my poor brother has been discovered in the woods at the same spot, and in the same condition, as his wife was found last week. Is it true?'

'I'm afraid so. He is dead.'

I wished I could see her face to read its expression. But the veil was impenetrable.

'So death still sits on the roof of our house. First Dolores, then Woodley and the idiot labouring man, and now poor Ramilles. If I wept for him, I would have good reason.'

'You are veiled, Sarah. But I think you do not weep.'

My remark was presumptuous but Sarah seemed pleased.

'You are right, I don't weep. As his sister I should, but these poor eyes are good for nothing, it seems, not even shedding tears.'

'Tears can do Ramilles no good now. You must look to yourself.'

She turned her head sharply towards me.

'*Look*, Titus? Must I *look*?'

'You know what I mean.'

She sighed with a long out-breath, and followed it with a reflective silence.

'So much of language is taken up with looking and seeing,' she said at last. 'Most people don't notice, but I mark every instance as soon as it hits my ear. See here! Kind regards! In my view. I'll look after you.'

She gave another sigh, but more business-like.

'Who will look after me now, Titus? I have hopeless prospects.'

She gave a single, bitter laugh.

'And there's another instance,' she said. 'Prospects!'

'You have no reason to abandon hope, Sarah.'

'Then tell me without equivocating, has my brother taken his own life? I need to know, for if he has, I am ruined.'

'It isn't for me to rule on whether he did or not,' I said, with a glance at the maid, who sat demurely looking into the fire. She was listening intently, though pretending not to. 'There will be another inquest and the jury will decide.'

'Then tell me exactly what you know.'

323

So I told her, not sparing any of the detail of the previous night's events at the Turk's Head, nor of what had been later found in the woods.

When I had finished, she said, 'I am touched that Ramilles thought of me, and held back at first from the awful act of suicide. But I am very sorry he tried to force you to do the office for him.'

'Well, I am a public servant, after all.'

'Is that an attempt at levity, Titus?'

'I am sorry. It is because I find it difficult to tell you the truth. I'm afraid it is possible that the inquest jury will find for suicide, after all. He died by the shot of his own gun, you see.'

I heard the sound of the long-case clock in the passageway striking the half-hour. Sarah did not comment and at that moment I made a pledge which, looking back, still frightens me.

'But you must trust me, Sarah,' I said. 'You will not go destitute. I will make sure of it. But I need to leave you now. The inquest on Dolores must continue, and that on your brother must begin.'

There was still uproar in the inquest room. Forcing my way in, I quickly briefed Furzey, then returned to my chair and hammered them all down to silence.

'As everyone already appears to know,' I said, 'Squire Brockletower has been found dead. I have already been called to the body, and have determined that an inquest is required. Since we are already in the midst of such a process on Mr Brockletower's wife, I propose to swear this same jury on the new matter and allow the two hearings to continue in parallel. Let's proceed.'

I then turned to the jury and swore them one by one, as

before. The excitable Pimlott's mouth was working, as if chewing on something very hot. Of the others, Gumble, who I knew had hated Brockletower, looked anxious. He might not have liked the terms of his tenancy, but the uncertainty of change appealed even less. The reserve juror Tom Avery, on the other hand, appeared exultant. I was glad he was not a voting member, for his fanaticism would surely have distorted any verdict out of recognition.

I now addressed the court again, formally adjourning the hearing until such time as the jury had viewed this latest body. The bailiff, who had bullied his way into a seat near the front, immediately rose to his feet. He was bristling and (when he spoke) booming. He had come all this way expressly from Preston to hear the evidence, and he demanded to know if he was to be kept waiting all day, and if so why? I carefully controlled and articulated my reply for all to hear.

'Mr Grimshaw, may I explain? All excepting the jurors and the notified witnesses are at liberty to return to their homes and businesses. Their waiting in this room is neither legally required nor (in these numbers) particularly desired, though they are welcome as ever to stay for the outcome, if they so wish and have the leisure. But let it be always remembered, please, that the pace of this inquiry is not set for their convenience, but in the interests of finding the truth. Now, let us get on.'

Grimshaw's mouth worked open and shut, but there was nothing he could say. Deflated, he sat down while I beckoned the jurors to follow me out to the waiting wagon.

Wigglesworth's wagon was furnished with a wide bench seat running lengthwise down its centre, so that the passengers, ranged in two rows back to back, could sit looking outwards at the passing scene. I hoped the arrangement would discourage them from disputing with each other. Once Pennyfold had disposed them in their places, I mounted my horse and signalled to the driver to follow behind me along the road. For several hundred yards a small crew of village children trailed us, dancing along and shouting. Some tried to clamber onto the wagon's tailgate, only to be cuffed off by the backs of the passengers' hands.

As we passed the vicarage I suddenly had the idea that I would go in to the Reverend Brockletower, to advise him of his nephew's fate, and perhaps see if he could throw any light on it. I sent the wagon on ahead, saying I would catch them up.

A servant in a mob-cap and holding a feather duster opened the front door.

'He's in his study, sir,' she told me when I'd enquired after her master. 'Though whether you'll get any sense out of him, I doubt. Been there all night, he has.'

She showed me to the study door and I went in. The room was curtained and the fire had died. The priest lay on the hearthrug flat out and unwigged with his round stomach upwards, his legs splayed and his mouth open, snoring gently. A spilled stem-glass lay on the carpet near his hand. An empty decanter stood on the little table beside his fireside chair. Two equally empty port wine bottles had been placed together on the mantel-shelf and below them, in the hearth, lay a mess of broken tobacco pipes.

The Brockletowers, I thought, contemplating this sight, had been a blighted family indeed: their young head given to anger and unnatural attachments, and regarded as a tyrant by his tenants; his sister stone blind; his clergyman uncle an incapable sot.

'Ahem.'

I coughed into my fist, as loudly as possible. The recumbent parson did not stir. I called more loudly.

'Mr Brockletower, sir?'

With a snort he came awake and the eye nearest to me rolled open, followed by its companion. Both eyeballs were bulbous and mottled with all the yellows and pinks that might conceivably be available on the largest of Mr Winstanley's palettes. After a moment's dazed reflection the Reverend Brockletower groaned and began levering himself up until he was hoisted on one elbow. He blinked at me without recognition.

'Mr Brockletower,' I said, 'it is Coroner Cragg. How do you do?'

He rubbed his free hand across his face, rasping the stubble of his beard.

'How do I do? How do I do? I'm sorry, but at this moment I don't, sir. And shall not for some hours. Too much port after dinner, you know. That's all it is.'

'Well, I have called to enquire if you've heard anything of Ramilles.'

He looked at me as if through fogged eyes.

'Ram, is it? My nephew? Take a seat, take a seat! Have I heard from him? Let me think. Yes, yes. He was here. Of course he was. That was last night. He rode here like a fury. He would not drink, all he wanted to do was talk. It's all coming back to me. He talked like a maniac. He accused me of breach of confidence and telling mischievous tales about him and then he said I had killed him. *Killed* him? I said how could I have killed him when he stood before me as full of life as a March hare. But he kept saying it – I'd killed him, I'd killed him.'

Suddenly the Reverend Brockletower's mouth dropped down at the sides and, turning his head away, he squinted into the farthest corner of the room.

'Or did he? Did he *really*? Perhaps I dreamed the whole thing, lying here on the floor. These details certainly resemble those of a nightmare, but I do not remember. Too much port after dinner, eh? I can't be absolutely sure that it isn't making me lose my mind.'

I hastened to reassure him.

'I saw him at a coffee house in town last night, sir. He told me he had been with you, so I think you may comfort yourself, at least, that your mind is not playing tricks. And, after he visited you, he was in a peculiarly deranged state in the evening, by which time I saw him.'

'But what did he say to you? Did he accuse me of killing him?'

'Comfort yourself, sir, he did not. However, I am very much afraid you must prepare yourself, for your nephew is indeed dead. They found him at daybreak in the Fulwood. It was the same spot where his unfortunate wife was discovered. But it was an accident, I hope.'

The vicar put his hands to his cheeks.

'Oh! Oh! Dead, is he? Not dead! Oh! Poor boy! Poor boy!'

Sitting there on the floor, he moved the hands towards each other until they covered his whole face and slowly lowered his head onto his knees. I said a few words of condolence, to which he did not respond. So I turned to the door and quietly turned the knob. I could still hear the muffled lamentation as, retreating across the hall, I let myself out.

When I caught up with the jury, the village children had given up the chase, and the wagon was jolting along without its ushers. Its passengers were arguing loudly about the relative merits of two prizefighters, the Long Ridge Lammer and a Garstang man known only as the Churchwarden, who were due to meet in combat the following week in a tent on Town Moor. So much for my hope that the seating arrangement would pacify the jurymen, but I left them to talk, for I had heard a horse galloping to catch up with us. It was Luke Fidelis.

'Luke!' I cried. 'We are going to view the body *in situ mortis*. Come with us.'

So Fidelis and I trotted side by side along the Preston road, as the argument about whether the Lammer's granite jaw would prove susceptible to the Churchwarden's cast-iron fist, lurched and swayed along behind us.

I find that puzzles are either canine or feline. Some are like a dog that barks and wants to play. The dog runs and leaps around, just out of reach, but you can be confident that, sooner rather than later, it will tire and be mastered. Much worse are the problems that retreat from you, like a cat that creeps under your garden shed. No amount of cajoling will bring it to hand. No words or foodstuffs are sweet enough to persuade it out. The only thing is to go about some other business and only then will it emerge into the light and lap the milk you left for it.

The problem I was presented with at the start of this narrative – the bloody death of Dolores Brockletower – had been of the feline kind. The more strenuously I had pursued the solution, the more elusive it became. Only as the means of her husband's death preoccupied me would I stumble upon exactly how his wife had died.

As we came in sight of the tongue of the Fulwood that licks across the Yolland road I was worrying over this question of Brockletower's death. I told Fidelis of the decision I had made while speaking with Sarah: to do all I could for her sake to deflect the jury from such a verdict.

'The difficulty is that there is evidence for it. His life was manifestly in great disorder. In addition to which he told me he wanted to end it.'

After a moment's consideration, Luke made an astute remark.

'He must have been forced to a choice by Woodley's letter. He could not actually pay Woodley – that would have been an impossible indignity. But Woodley's demands made him realize his life's continuance was now impossible.'

'Yes. But, though he could kill Woodley, he could not kill himself. Someone else had to do it. Last night he was trying to persuade me to blow his brains out for him, in return for having mine blown out simultaneously – not much of a bargain. Yet it seems he had already developed a deranged alternative: a conviction that Uncle Oliver was his real murderer.'

'The vicar?'

'Yes, the vicar, whom I have just been to see.'

I told Luke how I had called at the vicarage and discovered its crapulous tenant. He asked me to repeat exactly what Oliver Brockletower had said about his nephew's accusation.

'Of course,' I added after doing so, 'he'd already guessed his uncle had betrayed him by telling me about his desire for a divorce.'

'A betrayal that might have led to his being reasonably suspected of her murder,' said Luke. 'And to the publication of details about her unusual physical nature. Either event might have been enough to drive him to seek his own death, an event traceable back to his uncle's indiscretion when he talked to you in the churchyard. In which case, he would have been "killed" by his uncle. Have I got it right, Titus?'

'It is the construction I put on it.'

Luke leaned forward and clapped his hand repeatedly against his horse's neck, in sheer delight.

'The capacity of the human mind for deluding itself is truly wonderful,' he crowed. 'You would think if there is one person we should each be able to rely on never to lie to us, it would be ourselves. But it isn't the case. We constantly abuse our own trust.'

We drew close to the belt of trees through which the road passed. Compared with the previous week, they were greening doubly fast now in the spring sunshine. From within, where the road curved around, I heard the sound of the woodsmen, whom I had encountered the previous Friday and whom, when we rounded the bend, we came upon, still sawing and loading wood from the great beech tree they had felled.

I caught sight of Shipkin and rode straight across to him. Having been given his evidence on the inquest's first day, I had exempted him from attending the second. But I was surprised to see him working all the same.

'Have you not heard the news of your master?' I asked when I reached him.

'We've heard,' the woodsman growled, as he moved crab-wise around an enormous bundle of logs, testing the knots in the ropes that bound it. 'But we still must see to the timber, before it rots.'

The men had erected a triangular structure of spars to make a crane or hoist. They were about to haul the logs into the air before swinging them over and dropping them onto the bed of the wagon. The structure consisted of three spars forming a tripod, from the apex of which was suspended asymmetrically a beam that could be raised and lowered by means of a pulley. One end of the beam was to be attached to the load while the other, the longer end, was for controlling – lifting, swinging, lowering – the logs as required, using Archimedes's law of leverage. I had of course seen such contraptions before, and paid little attention to this one.

I cannot say how the idea came to me. I had said goodbye to

the woodsmen as they began hauling the load of logs into the air. I could hear behind me the squeak of the pulley and the rope creaking as I regained the road, where Luke and the jury on their wagon were moving off again. We made a few hundred yards more when suddenly I remembered what Ramilles Brockletower said to me about his wife's intention. *To have the world believe that he killed her.* With the squeak of the woodsmen's pulley still in my ears I stopped my horse. Another image had come into my head, as if lit by a flash of light: Solomon Miller being plucked into the air by the builders' rope.

Immediately I wheeled my horse again and cantered back to the woodsmen.

'Shipkin!' I called. 'Will you lend me your axe?'

Chapter Twenty-nine

WE LEFT THE wagon in a sunken lane that skirted the edge of the Fulwood, about a quarter of a mile from our destination. Led by Fidelis and myself, the jurors plunged down through the trees, dead twigs popping like small firecrackers under our feet. Having given up the prizefighting argument, the group was murmuring together as uneasily as a gaggle of driven geese.

We came to the clearing where Ramilles Brockletower's body had been found and was still lying, close by the dead oak. I looked at the tree itself, up and down, and felt a thump of excitement in my chest. But that matter would have to wait. The prime reason for our journey must come first.

The two finders of the body were sitting side by side on the stump of another old tree, as far as possible across the clearing from the body. They had unfurled a chequered cloth in front of them and were eating the sort of oatmeal rock that passes for bread amongst the poor, and a couple of cold boiled turnips. The old man still had a few teeth. He bit off a chunk of turnip and masticated doggedly until I saw him hook the food out of his mouth with a grimy forefinger, and pass it to his toothless wife. She took it gratefully, gummed it for a few moments, then swallowed with a great show of satisfaction, smacking her lips. Quite unreasonably, the sight revolted me.

'Are you not ashamed to be feasting in this solemn place of death?' I asked sternly.

I knew as soon as I had spoken that my words were ridiculous, but it was too late.

The woman cackled with laughter. 'Feasting, you call it?'

'I mean, would you eat in . . . well, in church, woman?'

She looked around her.

'*Church*, you call it?'

Her consort, swallowing his own mouthful, put a warning hand on her arm, then turned to me.

'You've been hours coming back to us,' he grumbled. 'I tell you, without us eating, there'd be a couple more bodies here for you to find.'

'You exaggerate. There is such a thing as self-control, I believe.'

'Yer, and there's such a thing as starvation, an'all.'

The argument had no point and I gave it up, beckoning to the jury to gather around.

'Since we are all present,' I told them, 'we will reconstitute the court *ad hoc* and take evidence from Jeremiah Holden here, who, with this woman, was first finder of the body of Mr Ramilles Brockletower. For the purposes of the moment I will double as Coroner and clerk. Are you all agreed?'

There were murmurs of assent. Although this was not regular procedure, a coroner's powers of variation are not negligible and I could see every reason to proceed in this way. It would save time and some money.

'Tom!' I called, beckoning to pious Tom Avery, the reserve juror. 'You have a pocket scripture about you, I am sure.'

Avery felt in his coat pocket and reverently produced a handy volume.

'It is but the Pentateuch, Coroner.'

'That'll do. It's Holy Writ, and doesn't have to be the entire Bible. Jeremiah, place your hand on this book, and repeat after me.'

So I swore Jeremiah Holden as a witness. Then I asked him to tell us when, and how, he and his woman had found the body, what state it was in and what they did about it. After he had given his account, I walked the jurors across to where the body lay. We examined the head wound.

I told how I had witnessed the accident and added, 'Dr Fidelis will tell us that, having sustained the break to his head, he would have been in danger of fainting at any time, especially if seized by great emotion. Under this danger he rode here, who knows why? It is enough to remember that this is where his wife died on the Tuesday of last week. Once here, he suffered a fit caused by his injured skull, fell from his horse and on impact the gun in his pocket went off. So he died, to be discovered some time later by Mr Holden and his wife. Now, of course, it is not for me to determine if this is true. It is for you. But that is how I suggest it happened.'

Through all this I had not mentioned the letter that I'd also found in Brockletower's pocket. In its way, it was material and perhaps I should have placed it before the jury. But I did not, and was prepared to bear the consequences of that decision, should there be any. But, I reasoned, the deaths of the Brockletowers were simple facts, and could in plain truth be simply accounted for by publicly known facts. The secret ramifications around them were complications and curlicues, and better safely out of sight, I reasoned. For a lawyer, avoiding the unpredictable is a matter of instinct.

Besides all this, I was impatient now to get back to the

hollow tree. So I dismissed the Holdens and invited the jurors to gather around the oak.

I picked up Shipkin's axe and began hacking a hole in the tree's bole, a little less than three feet off the ground, just above where the bole had thickened and bulged, as happens to old trees near the ground. I was making hard work of it and after a few chops, Pennyfold stepped forward and held his hand out for the axe.

'I can see you are not an axeman, Coroner. Let me.'

I thanked him and asked for a hole large enough to reach into. Soon he stood back, having opened a triangular slot big enough to take a man's hand and arm. Bending and squinting, I could see nothing inside. The hollow interior was dark.

'Anthony, would you be good enough to feel inside the tree? Your arm is longer than mine.'

Maybridge shrank back.

'Not me, Coroner! There may be vipers, or worse.'

'Very well. Has anyone got a candle?'

Peter Gardner had. He drew it from his pocket with a tinder-box and struck a light. I held the lighted candle inside the tree and could see glints of reflected light, but they were out of reach.

'There's something there. It is a job for someone with longer arms than mine.'

The jury looked at each other. None fancied it. Then, with an expression of amused sufferance, Fidelis pushed through the crowd, holding his riding crop, with its hooked ivory handle. He knelt and used the light to inspect the dark interior, then thrust his hand and crop, hook end first, through the hole. He cast about for a moment and then withdrew the crop, put it down and felt inside with his hand once more. This time it came out holding a horseshoe.

In my pocket was the shoe that had been found cast aside near Dolores Brockletower's body. Immediately I produced this and held it beside Fidelis's.

'Are they from the same source, George?' I asked.

Pennyfold took a close look and nodded his head.

'And I reckon they're my work,' he said.

'The one from the tree has a line tied to it,' said Fidelis.

A green line, like a fishing line, was tied neatly around the exact middle of the shoe, with its other end still lying inside the tree. Fidelis dropped the horseshoe on the ground and began drawing the line out. With about ten feet smoothly and rapidly withdrawn, it snagged. Fidelis put his hand back into the hole and felt down the inner wall of the trunk.

'Ah! What's this?'

When he pulled his hand out again, it was holding the very thing I now expected: one half of a pair of scissors, attached to the end of the line through the finger-loop.

'Be careful,' I warned, 'the blade is sharp.'

But Luke could see that. He was examining the blade closely, turning it in the light.

'Feel inside the tree again,' I urged. 'I rather fancy you may find another. But be cautious.'

After further exploration, the doctor's hand came out again and it was now holding two more horseshoes, tied together at the end of another length of line. Pennyfold confirmed they were identical to the others.

'Pull on the line! Pull on it!' I exclaimed.

And securely fastened at the extreme end of this second line was, as I knew it would be, the other half of the scissors.

'This one is different,' Luke stated calmly, examining the second blade as carefully as the first. 'It is stained.'

'What with?' I asked, though I knew the answer.

'It might be blood,' he said tentatively. 'Dried blood.'

'That is exactly what I think it is,' I said, quite unable by now to conceal my satisfaction.

Thoughtfully, Luke turned the blade in his fingers once more. Then he turned back to me with sudden vitality.

'Of course, of course! I've been slow-witted about this. It is the blade that cut her throat. Of *course*!' In Fidelis's voice was a mixture of awe and surprise.

One member of the jury swore, another whistled.

'So,' I said, 'how come it is in the tree, on the end of a line? Can anyone tell? Can you, Doctor Fidelis?'

Fidelis frowned, thinking furiously. Suddenly his face brightened.

'Yes! How dull I am! She cut her own throat, but she wanted to leave no trace. She contrived a way of making the blade disappear as soon as it had done its work! Come on – we can prove it.'

He pushed the circling jurymen aside and ran to his horse. A moment later he was in the saddle, walking the horse back to the tree. Reaching down, he held out his hand and I gave him the two horseshoes and the blade, which were still connected by the length of line. He stood up in his saddle, steadying himself by holding the tree, and then reached up as far as a round hole, a foot across, where a large branch had once been attached. Through this, he dropped the horseshoes.

Watched by the open-mouthed jury, he lowered himself again into the saddle, still holding the half-scissors. The line tied to them was tautened by the weight of the horseshoes dangling inside the tree.

'Do it, Luke,' I said. 'Let go the blade.'

He let go and it flew up at once, out of his fingers, being instantly dragged into the tree by the two horseshoes falling inside. We heard the clunk of them as they hit the ground, and then a lighter thump as the blade itself fell beside them.

Fidelis reached through the aperture made by Shipkin, and brought out the evidence a second time. He studied the horseshoes and blade as they lay in the palm of his right hand. With his left he picked up the other blade and horseshoe from where they lay on the ground, and weighed the two of them thoughtfully.

'The second blade's puzzling me,' said Abel Plint, 'what's *it* doing in the tree?'

'A pair of scissors has two blades,' I said.

'Yes, but she only needed one to kill herself with.'

'And why does the first have two weights on the end of its line?' asked Peter Gardner, 'and the second only one weight?'

'I do not think the blade in your left hand was the second, but the first,' said Luke, quick as ever to perceive the truth.

'Why's that, sir?' asked Thomas Thorne.

'It was a trial throw. The single horseshoe was slung through the hole on the end of its line into the hollow trunk. The blade was then released to see if it would indeed disappear safely into the tree-trunk. The test went well enough, but it was judged better, the second fateful time, to double the weight. Just to make sure the blade did not catch at the lip of the hole.'

I clapped him on the shoulder.

'And the horsehoe we found near the body?' I prompted.

'The fourth of the set. She threw it aside because it wasn't needed.'

As I spoke I heard the cracking of twigs, and two voices, from lower down in the wood. Pearson was with us at last.

'Luke, will you drop these items into your medical bag, just for the time being?' I said in a low voice. 'We will say nothing of this until we are back in court.'

'Who's with Pearson?' asked Fidelis.

I listened again.

'Well, by the sound of it, it is Mr Grimshaw, the bailiff, come to visit us.'

Chapter Thirty

Pᴇᴀʀsᴏɴ, ᴀs ɪᴛ ʜᴀᴘᴘᴇɴᴇᴅ, had received a message from the bailiff at Garlick Hall. He was to await Grimshaw, and be at his disposal, for the bailiff wanted to see for himself the spot where Ramilles Brockletower met his death. But before I could hear these details from Pearson himself, Grimshaw's finger was pointing, and his complaint was directed at me.

'I am surprised at you, Cragg, surprised beyond measure. Is this the way to conduct Coroner's business, traipsing off in the woods with your jury? One would think they were here for a picnic or some other diversion. And then you expect the borough to meet your fee.'

I shrugged. My inquest fee was always the same, a paltry thirteen shillings and fourpence, fixed by statute in 1487. Every inquest in the land was subsidized out of the coroner's own pocket: only men with successful legal practices, or private means, could afford to do the work.

'I expect only what the law allows me,' I said. 'But you will be glad to know that our business in this place is concluded.'

Grimshaw's curiosity was aroused.

'With what consequence? You must tell me!'

'I fear these are matters for the court and the jury in the first instance, Mr Grimshaw. But if you care to attend the inquest's conclusion, you will find them out with the rest of the public. Now, Pearson, are you ready to take Mr Brockletower home?'

It gave me great satisfaction to see how Grimshaw fumed, while I made arrangements with Pearson for the return of the squire to his former home. He was still fuming as Pearson and the corpse went one way, down towards the Hall, while Luke and I took the jury up through the forest to the track, where their conveyance waited. Not knowing immediately what to do, the bailiff hesitated, then spurred his horse up the slope, going past us at speed.

'He won't lower himself to ride along with us,' murmured Luke. 'But I would bet he's straight back to Yolland for the end of the hearing.'

'Yes,' I said. 'He's thinking about those daughters of his cousin in Lancaster. Their prospects of inheriting Garlick Hall lie in this jury's hands.'

We had ridden for a while behind the jurors' carriage, when Luke asked airily, 'How did you know we would find those blades in the hollow tree, by the way? I am rather crestfallen that I did not reach the solution before you.'

'I knew she had asked for a line. And her dressmaker had lost a pair of scissors on the day she had been in the shop. Perhaps these things, and the discarded horseshoe they found near her body, might have led me earlier to the discovery. But none of it made sense until this morning. I saw the woodsman's lifting machine, and remembered the death of poor Solomon.'

'Ah yes, I see. All instances of Archimedes's mathematics. Pulleys. The association of ideas really is the father of all genius, isn't it?'

'Well, we know she killed herself. The question now is, do I publicize exactly *why* she did it? Do we need to tell her very particular secret?'

'What harm does it do? The unhappy couple are both dead.'

'There may be harm to this little commonwealth, of which we are all members. Its survival requires order and stability, Luke, in its general mind as well as in its body. Some truths can make folk doubt the divine order, and shake their faith in the future. Knowing this *anomaly* has been in our midst . . . well, it is – or it might be – destabilizing.'

'But truth must be told, Titus, surely!'

My friend sounded shocked.

'There are many truths in a single circumstance,' I said firmly. 'I am of the opinion that not all of them must be told. The strictly material truth shall out. Let's confine ourselves to that, and just leave aside the matter of Dolores's . . . ambiguous anatomy. Do you agree?'

Luke was silent. He was pulling at a moral knot, trying to loosen it. Finally he said, in a wounded voice, 'I could publish this as a paper to the Royal Society. It could make my name in London.'

'London is a fine place,' I conceded, 'but it is not where we live.'

He reflected a little longer and then sighed deeply.

'Very well. I shall find another way to conquer London.'

'Thank you, Luke. Only four remain who know about this matter: you, I , George and Dapperwick. Dapperwick never goes anywhere or sees anyone, and is thought to be half crazy. But what about George? Will he keep his word never to speak of this?'

'George is a paragon of discretion, Titus. And he does not come often to this town.'

'Where you and I shall keep the truth between ourselves. That's good, because I intend to call you at the inquest to explain in your most lucid terms what we found inside the tree, and what it means.'

'That Dolores Brockletower killed herself because she was mad for a child, but did it in this peculiar way by being afraid of condemnation as a suicide.'

'Yes and further – and I rely on you for this – that Ramilles Brockletower died by accident. It must be so, Luke, for his sister Sarah's sake.'

'And for the sakes of Grimshaw's cousins,' he added drily.

'That can't be helped,' I said.

Back at the Plough's public room, there was none of the previous day's jollifying. What had happened was too enormous, with implications for every other family in the area. Grimshaw was there again, as we had felt sure he would be. So was Sarah.

There were only two more pieces of evidence to hear. The first was that of Abigail Talboys, and she came to the witness chair looking calm and resolute. She gave her evidence in a firm clear voice, according to the terms we had agreed. Without mention of her pregnancy, she stated as a fact that Mrs Brockletower had repeatedly lamented her childlessness, and even mentioned adoption, during their private fittings at the shop on Friar Gate. I thanked her and let her step down, before calling Luke Fidelis.

'She bled to death after receiving a slashing injury to the throat,' he replied.

'Was there any indication of how this was done?'

'It must have been by a sharp blade, drawn from left to right, like this.'

He mimed with his finger the movement of the blade just as young Jonah had done in my parlour on that first morning.

'Was it done by human agency?'

'Undoubtedly. It could not have been brought about otherwise.'

'And were there any other conclusions about this unfortunate death that your medical knowledge leads you to?'

Luke shook his head.

'No. Not from medical knowledge. But from discoveries made inside the hollow tree beside which she fell, I can say without doubt that she died by her own hand.'

The public gave a collective gasp, exchanging shocked glances.

'Will you explain, please, Dr Fidelis?' I asked.

So he did, carefully taking the court through Dolores Brockletower's preparations, and then her execution of the plan she had made.

'This will seem to many an extraordinary and elaborate procedure,' I remarked. 'Can you think of any motive for a person to follow it?'

'I can think of two. One would be to cast suspicion upon someone else. If no weapon is found beside the body the investigators would naturally think of an attack by another party. Another motive would be to prevent an inquest – *this* inquest for example – from bringing in a verdict of suicide.'

I turned then to the matter of Squire Brockletower, inviting the doctor to give his opinion as to the squire's death. He thought that death had been accidental, a seizure of the brain following directly and causally from the earlier injury to his head, causing him to fall from his horse and discharge the pistol in his pocket. That it had happened at the same place where Dolores had died was a coincidence, though, as he put it, 'I cannot discount the possibility that, when he visited the place of his wife's demise, a sudden excess of emotion tipped his damaged brain into seizure.'

So I let him down and turned to the jury, summarizing all the events and relating my own experience in the room at the Turk's Head. Having seen the bodies, and having heard this and all the other evidence, I told them they must now put their heads together and consider verdicts on the two deaths before them.

'You may be led to the conclusion,' I warned, 'that they died by their own hands. Or you may think it was by the hands of another. If by those of another, and you cannot name the owner of those hands, you should say it was done by a person or persons unknown. If you think it was done by their own hands, I ask you to consider very carefully whether they were in their right mind. There is a very large difference in the consequences, not just for the mortal remains of the deceased but for the prospects of their surviving relatives, between on the one hand a verdict of premeditated self-murder, and on the other of suicide whilst insane.'

I glanced meaningfully towards Sarah, fully intending that the jury noticed the direction of my gaze. She was sitting forward in her chair, her face tilted upwards, as she listened attentively to my words.

'Go now to the room Mr Wigglesworth has prepared for you. I have asked him to provide some refreshments there, but do not allow the pleasures of eating and drinking to delay or interfere with your verdicts.'

With the twelve principal jurymen gathered in conclave inside the inn parlour, the public audience in the hall began their own speculations upon the issue. This debate, which started like the whisper of wind in the reeds, swelled by imperceptible increments until, after ten minutes, it had become a zoological roar. I did not interfere, preferring to dictate to Furzey some notes towards my inquest report, sketching in the general background to the case such as would have to be included irrespective of the final verdicts – though I was confident that I knew what these would be.

After thirty minutes, as I was still dictating, the room suddenly quietened, and then fell completely silent. George Pennyfold had come in and was asking to speak with me. I took him into a corner and we whispered together, while the entire public watched us, trying to discern from our movements and posture what was being said.

'We have agreed on the squire,' Pennyfold murmured into my ear. 'But we are split over his wife.'

'You must be unanimous,' I told him. 'You must somehow find a safe verdict on which you can all agree.'

'I don't know how we may do that,' he complained. 'Our differences are great.'

'You must exercise leadership, George. You are foreman. Marshal the arguments, persuade the doubters. I can't help you further, except on legalities. Otherwise I've done my part and it's for you and your fellows alone to decide the question. But no one here wants a prolonged wrangle, and certainly not a hung jury. So remember: leadership's the word!'

He nodded his head, walked back the length of the room and out to rejoin the others in the parlour. I thought Pennyfold a sensible, opinionated man whose opinions would coincide with my own. I also considered an initially divided jury was good: it seemed more likely that, when they did settle on something, it would be an ameliorative verdict – the very kind I was hoping for.

When, forty minutes later, they came back at last and

arrayed themselves in the jury seats, their faces told me they had done something momentous.

'Well? Have you agreed?' I asked George.

Pennyfold stood up.

'We have.'

At this moment the foreman looked peculiarly imperious. His nostrils were flared, his back erect, as he looked around the room like an actor surveying his audience, or a general his army.

'In that case, will you first give me your verdict on the death of Ramilles Brockletower?'

Pennyfold briefly cleared his throat and spoke, his voice resounding from every corner of the room.

'Our verdict is accidental death. We think the pistol discharged itself as he struck the ground, and fatally wounded him.'

Good, I thought. Very good. And, by its approving murmurs, it seemed the public agreed with me. I checked that Furzey had recorded the verdict and went on.

'And now your decision on Dolores Brockletower, please.'

The foreman cleared his throat again, more thoroughly this time, and intoned.

'We are of the opinion, sir, that she committed self-murder, after long premeditation and in full possession of her reason.'

As a wave of comment washed around the room, I am not sure if my jaw did not drop a fraction, or if my eyes did not shut for a second longer than would be natural in a blink. It was clear anyway that I had misread George Pennyfold. If he had exercised his leadership as strongly as I hoped, it could not have been in the cause of my private hopes. Dolores Brockletower had been condemned for *felo de se* without mitigation, and there was nothing I could do about it.

The public was immediately twittering like starlings in

reaction. Sarah showed no emotion, but the bailiff was looking this way and that, unsure of what the verdicts meant for the prospects of his cousin. I rose to my feet and waited for silence. Then I said the words that I had to say.

'Thank you, foreman and your fellow jurymen. In view of these two verdicts I pronounce that Ramilles Brockletower be eligible for Christian burial. His property is not forfeit to the crown. However, Dolores Brockletower has been found a rational self-murderess and I must accordingly declare that her personal fortune, whatsoever it be, shall not form part of Mr Brockletower's estate, but pass instead to the crown. I further direct that she be buried in unconsecrated ground, in the manner prescribed by the law. As for you, I enjoin you to speak in no way, to any person whatsoever, of your deliberations this afternoon. And so you are dismissed and this inquest is closed.'

In twos and threes the jury rose, yawning and stretching and looking about them for their relatives and friends among the public, amongst whom the starling discourse had fiercely resumed. I hurried from my place and caught George Pennyfold by the arm.

'What on earth persuaded you she killed herself in reason, and with forethought?' I asked, drawing him away from the others.

'I didn't want it, Mr Cragg,' he said. 'I agree with you that suicide is rarely a rational act, and that the punishments it draws are not in proportion. Like you I would have preferred a verdict of accident, or madness, to avoid what must follow a finding of self-murder. But we witnessed your discoveries inside the tree. We know what she did.'

'But still you could have found her mad, surely.'

Pennyfold shook his head.

'No. There was clear forethought, and undoubted reason.

Mrs Brockletower was not mad for want of a child, but angry with her husband. And your discovery showed she had coldly calculated and prepared a means of killing herself that would, as she hoped, incriminate him.'

'So you saw her as perverted, but not insane?'

'Yes. And to have behaved with unmixed wickedness. I'm right sorry, Coroner, but that is how we all saw it in the end.'

I patted his arm consolingly. There was little point in reproaching him.

'Don't be. Go on, back to your forge. There must be many a horseshoe waiting to be bent.'

'So!' exclaimed Elizabeth, 'Dolores Brockletower killed herself just to trap her husband! She hated him so much she wanted to see him hang.'

We were sitting side by side in bed, my wife's head resting on my shoulder, and I had just told her of the jury's decision, and of our discoveries inside the hollow tree earlier that morning.

'It's what the jury concluded,' I confirmed. 'Of course, she could only see that outcome from a seat in the hottest room in hell.'

'It is mad indeed to wish for one's own damnation, Titus, in whatever cause.'

'I wish the jury *had* found her mad,' I said. 'That would have allowed her a Christian burial and saved her fortune for the family. But the plans she hatched were in such detail that the jury was convinced of her rationality.'

'She was jealous of the architect Woodley, you say. I do not think jealousy is rational, Titus. It made Othello mad in the play.'

'I agree, but I'm not sure it was only jealousy that drove her.

A storm of competing furies raged in her mind. One of them came from her childlessness, too, I believe.'

Elizabeth looked at me, with sudden concern. I put my hand gently up and stroked her cheek.

'Do not distress yourself, my love. The Brockletowers' case was not at all like . . . like anybody else's. You see, Luke Fidelis made a discovery about Dolores that means she always knew she could not conceive. By marrying   she embarked on a course of wicked deception – or was it merely a desperate contrivance to escape from her bad life in Jamaica? I wonder about that.'

'What do you mean, her bad life?'

And so, because there could be no secrets between us, I told my wife about Luke Fidelis's post-mortem discovery, and the outburst of her husband in his library, when he described to me the circumstances of their meeting. Elizabeth sat up. Her hands went to her face. Her eyes widened in disbelief.

'Dolores was not a woman?' she gasped.

'Not entirely, no.'

'She was a *man*?'

'Not quite that, either. She was hermaphrodite, according to Dr Dapperwick – half man, half woman. He is an authority in such things.'

'Such things? *Are* there such things? Oh Lord, a monster, a foul mistake of nature. Poor Dolores, poor thing. How she must have suffered!'

We fell silent for a while, Elizabeth sitting still as a funerary monument, staring at the counterpane. Then she roused herself again.

'So what is Sarah Brockletower's position now, Titus?'

'She loses Dolores's fortune, settled on her by the father in Jamaica. But I have had Furzey check on the quiet with the clerk at Rudgewick & Tench, and by the squire's will, she has a life interest in Garlick Hall, but without any responsibility for her brother's debts. They will be in the care of the bailiff's wretched cousin in Lancaster.'

'I'm glad of it,' said Elizabeth. 'It doesn't matter that the sugar fortune is lost. My father would say it is tainted money, anyway, because it is earned by the slave system, which he always says is unjust. But now, at least, she will continue to have a home. Yes, I know she once meant something to you, Titus, and it does you credit that you still care for her future well-being.'

How many women would have such clear-headed charity? I told her I loved her for it, adding, 'But the whole thing leaves me with a very melancholy duty to perform, which will be hard to bear.'

'I hope it is not something very unpleasant.'

'I'm afraid it is. That is why these days there are so few verdicts of self-murder.'

And when I told her what had to be done, she crossed herself three times.

'The angels and saints preserve us against such barbarism!'

'We must hope they will. But there is nothing the saints can do for Dolores Brockletower, at all events. It is too late.'

And so I kissed her, then reached over and snuffed out the light.

Chapter Thirty-one

As we made our way along the Moor Road, with the axle of the cart that bore the coffin squealing and its rusty wheel hoops grinding over the stony sections, we glimpsed Robert Crowther standing up ahead on a rise in the ground. His form was silhouetted against the full moon, with hands on his spade, and head bowed. No doubt he was only resting, but he looked like a sentry mourning at the corner of a royal catafalque. As we came up to him we saw that he had chosen a spot at which a bridle-path intersects with the road, making a crossroads of a kind, for the unmarked resting place of Dolores Brockletower. I pulled out my watch and, tilting the face to catch the moonlight, read the time: a quarter before midnight.

'How do, Coroner?' said Crowther, tipping but not removing his hat.

I gave him how-do in return and dismounted.

'The digging is finished?' I asked.

'Aye. Once I got through the heather roots it made easy work. Just the one big stone to shift.'

We had set out from Market Place twenty minutes earlier, with me riding a few yards in the lead of Dolores's pitiful cortège. This was made up of the decayed Corporation cart, with its equally old horses, and similarly decrepit driver, whose name was Wintly; Sergeant Sutch and a fusilier from Lord Derby's regiment in military support; and, bringing up the rear, the hangman, Stonecross from Lancaster, who had ridden down during the day to perform his duty. Waiting for them to catch me up, I stood beside Crowther and we looked together down into the grave, a deep, black, wet slot that even this moon, high and round, could not penetrate. I had a sudden apprehension of a bottomless hole which, if one fell in, would tumble you all the way to hell.

With Sarah's consent the body of her sister-in-law had continued to lie locked in the Garlick Hall Ice-house for a week past the inquest. For all that it was a body condemned and cursed by the jury's decision it had undergone little additional decay.

In the meantime Reverend Brockletower had read his nephew's obsequies and laid him decently to rest in the family vault, under the chancel of Yolland Church. The funeral was the last time I had seen Sarah, and it had brought an unbidden, sad and sudden memory of my first-ever glimpse of her, across those same pews. But at least I could assure myself that she would in future be provided for, if not luxuriously, then decently. I knew this because one of Sarah's first acts as mistress of Garlick Hall had been to remove her affairs from the firm of Rudgewick & Tench, and return them to my office. I found looking over them that there were heavy debts and encumbrances, but by arrangement with her banker I had ensured that the Hall's dairy income would be hypothecated to her personal needs and costs, while the rents from tenant-farms would furnish the bank interest.

Wintly brought the cart to a standstill, but stayed on his box, keeping firm hold of the driving reins. His jades tossed their heads, stamped their hooves, and looked for a moment as jumpy as unbroken colts in the edgy and desolate moonlight.

But Wintly was a man of faint courage, and I could tell he, too, wished himself elsewhere at this moment.

So it was left to Sutch and his trooper, with Stonecross and myself, to seize the box between us and slide it over the cart's tail, then heave it clear. We carried it without ceremony to the graveside and placed it across two bands of strong webbing that Crowther had lain in parallel on the ground, so that the coffin could be lowered hand over hand into the grave.

But one awful piece of ritual yet remained before that descent, and it was Stonecross's to perform. The celebrated executioner was a strong, well-set man in his fifties, wearing a sober and gentlemanly black coat, almost clerical in cut, and a neat, business-like wig. He fetched his saddlebag and laid it beside the box, before kneeling himself and drawing on a pair of white kid gloves. He took a short crowbar out of the bag and began, with infinite care, to jimmy the crowbar under the coffin lid. As he exerted leverage the nails creaked and finally popped loose, allowing the lid to be opened. We all peered down at what was revealed. Dolores Brockletower was wearing the clothes she had died in. The caked wound to her throat was plainly visible, the hands were crossed on her chest and the eyelids lay closed. In form she looked frayed, and dirty, but anyone would have said that she also looked peaceful.

Not for long, Stonecross returned the crowbar to his bag, and rummaged in it again. Finally he produced a short-handled mallet and a stake, whittled in white wood and sharpened at one end. With these in his fists, he looked back questioningly towards me. I held up a hand in warning and, once again, extracted watch from pocket. It was now five minutes to midnight.

'Not yet,' I told him.

It was a long-drawn-out five minutes. The feathering breeze was from the north and chilly, but I felt hot. I had twice before presided over this ritual of purgation, if that is the right word for what we were about to perform, but one did not become accustomed to it. Fidelis, who refused to attend though I had invited him, called it a damnable desecrating act. But how can one desecrate a suicide? I asked. By decision of the law she is found to have desecrated herself.

'But the procedure is abominable!' he spluttered. 'It is intolerable to reason. And, besides, she might have repented between letting go the blade and falling from her horse. She might have saved herself after all.'

This was just like Fidelis. He could speak of reason in one breath and mouth papist quibbles the next. That, however, was his personal confusion, and my Elizabeth, though she shared his religion, had clearer thoughts.

'If it must be done,' she said, 'it is better supervised by a good man like you, Titus, with a pure heart. The people are bound to be afraid of one that dies by her own hand. They cannot help believing she will wander the earth, spreading alarm and doing all sorts of evil, until Judgement Day. In their eyes it is for you to stop her, and so you must.'

'Thank heaven it will not be me, but the public executioner who does the stopping. I doubt he has a pure heart.'

'Oh, I'm sure he has!' she exclaimed, charitably.

'Are we ready yet, Mr Cragg?' said the pure-at-heart now. 'Shall I proceed?'

His voice was dark and musical, its sounds intoned on one melancholy note. My watch said it was still one minute before midnight.

'Wait for my signal,' I told him.

The two soldiers took up positions one at each end of the coffin. Crowther and I stood opposite Stonecross, on the other side of the box. We watched as Stonecross bunched his left fist around the stake and poised its sharpened point directly over Dolores Brockletower's frozen heart. I waited, watching the alignment of the minute hand as it imperceptibly moved towards the vertical.

'Now!' I whispered.

With sudden dispatch, and not a second's hesitation, Stonecross struck the head of the stake hard with the mallet. And, as the point penetrated, the body seemed to convulse for a moment, to convulse again, and then the eyelids flipped open.

The fusilier swore. Crowther gasped, and I felt that a clammy hand had clutched at my guts. The eyes of Dolores Brockletower were staring upwards. They were not directed towards the five of us who gathered around. They were staring beyond, far beyond, at the full moon.

'Put the lid back on, quickly!' I ordered.

And so we returned her to the dark.

My pledge to Sarah had left me with one more task. If the jury in the inquest on Benjamin Woodley should happen to give the true verdict – his murder by the squire – the law would after all require the forfeiture of his estates, and leave her destitute as she had feared. Yet, to prevent this was easy. I had only to maintain a judicious silence. Apart from myself, only Fidelis and Elizabeth knew the truth, and I trusted them to follow me. Without the letter that I pulled from the squire's pocket and never made public, there was no other material evidence.

So I was faced with the question that bedevils many who hold official positions: which ought to take precedence, the public or the private duty? It was Elizabeth who made up my mind.

'Titus, you gave the woman your word. You owe nothing to Woodley and, anyway, he and his killer are both dead and beyond the reach of human justice. You must keep your peace now, and save poor Sarah.'

So it happened at the inquest that twelve men of Preston, destitute of evidence, sent Woodley into the ground under the rubric 'murder by person or persons unknown'. A few weeks later, after getting my inquest fee of thirteen shillings and fourpence, I slipped one day into St John's Church. After muttering a few words of prayer for Woodley's soul, I quietly dropped the money into the poor box.

Historical Note

MID-GEORGIAN PRESTON, where this story is set, was one of England's ancient self-governing charter towns. By the 1600s it had grown into the prime social and legal centre of Lancashire, being pleasantly and strategically located in the heart of the county, with a busy agricultural market, and a significant community of craft workers amongst its stable population of about 5,000. It remained like this until the end of the century when industrialization transformed the town into the grimy, overcrowded manufactory that Charles Dickens called Coketown, his setting for Hard Times.

Today hardly anything pre-Victorian remains except the central medieval street-plan: the three principal streets of Church Gate, Fisher Gate and Friar Gate, leading east, west and north-west from the focal point of the flagged market-place and the site of the medieval Moot Hall. This building collapsed in 1780 to be succeeded by three further civic structures, the latest a 1960s office block of remarkable ugliness. So, to conjure up the pre-industrial scene, you have to vault back from today's ring-roads, pre-stressed concrete and glass, over sooty Victorian stonework and uniform red-brick back-to-backs, to imagine a vanished townscape mixing medieval, Tudor and Georgian styles.

Administratively eighteenth-century Preston was, like most other borough towns, an oligarchy. The council's twenty-four members (or burgesses) appointed each other and parcelled out the senior offices, including that of the Mayor and two bailiffs, annually between themselves. Charter towns like this were virtual city-states where (in Tom Paine's scathing words) a man's 'rights are circumscribed to the town and, in some cases, to the parish of his birth; and all other parts, though in his native land, are to him as a foreign country'. These communities reserved the right to run their own affairs, and keep 'foreigners' away at all costs.

I have taken liberties with a few local details, not least in the coroner's own office. In historical Preston the unusual custom was for the annually appointed Mayor to sit as coroner *ex officio*. But, preferring him to stand apart from local politics, I impose the more typical English model whereby Titus Cragg is directly appointed by the crown, with life-tenure. My other inventions include Garlick Hall, the nearby village of Yolland, and most of the cast of characters.

'Mr Spectator', one of Cragg's heroes, is the imaginary writer of the London periodical *The Spectator*, written in the reign of Queen Anne (March 1711–December 1712 and June–November 1714) largely by Sir Richard Steele and Joseph Addison. Cragg also reveres 'Mr Isaac Bickerstaff', the persona behind Steele's earlier *Tatler*, which appeared in 1709. These single-sheet papers had a character very like today's Internet blogs: they appeared several times a week to ruminate on public issues as they cropped up. Both *Tatler* and *Spectator* were then collected in book form and their contents remained hugely popular as arbiters of taste and good sense throughout the Georgian age.

Bodies Politic

By Robin Blake

A Cragg & Fidelis Mystery

PRESTON, 1741

The drowning of drunken publican Antony Egan is no surprise – even if it comes as an unpleasant shock to coroner Titus Cragg, whose wife was the old man's niece. But he does his duty to the letter, and the inquest's verdict is accidental death. Meanwhile the town is agog with rumour and faction, as the General Election is only a week away and the two local seats are to be contested by four rival candidates.

But Cragg's close friend, Dr Luke Fidelis, finds evidence to cast doubt on the events leading to Egan's demise. Soon suspicions are further roused when a well-to-do farmer collapses and it appears he was in town on political business. Is there a conspiracy afoot? The Mayor and Council have their own way of imposing order, but Cragg is determined not to be swayed by pressure. With the help of Fidelis's scientific ingenuity the true criminals are brought to light . . .

An extract of the gripping sequel to
A Dark Anatomy follows here.

Chapter One

A HUMAN BODY IN the salmon traps was not such a rare event. The one they caught in the spring of 1741 was the fifth during my eight years as coroner in the borough of Preston. On the other hand, from my point of view, there was something very particular and personal about the latest one. This corpse was my kith, if not quite my kin.

But I had no idea of that when the call to the riverbank came early on that Monday morning, exactly seven days before we were due to begin a week of voting in that year's General Election. I immediately hurried out to perform the coroner's first duty – that of answering the summons to a questionable death, and judging the need for an inquest. On my way to the stretch of the River Ribble in which the traps were laid, I naturally had to pass along Fisher Gate, where my friend Luke Fidelis lived on the upper floor of the premises of Adam Lorris, the bookbinder. Reaching Lorris's address, I mounted the steps to the door and pealed the bell. If Fidelis was at home he could be of some use to me. When bodies were found floating in the river, the initial questions were always the same: How long had they been there? How far had they travelled? Doctor Fidelis's knowledge of physiology, and such things as the progressive effects of total water immersion on a corpse, was far ahead of mine.

Mrs Lorris went up to tell Fidelis I had called and of course, as was his habit, my friend was still lounging in bed. I chatted for a few minutes at the foot of the stairs with Lorris and Mrs Lorris. He told me of his progress with my old childhood book of *Aesop's Fables* that I had brought to him for rebinding.

'I read the book through with Mrs Lorris before I started, and we were vastly entertained, were we not, my heart?'

'Oh yes, Mr Cragg!' Dot Lorris exclaimed, her face breaking into creases of remembered enjoyment. 'Such tricks those animals got up to.'

'Yes, Mr Aesop was a clever fellow,' I agreed. 'He had a charming way of translating human nature into the behaviour of beasts.'

I glanced up the stairs for a sign that Fidelis might be stirring himself. There was none.

'There's some of the fables, mind, that a husband would do better not to put before his wife,' observed Lorris.

'Oh? And which are those, Husband?' Dot challenged.

'*The Fox and the Vixen* for one. Remember it, Mr Cragg?'

I said I had a vague memory of it.

'That vixen,' said Lorris, shaking his head, 'she stayed under cover and let the fox run from the farmer by himself. There's little wifely love in that, or trust.'

'Trust!' laughed his wife. 'What was there to trust? He calculated that if both of them ran, his wife would be caught and he would get away. The farmer could only chase after one of them, and that would be the vixen, as she was the slower.'

'No, *she* calculated that if she stayed under cover, she'd save herself and damn the fox.'

'The fox damned himself when he lost his nerve,' was Dot Lorris's pitiless rejoinder.

Before the discussion grew too heated I steered it towards

the election. The people of Preston were excited at having a contested vote at last. In the previous parliament, and the two before that, our borough members had simply walked-over, as no one could be found to stand against them. This time four men would be fighting over the two seats, making for a much livelier prospect.

After a couple of minutes we heard Fidelis's voice calling down.

'Cragg, I'm in my nightshirt, but come up if you like.'

Instead I called up to him.

'Get dressed, Luke. It's almost seven and I'm taking you for a walk by the river.'

'A walk? Before *seven*? Surely it can wait.'

'No. It is now or not at all.'

At length, the tall, fair-haired figure of Preston's youngest and most adventurous doctor appeared on the stair. He was grumbling, as usual, when asked to do a thing before eight in the morning.

'I only wanted half an hour more of sleep, Titus,' he growled. 'I was drinking until past midnight.'

In consideration of Luke's aching head I did not set too sharp a pace as we went along Fisher Gate and then, by a turning to the left, into the lane that passed the playhouse and headed down from the bluff, along which the town is ranged towards the riverbank.

'Well, what is it?' Luke asked. 'I don't suppose this outing is for the improvement of my health.'

'No. There's a body in the river.'

'Ah!'

We walked on in silence to the bottom of the steep path, before striking across the meadow beside the riverbank. But I sensed an increased spring in Luke's step. He was stimulated by the opportunity to assist me in my inquiries; more so, I think, than I was in leading them.

In many towns, the river is a high street. The buildings line up expectantly alongside it, waiting for trade to come across its wharves and quays, while locks upstream and down regulate the water for the traffic of lighters and barges. None of this is so at Preston, for the river is at a distance, and on a different level. Abreast of the town to the south, it is at this point wide and, being close to the estuary, tidal. But it drains a great area of uplands to the east and, after heavy or prolonged rains combined with a tide, it can go so high that the water meadows flood up to a hundred yards on either side. To keep its skirts dry, therefore, the town stays aloof on its ridge, a quarter mile distant from the waterside, and it is possible to live one's life there without any particular consciousness of the river, except as a barrier to be crossed when travelling south, and as the regular provider of fish suppers.

On this morning, breezy after yesterday's downpour, the current was big and tumbling, but it had stayed within the banks. A group of men wearing knee-length boots of greased leather were working the traps from boats that bobbed and pitched in the boiling stream. They were gaffing the last of the fish that had come into the traps during the night, and bringing them ashore to add to the neat row of those already landed. As we came near enough to see the display of salmon, like spears of bright polished pewter in the riverbank grass, we saw a gaggle of women in bonnets and full-length cloaks, advancing along the bank towards us, laughing and singing. It would be their job to pack the fish in rush parcels and carry them up to the market.

The women arrived at the same time as we did, and

immediately their laughter died as they saw the thing lying, stretched companionably alongside the row of fish, as if it was itself an enormous example of the species. It was wrapped in a net like a parcel, but this did not fully conceal the fearful truth: the head end was rounded, from which the shape swelled smoothly up to the belly in a small mound before tapering away again. At the end where – had it really been a monster salmon – the tail should be, two splayed feet protruded. They wore the wooden-soled clogs of the countryman, strengthened like a horse's hoof with curves of steel nailed into them.

The sight provoked immediate cries of dismay from the women.

'Quiet yourselves,' shouted one of the men, as he carried the last of the fish up from his boat and slapped it down with the others. 'Coroner's here. You should be respectful.'

I asked who was in charge of the fishing party. It was the man that had just spoken, whose name was Peter Crane.

'Was it you that first saw it in the water?' I asked.

'It was. Me and the lad spotted it first.'

Crane nodded towards a youth who looked a younger edition of himself.

'What time was that?'

'An hour ago, or a bit more.'

I took out my watch. It was half past seven.

'Before half past six, then.'

'If you say so.'

'And did you find him just like that?'

'How do you mean?'

'Wrapped in the net.'

'Oh no. We wrapped him when we brought him ashore, like. Out of respect.'

Or, I thought, *to stop him getting up and running away*.

367

It was a common thought: you can never be too sure of those that drown.

'Would you kindly uncover him for me now?'

It took three men to undo the parcel, so heavy was the body, and so well-wrapped.

'Did you know him?' I asked as they struggled.

'Oh, aye, we knew him.'

'Who was he?'

'Don't think you won't know him yourself, Mr Cragg. Take a look.'

Finally, with two of them pulling his feet and a third at the other end hauling the net, they had managed to disencumber the body. The dead man was wearing a coat, shirt, breeches and the aforementioned clogs. His grey hair was tied at the back. His eyes were closed.

'Good God!' exclaimed Fidelis. 'Look who it is.'

We all drew closer, and there was a murmur of recognition from the women. I knew the man better even than the others and, for a moment, was so disconcerted I could not speak. Not only did I well know his identity, I knew also that the contented impression conveyed by the corpse was false. For these were the mortal remains of poor Antony Egan, landlord of the Ferry Inn and the sadly troubled uncle of Elizabeth, my own sweet wife.

'Did you close the eyes, or were they like this when you found him?' Fidelis asked Crane.

'No, Doctor, staring open they were. I closed them.'

As a simulacrum of sleep it made the man look at peace, an appearance reinforced by the hands being arranged comfortably over the swollen stomach.

I knelt down on one knee beside him, opened his sodden coat and went through the pockets. They were empty except for a tobacco pouch, a few coppers and his watch, its chain securely attached to a waistcoat buttonhole. Then I stood again and looked at Fidelis who was on the other side of the corpse.

'He has his watch,' I said.

'He wasn't robbed, then.'

'When do you think he went into the water?'

'I doubt it was long ago.'

'Did he drown?'

'Let's see. Mr Crane would you and your men kindly turn him over for me, and bring him round so his head's over the river.'

The dead man was placed, according to Luke's instructions, on his stomach with head and shoulders over the stream and arms trailing in the water – the posture of one who throws himself down to drink, or a boy attempting to tickle a trout. Luke then crouched beside him and placed both hands palms down, with fingers spread out, flat on his back.

'Look at the mouth, Titus, while I palpitate.'

I placed myself on the other side of the body and sank down on one knee, leaning a little over the water to see the profile of Antony's head. Luke pressed his hands down sharply three or four times in a kneading motion just below the rib cage and immediately water gushed up and out of the mouth, like water from a parish pump. Luke stood up.

'You saw it?' he asked. 'Lungs full of water. He sucked it in trying to breathe. It means he was alive when he went into the river. He died by drowning.'

I rose from my genuflection and considered for a moment. The cloud cover was disintegrating and patches of freshly minted blue sky had opened up over our heads. Then, in the east, the morning sun broke free and shafts of light set the swollen river surface glittering.

'Well, Luke, I have a ten-minute walk upstream ahead of

me. It's a fine day. Will you come along, or have you other business?'

He said he had no patients to see immediately and would be glad to go with me. I asked Crane to get some sort of conveyance, and use it to transport Egan's body along the bankside path behind us.

'There will be an inquest but I see no reason why he can't lie at home, and be viewed there by the jury. There've been inquests at the Ferry Inn before. It's better that I go ahead, to break the news to his daughters. They will need time to prepare.'

Luke and I set off at a brisk pace to walk to the inn. It stood half a mile above the salmon traps, rather less than midway to the big stone bridge at Walton-le-Dale that bears the southern road for Wigan and Manchester. A road of sorts branched from there to connect with the ferry-stage, and for uncounted centuries traffic from the south had been transported across the stream in competition with the bridge. The Ferry Inn, lying on the southern bank, had served the needs of those waiting to cross, and a good business it had been, for the reason (which was really unreason) that, while a ferry crossing was cheaper than the bridge toll, many of those waiting to use it were happy to spend the saved money on drinking, eating, card-playing and, sometimes, a bed for the night. So business had come to the inn as naturally as fish got into the salmon traps.

But under Egan its prosperity had progressively dwindled, to such an extent that for the past few years the inn had been hesitating on the edge of ruin. It seemed to keep going only by the tenacity and good sense of his twin daughters, Grace and Mary-Ann.

'Poor Egan,' said Luke as we trudged along the bankside. 'I was drinking at the Ferry only last week, on my way back from visiting a patient.'

'I hadn't seen him for a month or more,' I said. 'We see his daughters, of course, because they're Elizabeth's cousins. But we gave over inviting Antony two or three years ago. It had become impossible. What condition was he in – on the day you were there?'

'Same as always; no better, no worse.'

'I don't think he'd enjoyed a waking hour of sobriety for five years.'

'Is *enjoy* the right word, Titus? I enjoy a drink. But men like that can do nothing without a drink. Drunkenness is their sobriety; their accustomed condition.'

'If so, what is their drunkenness?'

'Unconsciousness, I think. Oblivion.'

'Well, now poor Antony has found an eternity of that.'

'What made his life take the turn it did? Was he always a sot?'

'No. Once he was the model of moderation.'

'Then what happened?'

'The son that he cherished above all other creatures deserted him, and went south, without ever writing or sending word. And then, when word came at last, it was that the boy had died. His father took to drink because he could not bear to remember it.'

By now we had left the water meadows behind and reached the ferry's landing stage, on the northern side of the river. From here we had to cross to the inn on the far bank, which meant waiting for the ferry. We could see the flat, raft-like conveyance labouring towards us, fighting the flood as two men turned the great winching wheel that hauled along the fixed rope that stretched from bank to bank. A short distance upstream, smoke was rising from the chimneys of the inn, which stood among a small cluster of houses and trees known as Middleforth Green.

The day had started at the inn as it did every day. There was no sign yet that this might not be one like any other.

The ferry reached land with a crunch and lowered its ramp. Half a dozen passengers came off, and with them a cart laden with leeks, sparrowgrass, watercress and other market vegetables. The ferryman, Robert Battersby, a fellow famous for his bad grace, tied off his ropes and came ashore with his son and crewman, Simeon, a muscular boy of seventeen. As they ambled towards the wooden hut, in which they sheltered from rain and sold tickets between crossings, I stopped them and said we required immediate transport over to the Ferry Inn. He muttered something about his timetable but I cut him short, saying it was Coroner's business and that as soon as he had transported me and Dr Fidelis, he was to return and await the arrival of a body from downriver, for bringing across after us.

When he heard this, a smile broke across young Simeon's face, and be began jiggling up and down.

'Another one gone in, is it?' he said, his voice lifting with sudden delight. 'Another sacrifice to the water? Oh, aye. She's a cruel one is the river goddess.'

'Shut it and don't be daft,' said the father savagely to the son, then turned back to me. 'Pay no mind, Mr Cragg. His head's full of nonsense. We'll take you now. It'll be tuppence.'

I gave him the money, and a warning.

'Let's have a little reverence when the body comes after, Mr Battersby, if you please.'

extracts reading groups
competitions books new
discounts extracts
competitions extracts
books new
reading groups events
events books
extracts
new titles reading groups
interviews
events extracts
discounts books
new books events
events new events
discounts extracts discounts

www.panmacmillan.com

extracts events reading groups
competitions books extracts new